SHOULD HAVE TOLD YOU SOONER

SHOULD HAVE TOLD YOU SOONER

a novel

JANE WARD

SHE WRITES PRESS

Published in 2026 by
She Writes Press, an imprint of The Stable Book Group

32 Court Street, Suite 2109
Brooklyn, NY 11201
https://shewritespress.com
Library of Congress Control Number: 2025918559
ISBN: 979-8-89636-066-7
eISBN: 979-8-89636-067-4

Interior Designer: Andrea Reider

Printed in the United States

What might have been and what has been
Point to one end, which is always present.

—T. S. Eliot, "Burnt Norton," *The Four Quartets*

Love's
merciless, the way it travels in
and keeps emitting light.

—Kim Addonizio, "Stolen Moments"

I turn ten years old today. I'm sure that's something you'd remember and perhaps think about. I am hoping for a new bicycle for my birthday, a big one with five speeds to replace my smaller baby bike, the one I learned to ride on. I showed Mum and Dad a picture of the one I want, but I don't know if they will buy it for me. Mum worries that I will fall from a taller bike. She's always fussing when I have accidents, like tripping when I run or getting knocked about when I play football at school. "You have to be more careful, love! I want to keep you in one piece!"

This place where I live with Mum and Dad is called Chapel Allerton. It is outside the city of Leeds, in case you don't know it. Or if you'd like to visit someday. I am having a party this afternoon, in our back garden, Methley Mount, number 7. Mum invited all the children from my class at school, but not all of them are my friends. I know them and they know me and we get on. But I really only have two good friends, Daisy and Martin. Daisy lives behind us, and she and I grew up playing games like Snakes and Ladders on the outdoors table where her parents like to have supper on warm days. Like the Italians, Mum says whenever she sees them eating there. Now, though, Daisy and I mostly read books together at my house or do schoolwork. Martin and I ride our bikes on the street after school. His is taller than the one I have now. It has five speeds, which is how I got the idea for my new bike. If I had a new, bigger bike like the one in the picture, I would be just like Martin. I could keep up with him.

But if I don't get it because Mum thinks it's too dangerous, I hope I will at least get some new art supplies. I like to draw as much as I like to cycle, maybe more because I need to draw. I carry so many pictures in my head and they are noisy until I let them out. My friends' faces, their bicycles, the neighbor's dog lying in the sunny garden, Dad's favorite rose bush, all the objects in my mum's kitchen—everything knocks about in my brain until I put what's inside there on paper. Now I have pages and pages of drawings.

Right now, I can only use crayons and colored pencils and the sketchbooks Mum picks up from W.H. Smith, but I would like pastels and charcoal sticks and acrylic paints and heavy paper from a real art supply store. And brushes, too. Before I had the crayons and colored pencils, I used to borrow the lead pencil my father used for his crossword puzzles. Dad would leave it on the side table next to his armchair and he never minded that I took it as long as I put it back so it was there for him after tea, when he opened the paper to the daily puzzle. I showed Dad my sketches and told him that I want proper paints because paint moves easier across the paper than crayons and helps me capture what I see before it has a chance to disappear. I said I hoped he would convince Mum that I wouldn't make a mess with the paint. But I think he didn't hear me properly. He was looking at each drawing I gave him. "I don't even have a favorite color, never mind any artistic talent. Nor can your mother sketch to save herself," he said. "Where does this talent come from, I wonder?"

Sometimes I wonder that too. Where it all comes from. I wonder how I got to be so good at art. I wonder where I got my colorful, noisy brain. Maybe it is like yours. Does this sound like you? I would like to know. I will keep writing to you with stories and with questions, and I will hold these letters under my mattress until I know where to send them.

Signed,
Your son

PART I

FOOTFALLS ECHO IN THE MEMORY

CHAPTER 1

YMCA POOL, MASSACHUSETTS, OCTOBER 2022

Noel Enfield found an open lane at the Y pool and slipped in. This early in the morning, there was little risk of sharing lanes, and she could swim without worrying about keeping clear of another body. She had enough on her mind.

Swimming laps—concentrating only on her body pushing through the water—usually helped her manage the stress in her life. But by the time she had launched her first turn off the far wall, she knew today would be a struggle. She couldn't shake the worry that had weighed on her since yesterday afternoon, when Deb Stone, the Field-Lyons Museum's deputy director, had sent her a last-minute request for a lunchtime meeting today, adding as a note: *Sorry to squeeze this in during lunch, but the subject is time-sensitive and this is my only free block.* No word about what the subject might be, but Noel knew that meetings scheduled with less than twenty-four hours' notice generally indicated crises.

"Maybe it's about a new project coming in, something we haven't planned for," her assistant, Paula, had suggested.

Or maybe she's "restructuring" again, Noel had thought to herself, the euphemism for downsizing staff. *Maybe some of us are about to be let go.*

She had kept all that to herself, though, and simply nodded in agreement with Paula—*Yes, I'm sure it's something like that*—to avoid making her assistant nervous too.

Part of Noel felt her own fear was irrational; she knew she was hardworking and dedicated and necessary. Over the years she had transformed both the department and her role as Director of Collections, changes that had led to better, more streamlined operations—somewhat of a feat within a not-for-profit organization. However, she also knew those achievements weren't always taken into account when jobs had to go on the chopping block. And she couldn't afford to lose her job now that her six-year marriage was coming to an end.

Her choice, she reminded herself as she powered through another lap. It had been her choice to end the marriage and thrust both herself and Andy into endless phone calls with attorneys and discussions of demands being made and whether or not to accommodate them. Who got what, who lost what. Most recently, Andy had requested that Noel sign over her half of their house to him. "It's the only home Alice remembers," he had argued, "and she'll need stability now that you've decided to blow up her life. Especially if you're no longer going to be in it."

The threat of losing Alice altogether, though veiled, was clear enough to Noel.

The day Noel met Andy, she'd excused herself to use the ladies' room to freshen up at the end of lunch out with a girlfriend. Outside the restroom door had stood a man with his young daughter. Noel could tell by the way the girl hopped from foot to foot that she needed to use the toilet, but she was refusing—loudly—to go into the men's room with her father.

As the girl's father explained that he couldn't take her into the ladies' room and she wasn't old enough to go in by herself, she stamped her foot and cried out, "I'm a big girl! I'm four!"

"Four!" Noel exclaimed as she approached. "That is awfully big." She smiled at the man. "What if I check inside first to make sure the room is empty? Then we can stand guard out here while she goes in by herself."

"That would work. Thank you." Noel could hear the relief in the man's voice.

"Of course. Be right back."

When Noel nodded an all-clear, the man hustled his daughter into the restroom. "Be quick. But if you need me, I'm right outside the door. And don't forget to wash your hands!" he added as the girl disappeared inside.

Noel laughed and the man shot her a sheepish smile.

"Believe it or not, that was my first single-dad fail," he said. "She's very headstrong lately."

"It was bound to happen," she said. "You handled it well."

"With help," he acknowledged, and he smiled again—full wattage this time. His intensity made Noel feel bashful for the first time in a long time. She thanked the squeal of the bathroom door a few moments later for ending the awkward silence between them.

"I'm Andy, by the way," the man said as he stopped his girl from running past them, "and this is Alice."

"I'm big," Alice said again, shaking herself free from his hands on her shoulders.

"Yes, you are," Noel said, laughing. "It's nice to meet you, Alice. And Andy. I'm Noel. Yes, like the man's name," she added when Andy frowned in confusion. "I was named for a grandfather I never met."

In those few moments, while grinning down at a stranger's lovely, defiant daughter, her heart had stirred with so much yearning for a life that had eluded her in her forty-three years.

Here, she'd thought when Andy had asked her for a first date on a whim, *here is my haven.* She'd thought it again each time he asked her to come with him on outings with Alice after that. Finally—after the break from her partner, Ed, who'd admitted after ten years that he didn't want children; after the devastating diagnosis of premature menopause that had followed their split;

and long after the two-plus university years wasted on Bryn, her first love who hadn't loved her enough in return—finally, a child, and someone who loved a child this much. Her own family. And she would love them, not as second or third best but as *hers*, as if all the missteps of those younger years could be forgotten because she had arrived here. Andy's wife. Alice's mom.

But no, she wasn't. She was Alice's stepmother. Going forward, her visits with Alice would always be up to Andy. Her choice to leave him had consequences, and there was no going back anyway. "What's done is done," as Noel's grandmother had so often said—one of her most frequent platitudes.

"What's done is done," Gran said when Noel was nine and the car her mother was a passenger in went off the road and careened into a tree. That night, Noel showed up at her grandmother's front door near midnight in the company of a social worker who'd had the task of explaining that Noel was now orphaned. If not for Gran walking away from her retirement plans and taking on the raising of her, she would have ended up in foster care for sure. And she would be forever grateful to her grandmother for taking her in, for loving her as best she knew how. But after the social worker told her grandmother about the crash, and after Gran expressed her bewildered frustration at her daughter's getting into a car with a man who would turn out to be a reckless driver, she'd turned and looked at Noel. "Ah, what's done is done," she'd said, "and here you are."

Yes, there she was, and there she stayed for the next nine years before going off to university. Gran had intended the lesson as a kindness for Noel: a drawing of a firm line under something awful, a way to tell her that what came after could be and would be better—and because of Gran, Noel had put the same platitude into practice for decades.

"Let him have it," she'd told her attorney, against the woman's best advice. "The house is not important to me. Alice is." She would make any concessions that might help her keep that little girl in her life.

She pushed herself up and down the pool lane, her hands slapping the surface of the water instead of slicing into it. Bad form. She knew it but couldn't correct herself. Lately, when thoughts of Andy and the looming end of her marriage invaded her mind, she lost focus. She'd sworn to put this failure out of her thoughts for the one hour she had to herself, but here it was anyway—a greater pull than the peace she expected in the water. She hoped Paula was right that Deb wanted to discuss a new, last-minute project. She really hoped this would not be another setback.

Crawl, crawl. She persisted through water that felt like sludge until her limbs were heavy. Had she done her hour? Less? Did it matter?

Her first swim teacher's advice popped into her head: "Mastering the water doesn't always mean pushing through it. Sometimes a swimmer has to conserve energy; sometimes it is enough to stay afloat."

Noel rolled onto her back and, with a few flutter kicks, allowed the water to carry her, exhausted, the last few feet.

CHAPTER 2

FIELD-LYONS MUSEUM, OCTOBER 2022

After the arduous swim, Noel's morning passed quickly as she and Paula pulled and cleaned pieces for an upcoming in-house exhibit on daily life in Colonial Massachusetts. The pewter tankards and wooden trenchers weren't her favorite pieces, but everything from this period drew visitors to the museum, and being stuck in the collection for a few hours provided a good distraction. When she finally looked at her watch, it was thirty minutes before she needed to be in Deb's office.

Paula caught her checking the time and shooed her off. "I've got this under control. You go get ready."

"It would help if I had an inkling of what she wants to discuss," Noel complained.

Paula smiled. "I don't think it's bad news. If Deb planned to drop bad news, we'd have heard rumors of it by now. No one around here keeps secrets very well. I bet it's either a last-minute loan request or she's going to offer you a promotion."

"I'm sure you're right about the loan request." Noel shrugged. "Whatever it is, I hope I can get out at two as planned. I promised I'd be at Alice's skate practice today, and I can't let her down. It's the first time she's wanted to see me since . . ."

"I get it," Paula said when Noel faltered. "No matter what Deb needs, the department will handle it and you'll get out on time. Now, go."

Noel tucked a lock of hair behind her ear as she walked back to her office to collect her task book and tablet in case she needed her calendar. She doubted they'd be discussing a promotion. She'd been offered new jobs within the museum before—had even been recruited by other museums, both nearby and in other states, for positions that included longer hours or more travel—but offers had dwindled over the past seven years. After meeting and marrying Andy and becoming a mom to Alice, being home as much as possible had been more important to her than advancing. And Andy had been adamant that Alice needed a reliable motherly presence after Marisa's defection. Noel had agreed, but meeting that need had meant compromise in her career. With every year she'd stayed in Collections, the opportunities had dried up.

When Noel arrived at the deputy director's office, she found her on the phone. Deb mouthed "sorry" and motioned for Noel to take the seat opposite her while she finished her call.

It wasn't an unpleasant conversation, Noel gathered from the smile on Deb's face. In fact, her boss seemed in a buoyant mood, and Noel wondered if she too might relax—if, instead of the routine glitches and problems that the deputy director often addressed with her, today's agenda might be problem-free. She wasn't sure she could handle any more problems.

She was so absorbed in trying to figure out why she was there that she almost missed Deb ending her call and turning the conversation to her.

"Noel. Thank you for your patience."

"Oh. Of course."

"And thank you for agreeing to see me last-minute. I'll try and keep things brief." Deb relaxed back into her chair. Then she smiled. "I have a proposal to talk to you about. This may be a project that proves too disruptive, so when I've finished, I want you to tell me exactly what you think. And be completely honest, okay?"

A new project? Both relieved and intrigued, Noel nodded.

"Back in February," Deb began, "we were approached by the Addison Gallery in London. Do you remember, Noel, that we sent them a couple of small Pre-Raphaelite sketches for their comprehensive show about the brotherhood in 2018?"

The request had created a flurry of excited energy among Noel's staff. The Addison was prestigious; inclusion of even these minor pieces—a pair of Rossetti ink studies of the model and painter Lizzie Siddal—had been a huge honor.

She nodded. "I remember. Do they have another show on the horizon? Another request for a loan?"

"A loan, yes, but it's not for art. Their head curator, Jean Rayburn, is seconding one of her staff with us. This isn't general knowledge yet, but the Addison will be expanding one of their regional outposts soon, the one in the north of England, and part of the expansion plan includes turning the building's outdoor space into a sculpture-exhibit park. Jean and I have become good friends over the years, and she knows we can help her staff member get up to speed with interactive outdoor exhibits. Our Board approved it, we have lodging, we can dedicate staff time to the project. The six-month secondment will overlap with the months leading up to the art student sculpture show we put on every May, and honestly, it will be great to have the extra set of hands."

"That sounds wonderful for the museum. So how can Collections help?" Noel asked.

"Ah." Deb smiled. "Collections can't help, but maybe you can. Jean and others at the Addison had the idea that we make the secondment reciprocal. Meaning we send someone from here to them for six months' worth of skill building. The secondee would become part of the Addison team responsible for the exhibition showcasing the 2023 UK Rising Artists Awards. That person would also write the show's exhibition guide with input from the competing artists—gathering bios, artists' statements, assessing the paintings. I nominated you for this secondment."

Noel sat in stunned silence for a few moments. She could hardly believe what she'd heard. "Me? Over curatorial staff?"

"Oh," Deb said, "there are always people who would love to go to London, but—and please don't share this news with anyone just yet—someone on staff gave her notice; she's leaving for an opportunity in Illinois. Which means I'll have a curator's job to fill soon. After some reorganizing, I'd like to put you in charge of American Art and Artifacts. You could come back here and step right into the new role."

A secondment *and* a curatorial job? Noel sat back in the chair. Paula's promotion comment she had dismissed as ridiculous was not so ridiculous after all. She was being given one more opportunity to advance. "I hardly know what to say."

"Say yes; I want you in that spot," Deb said. "You've dedicated yourself to this place and it's high time we invested in you. If you come back with these skills under your belt, the open job will be yours. I'll have to advertise the position, of course, but that will be a formality. I'll hold it for you. The only question is, is it the right time for you to make a change in your career?"

Noel's heart raced with excitement. She had started her museum career full of ambition to advance, and for years she had moved steadily up the ranks—until she'd pressed pause to establish herself as mother to Alice. But she had more flexibility now.

She felt so overwhelmed by this generous offer that she was speechless. The secondment experience would be invaluable—her ticket to moving into the curatorial spot or moving to any museum of her choosing, really. More responsibility, more rank, likely more much-needed money. She really was poised to leap, to put her career pause behind her, to take a chance on herself.

"Are you unsure?" Deb interrupted Noel's thoughts. "You've passed up promotion offers in the past, but now that your daughter's older and your circumstances have changed . . . well, I did wonder if you'd like the change of scenery. My divorce motivated me to come clear across the country to the Field-Lyons—but of course, my ex and I didn't have children."

"I can say emphatically yes, yes I want this," Noel said quickly. "I would jump at this opportunity without question if I only had myself to think about. But I do need to think about what this would mean for visits with Alice. Six months is a long stretch to go without seeing her and I really have to—"

"Forgive me," Deb interrupted, holding up a hand. "There's something I should have told you straight away. If you weren't separated, I'd have suggested that your whole family should accompany you. The Addison is offering a two-bedroom apartment, which would have been big enough for all of you. Meaning it's big enough for you to have Alice come and stay with you a time or two."

Would Andy go for that? Noel wasn't sure. She remembered back to the morning she told him she was leaving—his awful, awful words, his face contorted with anger. Ugly. Ugly, ugly, ugly. She had known it would be. To him, her decision had come out of nowhere, and the more he'd pressed her for reasons, the quieter she'd grown.

Of course he'd been irate. But explaining herself to Andy's satisfaction would have meant having multiple conversations about herself, her past, the mistakes she'd made—so many things she had never told him about before they'd married, decisions made that she knew he would have disapproved of. So she'd simply left, and left Andy exasperated.

However, in the months since, as lawyers had taken over the most difficult conversations and allowed them distance from each other, Andy's anger had abated somewhat. He remained short with her, yes, but he was also coming around to letting her have time with Alice. She hoped he'd see reason. His first wife had abandoned him when Alice was an infant; Noel was the only mother Alice knew. Surely he wanted Alice to have a mother in her life.

Her relationship with Alice was strained right now too, but Noel allowed herself to imagine taking her to London's parks and museums and shops, taking her for tea, having her with her for an entire school vacation week. They might get their relationship back on better footing. All this, and an opportunity to pursue the work that excited her, the work she had trained to do when she started the art history course in London all those years ago.

London. Thinking the city's name brought her excited anticipation to a quick halt. The last time she had lived there, she had experienced both the happiest and darkest moments of her life, with the lowest points leading her to withdraw from university to return to the States to finish her degree. No one except her grandmother had known the circumstances behind her departure, that she had left the city broken. Even if she could go back, should she?

Deb studied her face carefully. "I can tell you're thinking through all the pros and cons, and if you come to the conclusion that it's not the right move for you, that's fine," she said. "I do want you to be honest. I won't hold a 'no, thanks' against you, I promise. You can stay where you are. But if it's only the details that are overwhelming you, let me say there are things you won't need to worry about at all. Between them, the two museums will work out travel arrangements, your lodging, and help you secure any necessary visas."

The moment Noel was given an out, she knew for certain that she wanted the position; she wanted to keep moving up; she wanted to get away. This time around, she would stay on an even keel—go to work, do her job, dedicate herself to doing well, be professional. Going back to such a place didn't mean going back in time. She could put the lid back on this particular box of memories and keep it as firmly closed as she had for decades. Maybe it would be cleansing, standing up to the past so that she might be free of it once and for all.

The longer she thought about it, the more certain she felt she could face London. It was a different city to the one she'd known in the 1990s, and she was a different woman. Stronger. That part of her life was well behind her.

"I won't need a visa," she said, thinking aloud. "I have a British passport."

"There you go." Deb smiled. "You're speaking like a woman who is packed and ready to board the plane, and I'm so pleased. I won't lie, you'll have a busy few weeks before you leave, but there are relocation teams on both ends to make the transition as smooth as possible."

Noel looked at Deb. The hopeful expectation on her boss's face made her feel as if she should agree on the spot. "I know you'd like an answer now, but I do need to talk to Andy. I can tell you this, though: I've put advancement on hold for years—with no regrets, honestly—but the time feels right for a move. I feel ready."

"I agree; you are ready. Go home and think. Talk it over with the family. I will need you to let me know by end-of-day tomorrow, however. I wish I could give you more time than that, but I can't. Speaking of time . . ." Deb looked at her watch. "We've finished a little early. How about a cup of coffee downstairs, now that the business is behind us? Or a quick bite of lunch, since I've kept you from yours?"

If the cafeteria wasn't crowded, Noel calculated, she had time to eat and still leave early enough to catch Alice's skating practice and take her out for pizza as promised. Leaving here by two thirty or three would not be disastrous. There was no reason to say no to her boss, and in fact, she didn't want to.

"A quick lunch? I'd like that very much."

CHAPTER 3

SKATING RINK, OCTOBER 2022

The ice rink during practice hours was a noisy place. Several songs played at once, blaring and tinny through individual players instead of the rink's sound system. Three instructors stood at the barriers, calling out instructions and corrections to several pupils, while parents in the stands either augmented those calls with their own advice or chatted with their nearest neighbors. Sometimes there were angry shouts from the skaters, or loud sobs of frustration. Some of the parents continued to talk through these interruptions or scroll their phones, paying attention to the ice only when their own child was on it.

Andy was one of those parents—uninterested in anyone but Alice, even taking notes when she skated. But not Noel. She loved the athleticism and the grace of each skater, even the youngest ones who hadn't quite mastered grace. It took courage to be out there, gliding across a sheet of frozen water on thin blades.

She stood inside the entry and assessed how late she was by locating Alice, figuring out what she was working on. Footwork sequences. Noel had arrived pretty far into practice. All her daughter had left to do were her final endurance laps around the rink and a cooldown.

After they'd wrapped up their meeting, Deb had whisked her off to Craftsman, the museum's white-tablecloth restaurant, and not the cafeteria as Noel had expected. "To celebrate," she had said while leading Noel to the elevator. "I have a good feeling your answer will be yes. I'm an optimist."

Even though Noel had passed on dessert, lunch had taken longer than anticipated. And after lunch, feeling a little light-headed from the glass of prosecco Deb had insisted on ordering, she had gone back to her office instead of getting right in the car and passed some time finishing up paperwork and sharing with Paula the news that had been discussed at the meeting.

Paula had been as surprised as Noel, then alternately thrilled and anxious when she learned it was likely that she'd be Acting Director in Noel's absence. Perhaps full-fledged, once Noel's promotion was made official—but Noel kept that part to herself, as Deb had asked. There was enough for the two women to celebrate, in any case, and they had, hugging and congratulating each other and hugging again. It had been a joy to tell someone who was simply happy for her. Telling Andy when she dropped Alice at home later would be far more complicated.

It turned out she wouldn't have to wait until she brought Alice home to talk to him. As she scanned the crowd looking for a seat with a good view of the ice, she spotted him. He had a favorite bleacher, and most of the seats around him were empty. She stood for a moment longer, watching him. He leaned forward, elbows resting on knees, chin on his fists, watching Alice work through her sequence, his eyes taking nothing else in.

He wasn't supposed to be here, and it annoyed Noel that he was encroaching on her time with Alice. Had he forgotten that he'd agreed to her pickup and pizza after, she wondered?

Uncertain but determined, she composed her face, relaxing her frown into a smile, and walked across the rink to him.

He didn't track her approach and only looked her way when she sat next to him.

"I wasn't expecting to see you here," she said. "I thought this was my day to do the pickup. Pickup and supper out. Or did I get the day wrong?"

"Hello to you, too," Andy said, his eyes already focused back on the ice. "You know I always catch practice."

Noel didn't engage. It was awkward to be in Andy's company since she had moved out. But with Alice and her best interests in common, they could be civil. Noel located Alice on the ice. "She's doing very well."

Andy laughed. "She's got a special talent, and it helps that she's determined. I know you think we all push her too hard. Me. Coach." He held his hand up, somehow knowing Noel was about to open her mouth to protest even though his eyes were back on the ice and his daughter. "You do. But it's all Alice. Some of these kids are good but they don't practice the basics enough. And that's where she stands out."

Before Noel could think of the right thing to say in reply, Andy changed the subject. "You're later than you said you'd be."

"A last-minute meeting with Deb ran a bit long," she said, seeing her opening. "I got here as soon as I could. Turns out there's an opportunity she wanted to discuss with me. A work-related opportunity that I need—"

"Did you see the triple, Dad? I nailed it!" Alice had skated over to the dasher boards, excited to celebrate her accomplishment.

"Stay focused, Alice!" her coach called from behind her.

Alice swiveled in her direction. "I know, I know," she said, "time for laps." She looked back at Andy and rolled her eyes.

When she lingered a moment longer, Noel lifted her hand in a wave. "Nice work out there!"

Without acknowledging her presence, Alice pushed off from the side and skated right into her laps.

Taken aback, Noel said, "I thought she was looking forward to tonight."

"She changed her mind," Andy said stiffly. "She's still not ready for a night out alone with you. To be honest, I'm not ready for it either."

Noel looked at him. He was still only showing her his profile, intent as he was on Alice. "We discussed—"

"I know what we discussed. But she's still upset. She asked me to ask you . . ." He paused, as if searching for the right way to say whatever was on his mind.

"Ask me . . ." she prompted, even though she was worried by the change of plans.

"She wondered, and I did too," he began, "if instead of taking her out for pizza, you might come to ours for supper? I put together a lasagna last night. Alice's request."

Come to "ours." Of course it wasn't hers anymore, but the reality gave her pause.

When Noel didn't answer, Andy continued, "She told me she wants to take this slowly. I thought you'd agree. Unless you have other plans?"

My only other plans were pizza and spending time alone with Alice, Noel thought to herself, but she kept the sharp remarks in check. This was about mending the rift with her daughter, she reminded herself, and if this was what would make her daughter happy, then she'd save the pizza plans for next time. "Of course, that would be nice. Thank you."

Andy nodded, and after a few seconds he said, "I need to stretch my legs. I'll go get Alice a hot chocolate for when she's finished. Can I get you something?"

"No, I'm fine. You go. These bleachers are killer, and you've been sitting for a while," Noel said, trying to keep things light.

Andy nodded and stood up. He took a few steps but then stopped. "You started to say something earlier. About work? Some kind of work opportunity?"

"It's nothing important, really. We can talk about it later. Actually," she added as Andy smiled and started off again for the snack stand, "I will have a hot chocolate, if you don't mind."

Without a backward glance, Andy lifted a hand, acknowledging he'd heard her.

When he was out of sight, Noel exhaled the breath she was holding. It would only be a matter of minutes to make the extra drink, but she needed the time alone to prepare herself for this change in plans: spending an evening in the home that was no longer hers with a daughter who didn't want to be alone with her and an estranged husband who no longer trusted her.

She didn't blame either of them; there was much for her to repair. But the fractured situation made it the worst possible time to bring up the secondment news and her idea of having Alice visit her in London. She'd let herself be carried away by what might be instead of coming to terms with what was.

CHAPTER 4

OUTSIDE ANDY'S HOME, OCTOBER 2022

Once practice ended, the skaters raced each other for the gate and left the ice. Noel knew Alice would emerge from the locker room only after she had changed into street clothes and packed up her equipment so she stayed put in the bleachers, sipping her cocoa.

Andy stood and picked up the cup of cocoa he had bought for Alice. "I'll go wait outside the locker room."

"Okay. Good idea. We'll wait there instead." She reached under the bleacher for her bag and then stood up.

Andy didn't move. "There's no need for both of us to be here. Why don't you go on ahead to the house?"

"I really don't mind hanging around for a bit," Noel said. "I can say hi to Alice and then follow you home."

"Noel, I think it's best if we meet you there," Andy said firmly.

"Oh." Despite the rink's cold, Noel's face felt warm with embarrassment. She'd thought Andy was being considerate of her, warning her it could be a long wait. The truth was, he didn't want her to wait with him. "Sure. I'll see you there. I can check work email while I wait."

Noel relived the embarrassment of misunderstanding Andy as she pulled up to the curb in front of the locked, empty house and parked.

Here she was, back. Under the streetlights, the bright yellow leaves of the sugar maples in the side yard glowed. The lawn was clipped and edged, the shrubs trimmed, and the house as tidy as ever. Even parking where she just had was typical. Yet her car felt out of place; she felt out of place. She could imagine the neighbors peering out their windows, surprised to see her car again and curious to know why she was here.

The last time she had been at the house was the morning after she and Andy had thrown a party, with his new boss and colleagues in attendance, to celebrate him landing a new job.

Hands still on the steering wheel, Noel closed her eyes. She could picture all of them in the last throes of that party as clearly as if it had happened yesterday. Could picture herself walking around the dining table, clearing the half-empty and nearly empty serving bowls, sauce boats and baking dishes, crumpled napkins, used utensils, and emptied wine glasses. Could see Andy in the living room, having a one-on-one conversation with the man who'd hired him, Christopher Murray—Chris, as he'd invited Noel to call him when he introduced himself and his wife, Hayley, at the front door. The circle of women, wives and partners, chattering about children balking at college application deadlines and how once-sunny babies had become such sullen, stubborn teens. She remembered smiling at the complaints but not engaging, instead going about the business of clearing the table clutter to make room for dessert.

But then one of the women had called out to her. "How about you, Noel? I know Alice is only eleven, but do you and Andy have older children applying to colleges this year?"

Noel recalled how she had turned, her arms full of dishes bound for the kitchen sink, and looked at the well-dressed woman who had asked the question. Nancy. Her smile was warm and her eyes held genuine interest. Still, Noel dreaded questions like hers in case they prompted even more personal questions. *Is Alice your only child? Did you choose to wait, or . . . ?*

She must have looked stricken, because before she had a chance to say, "No, Alice is our only," Nancy had apologized.

"That was too personal, I'm sorry. I'm always doing that, speaking without thinking."

"It's fine." Thinking of what the night meant to Andy, Noel had smiled through her answer, although she hadn't felt like it. "No older children. Andy and I have only been married six years."

Once she'd said that, though, Nancy had looked puzzled, and Noel realized she had done the opposite of heading off further questions. Cursing herself for the mistake, she'd added, "Andy was a single dad when I met him. I'm Alice's stepmom."

"Oh!" exclaimed Chris's wife, Hayley, before Noel could exit the conversation and the room. "I'm a stepmom like you, Noel. Chris has three boys from his first marriage." As Hayley spoke, she rubbed her hand over her stomach, the circles drawing Noel's attention to a small but unmistakable bump. A pregnancy. Unlike Noel, she would have the stepkids and her own child too.

In the quiet of the car, Noel rested her forehead on the steering wheel. If only the reminders had ended with Nancy's and Hayley's innocuous attempts at bonding with her. Noel might have been able to shove those conversations and everything they stirred up in her to the back of her mind. She might have gotten through the evening with her marriage intact.

But not long after she'd gone into the kitchen to escape the group of women, Andy had followed.

"Noel?"

She was so engrossed in her tasks, she jumped at the sound of Andy's voice. He was standing in the doorway.

"I was wondering what happened to you," he said.

Noel managed a smile. "Wrangling these desserts was more than I bargained for."

"Oh, right," he said, looking over at the counter and the spread of cakes and tarts waiting there. "Before I forget"—he looked back at Noel—"do we have sparkling water? Chris asked if we had any. Hayley's stomach is bothering her and we only have still on the table."

Noel pointed to the fridge. "There's some chilling."

"Thanks," he said, but he didn't make a move for it.

"What is it?" she asked him.

"You don't think there was something wrong with the food you served, do you? You didn't let anything sit out too—no, forget it. I know you're careful."

His tone conveyed that he wasn't 100 percent certain that Noel had taken care, and that irked her. Without thinking, she blurted, "It wasn't my cooking. She's pregnant."

Andy gave an incredulous laugh. "What are you talking about?"

"Hayley is pregnant. It's a logical guess," she said, holding up a hand, when she saw his skeptical look. She began counting off: "You said her stomach is upset, one. Two, she keeps putting a hand on her belly. And, three, she didn't have any wine all night."

"Lots of people don't drink in these kinds of social situations. You didn't," he pointed out. "For a person who's never been pregnant, you sure seem to know a lot," he added, grinning. A picked-over bowl of shelled pistachios she'd yet to empty into the trash caught his eye and he grabbed a handful, popping them one by one into his mouth.

Noel said nothing. For what was the rebuttal, she wondered? Not the truth—not with a houseful of strangers, not at this point in their marriage.

"Why don't you head back and let everyone know I'll be right in, okay?" Noel said, the most efficient way she knew to dismiss him from the kitchen. "I'll bring the San Pellegrino in a minute."

Noel lifted her head from the steering wheel, recalling how, after Andy had rejoined the conversation in the other room, she had looked around their familiar, well-loved kitchen. The creamy yellow walls, the family photos on the fridge, the cool tumbled surface of the granite island. It had always been her favorite room in the house—the place where everyone gathered, foraged for snacks, poured wine, laid out homework, baked cookies, talked. The room where she dropped her work bag and changed from working professional into wife and mother, and where she dressed Alice's skinned knees and nursed her less obvious but equally painful friendship wounds. That kitchen meant home, the place where she'd landed after believing she could move on.

And Andy, the doting father she'd met outside the ladies' room door almost seven years earlier, had felt like the person she could move on with. *Andy is someone,* she'd thought, *who, despite his pain, is open to meeting new people, talking, having new experiences.*

In those early days of their relationship, when she was still crushed by Ed's leaving and her infertility, Andy had been an inspiration, a model for her of the kind of person she hoped to be after too many years of regretted decisions and false starts and disappointments. How resilient he was, she'd thought, to take a chance on starting over with her after he'd been so deeply hurt by Marisa and her "unnatural decision," as he had called it on their second or third date. ("Who has a child and then leaves? What kind of woman leaves her child?")

She'd never answered him; instead, she'd left the question hanging in the air between them. After all, decades had passed since that day when Gran had arrived at her London flat with a suggestion to help in a way that twenty-year-old Noel had not considered, not in a million years. "Why not put it all behind you and come home with me, unencumbered?"—as if what she was leaving behind was nothing more than excess luggage, a drag on her.

And she had. She'd gotten on that plane. She'd left London and everyone who was important to her behind—and, with time, the worst of her anguish had passed. She'd begun to believe that Gran had been right, that leaving had been for the best. She'd come to believe that she could keep the past to herself—her business, no one else's. But the truth had followed her, and Andy, on the night of the party, had unwittingly stumbled into it. *For someone who's never been pregnant, you sure seem to know a lot.*

She wasn't ever going to set him straight, but once he'd spoken those words, she couldn't continue living a lie either. That was the moment she knew her marriage was over. Telling him the next morning that she was leaving had only been a formality.

Headlights coming up behind her and lighting the interior of her car brought her back to the present. It was Andy and Alice slowing down, then passing her on their way to the garage. Noel straightened up and shook her head, clearing her thoughts. It was time to see Alice; it was time to talk to Andy about London. She took a breath and popped open the car door.

CHAPTER 5

ANDY'S HOME, OCTOBER 2022

By the time Noel made it to the garage, Alice had already bounded into the house.

"She has homework," Andy told her. "I want her to get a jump on it."

Noel nodded, then trailed a few steps behind as he followed Alice's path from the garage into the kitchen.

After switching on the oven, Andy walked over to the fridge, took out the lasagna, and set it on the counter.

"Can I help with something?" Noel asked. "Set the table? Make a salad?"

"That would be weird, don't you think?"

Before she had a chance to ask what he meant by that, he said, "Salad's made already, and Alice is responsible for the table, remember?"

She nodded. "I remember."

"By the way . . ." He walked back to the sink and grabbed a serving dish that was set off to one side. A Meissen serving bowl, an heirloom from Noel's grandmother. "You forgot this when you packed up." He slid it across the island toward her.

She put her hand out and stopped the slide of the bowl. As she did, a loose chip of porcelain inside rattled.

"Oh." She reached in and picked up the shard, smaller than a dime. "What happened?"

"I figured you knew. It was like this when I got down the stack of bowls the other day." He peered closely at the dish's chipped rim and shrugged. "It's barely noticeable."

She nodded, holding her tongue. It might be a small nick, but the bowl was all she had left of her grandmother. "Sentimental people are drawn to the museum world," Andy had teased early on in their relationship, implying that a desire to work with art and artifacts meant she preferred to live in the past.

That simply wasn't true. Rather than dwell in the past, she had moved forward. Gran had taught her that—to keep going, to see her own history as being malleable, the future not defined or fixed because of anything she had done or that had been done to her. The attachment to the bowl had nothing to do with a desire to turn back time and everything to do with remembering the lessons in her grandmother's steely will.

Maybe it won't look too bad if I glue the piece back on, she thought, but it bothered her that it would always be marred now. The bowl had been intact the last time she used it, she was certain. The night of their party. Certainly she would have noticed a chipped rim before filling it with salad.

She was so lost in these thoughts that she only heard the tail end of a question Andy was asking her.

"Tell you . . . ? I'm sorry, I missed most of what you said."

"I said, it felt like you were being evasive at the rink when I tried to follow up with you about the work opportunity you mentioned." He frowned. "'Not important.' 'Tell you later.' Do you want to tell me now? It's later, after all."

"The rink was noisy and the girls were winding up their practice—it didn't feel like the right time," she said evenly. "But sure, we can talk about it now if you'd like."

He gestured with his hand, yielding her the floor.

"Okay, well, the opportunity. Deb made me an offer that might turn out to be fun for all of us."

"For all of us?" he echoed with a dubious look. "Go on."

Encouraged, she continued. "She offered me a six-month secondment to the Addison Gallery in London. From the beginning of November through mid-May. They want me as part of the team responsible for curating and mounting the UK Rising Artists Exhibition in conjunction with the awards. I'll help make decisions regarding the show, I'll interview the artists, review their entries, write the exhibition catalog—all that."

He made a face. "Your boss is giving you a six-month . . . trip? Why? What's in it for her?"

"She wants me to get this experience under my belt so that I can move from Collections to Curatorial in the spring. She's told me I'll be promoted when I get back. Different responsibilities, work I've always wanted to do."

"But couldn't, I get it. So training, essentially. When she could hire someone who already knows this stuff." He shook his head. "That sounds like a waste of time and money, if you ask me. But that's a nonprofit for you."

She tamped down the anger she felt at his dismissiveness. "Loads of for-profit businesses use secondments to develop their staff," she said with more patience than she felt. "If they like a person, they invest in the person." She waited a beat, then dove on. "If I go, I'd like Alice to come over for a visit, or even two. She has three school breaks during those six months. What would you think of that?"

Time passed as Andy stared at her and said nothing. The kitchen was quiet, no noise but the wall clock ticking away the seconds and the oven fan whirring as the oven preheated.

Finally, he spoke. "If you go?"

"I haven't accepted the offer yet. I told Deb I'd talk to you before I gave her an answer. But she does need an answer quickly—tomorrow, she said. I'd have to leave in a couple of weeks."

"If you go."

"Yes." She waited a moment and added, "Of course. *If*. But I do think it could be a lot of fun for Alice. The Addison is offering a two-bedroom flat. She and I could have a mother-daughter adventure. And you'd have a break back here."

He waited another few moments, then shook his head. "Flying Alice overseas for a week when she's not comfortable with you right now? How could you possibly think this is a good idea?" He glared at Noel and then walked away, opening cabinets, grabbing dishes, setting them on the counter with a clatter. He strode over to the refrigerator and stopped abruptly at the door. "'I'm divorcing you, not Alice,'" he said, looking back at Noel. "Your words. You promised you'd work hard to stay in her life, but now you want to disappear from her life for months?"

"I'm not . . ." She bit her tongue.

Do not let him bait you into arguments that you will lose. Her attorney's instructions came back to her loud and clear.

"I'm taking a job," she continued. "A temporary job. I can make some weekend trips back and forth. I won't be that far." She paused. "And I honestly thought it would be fun for Alice, a chance to travel and see new places." As she said it, she realized how hollow this sounded, how wishful and unattainable.

"Or is it fun for *you* to punt on your responsibilities for six months?"

"Andy." Noel pinched the bridge of her nose. "I get it, I sprang this on you two weeks before I have to leave. You must feel rushed. Why don't we—"

"Leave for where? What's going on?"

Noel and Andy both turned, surprised by the interruption. Alice stood in the doorway of the kitchen, a wary expression on her face. How long she'd been standing there wasn't clear. Noel started to explain but Andy talked over her.

"Noel is going to London for six months. For a job."

Noel looked at him. "Come on. It's a little more involved than that." She looked back at Alice. "I've been offered a six-month job at a London museum, to learn some new skills. Of course I'll travel back to see you. But I also thought you might like to come and see me over your school vacations. I'm going to have an apartment in a great part of London and we could do lots of sightseeing. All the historical sites you've ever heard about—Buckingham Palace, Tower of London, Westminster Abbey—but also museums and plays and music and walks in the parks." Noel paused and then added, "We could have a lot of fun."

"Would my dad come?"

Noel shook her head. "It would be just the two of us. For one school vacation week, or maybe two. And in between, I'll make plans to see you here on some weekends."

Noel kept her eyes on Alice. She looked a little curious—until she turned to her father to gauge his reaction. As soon as she saw the scowl on his face, her shoulders dropped and she looked back at Noel. "I don't think I'd like to fly by myself. And I'd miss my friends and skating if I was away. Thanks, though."

"Exactly what I thought." Andy smiled over at Noel, triumphant. "Now," he added, clapping his hands together, "we've settled that. Alice, go wash up for dinner. I'll call you in a bit to set the table."

Alice ran upstairs and Andy returned to preparing for dinner, avoiding Noel—not speaking to her, pointedly not looking at her. He pulled a bottle of wine from the rack, opened it, and poured himself a glass as he looked out the window that overlooked the backyard.

"She takes her cues from you, Andy," she said, unable to take the silence any longer. "Maybe give this some more thought and—"

"I'm not going to change my mind," he said, still looking out the window. "Do what you want, Noel. Go, don't go. But tell me"—he turned around—"why did we spend all this time these past few weeks negotiating about visits if you are just going to turn around and leave her? 'I want to be part of her life,'" he mimicked in a falsetto.

"Stop. I do—"

"That's not the message you're sending to Alice. You're telling her that your career is more important than she is. You forget, she and I have been through this before. I don't know why I thought you were different."

"I said, *stop*." Noel fought to keep her voice down. "I'm not walking out of her life. This is a conversation about how I might stay in it and be an active part of it. Visiting me is one idea, showing her a place that gives her an idea of my history and hers. You know my mother and I were both born in London, my grandmother lived there for a good part of her early life. I could show her where. Visiting my grandmother's childhood home was one of the first things I did when I went over for uni—"

"*Your* family."

"Yes, I'm talking about where I come from, I said that."

"You're saying 'her history,' when really, you're talking about *yours*. It has nothing at all to do with Alice. She's not your daughter. She's mine. I think I've been mighty generous, but I won't be taken advantage of. In fact," he said, eyes narrowed, "it's probably best if you don't stay for supper. You asked to get out of this marriage and this family for reasons you can't even articulate, and you know what? I'll give you exactly what you wanted. Go on up and say goodbye to Alice, and when you're done upstairs, please let yourself out."

Upstairs, Noel stood outside her daughter's bedroom door, her hand poised to knock. Before she had a chance to, the door opened. Alice still wore the beanie that kept her head warm while she skated.

“May I come in?” Noel asked.

Alice shrugged and pulled off the cap. Strands of her dark, silky hair, full of static electricity, stood on end.

Noel had seen one photo of Marisa, Andy’s ex-wife, years ago, before Andy had found her snooping and stored the few remnants left of Alice’s mother away in the attic. Alice shared her mother’s dark hair and pale skin; the rest of her was all Andy.

She reached out to smooth down the flyaways but Alice ducked out of her reach. “Don’t.” She planted herself in the narrow opening between door and doorjamb, blocking Noel from entering. “I heard my dad,” she said. “I heard everything he said to you.”

“I see,” Noel said, and Alice began to step back into her room, closing the door behind her.

“Alice—Alice, wait a minute,” Noel pleaded. “I understand why you wouldn’t want to leave home and visit me in London. I can also understand why you’re upset with the idea of me going. If you want to talk about it, I’ll listen.”

Alice shrugged. Her eyes were dark, flat. “You’ll just leave anyway. What difference does it make?”

A few years back, Noel had found Marisa Bautista’s profile on Facebook and, in a moment of generosity—and gratitude, she’d told herself, for all she’d inherited from Marisa’s loss—she had reached out to her on Messenger. She’d attached Alice’s most recent school photo, along with a note explaining who she was to Alice and what a wonderful person Alice was growing into. The door, she’d said, was open for Marisa to have a relationship with her. A few days had passed before Marisa replied. “I know Andrew doesn’t think that way,” she’d written, “and he won’t be pleased if he knows you contacted me. I’m sorry, I’m sure you’re a very nice person, but don’t contact me again.”

In the moment, Noel had felt embarrassed by both the reply and her impulse to send the message—but also, if she was being honest, the tiniest bit smug. *Andy was right all along,* she'd thought, *you weren't a mother, and I'm better than you.* She felt humbled by that memory now, by how black-and-white she'd seen the situation as being, by how superior she'd felt.

I want you to come visit me! I want to keep seeing you! I want this to have a different ending! The urge to profess all that in her loudest voice was great, as if saying these things at the top of her lungs would convince Alice that the divorce didn't mean she was being abandoned. Instead, she remained calm.

"It's an opportunity to do something I've always wanted to do," she said. "Remember how I tell you to take a chance on yourself and your dreams? If I take this job, it doesn't mean I'm leaving *you*. I love you." She walked closer to Alice, gently took her face in her hands, and looked into her eyes. "I'm still your mother, Alice. I'll always be available to you, no matter where I am, whenever you need me."

Alice opened her mouth, then changed her mind. Instead of speaking, she pulled away from Noel, quietly slipped behind her bedroom door, and closed it.

CHAPTER 6

NOEL'S AIRBNB, OCTOBER 2022

Once back at her temporary home, Noel set her handbag and the Meissen bowl on the tiny rectangle of kitchen counter. The whole kitchen was compact and only very basically equipped with cheap, silicone utensils and the flimsiest set of knives she'd ever used. Not that she was doing much more than sleeping in this dim basement rental. She'd discovered early on that the vent above the range did nothing more than stir the air, which meant cooking smells lingered between the two rooms. It was easier and more pleasant to bring home takeout meals from the grocery store's cold food bar.

Tonight, though, she reached past the boxed salad in her small fridge and went straight to the wedge of cake she'd bought with it and stashed away. The rich chocolate tasted delicious at first, the buttery frosting hitting her tongue and making her mouth water. But the pleasure didn't last; the cake rested heavily in her stomach. Leaving the last few bites uneaten, she dropped the fork onto the plate and put it all into the sink before filling the kettle and putting it on to boil.

While she waited for the kettle's whistle to sound, she picked up the Meissen dish she had brought back with her. She felt the cool glaze on the rim against her palms and then the jagged roughness of the new flaw under her thumb. The piece was the only sentimental gift her grandmother, the most unsentimental of women, had ever given her. "My mother gave it to me when I flew the nest," Gran had said when she presented it to Noel, a congratulations of sorts for picking herself up after London and finishing college. "Now that you're on your way, it's yours."

She was surprised she had forgotten it when packing up her clothes and books and other important personal items for storage—but then, she had been working in a hurry that day, trying to get the boxes filled and ready to go before Andy brought Alice home from school. Otherwise, ever since it had been given to her the bowl had moved everywhere she had, waiting on shelf after shelf, biding its time for that right apartment, home, family. As if it might help her fulfill her desire for those, like a talisman.

The kettle began to emit a low whistle. Noel sighed and looked at the bowl one more time before setting it down. Tomorrow she could find some glue and make the repair. The bowl could come along with her to the next apartment, a more permanent one, once she'd found it.

The kettle went from whistle to high-pitched shriek. Noel took it off the burner but made no move to pour the water into her mug. Instead, she paused. In the wake of tonight's argument with Andy, she hadn't entertained any idea but staying put and doing her best to find a way forward with Alice. But maybe she should bring the bowl to her storage unit instead, pile it on top of the haphazardly stacked boxes in there. If she said yes to the London job, she wouldn't be needing fine serving pieces or a new apartment for a while.

Noel reached for her handbag and slid it in front of her. She felt around inside for her cell phone, found it, and scrolled through her contacts until she landed on Deb's entry. Her thumb hovered over the text icon. Was it unthinkable to go to London and put such distance between them all, she wondered? It was a risk. A six-month absence might make the rift harder to mend. Perhaps, though, with space, Andy's anger would cool and Alice's chill would thaw.

Or perhaps this was pie-in-the-sky thinking. Maybe this was nothing more than Noel drawing that imaginary line once again, preparing to move on from here and leave her mistakes behind. Or maybe she would be jumping from one problem to the next by wading into her unresolved past in London.

Nothing was clear. But she didn't think things could get much worse than they were at this moment. She tapped the icon and a fresh text thread opened.

My answer is yes, Noel typed. *Yes to London.*

Before she could change her mind, she hit send.

I was six when I found out about you. I was standing in the queue for school, holding my mother's hand, waiting for the doors to open so I might walk through them for the very first time. I was so bored that I kept kicking the paved walkway with the toe of my shoe. Mum tried to make me stop—"You're scuffing the leather"—and I would, for a few moments, until I got bored again.

After another minute of kicking, Mum squeezed my hand, reminding me to behave. "We're not made of money, are we?" she said and nodded in the direction of my restless foot.

A woman behind us, a woman my mother sometimes waved to at the market, spoke up.

"I don't know why we all arrived so early. It is hard to keep still for so long."

"Oh, hello!" my mother said. "Yes, it is. Although your daughter seems to be managing quite well." She smiled. "I believe we're neighbors across our back gardens."

"Yes, we are," the woman said. "We're the next street over. I'm Sandra. And this is my Daisy." She tipped her head at her daughter; she was holding her by the hand too. "And am I right that this is the lovely lad you got from the American? We heard something about it when you brought him home."

My mother gripped my hand so tight then that I said, "Ow!" I looked up at her in time to catch her shaking her head at the neighbor, a funny look on her face.

"Yes, this is my son," Mum said, a little too loudly.

Daisy's mother blushed. "Well, it's lovely to meet you. Maybe you and Daisy can play some—oh look, children, the doors are opening. Isn't this exciting!" She turned away from Mum and started fussing with Daisy's school uniform.

"Are you ready?" I looked up when Mum spoke, but she was staring straight ahead.

"Mum?"

No answer.

"Mum?" I asked again, because maybe she had not heard me now that everyone was laughing and talking.

She finally looked down. "Yes, love?" She had a different funny look on her face now, as if she was worried instead of bothered.

"What's The American? Where is it?" I remember thinking that our neighbor meant a place where parents found their children. The year before, when I'd first started asking questions about being born, my parents had told me I was delivered by the stork, but maybe I'd been picked out first at a shop called The American. Maybe this place was somewhere in town and I'd never noticed.

Mum relaxed a bit at my question. "Never you mind," she said, but then added, "It's something we can talk about at home. I promise. Right now, the only thing you should think about is having a wonderful time at school."

We did talk later, once Dad came home from work. And at the end of the conversation, I was no longer the boy brought by the stork to two parents who had waited for their very own child for fifteen years. The new story—the true story, Dad said—was I had been given to them by an American girl, a student who couldn't return to the United States with an English baby.

"But why couldn't she?"

"She wanted to finish her studies, love," Dad said. "She wasn't ready to be a mum. But she knew you would find a good home, and you did, didn't you?"

"She can come and find me someday, can't she?"

"Oh, son, no," Dad said. I remember he looked very sad as he told me this. "She has a new life and you do, too. That's what it means to be adopted. You are ours now. Remember, we had waited for you for years, and there you were. A child of our very own."

"But that isn't true. I'm not your very own. I belonged to someone else first, didn't I?"

As I looked at him, he sighed. "We didn't know the best way to explain how you came to us. Or the best time. But you're right, you belonged to someone else first."

"Will you and Mum be punished for telling a fib?"

"I feel very, very sorry that we told you something that wasn't true, son. That will be punishment enough, I expect." He looked over my head at Mum.

Mum had kept quiet the whole time Dad was talking. But later that evening, as I sat in the middle of the staircase when I should have been tucked up in bed, she and Dad talked more while I listened.

"This was always the risk of not telling him sooner," Dad said. "I knew that someone from town or someone from our families would put a foot in it. The social worker told us, remember? 'When he begins to ask questions, give him as much honesty as he can handle at his age.' Instead, we gave him storks and cabbage patches."

"And I'm saying we did tell him as much as he could handle," Mum said. "What other explanation could a young child possibly understand? I'm not even sure he understands now we've explained about the adoption, not really."

"He understands that we haven't been truthful with him. We didn't mean any harm, but if the time comes when he decides to look for his birth mother, we'll be the ones who kept the truth from him, and she'll be the one who can do no wrong."

"You're worrying about things that may never happen. He's loved, he's looked after. Likely he'll stop asking questions in a few days, once he gets caught up in the routines of school."

Mum was right. I did stop asking questions, just after. But not because I got caught up in school and forgot everything they told me. I stopped because my father was right too. I couldn't know if they would tell me the truth. But I never stopped having questions. About the words adoption and birth mother. About why you left and I stayed. And I never stopped believing you would look for me and find me. I know you will, you see. Someday.

I am—
Your son

PART II

DOWN THE PASSAGE WHICH WE DID NOT TAKE

CHAPTER 7

THE DISCO, NOVEMBER 1990

The dance beat pounded, steady and unvaried. At the song's chorus, the press of people on the disco floor raised their arms into the air in unison while colored lights strobed, illuminating the floors and walls and bodies. "Take me dancing naked in the rain!"

Noel stood apart from the scene, looking down from the balcony where the drinks were sold. She nursed a gin and tonic; she couldn't stand the sweet, yeasty smell of ales or cider. Discotheques were unfamiliar to her and she was too self-conscious for dancing. Alone up here, she felt out of place and conspicuous.

She had come at Calum's urging but knew no one in the crowd well except for him, and he was currently one of the arm wavers down in the crush of moving bodies. As she watched them, her overactive imagination conjured a fire breaking out, a stampede that might block a mass exit from the disco, the newspaper story she might not live to see the next day: *Death, Disaster at the Disco.*

"I should go home," she whispered to herself.

"You must come out tonight," Cal had said earlier that day on their way out of the lecture hall. He had linked his arm through hers and batted his eyes at her until she laughed. He was the first friend she had made at university, and now her closest one.

"You know I'm hopeless in crowds," she had protested while still laughing at his mugging.

"Even introverts need to blow off steam after the grind of exams and papers. You'll see, the minute you get out on the dance floor you can be alone in your own world, if that's what you want."

She'd taken a beat to give some thought to what he'd said. "Oh, all right," she'd finally agreed, "but only because you look so pathetically sad when I tell you no."

Cal and his easy-going ways had put her at ease from their first meeting over books at the bookstore. Other students in her course had acted aloof at first, wary of potential rivals. The art history college was competitive; museum jobs in London were scarce and highly sought-after. Such circumstances didn't breed easy camaraderie, and it didn't help that she was from America, still trying to find her way so many miles from home and her grandmother. But in a few short months, Cal had managed to endear himself to a large network of friends and acquaintances—male and female, foreigners and locals alike—both in and outside of university. He especially believed in balancing study with dancing.

He was also a good friend. Noel knew he'd look for her when he came up for air, and if she wasn't there, he would be disappointed to find out she had ditched him.

Resigned, she sighed and sipped her drink. It was warm. She had asked for ice and the bartender had given her one ice cube in return. She turned to look back at the bar, wondering if there might be a different server tending who would be more generous. Blocking her view was a young man dancing by himself, eyes closed, shoulders loose, his head bobbing and keeping time with the synthed beat.

He was breathtakingly good-looking. Not cute, not even handsome. *Beautiful* was all she could think about him. Sleek, dark hair that looked blue-black under the recessed lighting of the bar alcove and long enough to curl slightly at the nape of his neck. Olive skin, maybe; looked it, but it was hard to tell in the low light. He was compactly built—not short, not tall—and supple, at one with the rhythm of the music. *Soccer player, maybe,* she thought. *Football,* she corrected herself, and she watched him a moment longer, certain he was too lost in the music to notice and take offense at her staring.

She smiled, shook her head at him and at herself for watching, and then looked back out over the crowd. The song was ending finally, and she could see Cal below, searching the balcony for her. When their eyes met, he held up a finger for her to stay put, and he started to push his way through the other dancers.

As she waited for Cal to climb the stairs, a new song started, opening with an odd trill of plucked guitar strings followed by a simple chord progression on the keyboard. It was a song she knew, she realized, one her mother had sung to her often when she was in second or maybe third grade—in any case, only a short time before she'd had to pack up and go live with her grandmother. Ellie would play this one song from her favorite album over and over, picking up and dropping the needle each time it ended, saying to Noel as the song opened again with those first few, funny, plucked notes, "This is a song about us, sweetie, about how we'll always be together."

She hadn't heard this song since she was a child. Slow, a love song—nothing like the hard-driving dance music that had been playing all night.

Cal appeared at the top of the stairs. "Noel," he called across the room, "you missed . . ."

But the rest of what he said was lost, because someone behind tapped her on the shoulder and she turned to find the beautiful boy standing before her, his hand outstretched, palm up, fingers wiggling, calling for hers. He was smiling, and now that his eyes were open, she could see they were blue.

"Dance with me," he said. "I can't dance to this one alone."

"Do you know who that was?" Cal asked Noel as they headed for the doors to leave.

Noel shook her head. The beat-driven music had picked up again—ka-thunk, ka-thunk, ka-thunk—and she needed to be away from it and in the night air. She reached for Cal's sleeve and pulled him along. "Please, let's hurry. I'm awfully warm."

Cal offered her a raised eyebrow and a hearty laugh. "I'm sure you are."

They pushed their way against the tide of people coming upstairs for drinks and then through the smaller groups milling about the club's foyer until they finally made it outside.

The chilly November air was welcome. When Noel exhaled, she saw her breath float forward in a cloud.

"Bryn Jones," Cal said.

"I'm sorry, what?"

"Your dance partner." He tipped his head in the direction of the front door. When Noel shrugged, he said, "Bryn Jones. He's in fine arts, already won some prizes prior to uni. I mean, I hear he's quite good, quite focused. He's also quite gorgeous, which is objective fact, not hearsay like the rest of it. I must say, I'm a bit miffed you wouldn't dance with me down on the floor but you picked a stranger on the balcony to do it with—and to a song by Genesis, of all things."

Genesis. Yes, that was the name on her mother's favorite album. She could remember its title now too. *And Then There Were Three.*

"I didn't pick him," she protested. "I didn't even speak to him. I was standing with my drink, minding my own business, and dancing sort of happened."

"Did he ask for your name?"

Noel shook her head. "For the longest time, he was dancing alone—oblivious, I thought. I think he only wanted someone to dance with during the slower song." She tilted her head. "Genesis? Is that Phil Collins?"

"Phil is from the naff phase of Genesis, but yes. Wait." He grimaced. "You're not a fan, are you? Please say no."

"It was a song my mother liked. She used to sing it to me when I was little."

"Oh, no. Sorry." She had told Cal about her mother's death and growing up with her grandmother. "Makes sense you'd find yourself dancing to it instead of keeping me company. I'll let it go this time."

He poked out at her ribs with his elbow, but Noel hardly noticed.

Bryn Jones. She repeated his name to herself silently. She hadn't known it when she stood in his arms, held close by his hands clasped at her lower back. Names hadn't mattered. She'd kept her hands on his chest to feel the steady beat of his heart and her gaze off into the distance over his shoulder. She was almost his height, which was a good feeling. With taller boys, she often felt reduced, as if their height assumed some mantle of protection over her that she neither needed or wanted.

It was true he hadn't asked for her name. But he had instead given her another one. His breath had felt warm in her ear when he whispered, "I think you are my Lady of the Lake."

Noel had drawn back at that and looked him in the eye. "I'm sorry, what lady? Is that something to do with Sir Lancelot?"

Bryn had smiled at that and shaken his head. The song was coming to an end, the chorus repeating over and over into its final fade. He'd moved his hands from her back to her shoulders and kissed her cheek. "Thank you for the dance," he'd said before walking away.

"Cal," she said now as they strolled along Bloomsbury Street on the way home, the side of the British Museum to their right, a private park to their left. There were no neighbors or dog walkers in the small garden this late at night, no people with the keys to the gates taking one last turn. It would've been busier on Tottenham Court Road; tonight, Noel was grateful for the quieter walk. "Cal," she said again, "do you know the Lady of the Lake?"

"Is that King Arthur?"

"I think probably not," Noel answered, remembering her own similar question and Bryn's shake of the head.

"Och, Nessie, then," he said, dialing up his Scottish accent. "She's the only other lake lady I know."

They both laughed at that.

"Why do you ask?" he asked after a moment.

"Nothing important."

And it wasn't, was it? What Bryn had said to her had only been him being cryptic. Probably there was no answer. Anyway, they studied in different circles. It wasn't like they'd ever see each other again.

CHAPTER 8

UNIVERSITY COLLEGE, NOVEMBER 1990

Noel waved to a couple of acquaintances across the lecture hall when class ended, but she left the building alone. Most of her peers were heading down the road to a nearby café for the break between morning and afternoon lectures, but on Wednesdays, Noel had no late-day classes—so, instead of joining friends on those afternoons, she walked from campus to the Central YMCA, where she swam laps for an hour.

She'd learned to swim in the ocean and lane swimming in a chlorinated pool would always be second best, but she wasn't choosy lately. She needed the exertion of a hard swim to turn off her thoughts after being stuck in her head for hours on end. Swimming offered relief from the pressures of coursework, more so when she found herself sacrificing her well-being to it.

When trying to sway Noel's college decision, Gran had spoken reverently about the rigors of a British university education, although she herself had never gone. "Of course, I had to go straight from school to work in my father's fish shop," she'd explained. "And then I got married—you know the rest. But I always dreamed of going, studying literature, talking to chums about Jane Austen over cups of tea."

Cal had whooped with laughter when Noel told him that this romantic notion was what had finally persuaded her to come to London instead of studying closer to home. "If only it was cups of tea and an intellectual salon!" he'd said. "Little did you both know it's just bloody hard work."

It was, Noel had come to agree. Thrilling at times, always interesting, but demanding. The large lectures, the small seminars, the reading in between in preparation for the tutors' random questioning. It only took one time being poorly prepared and stumbling through an incomplete answer for Noel to understand there was nowhere to hide if she didn't know something or hadn't finished the assigned reading.

She hiked her swim bag to her shoulder and moved quickly to the building's front doors. She needed respite from the day's long, eye-rubbing sessions of reading and revising.

Outside, the day was gray but dry, cold but no colder than November was back at home. She wound her long, knitted scarf around her neck three times and then started down the building's front steps, paying little attention to the students seated on the stairs or leaning against the railings as she skipped by.

"Lady of the Lake!" she heard a male voice call at her back.

The name brought her to a stop. She turned. The young man she now knew was called Bryn Jones rose from the step he had been sitting on. His pants were spattered with paint.

"I'm sorry I had to call you that," he said. "I don't know your name. Mine is Bryn." He held up the carrier bag he had with him. "I brought you lunch. I thought we might have a picnic."

"A picnic?" Noel looked at Bryn quizzically. "Don't you think it's a little chilly?"

Bryn laughed. "Not outdoors. At the fine arts studios. I want to talk to you about something—a favor—and I thought, why not sweeten the favor with some food? Do you like cheese?" He held up the bag again and shook it a little.

Noel ignored the question. "How did you know to look for me here?"

"I didn't. But I recognized the bloke you were with last week at the club. Calum. I took a chance that you two were doing the same course. If I didn't find you on my own, I would have asked him about you eventually."

Re Cog Nized. Noel tilted her head. Bryn spoke with an unusual cadence, as if the three syllables were three separate words.

"Have you been waiting long?"

"Two mornings and two lunches, but who's counting?" He smiled. "Different food though, don't worry." His animated face was even more beautiful than she remembered.

Look out, a voice inside her—one that sounded remarkably like Gran's, the one she adopted when warning Noel away from all the pitfalls that awaited young women striving to make something of themselves—said. In Gran's world, most of these pitfalls took the shape of striking young men. *What kind of favors do you suppose every young man wants?* Maybe she'd tried so hard to warn Noel because the advice hadn't worked on her own daughter. Ellie hadn't listened, and had wound up with Noel when she was eighteen.

It had been easy enough for Noel to steer clear of sex before she arrived at university. The boys she had known in high school were either silly or cruel, drunkenly singing into empty beer bottles at parties or hip-checking smaller, more studious boys into locker-lined walls. But this one? With his quirky charm and disarming smile? She wrapped her arms around herself, stalling for time, as she wondered what Gran would think of his efforts to divert her from her plans, what she would think about her willingness to be diverted.

"Come on, then. When I've too much time on my own, I find myself getting homesick. Wouldn't you like to keep me company for a bit?"

Home Seck. Again, he spoke the two syllables like stand-alone words. And then, like he had in the disco, he held out his free hand and beckoned with his fingers. His eyes, she noticed, were the turquoise blue of light trapped in ice.

She put Gran out of her mind and made her decision. She took his hand. "My name is Noel."

"Noel," he repeated. "I like it, it suits you. Well, Noel, let's go have some lunch."

"Where is home?" Noel asked after a few minutes of walking in silence.

"Home," Bryn said, as he pointed to the right and led the way around the corner, "is the southwest coast of Wales, outside a little town on the sea called Tenby."

"I haven't been to Wales yet."

"And I'd never been anywhere else until I left to study at the Slade. I'll take you to see it someday."

"But I—"

He came to a sudden stop and looked at her. "We're here."

"Here" was the end of a mews and an unremarkable single-story brick building with a flat roof. It looked abandoned.

"This is the art studio?"

"It is. Painting only." He smiled and opened the door. He pointed. "I'm straight ahead. Go on. I have to latch the door."

She stepped inside and looked around. Many of the interior walls had been removed to make a mostly open floor space. Screens had been propped up here and there to create some privacy. There were several students in the large space, all of them hard at work. No one spoke.

As she walked across the poured concrete floor, her shoes squeaked, the rubber soles tacky against the painted surface. Her intrusion got looks ranging from dismissive to mildly interested to vaguely hostile. Only two people didn't take notice of her: a woman painter wearing headphones—big, puffy, padded ones, presumably to paint free from the squeak of interlopers—and her nude model. The model never broke her pose.

Noel whispered apologies as she went by but got no acknowledgment. She turned to Bryn and apologized to him too.

"Don't worry about it," he whispered in her ear. "It's only quiet now, but it won't stay this way for long. Trust me. The pretense of being devoted students is all for your benefit." He paused to look closely at Noel. "I'm glad you're here."

For a moment, she thought he would kiss her cheek again, as he had after their dance in the club. She felt her cheeks flush and she looked away from him and around the open space. "Where will we eat our picnic?" she asked.

"Straight down to business." Bryn mugged a serious face—eyebrows drawn, lips set in a line—but he couldn't hold it. The next second, he laughed. "Come around this side." He took her hand and drew her over to the far corner. "This is my space. You can sit here." He pointed to a wooden crate set in front of a large canvas on an easel. The painting—unfinished—was of a lake, flat-topped mountains, blue sky, the few clouds in it reflected on the calm surface of the water. Bold strokes and varying thicknesses of paint suggested textured fields in the distance, remnants of snow on the mountains, red flowers—or were those lichens?—dotting the rocks lakeside.

"It's pretty," she said as she sat down.

"Mmm."

She looked over her shoulder at him. He seemed in no hurry to discuss the work he'd sat her in front of or to mention the favor he wanted from her. Instead, he pulled a second crate over from its place under a small work table spread with paints and empty soup tins and a variety of brushes and rags stiff with dried paint, and carefully unpacked the plastic bag he said he'd carried around all morning while waiting for her. She watched him unwrap a wedge of very yellow cheese, take a loaf of wholemeal bread from its paper sleeve, and fish around the bottom of the sack for something else. A small knife, it turned out. When he laid his hands on it, he held it up in triumph. Then he sat on the floor and immediately pared a piece of cheese from the wedge and tore a hunk of bread from the loaf. He handed these to Noel and then sandwiched another large chunk of cheese inside a piece of bread for himself.

"Eat," he said, as he himself took a bite.

Her stomach rumbled but her curiosity about the painting in front of her won out over her hunger. "Does your painting have a name yet?"

"Ah," he said. "It does. For now I'm calling it *Lady of the Lake*."

She set her bread on her lap. "That's what you called me."

"Yes. I've been calling you by her given name since I met you. Nelferch, the lady of Llyn Y Fan Fach. Her story is one of the most well-known Welsh folk tales."

She laughed at the incomprehensible string of words he rattled off. "Nell Verk? The lady of what?"

"Nelferch," he repeated, emphasizing the guttural rumble at the end of the word, not as hard as the K sound she had used. "And Llyn Y Fan Fach is the lake from which she rose, this otherworldly creature who would fall in love with a mere mortal farmer named Gwyn. You reminded me of her, how you seemed to appear to me out of shimmering nowhere."

"Out of the beery haze of the disco, is more like it."

He smiled. "In the tale, the second time Gwyn saw Nelferch, he offered her bread and cheese—food of the mortals—which she didn't eat either." He pointed to the rough sandwich left untouched on Noel's lap.

"Oh." She flushed, then picked up the food and took a bite.

They ate for a few more moments in silence.

"Listen," Bryn finally said. "The favor." He stood, brushed crumbs of bread from his lap, and walked over to the easel. As he did, Noel remembered how much she liked his height, how sturdy and yet sleek he looked. "You had a good look at *Lady* before you sat down, and you can see it's not finished. Pretty, you said, and that's fine. I agree—it's a pleasant enough landscape. But it's not at all the Wales I'm trying to paint." He lowered his voice, as if preparing to share something confidential with her. "There are many beautiful places around where I grew up, and then there are the places that are both beautiful and magical. We have a folklore all about them, stories that have been told for generations about how these places exist as a . . . a bridge, I guess, between the natural and supernatural worlds. We've grown up believing if we sit long enough beside a lake like Llyn Y Fan Fach"—he pointed to the lake in the painting—"a magical creature like Nelferch will appear and speak to us. That's the Wales landscape I am trying—and failing, so far—to capture."

"That's really intriguing," Noel said. "But I can't imagine how you think I can help. I'm not a painter."

"Noel." He squatted to look her in the eyes. "The landscape needs its Nelferch, and I'm certain that's you. I'd like you to pose for me, I'd like to paint you."

"Paint me? Into this landscape?" She couldn't say what she had expected the favor would be, but this request had never crossed her mind. She couldn't possibly stand here or sit here—whatever—for hours in front of all these people while he painted. He had to see this. "I've never posed for anything—I mean, there are other models who know what they're doing. The girl on the other end of the studio?" Noel waved her hand in the direction of the artist who wore the headphones. "The naked one? She looked like she knew what she was doing. What about her?"

He smiled and shook his head. "I don't need just any model. I need the person who understands Nelferch. The person who can understand how hard it is to live between two worlds. I think you are that person."

She stared at him. After one brief dance and a cheese sandwich, he could see into her. Into the girl who had spent her lifetime moving from place to place at the whim of circumstance and other people, living everywhere and belonging—no, not nowhere, but rather in some place that was hers alone, the one comfortable place that she needed to claim, the one place she had yet to find.

She looked at Bryn a moment longer and then away to the other side of the room. She thought about what he'd asked her. Sitting for him would ensure this hole inside her would be exposed for days, more exposed even than the nude woman across the room. And she found herself drawn to him, more attracted than she should be. What if he, too, wanted more—until he saw how uncertain she really was inside? She wasn't ready to have her life laid bare for him to see and then reject. No. No, she should be in the water, swimming away from favors, putting impromptu picnics and observant blue eyes out of her mind.

She checked her watch. It was getting late in the afternoon. Soon it would be too late to find a free lane without waiting.

"What's the matter?" he asked.

"I'm supposed to be swimming. I need to get back."

"See? You really are Nelferch, going back to the water." He smiled as he made his point.

She shook her head. "It's not funny. I'm not Nelferch. I'm an art history student who swims at the Y. Look, I can't pose for your painting. It's too important and I'll only disappoint you."

"You will not. You couldn't." He looked at her then, an assessing look that took in all the features of her face. She felt how tangled her hair must look, tossed by the November wind. She reached up and tucked her hair behind her ear.

"Right." Bryn stood up, went over and crimped the paper bag around the torn wholemeal loaf, re-wrapped the cheese in its oily paper, and tucked everything back into the carrier bag. "I know how to prove it to you. If you'll come with me."

"I don't—"

"Well, I do. I think it will help if you could see with your eyes what I see with mine." When she didn't budge, he said, "Please let me show you. And if you still don't want to sit for me, I'll take your no for an answer. I promise." He put his hand on his heart.

The swim could wait, Noel decided. "All right," she said slowly. "You can show me."

CHAPTER 9

BRYN'S FLAT, NOVEMBER 1990

Bryn's flat was only one room but it was tidier than Noel had expected it would be. The bedcover was pulled up over the pillows and tucked under the mattress at the bottom to hold it in place. The only clutter came from stacks of sketches covering a small table in the corner, two chairs that tucked under it, and the patch of floor underneath them all.

Bryn started to gather all the paper into a pile the moment Noel followed him over the threshold.

"Don't fuss on my account," she said, shaking her head.

"I was clearing the clutter to find this." He held up a slim book. "Welsh tales for children, best I could find in the local bookshop. My granddad had a lovely old volume, but I've left it at home."

He held out the book to Noel. She took it from him and leafed through the first few pages.

"Page thirty-two," he said. "I'm making tea. Would you like some?"

"Yes, please." She took a seat on the end of his bed, one foot on the floor, the other tucked up under her, and flipped her way to the page number he'd given her. *The Girl from Llyn Y Fan Fach*. As she skimmed the story, she recognized the part about the bread and cheese Gwyn tries to share with Nelferch from Bryn's earlier recounting, and she smiled.

When she reached the end, she closed the book, marking the page with her finger. The kettle whistled and she waited a moment for Bryn to take it off the heat. As he poured boiling water over the tea bags, she said, "After Nelferch leaves, Gwyn imagines he sees her face every time he looks beneath the surface of the lake. Is that what you're trying to paint?"

"Something like that." He paused, seemed to consider something. "Tell me, what do you think of Nelferch and Gwyn?"

Despite her earlier reluctance, Noel found herself drawn into the moody story and the questions raised by it. "So far? It's a strange combination of completely fantastical and emotionally real. The part about Nelferch warning Gwyn that if he harmed her three times, she would leave him? It's as if she could see her future and she married him anyway. Why?"

"Maybe she thought things could turn out differently. People don't often start a relationship intending to be careless with their person, do they? We don't intend to do harm. Although I don't suppose intent matters if we grow complacent and do harm in the end."

She nodded. "It's all very sad." She was sitting but not quite, one leg folded, foot tucked up under her thigh, the other foot on the ground as if she might bolt. Instead, she turned slightly to look out the window. It was dark outside already; the streetlights were on. When she turned back to Bryn, she pushed a stray, heavy lock of hair off her face.

"May I take your picture?" he asked. He left the tea behind on the small table, walked past Noel to his nightstand, and reached for the camera resting there.

She shrugged. "All right. But why?"

"All in good time," he said, "but first." He sat at the top of his bed, near the pillow, to be at her level and brought the viewfinder to his eye. The camera, a Polaroid, was large and covered a good part of his face. He lowered it to speak to her. "Would you look to the side again, over your right shoulder? Yes. Thank you." He lifted the camera again and shot.

She heard a funny whirring noise followed by the spitting out of the instant photo. She looked back at him. "I haven't seen a Polaroid camera in years."

"I still find them handy. Here." He handed her the rigid square.

She watched as liquid seeped upward in waves from the bottom of the image. As it did, her form appeared—silvery at first, then gradually giving over to the colors she wore: blue, the black of her belt, her white shirt from Oxfam with its central fuchsia and gold floral mandala design, and finally the chestnut of her hair. She handed it back to Bryn before her facial features started to become defined.

He tapped the corner of the photo. "It was like this the night at the disco: I opened my eyes and you took shape before me. You were standing under one of the few lights—remember?—and you glowed up there, the one beacon in the dimness of the bar. I thought you were very beautiful, but more than that, you looked otherworldly, and I wanted to touch you to see if you'd disappear. So I asked you to dance. And I came looking for you the next day and the next and the next, because that moment of meeting you continued to feel a bit unreal to me. Still does."

"Is that why you took my picture? To prove I'm real?"

"You have a lot of questions." He took a last look at the photo and then propped it against the bedside lamp. "I took your picture because you showed me how to fix my painting. Also, because I wanted a photo of you. Here, then." He smiled. "Would you come over here?" He relaxed against the headboard and stretched his hand out to her.

She paused, considering what he'd said. She'd shown him how to fix his painting. Did he see her as Nelferch, then, poised not at the edge of a bedspread but at the edge of Llyn Y Fan Fach, just out of his reach? As an otherworldly creature that would help him capture what he hadn't yet—the dichotomy of the Welsh landscape, the tension between natural and supernatural?

She looked at his fingers, waiting for hers. They were strong and certain, with paint and ink trapped in the creases of every knuckle and under every nail. All she had to do was take this hand. She was afraid, though—afraid of this moment, of surrendering herself to it only to have it all disappear once he no longer needed inspiration for this painting.

Or she could trust him, herself, this moment they were sharing, how right it felt.

"I'll pose for you. But here, not in the studio, not with other people around." She reached her hand out, palm up. "And I'd rather you come to me."

He smiled wider, his eyes crinkling. He leaned forward and let her clasp his hand in hers, allowed himself to be drawn to her. "I can do all that."

CHAPTER 10

BRYN'S FLAT, JANUARY 1991

Bryn. Those hands, those hands of his—beckoning, reaching for hers, touching her face to know the bones there; gripping charcoal, racing across a sheet of paper, turning page after page of his sketchbook; finally, heavy on her shoulders, turning her toward him and then away until the light landed just right, a finger under her chin to lift it.

"You will look slightly defiant, because you are," he told her. "Remember, you've warned Gwyn, he's paid no heed, and your departure is nothing more than the consequence of that. Yes, that look, resigned but also annoyed: 'I told you so; why didn't you listen?'"

After what seemed like hours of touching and sketching, Bryn had filled several pages. He stopped working finally and went back and leafed through the book, his eyes resting on each drawing for several seconds. Noel could see he wasn't satisfied, that something was not quite right. She waited.

When he reached the last page, the same hands that had held her face and moved her body grabbed the sheet and tore it out. He crumpled it into a tight ball and groaned in frustration.

"What is it?" she asked nervously.

"It's not you," he explained. "You're brilliant. Look." With his finger, he traced the outline of her form on one of the pages. "It's about how the water around you looks, and the way you look descending into it. I can't quite capture the way the water welcomes you back. Before I can start painting, I need—"

Need what? she wondered when he didn't finish, but she waited patiently, watching the way his eyes flickered as he considered several ideas.

Finally, he smiled. "I know what we have to do."

Suddenly energized, he walked across the small room for his satchel. Into it, he packed a fresh sketchbook and pencils. When he reached for his Polaroid camera, though, he paused, his hand hovering over it as if he was having second thoughts.

He looked over his shoulder at Noel. She hadn't moved.

"I'm getting ahead of myself," he said. "You may not be pleased."

"Go on."

"How would you feel about bringing your swimming gear and trying out some of these poses in the water? In your pool? I know you aren't keen on doing any of this in a public space, and I shouldn't ask, but—"

"But you need to see me in the water," she said. "You need to know what Nelferch's body looks like underneath."

"Yes. That's exactly what I need. If it makes you uncomfortable to do this in front of other people, we can think of someplace else."

She looked at him. He looked hopeful but unsure of her answer. Back in November, she had been adamant about privacy, limiting the sessions to the two of them and the isolation of his flat. Maybe he could improvise. After all, Millais had painted Lizzie Siddal supine in his bathtub. But Nelferch was no Ophelia, lying still and succumbing to the shallows. Nelferch was intent on returning to her home in the lake's deep. Noel needed to have some of that same conviction. The pool was the only choice; she knew it.

Still, she asked, "Will you want to sketch at the pool? Or take photos?"

Bryn bit his lip, thinking. "Maybe a combination of both," he said. "I don't want to work solely from photos. Sketches will take time, but no matter what, this won't be something I can do quickly." He moved close enough to her that she could smell the charcoal dust on his hands. "If you'd rather not . . ."

He reached for her. Those hands, those hands of his. Marking her. Of course she'd do this.

"We'd better hurry if we want to get a lane," she said. "I'll get my things."

CHAPTER 11

BRYN'S FLAT, APRIL 1991

As it evolved, this painting of Bryn's captured the end of Nelferch and Gwyn—not their beginning, not the teasing or the mirth, not their new love, as Noel had initially imagined it might. Rather, it was darker. Bryn painted the tragedy of inevitability, of natural and supernatural trying and failing to merge. The lake, their meeting and parting place, was prominent and ominous. To the left, there was Gwyn, heading back to the mountains as if fleeing, his posture conveying an emotional range from shock to denial to regret to despair. Nelferch's face, meanwhile, appeared above the lake's central, deepest point, resignation written all over it as she welcomed the water closing around her. Her body underneath the surface was evident but distorted, swallowed and blurred by the rippling of the lake. An action that couldn't and wouldn't be undone.

The aura of despair became harder for Noel to shake after every session of posing. Each time Bryn announced he was finished for the day, she took to getting up, lifting her knees a few times, and stretching to rid herself of the fog of Nelferch's disappointment. Somehow, this simple movement would snap her out of it.

Then one day, as Bryn was fussing at the easel and she was sitting still, lost in the world of the old myth, he set down his brush, smiled at her, said, "That should do it."

"Done, done?" she asked. "As in, you've finished this piece?"

Bryn smiled, lifted one shoulder in a shrug. "Nearly. Close enough. At least, I don't need you any longer. The rest I'll do on my own over the next few days. Now"—he waved her off with both hands—"clothes on. Go on outside and walk around the block."

Dismissed, she grabbed her clothes and moved by him to the bathroom without a word. *I don't need you any longer.*

Now he will leave me, she told herself when she was outside, and she shivered. He'd been so brusque with her. Hadn't her grandmother hinted at something like this when they'd spoken a few weeks ago? Noel had gushed to Gran about this new relationship and had been met with a long silence on the other end of the line. In the space of waiting for a reply, Noel had heard her words echoing back to her. My "friend" Bryn. A brilliant painter. How silly she sounded, how vapid and young.

When Gran finally spoke, she asked, "A few poses? Not more than that?"

"Yes, of course," Noel replied, lying because she could hear the disapproval already and she didn't want to begin an argument while inside the phone box with the charge for the call adding up.

After a beat, Gran said, "The man driving the car your mother was in when she was killed? He was an artist, a musician. A third-rate musician."

As if Noel could forget. "Gran—"

"Flighty. Unserious. Careless. They're very self-centered, artists, and this is the time when you should be concentrating on you—your education, your career—without letting any man derail your purpose for his own."

Infuriated with herself for bringing up Bryn at all, she had claimed to be running out of money and ended the call as quickly as possible. She had avoided speaking to her grandmother since. But the seeds of doubt had been sown, and the ground within Noel had always been fertile for doubt. People she loved had left her. Why wouldn't he too, now his painting was finished?

When she returned to the flat, Bryn was busy. He had tidied while she was out taking turns around the park, moving until her breathing had pitched her mind from the folklore back into reality, and she found him now washing brushes.

He turned to her, and the broad smile on his face faded when he saw how dark and stormy her eyes were.

"Hey, hey, hey." He dropped the brushes in the sink. He had missed a streak of paint on himself, she noticed, a long dark gray one running down his forearm from the bone that stuck out on his wrist. "You look murderous. What is it?"

"You said, 'I don't need you any longer.'"

"As a model for this painting. Did you think I meant I wouldn't need you in my life, *cariad*?"

"No." She averted her eyes. "Yes."

"Then I was stupid to say that because it's not what I meant, not at all." He walked over to where she stood and put his hands on her shoulders. "You becoming Nelferch was playacting. Remember that. Their story has nothing to do with us. Only this does."

He took her clothes off her once again and led her into his bed. The paint on his forearm hadn't quite dried, and it smeared across her rib cage as he slid his hands from her waist to her breasts. She didn't care. Her back arched to meet him.

So this is being in love, she thought to herself, *all this feeling and longing and need.*

Bryn was the beating heart she couldn't live without, the drink of water in the desert. The idea that she no longer belonged only to herself was both thrilling and terrifying at the same time. Everything she felt was incongruous. Delirious and clearheaded. Giddy and serious. Joyful and terrified.

After some time in bed, he brought her over to the easel and they looked at the nearly finished landscape together. It bore little resemblance to its predecessor. Okay, yes, there was the lake with its rippled but clear surface, the broodiness of the fog slowly rolling out, the landscape opening up to reveal dark mountains full of looming shadows and reflections. But it was no longer simply striking and pleasant to look at. In this version Bryn had included, amid all the grays, blacks, and whites, a small red boat run up on the rocky water's edge, some kind of crude creel basket left in it. There was a sense of abandonment—Gwyn had grounded the boat and walked away bereft. In the lake, meanwhile, in the stirring shimmer of the water, Noel saw her poses below the surface—Nelferch at one with the water that swallowed her—while the outlines of the mountain shadows suggested something stolidly human. Gwyn, maybe—inflexible and dense, incapable of moving to hold her back from the dive, incapable of understanding why.

"Bryn, I . . . it's . . ." Everything she thought to say felt inadequate. She settled on, "There's so much sadness"—inadequate too, but true.

"There's a reason why the folk tale always ends with the sons of Nelferch and Gwyn becoming natural healers." He laughed. "Much as I despise that turn in the story, people like happy endings. The truth is always much more complicated."

CHAPTER 12

BRYN'S FLAT, MAY 1991

At some point during the month, Noel gave notice she was leaving her bedsit. Bryn's was basic but more convenient, and it would be cheaper to share. With *Lady of Llyn Y Fan Fach* completed, he spent more time at home, sketching, asking Noel to model when she could. He then took the sketches back to the art studio and painted from them there, hours at a time, juggling several large canvases. He took on more Welsh landscapes, more places where the real world met the folklore. Sometimes Noel's face or outline appeared in them, sometimes not.

Alone in the evenings, Noel threw herself into her coursework, something to occupy the hours until Bryn returned home, spattered with paint, ready to talk and to take her to bed. Study, work, sleep, talk, sex. She didn't feel nineteen; she felt older, wiser, full of experience, detached from the life her fellow students lived.

May brought Cal's birthday. He was going dancing with a group from art history, and he invited her to join them. Bryn was working so she said yes, but when she was there, she missed being home, waiting for him. After an hour, she feigned the spins, told Cal that she'd had too much to drink and the lights were bothering her balance, then hailed a taxi.

Cal had walked her out, and she waved to him through the window as he stood on the sidewalk, watching her leave. He frowned as he waved back. She knew he knew she was lying to him and was bothered by it, but it was too hard to explain that she needed to see Bryn—his face, the way his smile rearranged all his features into a portrait of joy, the fineness of his olive skin broken by the one small mole under his bottom lip, the dark, heavy waves of his hair as he tucked them behind his ears. She wanted to watch him walk up to the flat at the end of his day, to feel the flood of relief when he walked through their door. Relief that nothing had happened to take him away from her.

"Do you turn into a pumpkin if you miss one night of Bryn?" Cal teased when he caught up with her after class the next morning.

"Of course not," Noel said, and she looped her arm through his as they walked to their next lecture together.

A few days later, Noel went home to the flat after her last class, as usual, but the flat was unexpectedly still. Friday: his day for the shops, her turn to choose what they'd eat, and this morning she'd asked for some really good sheep's milk cheese from the shop they liked near Seven Dials. It was their weekly splurge: something delicious carried away, a loaf of good-enough bread from the good-enough bakery down the street, and a bottle of cheap Spanish Rioja from the off-license. But instead of Bryn busily laying out a sharp knife and a board, there was nothing, no one.

She stepped in, closed the door behind her, and looked around. His shoes were gone from their spot inside the front door, his coat missing from the peg. Maybe he'd gotten a late start; maybe he was out shopping.

Except. The windows she'd left open earlier had been lowered and locked—the drapes were limp and unmoving. Over at the sink, a few dishes rested in the drying rack. And the table was cleared of crumbs. And art supplies.

At this, she looked across to Bryn's painting corner. His most recent painting, a large one he'd been working and reworking but was still unhappy with, was off the easel and nowhere to be seen.

Maybe, in frustration, he'd taken it to the studio and lost track of time, lost track of the day of the week. Had to be. Cheese night could wait; there was always tomorrow.

Realizing she'd been holding her breath for several seconds, Noel exhaled. She dropped her bag on the floor, went to the windows, and opened them to let in the early-evening air and the noise from the street. For once, the noise of traffic and Friday-evening revel was welcome. But as she turned back to the empty room, she still felt anxious—something still felt not right.

Maybe the answer to that was in the piece of paper waiting for her on the turned-over crate they used as a coffee table, the one that caught her eye as she turned away from the window.

He's gone. He's left you, you know. The certainty washed over her.

"Shut up," she said aloud. It was Gran's voice that she heard in her head, Gran's words spreading doubt, as she'd surely intended in that last phone call. Why would she allow such doubt to take root? There had been no hint he would leave, no change in his behavior. He'd kissed her this morning, tried to pull her back to bed and then laughed when she'd feigned impatience and broken free. He hadn't been upset, or distant.

Bryn loved her. And yet. That tented piece of paper next to the heavy ceramic candle holder, a flea market find. A note with her name on it.

She took a few more steps and reached for it.

Noel, cariad—

The city is a distraction. So I've gone home for the week. Or maybe two. I don't know. I've told my tutors a week but

I'm telling you it may be closer to two, if anyone asks. I need some open space, I need the quiet—I only decided this in an instant, this afternoon. And I knew if I waited until you were home to tell you, I would have asked you to come with me—but that would be me looking for an excuse to keep from working on these bloody paintings. I'll bring you to Wales with me another time. I want you to see my home, but not when I'm lost in figuring out this work.

PS: I did get your cheese. And the wine, though Portuguese white not Rioja. Look in the fridge.

XX Bryn

Noel folded the note along the crease and laid it back on the crate. It explained the empty flat, and it made sense. He had been struggling with the noise, the demands on his time. She even understood the part where he wrote that asking her to come with him would have been active avoidance of the work at hand. Anyway, they weren't joined at the hip.

Even though this was all true, running through every point felt like she was trying to convince herself, and that left her body feeling heavy with exhaustion. She plopped herself onto their small sofa and leaned her head back against the scratchy cushion. As she tried to rest and come to terms with the empty flat, Gran's voice found its way into her mind.

You know what this is about, don't you? It's not about the city being a distraction. It's not about him fearing he'd be bringing you there so he'd have a reason to avoid working. He means you. You are the distraction. You're in the way of his success. And didn't I write and tell you this would happen?

Despite her fatigue, she sat up. Gran's letter. It was in her bag, left there unopened for days, unread because Noel was still angry with her. Was that what she had written? A big fat "I told you so"?

Her bag was at the door. She heaved herself off the couch and walked over to it. She pulled the letter out, looked at the stern block letters on the face, turned it over to its seal. Her thumb flirted with the affixed flap for a few seconds—and then she changed her mind. With both hands, she grabbed the envelope at the top and tore it in half.

"Shut up," she said, under her breath. She tore again—into quarters, then eighths. "Shut up."

She let go of the pieces and watched them flutter to the floor.

Fatigue came in a wave again, but at least Gran's voice had been silenced. No energy left in her for tidying the trash at her feet, Noel walked back to the sofa. The cheese could wait. The wine could wait. So could the cleaning up. What did it matter if she left a mess if she was the only person here to see it?

She rested her head back again, closed her eyes, and slept.

Bryn returned after two weeks, as he'd projected. With the passage of those days, Noel's upset eased, and when he walked through the door again she was so relieved to see him that confronting the careless way he'd left seemed pointless. He was home.

CHAPTER 13

SWN Y MOR, JUNE 1992

Another spring passed, and then it was summer—and as he'd promised, Bryn brought Noel to his grandfather's home.

A small place in need of modernizing, the cottage still felt like an idyll. For a week, they drank tea and coffee in the early morning before walking the steep path down to the beach at Monkstone, a spot remote enough to dodge the families on holiday, so Noel could swim.

The water was too cold to meet skin this early in the summer, so Noel wore a wetsuit that had been left hanging for more years than Bryn could remember on a peg in the cottage's garden shed. Back at the cottage, he would peel it off her, dry her body, and wrap her in wool that made her sneeze. Then he'd take her back to bed, where they would stay until empty stomachs prompted them back to the kitchen to eat—toast, yogurt, blackberries from bramble bushes growing wild on the lot. Gooseberries, sugared and stewed. Cheese bought from the tiny shop up the road.

Once full, Bryn would work all afternoon—outdoors when it wasn't raining, in all light. While he sketched and painted, Noel read or walked or simply pulled up a chair and watched him work. The need to do nothing was new yet easy to get used to, surrounded as she was by cozy house and sea and sky and days and nights alone with Bryn.

But in two days they would be returning to London, and something seemed to have shifted.

Lying next to Bryn, Noel watched the rise and fall of his chest. He'd fallen quickly into a deep sleep after they made love, and his face was smooth and untroubled in sleep. For the most part he was happy, she could tell, stopping here in this old, familiar place. Since yesterday, however, she had noticed how his eyes had begun to drift from his work and fix themselves in the middle distance every so often, his brush hand pausing while he stood still for those few minutes. The first time she saw this, she'd been watching from the window over the kitchen sink, and she'd thought he'd had a seizure. Worried, she'd put down the tea towel and gone through the back door to get to him. By the time she reached him, though, he had resumed work as if nothing had happened. He'd even turned to the movement of her coming up behind him and smiled. All was well.

Or maybe not quite. She wasn't sure.

She ran a finger down his arm. He opened his eyes and shifted to lie on his side. He reached over and brushed the hair back from her face.

"Maybe I'll be able to walk again, someday," he said. "What enchantment has come over you?"

"The sea air, maybe. The summer weather?" She shrugged. "Maybe it's just seeing you here, where you grew up. I haven't done much analyzing." She narrowed her eyes. "Why? Are you complaining?"

"I am not." His hand left her hair and his fingers followed the lines of her ear, her cheek, her jaw, before settling on her collarbone. "Noel," he said.

"Bryn." The sound of his name falling from her lips pleased her. She whispered it to hear it again and then reached for him, drew his body to hers. Despite what he'd said minutes ago, he could move just fine. She felt him grow hard against her leg and they shifted again so she was under him.

"Well," she said. "This is unexpected."

"Christ, you are so warm and soft." His breaths came quicker now that he'd entered her, now that they were moving together. He looked her in the eyes. "Noel, shall we get married?"

She laughed at him. "You're being silly."

"I'm not."

She laughed again and nudged him off her.

"Wait," he said, "I—"

"No, you wait." She pushed him onto his back and straddled him. Everything inside her began to feel syrupy—liquid and warm. She sighed. "Ask me again."

"Will you marry me? Noel?"

"Yes, Bryn. Yes, I will."

The next day was just as bright, just as lovely, and yet a gloomier atmosphere had settled inside the cottage. Noel had woken up with an upset stomach that toast and tea couldn't calm. She assumed it was her period, finally—it was so irregular—but so far she had only seen a bit of spotting and now had come this queasiness. She didn't want to swim, and the longer she sat, the more restless Bryn became, both unable to settle at the easel and unwilling to walk off his spare energy outdoors alone.

"We could talk about our move," Noel suggested as she sat with a hot water bottle clutched to her belly. "It's coming up not long after we return. We should firm up our plans."

Now that Bryn was finished with his course, they'd be moving out of the small flat in Bloomsbury and into a larger one, together, in Shoreditch—a longer trip to classes for Noel in the fall, but more generous in painting space for Bryn. Close to the art scene and new galleries that were popping up in the formerly neglected London neighborhood. Cheaper, too, for what they were getting. She felt more than willing to travel back and forth to her classes for a cheaper, larger space that would support Bryn's painting. It wasn't too long before she'd be out anyway, and, with luck, working. The time would fly by.

Bryn paced behind the sofa, picking up books from the bookshelves and decorative objects from the mantel, glancing at each before setting them down again. When his hand started for a bowl on the console table behind her, Noel reached out and stopped him from picking it up.

"What is it?" she asked.

"Eh. Our holiday is ending tomorrow and reality is sinking in, I suppose." He pulled his hand from hers and lifted the bowl that had caught his eye.

"We should be in the moment, then. Come on now. I know I'm not feeling great this morning. But unless I'm dying, I'll feel better eventually, and we can do something with the rest of the day."

He scowled at her. "See this?" He tapped the edge of the bowl he was holding. "There used to be fishing hooks kept in here. And it used to rest in the kitchen, on the counter. I don't know when this became décor. Did I move this? I don't even know." He set down the bowl and started pacing again.

"Bryn."

"Mmm?"

She patted the sofa cushion. "Would you sit down?"

He sighed but he obliged.

"Now," she said, "tell me. And before you protest that it's nothing, I know it's something. I know you. Is it about asking me to marry you? Maybe you didn't mean to, but you got caught up in the moment? If that's the case—I mean, we're young, we can not think about it for a while."

"Is that what you think?" Bryn demanded. "That I didn't really mean to ask you?"

Noel raised an eyebrow. "I think something's bothering you and you won't say. So why don't you say."

Bryn stayed quiet for a moment, as if organizing his thoughts. And then he took a breath. "Could you manage a walk? I can talk to you while we're walking."

Noel clutched the hot water bottle tighter for a few seconds before setting it down on the floor. The nausea seemed to have subsided, only to be replaced by a flutter of nerves. If it wasn't the spontaneous proposal bothering him, then what? What could be harder for him to talk about than that?

"I can manage a walk," she agreed. "Let me get my shoes."

The shoreline was empty, save for two other pairs of walkers farther ahead. It was a beautiful morning.

A beach near Noel's home in the States would be crowded once school was out, with rows of beach chairs and blankets, people sunning in place or batting beach balls around, children shrieking at the cold waves lapping at their feet, parents calling them in for more sunscreen. Someone, somewhere, would be playing loud music, assuming everyone wanted to hear what they did. But here—practically no one. The ocean water was calm, the sand stretched flat and empty and damp underfoot for yards and yards, the hills they walked in the direction of were low and flat-topped and lushly green.

Noel had taken off her shoes and she stared down at the prints her feet made as Bryn talked. And talked. About grant money for a painting course. Of the selection process. Being awarded the funds for the course. Being accepted to do the course. Studying modern applications of classical techniques at the Uffizi. Then painting *al fresco* throughout Italy—in Florence, in Urbino, Ravenna, Barolo. An amazing opportunity, hard to say no.

"It's poor timing, with the move and all. I get that. I should have said something sooner. It's been weighing on me that I haven't. I will say no, of course, if you want me to say no."

She looked out over the ocean. She felt like crying. If she were wearing the wetsuit she might walk out to where it was deep and swim away, swim and swim, letting her tears salt the ocean.

Objectively, she did not mind him going, but she did mind the expectation that she'd be okay with finding out last minute. Her responsibility had been to speak up the first time he'd done this, but of course she had not. Well, at least this time there was some advance warning because she'd pushed him to talk; she could prepare to be alone—in a new flat, in a new neighborhood where she knew absolutely no one.

"Why is it up to me to tell you no?" she asked. "I think you want to go, so it seems you've already said yes? At least to yourself?"

He reached for her hand, tried to bring it up to his lips, but found her resisting. He gave up but kept a hold of her hand. "I do want to go. I also don't want to leave you to settle in the new flat alone."

"Yes, I see that's the dilemma. It really has to be your decision, though. I will be fine, you know." She would be. She'd been self-reliant all her life. There had been little choice.

"I know."

He continued talking, but Noel's thoughts went a thousand miles away. Maybe Cal could help her set up the flat—if he was still speaking to her, after how unreliable she'd been. She hoped he would be happy to visit or invite her in for a meal once in a while, with Bryn gone. He might have a choice word or two regarding Bryn, but that would be okay too.

Bryn came to a stop. As they were still holding hands, she came to an abrupt stop too.

"Did you hear me?" he asked. "I said I'll be home by Christmas. Gone from beginning August through the week before the holiday. I can arrange to have the furniture moved, such as there is. You won't have to do that alone."

"This is a wonderful opportunity for you, and you should take it," she said. "But one thing."

Bryn smiled broadly. He lifted her hand to his lips again, and this time she let him. "Anything," he said.

"The next time, talk to me first, so that we might work out the details together."

"I'm sorry, I've been thoughtless. I will remember to talk to you first. Always." He reached for her, pulled her into him, and held on tight.

Noel slid her arms up his back, buried her face in his neck. She tried to concentrate on the feeling of security she had in his arms, on the steady certainty of the water that lapped up and back on the shoreline behind her. But in her head she turned over the three words her gran had used months ago to impugn Bryn's character, the words that had caused such discord between them. *Flighty. Unserious. Careless.*

Generalizing couldn't capture the whole of anyone. Bryn was also loving, kind, generous—a life force. But Noel hated that Gran might have been on to something, a tiny kernel of truth.

CHAPTER 14

UNIVERSITY COLLEGE, SEPTEMBER 1992

Noel fumbled her way out of the ladies' toilets in the basement of the building. Her nose was running, her eyes watery, after the violent bout of vomiting. She'd felt poorly off and on since Wales in June—and not long after Bryn had left in August, she'd visited the clinic for a pregnancy test. Positive. Although the extreme morning sickness had already told her all she needed to know.

A month later, and she still couldn't keep her meals down. Today she'd at least managed to make it to the end of class before running for the toilet; other days she couldn't even make it out of bed. She found it hard to rest, and still difficult to eat at times. Because she never knew when the nausea would strike, her coursework was suffering, as was her peace of mind. A couple of her tutors had already expressed concern that she was missing too much class time, and they were only two weeks in.

Despite the persistent sickness, her most recent scan had revealed a healthy baby and good growth. She had looked over at the sonogram screen, angled in her direction. There, the outline of her child, its spine glowing white and curled like a comma, the tiny umbilical cord a mere shadow, but there. And once she had seen the baby's physical outline, she'd wanted it more than anything.

If it was a boy, she would call him Sam. Samuel, after Bryn's beloved grandfather. She and Bryn and a baby. The timing wasn't ideal, but they'd be a family. She could see it, the three of them in their big new flat—Bryn working at one end, she and their child playing, reading, napping at the other. Those dreams kept her going when she felt sickest.

She blew her nose on the length of scratchy toilet paper she'd taken on her way out of the stall and rounded the corner of the adjacent corridor. Approaching the same corner and heading in her direction was Cal. He'd been trying to get her attention for weeks and she'd been avoiding him. Every conversation he started lately worked its way around to disapproval of Bryn, his leaving her in the middle of their move for the painting course in Italy.

She thought about backtracking, but it was too late. He'd spotted her. He came to a full stop, blocking her progress.

"What is going on with you?" he asked, his eyes full of concern.

"Nothing." She shook her head. "I've had a nasty flu and it's left me wiped out. But I do need to get to lecture."

"No. You should go home. You've been ill for days—maybe weeks? I've lost track."

His eyes flitted across her face. She knew he was taking in the puffy eyelids, the dark undereye circles, her lank hair, her sallow pallor. Thank god she did look like she was recovering from the flu. No one knew she was pregnant, and until she was able to tell Bryn, it would stay her secret.

"You need a doctor," he said.

"I don't. At least, I've seen the doctor. The worst of it's behind me. Once my appetite is back, I'll be fine. Now, please . . ."

She tried to sidestep him but he moved with her.

"Cal, please. This isn't helping."

"Have you told him? That is, if you can reach him? He should be here."

Him. He. Typical. He wouldn't say Bryn's name. But no, she hadn't told him, because she couldn't reach him. She looked away, afraid she'd start crying and not be able to stop if she kept looking at the worry on Cal's face.

"Noel." He reached out and took her hands in his. "Look at me. You're struggling. On top of it all, your partner isn't here with you. That's the truth, isn't it? Don't try any bull excrement on me."

Despite her anguish, Noel had to laugh at his phrasing—a reworking of *bullshit,* a word he'd picked up from her, but maintained sounded vulgar.

The next minute, though, she was sobbing, her head on his chest, her tears soaking his shirt.

"Oh, dear. Right." He put his arm around her shoulder and started walking. "I think you need a hot drink. Can you stand a cup of tea?"

She nodded. "But only if it's the peppermint tea at the Moroccan place down the road. It's the only thing that doesn't upset my stomach."

"Oh, good lord," he said under his breath. "Peppermint tea it is. Come."

CHAPTER 15

MOROCCAN TEA ROOM, SEPTEMBER 1992

"Talk to me. Does he even know you've been ill?"

When Noel shook her head, Cal rolled his eyes.

"I'll talk to you about this, but only if you stop being hostile to Bryn," she said. "I told him to go to Italy, I practically shoved him out the door. Will you promise no more criticism?"

"Promise, darling. Only listening."

At that moment, the waiter brought a large pot of tea to their table. They paused speaking until he poured and left them.

"Go on, have some tea first," Cal urged. "Then you can tell me what's going on."

Noel took a few small sips. The peppermint seemed to sit well, and she took a few more. When she set her cup back on the saucer, she said, "When Bryn left, we agreed we wouldn't worry about writing unless one of us had an emergency or whatever. You know they're moving from place to place, right? There's no way to know where they are and when they'll be there, no way either to ring each other. So, when I ended up . . . sick, I tried to reach him at the address I had for him. This was supposed to be some"—she waved her hand while she searched for the word—"fixed address, I guess, for emergencies, a place where they'd hold letters until they were able to forward them to the people in the program. God knows how." She sighed. "But we didn't think about logistics. We weren't going to worry over each other, nothing would happen, it would only be five months! That all made sense, until I did have something to tell him. I wrote, and my letter got returned to me. I sent another out, and back that one came too. So, no, he doesn't know, but not for lack of trying."

"O-kaaay." Cal opened his mouth to say something, reconsidered, and held his tongue.

"What?" she asked. She drew her brows together. "This is the truth, Cal. I'm not making it up so you'll think well of Bryn." Mostly all true. That her letters to Bryn were full of news about the pregnancy and not the flu was none of Cal's business.

Cal held his hands up. "I wasn't thinking that, I swear. And I am listening, with an open mind. But I do wonder if you—or he—copied the address wrong?"

Noel shook her head. "It's a photocopy of an official form that contains the emergency contact address. I don't have a telephone number for the organizers, but I suppose I could track that down in the fine arts office, somehow." She shrugged. "But then what? I pass along a message about . . . being sick, he gets it, he comes home, and by then I'm fully recovered? He's almost halfway through. I won't be responsible for him leaving now, not for this."

"You're really sick, Noel. You know I think he is awfully self-absorbed at times, but I can admit he does seem to love you. I think he'd want to be here."

"Maybe," she mumbled. When she picked up her teacup again, her hands shook. *Unless,* she thought, and a chill passed through her. Unless he didn't want the responsibility of a child, a family. Right now he was traveling, free to pick up at a moment's notice. What if he didn't want this freedom snatched away? Of course, she had none anymore; this baby's birth would yoke her in ways it wouldn't ever him, even if he did wish to be a father.

Acknowledging this inherent inequity, she seethed. Just as quickly, though, she felt guilty—how could she be so angry at Bryn when he was oblivious to the pregnancy? When she loved him so much?

The only thing worse than thinking all this would be putting it into words that Cal would be witness to.

She said nothing.

"Come on, drink some more tea." Cal slid the pot closer to her. "No big decisions when your stomach is upset. It's enough for now to know that you have a few more ideas of how to reach him, in case you start feeling worse. But it's good news you've been feeling better, right?" he added quickly. "Maybe none of this will matter in a day or two."

CHAPTER 16

SHOREDITCH FLAT, DECEMBER 1992

Eventually, food started to stay down. She ate pastina with butter and cheese, fig rolls from Marks & Spencer, and tinned apricots with yogurt until she put on some necessary weight.

In mid-October, when she could no longer camouflage her rounding belly, she had withdrawn from the semester, telling her advisor she needed to regain her strength after the bout with flu. It was true she was desperate for sleep, as much delicious sleep as possible. All she wanted to do with her free time was sleep curled up on her side, her arms cradling her growing belly.

With the onset of December's colder weather, she had to wear an old, oversized overcoat of Bryn's when she went out to do the shopping. This venturing out she kept to a minimum, preferring to stay at home, indoors, away from the prying eyes and frank stares of the market stall vendors and neighbors who wound their way around the fruit and vegetable displays with her. She knew that they judged her, the solitary, pregnant, odd American in the worn coat.

What would Bryn think, she wondered, when he came home to find her so transformed, so ungainly? It would be a shock. That a baby was on its way would be a shock. She looked down over herself. The toes of her shoes were barely visible now; at this rate, she wouldn't be able to button the coat by the twenty-first, when Bryn was due back. "The day of reckoning," she said to herself with a wry laugh, and she prepared herself for any reaction. Anger, remorse, contrition, joy. Joy, she thought, because he loved her. "I knew you'd be happy about the baby," she imagined telling him while pulling him close.

She crossed her arms over her belly and whispered, "I know he'll be as happy as I am, Sammy. I know he'll love you as much as I do."

Bryn's arrival date came and went with no sign of him. Then it was Christmas and she spent it alone, eating cornflakes. Cal called by on Boxing Day and for a moment, hearing the knock, her heart leapt. *Bryn!* She took a step toward the door, ready to fling it open, and then she heard her friend's voice, not Bryn's, and she shrank back, staying as quiet as possible, while he knocked and knocked and quietly spoke her name.

"Noel? Are you in? I've brought you some Christmas cake from home. Noel?"

She hadn't seen him since she withdrew from uni, he couldn't see her now, not like this. *Go away,* she willed.

Finally, he did. Why had he even come by, she asked Sammy, the only company she now had. Why had Cal assumed she was here and not off with Bryn; what did he know that she didn't?

Mum is ill. Yesterday, after she came home with Dad, he fussed over her, making her a cup of tea with milk and three teaspoons of sugar. I asked if everything was okay and Mum looked at me and said, "Yes, everything is fine, don't you worry. Tired, is all." Dad made beans on toast for supper and, distracted, he scorched the beans in the saucepan, leaving a charred ring at its bottom and the beans smelling like ash. Mum thanked him anyway and managed to eat a forkful, although anyone could see cutting through the toast exhausted her. "Tired, love," she said to me again, because I was staring at her, and Dad told me to go upstairs to my room, he'd do the washing up. I heard them begin to bicker when they thought I'd gone.

"You need to eat a bit more," Dad said. "Let me cut that for you."

Something fell to the floor, there was a metallic clang as it hit the tiles.

"Please don't fight me." Dad again. "I'm only trying to help."

"Stop treating me like a child," Mum snapped.

"There, there," Dad said a moment later, his voice gentler. I realized he was comforting Mum because she was crying, and instead of going to my room I crept quietly down the stairs and headed for the front door.

Once I was outside, I ran as fast as I could, unbothered that my trainers were loudly slap-slapping the pavement. I no longer thought about Mum and Dad hearing me running from the house. I only wanted to be far away.

I got as far as the primary school before I stopped. Martin was there, sitting on a swing, smoking a cigarette. I caught up with him although we're no longer such good friends. He hates school and wants to leave as soon as he is sixteen. He comes down here and sits in a swing and turns and turns, twisting the chain up tight before letting it go, spinning him back around. When he's had enough of that, he smokes.

Last night he told me he has an uncle—or not an uncle, really, but a close family friend of his dad—who fixes up rundown houses around Manchester, around Leeds, around York for people with buckets of money. He's been promised a job laying floors or carpet.

"I can really do it," he said. "Leave school, make some money."

"That's what you want," I said to him.

He took it as congratulations and said, "Thanks. My uncle could probably give you a job, if you like. Painting. You love to paint, and houses always need painting. It might not be bad to work together, knock off at the end of the day and go to the pub."

I smiled at him, at this vision of what my life could be. When he offered me the cigarette, I took it from him and drew in a lungful of smoke. I don't like smoking so much but I don't hate it either. I handed the cig back and tried to imagine myself standing in an empty home, laying a sheet over the floors Martin had just banged in, slapping boring but inoffensive magnolia paint on the walls. It didn't seem real. I thought about when Martin and I were young, before primary school, and went around riding our bikes and having no idea of what it would mean to do a job, any job, or to have a sick Mum. I envied Martin's big bike back then, and the way he always seemed to be winning some race I didn't even know how to be a part of. He'll be out in the world soon, and confident of it. Maybe that's the difference between us and why we've grown apart. He's always known how and where he belongs.

Several months ago, I started a painting for my art class. My teacher liked it and asked me about it. I told her I'd called it Origins. It was you, or rather a look into your belly as you carried me. There I was, baby me, floating upside down inside, cushioned by all the layers of you, held tight by the lifeline that connected us. I said, "Please don't tell my mum about this." She looked at me funny but encouraged me to keep going; and later, when it was finished, she encouraged me to enter it in the Sheffield arts council art contest.

"I can't," I said. "I can't get it to Sheffield. I can't ask my parents to drive me, because they'll ask to see the painting." It was then I explained that Mum could never have carried me like this. "I don't want her to feel bad," I told my teacher.

"I see," she said. "What if I take it to Sheffield for you?"

I agreed and it was settled.

But I don't much like that all the different parts of my life have fences around them, maintaining borders between each other. There's the part of me that writes to you and sneaks the letters under my mattress, off-limits to Mum and Dad. There's the part of me that has questions I can't ask. Another part that can't tell Mum or Dad about this painting because it may hurt them. I don't like that no one can see me put together and understand all of me. I don't like that you, too, have fences and borders and protections around you so I can't know you. I don't like that you put them there.

Martin continued smoking and I stood quietly with him as he did. After another couple of minutes, he finished the cigarette and I lifted my hand to wave goodbye. I hadn't said much, but I never do these days. I did not tell him about my mother. I did not tell him about the art competition I entered, how the painting I do could never be replaced by painting the walls of renovated homes. I did not say that I'm trying to find someone with my art, as if it's a visual letter, as if the right person will see it and know I belong to them. As if you will see it and claim me.

I am—
Your son

PART III

SHALL WE FOLLOW?

CHAPTER 17

THE ADDISON GALLERY, NOVEMBER 2022

Jean Rayburn concluded her address at the welcome breakfast and invited the guest of honor to speak. Noel stood, placing a hand on the back of her chair to steady herself. On top of the lingering jet lag from Sunday's overnight flight, she was also famished and feeling dizzy from it. She'd had little to eat since arriving and being deposited at the flat that would be her home for the next six months. Someone had kindly left eggs and an unsliced loaf of wholemeal bread, along with coffee pods for the Nespresso machine and some milk and orange juice, but Noel had been simultaneously too tired and too keyed up to cook or even eat. Instead, she'd fallen right into the comfortable enough bed, expecting to sleep hard—only to discover she wasn't sleepy enough to quiet the thoughts about Andy and Alice, their uneasy truce, and how stilted and uncomfortable their last few conversations had been.

Dozens of unfamiliar faces stared at her now, waiting for her to say something, waiting for her to be finished so they might grab a pastry and get back to work. She smiled and summoned a hearty hello as she looked around the room at her new colleagues. "Thank you for making my first morning so warm and welcoming. I'm pleased to join you all and get to know many of you. To my new team, I look forward to working together to launch the show. Now, I think I've kept you all from breakfast too long. Shall we have something to eat?"

The room broke out into a light applause. She was grateful for the noise. Her stomach was grumbling in a foreboding way. Earlier, while meeting in Jean's office with the Human Resources officer, she had been plied with cup after cup of tea. All that tea on her empty stomach wasn't sitting well.

Once everyone headed for the table piled high with breakfast pastries and fruit, she looked around her to see if she might slip off unnoticed to the ladies' room.

A man standing across the room was staring at her, his eyes crinkling as if there was a smile on his face behind his COVID mask. The attention was perplexing, but perhaps he was simply extra friendly. As she started to return his smile, she was struck with a sense of familiarity. Close to her in age, perhaps; balding; the hair he did have was trimmed close to his head and a sort of buff color rather than white or silver—no, she couldn't place him. Probably someone she had passed in a hallway once upon a time during one of her whirlwind visits to transport some artifact or other. Masks made it harder to make identifications, especially with casual acquaintances.

He raised his hand in greeting, and Noel mirrored the gesture—but when she looked away for a moment, a wave of dizziness overwhelmed her. The fear of fainting in front of this crowd cut short her curiosity.

"Excuse me," she said to the people standing in the way of the exit door. The pause as she waited for them to part was agonizing, but it gave her a chance to grab a bottle of sparkling water from the drinks table to her right. When the path cleared, she race-walked to the door. She had passed the ladies' room on the way to the meeting space and knew it was only a short distance down the corridor. She hoped she would reach it before collapsing, and she did, barely.

Once there, she opened the door to find a cleaner inside, her mop bucket and a plastic stanchion blocking access to the toilets.

The woman turned. "I'll be a minute, love. There's another ladies' down the stairs." She pointed in the direction of the door Noel had just entered.

"I'm sorry, but I don't think I can make it that far. I only need to sit for a minute. And maybe splash a little cold water on my face."

The cleaner tutted but helped her to a bench seat to the left of a bank of touch-up mirrors.

"I'm so sorry," she said again to the cleaner, who was now standing impatiently with her hands on her hips. "Jet lag," she explained. *Coupled with nerves and an empty stomach,* she added to herself as she cracked open the bottled water and drank half its contents down. Tepid, but it would do. *What an inauspicious, embarrassing start,* she thought, shaking her head.

"Would you like to use a sink before I start cleaning over there?"

Noel took a moment to assess how she felt and decided she was steady enough now to stand. "Yes, please. You've been very understanding," she added as she dampened a paper towel and touched it to her forehead and temples. Done, she crumpled the paper in her hand. "Thank you."

"Well, I was happy to help. Mind, them in charge"—the cleaner tipped her chin in the general direction of the restroom door—"like me to have the loos clean before we open. But I reckon I haven't lost much time waiting on you to feel better." She pointed at the plastic bin liner attached to the end of her cleaning cart.

Noel smiled and placed the balled-up wet paper in it. She exited as swiftly as possible, swigging more water as she pushed through the door. There was someone on the other side, though, someone she didn't see with her head tilted back to drink. They collided.

"I'm so sorry," Noel said, backing away. When she finally looked up at the face of the man she'd run into, she realized it was the waving man from the meeting. "Oh."

"Noel," he said.

"Yes," she answered. "I'm afraid I'm leaving bad impressions everywhere I go this morning."

The man's eyes crinkled again.

"Why do I feel like you're laughing at me?" she asked. "Did I say something funny?"

"One of the last times we spoke, you were leaving a loo," he said. "Maybe we should stop meeting like this." When Noel drew her eyebrows together, puzzled, he asked, "Do you not remember me? I'm wounded, as I'm sure I haven't changed a bit."

It was the word *remember* that did it, the assertive Glasgow burr as he rolled the *R*s. But the voice she associated with these hadn't been as deep and gravelly. Noel couldn't make it make sense. "Calum?"

He lowered his mask below his chin. She searched his face. The short beard he sported was more gingery than the ring of hair left on his head. When he grinned, she recognized the dimples and the mischievous twinkle in his eyes. Back when she knew him well, he had always been grinning.

"Calum Paterson! It is you!"

"Aye, in the flesh. I knew you were coming and I wanted to surprise you at the welcome this morning."

"But . . . here? How—"

"I'm the Addison's director of development. We'll be colleagues. You could have blown me over when Jean made the announcement a couple of weeks ago that you'd be joining us. Noel Enfield." He shook his head.

"And you remembered me, after all this time?"

"Don't be daft, Noel. Do you think I'd forget you altogether, just because some time has passed?"

Cal tried to sound as if he was joking, but his earlier jocularity slipped and Noel heard a hint of frustration in the ribbing. She dropped her eyes from his. She supposed she deserved it for the way she'd avoided him after that last time they'd met and he'd taken her for tea, and then for the way she'd left the country without saying goodbye. And now they would be colleagues for the next half year.

She felt Cal's eyes on her, urging her to look at him. When she did, he said more gently this time, "You truly haven't changed much, lovely as always. Whereas I . . ." He flourished his hands down length of himself, making a point of the French blue shirt, the cufflinks, the dark trousers with the slightest hint of a chalk stripe.

She took him in. Her past, right in her face on the first day. How had she forgotten how small the London art world could feel? Students, professors, gallery owners, curators, the artists themselves—all knew each other or jockeyed to meet so they would know each other. Everyone had coveted the same jobs, attended the same parties, shown their faces at the same openings, Noel remembered. She with Cal, and later with Bryn. Bryn had been much sought-after even then, his future all but sewn up. Hers too, or so she'd thought. But this was nothing she wanted to think about now, although here was Cal, reminding her. She flashed back to her younger days, watching him as he strode the halls of the art history building, his arms spread wide to show off his latest garish outfit: a mustard-colored sweater, a stripey Dr. Who scarf, the woolen tuxedo trousers from Oxfam with the moth hole in the seat.

"Different wardrobe," she quipped.

"No hair, either." He smiled. "But you're right. Our donors prefer bespoke suits. Listen," he continued, "I followed you out here to say hello, but also because you were looking a wee bit peaky. Are you all right?"

Noel nodded. "I am now. Too much tea and no breakfast. No dinner last night either."

"Then come along with me." He reached for her, put her arm through his as he'd always done, and patted her hand. "I'm taking you to the caff for a proper meal."

"I should get to my desk—"

"I'm not taking no for an answer. We old friends have some catching up to do. Decades' worth of it." He patted her hand again. "And you need some food in you before you pass out. Looking a bit green, still, if you ask me. Off we go."

"They do a mean fry-up, believe it or not, but I thought I'd start you with a currant bun and some yogurt with fresh fruit. And not a cup of tea in sight." Cal set a tray laden with food on the café table. "Cappuccino," he added. "Lots of milk. Plus more water."

Noel tore off a piece of the bun and popped it into her mouth. "This is delicious," she said.

"The scones are good too, if you want one for later." He winked. "So," he said, leaning back in his chair, watching her tuck in. "Noel. Here on loan from a museum in the States."

She nodded. "I'm here to get some new experiences under my belt. I've spent the last several years in Collections. My boss would like to move me into curatorial work when I get back, and I'd like that too."

"Why parked for several years in Collections? I'd always thought you were destined for running the show somewhere."

"It's a long story." She waved, dismissing the details. "You know, one thing and the other. Life."

He raised an eyebrow. "Tell me about that. Your life. Fill me in on the last . . ." He screwed his face up in concentration, calculating. "Twenty-eight years?"

"Twenty-nine. And change."

"Twenty-nine." He shook his head. "That's a long time between visits. I've gotten old in the interim."

"You don't look old." Noel picked up the cappuccino and sipped. It was creamy and delicious. "You look great, actually. Why don't you tell me about *your* life?" She was happy to change the subject.

"You've heard a little about my illustrious career managing big donors. Like you, not what I thought I'd end up doing, but I'm surprisingly good at parting people from their money." He laughed. "I settled down with a partner about twenty-odd years ago. Tim. We lived together for fifteen years and then married shortly after same-sex marriage was legalized."

"You got married?"

He nodded. "I was almost as surprised as you are. But Tim . . . well, he came along when I was at a very low point, after another relationship had taken a bad turn, and he made me laugh when I thought I'd never laugh again." He smiled. "Tim brought the light back. How could I let him get away?"

"He sounds special."

"Exasperating and stubborn, too. But yes, he was very, very special."

"Wait." Noel stared into Cal's eyes. "'Was'? What—"

"COVID is what," he said wearily. "We had almost made it to our sixth wedding anniversary when Tim fell ill—this was before there was a vaccine. In some sort of twisted miracle, I didn't even catch it. There were days I wish I had, let me tell you, after he died and I was alone."

"Cal." She didn't know what to say. Those were terrible days, between the fear and the isolation. Although the danger always loomed, she and Andy had managed to keep themselves and Alice safe. Nothing at all like this had happened to them.

She reached her hand across the table. Cal took it and squeezed.

"We had over twenty excellent years together," he said. "Some people don't get anything near that. You, though. Jean's memo mentioned something about you leaving a family behind. I assumed husband and children, since I recall you only had your gran growing up."

She let go of his hand, picked up her coffee again, and drained it. What would Cal think if she blurted out that her marriage was coming to an end? Probably he wouldn't be surprised to learn about another relationship she couldn't sustain. She gave him only the outlines. "I got married about six years ago. Andy—my husband—had a young daughter he was raising alone when we got together. Alice. I became an instant mom. Stepmom."

"They didn't want to come with you?"

"It's not that easy to tell an eleven-year-old she has to leave her friends and her activities."

He smiled. "There's always a school break, I suppose. They'll miss you. I look forward to meeting them, whenever that may be."

Noel looked into her empty cup. "What about you?" she asked, turning the conversation back to him again. "Did you and Tim have children?"

"No. Too busy, too complicated, or so we thought. I suppose we could've figured it all out. It might've been nice to have someone now, lives other than my own to focus on." He shrugged. "Unless I would've lost them too. Damn COVID."

A lump rose in Noel's throat. "I'm sorry."

His eyes glistened. "I know. Eat up now. You haven't touched your fruit."

"I might take it back to my desk," she said with a look at her watch. "My colleagues will be thinking the worst of me. Slacker." She smiled and rolled her eyes.

"That's the last thing anyone would call the Noel I once knew, but yes, we should both get back. We have months to get reacquainted, after all." Cal stood. "Are you jumping right into the project, then?"

"Yes." She snapped the plastic lid back over the fruit and yogurt bowl, then put all her trash and dirty dishes onto the tray. Cal grabbed it before she could. "Oh, thanks. Anyway, yes, we're getting right into pulling together the catalog for the exhibition. I've never been responsible for one before but I'm excited."

"It's going to be a wonderful show," he said. "There's some fabulous art this year. Exceptional, really. One artist—Henry Bell—is my personal favorite to take the prize this year. He's—well, you'll see. I don't want to influence the way you look at his work. I envy you, coming into this with fresh eyes and an unbiased perspective."

"I hope I do the show justice. It's all a bit overwhelming when I stop and think about it— the art, the importance of the award, being . . ." She was going to say being back in London, but stopped herself. "Being away from my familiar environment. Not to mention the jet lag. And less than an hour ago I learned that Jean had arranged for me to be interviewed later this evening, for a journal—*Art* something or other—and I have no idea what I'll say about what I'm doing here."

"*Art/Source*," Cal said.

She nodded. "That's it. Jean is very happy to have the publicity, and I want to keep her happy. But maybe I should go do a little work so that when I talk about my role, I'll have something informed to say."

"Let's get you on your way, then." He stood and led the way to the exit, depositing the cluttered tray at the bins on the way out. Outside the cafeteria, he stopped and turned to her. "I'm glad you're back. I have always regretted the way we dropped out of each other's lives. Maybe when you're rested up, we can have a proper chat. You might even decide you'd like to tell me why you left without saying goodbye."

"Cal, I . . ." She shook her head, suddenly defensive. "We were kids. Students get homesick and change their minds about where they attend school all the time. It's a pretty boring story, my leaving London. I don't know why you'd want to dredge it all up."

Cal smiled sadly and held up his hands. "I didn't intend to upset you. If you don't feel the same about reconnecting with an old friend, that's fine. But"—he waved an arm in an expansive arc—"this is a very small world, as you may remember. Being back here, you're going to bump into people from your past all the time. You and I will be seeing each other a lot within these walls. It would be nice to be friends. Or at least cordial."

Noel closed her eyes as if that would disappear her from this conversation she did not want to have. "Thank you for feeding me," she said finally, squaring her shoulders and resigning herself to meeting his intent gaze. "I was hungrier than I knew. And now . . ." She pointed in the direction of the elevators.

She had only made it a few steps when Cal called out, "Noel!"

With no other noise around them, there was no way she could pretend she hadn't heard him, so she turned.

His eyes surprised her. Gone was the earlier warmth she'd seen there; the genuine happiness he'd seemed to radiate earlier at seeing her again had been replaced by something more formal, more circumspect.

"I hope you settle in well," he said. "If there's anything I can do, please ring me." He looked at her a beat longer, and then he was off down the corridor, around the corner—gone.

She lingered, looking a moment longer at the emptiness he'd left in his wake. Her old, good friend. "Cal!" she called, and she jogged to the corner where he'd turned, hoping maybe he too had paused, stopped in his tracks.

But no, there was no sign of him. Others wandering in and out of the cafeteria had taken his place, and a couple of people looked curiously at her as they passed.

Noel knew it was time to leave the lower level and get upstairs to her new desk, but she couldn't make herself move. She'd signaled that she wanted no more reminders of her past, the way she'd left and why, and Cal had complied. Establishing her boundaries and having them respected ought to be empowering, right?

Why, instead, did she feel so lost?

CHAPTER 18

NOEL'S FLAT, NOVEMBER 2022

The rest of Noel's inaugural day was so hectic with meetings and introductions and on-boarding videos that the feelings stirred up by the encounter with Cal got pushed to the back of her mind. When the Human Resources staffer assigned to guide her through her first day approached her at half five and urged her to go home, she realized how exhausted she was and agreed an early night was a good idea. Before closing down her work computer, she emailed the artist dossiers and their digital portfolios to herself so that she could upload copies onto the desktop of her personal laptop. Reviewing all the work and the bios before bed would give her a jump on the work she would begin in earnest tomorrow.

The task would also fill the hours before bedtime, she thought as she unlocked the front door to her flat and stepped into its stillness. If she didn't manage her after-hours time well, fill those hours with work and getting outside and perhaps swimming, the flat's monotonous gray furnishings and the surrounding solitude would likely draw her into a melancholic state, give her too much space to wonder about the circumstances and the people she would rather not.

Along with the sundry food and drink left for her arrival at the flat, someone had seen fit to include a bottle of wine, a New Zealand sauvignon blanc. The wine even had a screw top so she didn't have to rake through drawers to find a corkscrew.

She poured a substantial amount into a juice glass—the glass closest to hand—and sipped as she scrambled two of the eggs and waited for toast to pop. If she'd had a little spinach, she would've treated herself to an omelet, but omelets could wait until she made a bigger shop over the weekend. She wrote "google nearest grocery" to her list of things to do tonight, paused, added "google pool near me," and then took the egg pan off the flame.

Wine in one hand, plate in the other, and notebook with to-do list started on it tucked under her arm, Noel headed for the small, glass-topped dining table where she had left her laptop after unpacking it the previous day. Once she had set her dinner down on a placemat and the notepad near her right hand, she uploaded all the files from her email, and soon enough she had the artist biographies and statements open on the screen. She ate and drank as she read, occasionally stopping to jot down facts about the artists she wanted to remember.

Cal hadn't been exaggerating—this was a highly accomplished group of finalists for the prestigious award. All had studied with some of the top instructors in the country. Most had amassed junior awards and significant recognitions; some had even exhibited widely. The individual artist statements gave more insight into what themes they explored and the various media they employed to create their works. Drawn in, Noel gave up on the last triangles of toast, slid her plate off to one side, and pulled her glass in front of her.

The wine was making her pleasantly drowsy, and while she could still keep her eyes open, she pored over each statement. The last was Henry Bell's, the artist Cal had told her was a serious contender for the top prize. Where his photo should be was an empty, shaded square; he was the only artist to have neglected to include a headshot.

His statement was also the briefest—a couple of sentences about intent and one detail about the paint he preferred to use. She copied, "I paint what's abandoned, and the liminal spaces between the letting go and reclaiming. But most important to me is creating something and leaving it up to the viewer to think about what they see and how the image makes them feel," underlining the words *abandoned* and *reclaiming*. She then set down her pen and clicked on his portfolio file, opening his collection before the others even though it was last in the queue.

When the first slide appeared, she sat back in her seat. It was a striking canvas, the top half of the field all blue sky and clouds, the bottom half terraced buildings, the trees around them full with brown leaves. Early fall. Some buildings in the terrace appeared to be homes, others clearly shops fronted with large plates of glass that reflected sunlight. Occupying the front field were electrical poles and powerlines, several rows bisecting and crisscrossing as they connected to the buildings. There were no people in the composition—no one walking the streets, no figures visible through the windows; some windows, she noticed, were broken, the interior beyond eerily blackened. Entering into the upper right of this forefront was a crow in flight. The painting felt as though it was larger than its purported ninety by sixty centimeters because of the proportions of the imposing black bird.

She continued clicking through each image, spending several minutes on every one. Some elements carried over from painting to painting: festoons of power lines; buildings that looked abandoned or derelict; flowering weeds—bindweed, groundsel, dandelions—growing in unexpected places; and birds—crows mostly, but sometimes a magpie or two, taking flight from sooty window ledges. Perhaps to enhance the urban nature of his landscapes, Bell had incorporated faint drafting lines into the canvases, subtly raised horizontals and diagonals, a topography of sorts. An impasto of thickly built-up paint, Noel wondered? Hard to tell from a quick look at a digital image, and she hoped she'd soon be able to see all the work in person.

The final slide in the deck was his competition entry, titled *Yours for the taking*.

She moved her face closer to the laptop screen. Bell had made a slight departure from the other cityscapes in this piece. Yes, there were power lines in *Yours*—long ones extending from the shell of what appeared to be an old brick-faced mill or factory to a pair of steel pylons, set off-center and to the right, looming ominously and apparently casting twin shadows. And there was a bird: a lone crow perched on a crossbar halfway up the latticed tower, not in flight but acting as observer or sentry. There were weeds too, not so showy as his others, but there. The ground in front of the mill was littered with discarded brick and slabs of mortar where persistent clumps of meadow grass and spreading shoots of petty spurge pushed through the cracks. A lone wild carrot flower stood tall in the foreground and, together with the invasive greens, interrupted the monochromatic palette, as above a slice of vivid blue sky did the same. Here and there, a shimmering gold light kissed several surfaces—ostensibly light rays from a sun that was above the scene, just out of the range of the canvas.

It was this light that made *Yours* so different. The eye was drawn from the concentration of golden light down to the ground rubble. She was reminded of examples of luminism in the religious paintings of the Renaissance, where gold light emanated diagonally from the heavens and fell on the pregnant stomach of the virgin mother of Christ. There was a similar spotlighting here, though of the mundane urban landscape. Noel tapped the magnifying glass icon several times to zoom in on the area her eye was drawn to by the light. Almost lost in the sameness of brick and debris was something lighter brown than the surrounding brick, something slightly larger. It was a parcel of some sort—a basket, she thought. The rippling in the sides conveyed the soft lines of something woven. The grayish contents inside the basket were similar in color to the scattered mortar, but this was definitely not a basket of mortar shards but rather folds of fabric—soft wool, from the texture.

Zoomed in at this level, Noel could see that the textural relief in the painting probably hadn't come from thicker daubs of paint. This technique was impasto-like, but its surface was smoother and without telltale brush marks. She made a note to ask how he'd accomplished it.

His line technique was used again in the shadows cast by the pylons. Or not by the pylons. She blinked and squeezed her eyes shut for a moment; the close work was taxing on her eyes. When she opened them, she leaned in again. No, not by the pylons. Could not be. The angle was off. And there appeared to be four shadows, not two. Curious. Whatever was casting these shadows was out of scene like the sun was, poised somewhere in front, onlookers like herself. Humans? The figures had none of the geometry of trusses. While tapering from narrow tops to wider bases, there was a softer roundness to the outlines that could never come from rigid steel. And there, reflected in the empty building's windows, were shadowy faces, or the suggestion of faces. Gazing, as she was, at the abandoned building, the basket, and what might be inside.

Noel sat back. Next to her the unfinished pieces of toast had grown cold, the butter she'd spread haphazardly congealed on its surface. Looking at this painting left her feeling frustrated, weepy, overwhelmed, and longing for something she couldn't quite name—all the same feelings that had overtaken her years earlier, after Bryn had dismissed her from sitting for *Lady of Llyn Y Fan Fach* and she'd seen the largely finished canvas for the first time.

That was the last time she had been so physically affected by a painting that she'd had to be shooed out the door into the bracing air to walk off the residual energy. Now, she was almost too exhausted, too weighed down with emotions to move, but maybe moving her body would be best.

She stood and brought her plate to the sink, thinking of what Cal had said earlier—that he envied her seeing Henry's work for the first time. She understood his envy. She too would feel it when the work was hung and the crowds who came to visit would approach the canvas with their fresh eyes and be so moved.

But there was something else affecting her. The subjects of the two men's paintings couldn't be more dissimilar—one a natural world, the other landscape gritty and man-made—and yet. Bryn's interpretation of a marriage between people of two different worlds portrayed grief and the weighty responsibility for the loss of Nelferch to the water from whence she'd come. And Bell's work, despite its title implying someone was gaining something tangible, overwhelmed her with that same feeling of loss, this time the loss of people destined to look but not touch, or perhaps touch but not know—people trapped behind glass instead of water. Perhaps because she was familiar with loss, she found it everywhere. "Yours for the taking," she whispered to herself.

She walked back to the dining table and looked down at the notebook she'd kept at her elbow, at one of the quotes she'd pulled from Henry's artist statement. She picked up the pen she'd written with and tapped the words on the page. "I paint what's abandoned." Was this work more about relinquishing than finding? Had something been abandoned at this factory? Was that something in the basket? Had these shadowy figures stumbled upon a tragedy rather than a gift? Or had they been the cause of one by relinquishing whatever was in it? She took notes as the ideas came to her. All questions for Henry Bell when she met him in advance of composing his section of the exhibition guide. Her interpretations would have to do his work justice, so the interview would have to be thorough.

Interview. Her eyes wandered across to the page opposite her notes to her to-do list. There it was: *Interview tonight at 7*. She looked up from the list to the wall clock; it was a quarter after seven. "Oh, no."

Somewhere in town, that journalist was either growing impatient waiting on her or furious thinking she'd been blown off. Briefly, she considered emailing her regrets, explaining that the dangerous combination of fatigue and hunger and immersion in dizzying art had combined to push all earthly concerns out of her mind. But this interview was the one thing Jean had urged her to participate in.

As she began searching for the meeting link in her email, Noel hoped she wouldn't disappoint her new boss on her first day.

CHAPTER 19

THE CITY, DECEMBER 2022

Four weeks passed. Every day of those four weeks, Noel spent working. On weekends, when she wasn't in her office, she parked herself at the dining table in her flat, which was where she was on this Saturday, three weeks before Christmas Eve.

That she might want plans for the upcoming holiday barely registered. There was so much to do. Right from day two, work at the Addison had become a whirlwind of activity as she, Jean, and Jean's permanent staff met daily to stay on top of each successive phase of planning. The steps taken in years past could only serve as loose guidelines this time around, as the world of public gathering had changed. So many aspects this year had to include COVID accommodations, considerations that added time and energy and cost to even the simplest of tasks. Equally important to the show's success was factoring in remediations to the actual events themselves. Hand-sanitizing stations. Advanced air-purification systems. Masking suggestions in print materials and on signage. All these additional steps required more attention—difficult, given the narrow window of planning time allowed.

Jean never missed a chance to express her gratitude for the extra pair of hands Noel was lending to these efforts. "We simply didn't factor in enough time, when of course we should have known better," she said more than once. "Thank goodness we have you, Noel."

Noel was juggling these intense team collaborations with meeting her own specific work goals. She had by this point personally contacted all the artists on the shortlist, consulted their calendars and hers, and begun meeting with them at the museum to discuss their exhibition entries. She was more engaged in this project than she had been with any work in a long time, and proving to herself that she was capable was invigorating.

The pace was also exhausting—something else she appreciated. Being physically and mentally tired by the time she returned to her quiet flat in the evening kept her from turning over and over in her mind the doubt she felt about leaving Andy and Alice behind.

She'd been checking in with Alice frequently with texts and emails and voicemails, and sometimes her daughter responded with a thumbs-up to photos attached to the texts, photos of her workspace, of the plates of food she ordered at the museum café, of artwork around the building that she thought Alice might like to see. But sometimes Alice didn't remark at all. Nor did she initiate any correspondence or reply with details of her own days—a sign, perhaps, that she didn't trust Noel was interested, despite the encouragement and open-ended questions.

Or maybe she felt chatting too much with Noel was disloyal to her dad.

From Andy, she'd heard next to nothing. A forwarded email from Alice's school about a volunteer responsibility she usually accepted but would miss this year. *Touché, Andy,* she'd said to herself when she opened that one. She'd received no follow-up and nothing personal, no updates.

It was better that way. She wanted to avoid arguing.

Something else she was avoiding, she thought as she looked around the flat and then at all the work spread out across the table, was London itself. Holing herself up with so many tasks meant no coming face-to-face with memories. They were around every corner since reminders of Bryn were everywhere—in familiar architectural details they'd once commented on, in the unchanged signage of the ubiquitous chain shops, even in her short walks to the corner market, which led her past a pub with a name similar to one they'd frequented in Bloomsbury. Younger Noel had loved this city so much—the landmarks, marquees, noise, unfamiliar scents. She was preventing herself from mixing into all that now. *Protecting myself,* she thought. Another voice inside popped right up to counter that: *Punishing yourself,* it said, and it was probably right. Museums and parks she loved at her feet, and here she was inside, denying herself access to them.

She shoved aside her laptop and put her forehead down on the cool glass of the dining table. What difference did all her hard work make if she refused to get out and see what was going on around her? For the first time in a long time she could do what she wanted when she wanted without giving thought to whether or not another person was comfortable, bored, happy, unhappy, tired, feeling slighted, about to have a tantrum. She could be fully engaged, totally in the moment. Maybe today, this Saturday, was best spent venturing out, at least a little. There was Christmas coming, too. She could distract herself from anything too harshly familiar by shopping for Alice instead of resorting to sending a museum gift shop gift. Baby steps.

She set out from the flat and headed south. Before she had time to consider a route, her feet carried her forward. Muscle memory, a well-worn walk. Central London highlights in a day, Cal had called it when he first took her around the city.

Kensington, South Kensington, all the way into Chelsea and down to the river. From there she went left along the embankment, passing one bridge and then a second at Millbank, just past which she gave a nod to the Tate but did not stop inside. After the four miles or so, she was feeling the rhythm in her gait, her body and her mind and her senses almost at one in the elements. When the walk began to feel forced, she pressed on. She didn't want to give in to anything that would make her stop and turn back for the flat.

She kept going along the river until she reached Waterloo Bridge, where she and Bryn had once stopped so she could tell him the entire plot of the melodrama of the same name starring Vivien Leigh. Going any farther east from this bridge, even this far from Shoreditch, was inviting too much grief. Instead, she headed north, the river at her back.

There was the Courtauld—days of strolling the collection and visiting exhibitions; the Opera House—one ballet with Cal; Seven Dials—her favorite cheese shop. Thirty years on and she was finding her way from memory, the same memory she had been wary of, no need for the map she clutched in her hand. A few blocks ahead was the Y where she used to swim, the very same one Bryn had diverted her from the day he took her to his studio. She was so close now to Bloomsbury and the university, but she sensed that, too, would be one memory too many, so instead of continuing north she went west on Oxford Street, straight into the shopping madness.

Christmas was everywhere. By keeping herself inside the house and inside the museum, she'd missed it all—the decorations, the preparations, the crowds. But she was here now, and she kept going.

In the window of a department store, there was a winter coat that Alice might like; Noel nipped in and fought her way through the crowds until she reached the right department, and didn't even look at the price tag before buying it. She had it boxed and wrapped, thinking she'd somehow get it to a post office on Monday.

Leaving the store, she took Regent Street to Piccadilly, Piccadilly to St. James Park, the park to the palace, the palace through the Green Park and under Wellington Arch, miles altogether, carrying the shopping bag heavy with a boxed and wrapped wool coat. As her arm grew tired, the bag began to twist back and forth in her grasp and the box corners banged into her shin.

She was hungry by then, her legs weary and maybe bruised, and it was possible blisters were forming on the soles of her feet despite her sensible boots. Time for a break.

She spotted a free bench at the Serpentine, not far from Peter Pan, and she sat. All around her were another palace, statues, memorial fountain alongside the lake, the wintery remnants of once-flowering gardens, many gracefully meandering pathways, and one of the world's most ornate tributes to love—the love of a queen for her prince consort. From her seat on the cold bench, she shot a few photos. For Alice. For herself.

Proof. She'd done it, made her walk. It felt like the end of something, maybe. Or, from another angle, it felt like a beginning.

CHAPTER 20

ADDISON GALLERY, DECEMBER 2022

On Monday, Noel tossed her handbag onto her desk and tore open a Twix wrapper, eating the two biscuit fingers nestled inside without savoring the chocolate or the crunch. She was starving and relieved she had thought to add the chocolate bar on top of her morning newspaper at the newsstand, as she'd had nothing for breakfast in the flat, not even a heel of a loaf, and no time to stop in the cafeteria earlier. She'd spent ninety minutes before lunch with one of her artists, standing in front of the young woman's large painting, asking questions, taking notes, and hoping that the growling from her stomach wasn't loud enough to embarrass her. Glancing at her open laptop, she reminded herself of the staff meetings coming up at three and four.

And Henry Bell was due at one. She had about ten minutes to finish her snack and gather her files before heading out again, she realized with a glance at her watch.

She groaned, sat up straight, crumpled the Twix wrapper, and lobbed it at the wastebasket on the other side of her desk. Just as it landed in the direct center of its target, there was a knock at the door. "Back to work," she muttered, and then, louder, "Come in!"

Her door, partially cracked open, opened wider and a brown snout poked in. An entire dog followed.

"What—who are you?" Noel asked aloud.

The dog took its time sauntering over to her, stopping to sniff the air and then the rim of the wastebasket before finally approaching and resting her head on Noel's knee, her brown, beseeching eyes looking into Noel's.

"Now, I know it wasn't you who knocked," she said as she scratched behind the dog's ears. She peered over at the door, halfway open. "Is someone behind the door playing tricks?" In a louder voice, she called, "Is this prank-the-newest-employee day?"

The door opened a bit more and this time a human head appeared. "Sorry about that. Not a prank. I knocked, then got distracted." He pointed his thumb over his shoulder. "Do you know there's a Fragonard sketch, unfinished, right on the wall outside your door? Well, of course you do. I assume it's bolted down, but still. Quite astonishing. Anyway, Gertie—that's Gertie," he said with a nod toward the dog, "gets impatient with my little distractions. She's meant to keep me on top of things, but today she decided to go ahead without me. I'm Henry, by the way. Henry Bell. I hope you don't mind dogs."

"Gosh, no, she's fine here. Come on in, Henry." She waved him in. "Have a seat. I appreciate your time today. We'll head over to the gallery to see your work in a minute, then take as deep a dive into your work and biography as is possible in ninety minutes."

"You're American," he said as he sat.

"Yes," Noel answered, not going into the "yes, but" territory of explaining her dual citizenship that she had with countless strangers since her arrival. "I'm on a secondment from a museum in the States, outside of Boston. I've been looking forward to our talk since I reviewed the slides of your work." She leaned forward, displacing Gertie's chin. The dog reminded Noel of her presence with a couple of pointed nudges and she sat back, laughing. "Okay, okay, I get it."

"She likes you." Henry smiled and his gray-blue eyes crinkled at the outer corners.

She responded with a smile for him, pleased that he was happy and ready to work with her. "I'm glad I pass her test. Do you want to get right down to it?"

"Actually," he said, dropping his voice to a conspiratorial whisper, "I'm really famished. I don't think I ate breakfast this morning." He screwed up his face in thought. "No, that's right, I didn't. And I haven't had lunch, and all I ate yesterday was toast. I need to do a proper shop but I keep forgetting."

How funny, Noel thought. Toast—like her, he'd been existing on it. They could both use a decent meal, and it would be easy enough to begin their conversation over lunch. Before she had a chance to think about propriety or museum rules, she blurted, "Let me treat you. It's only the cafeteria, but the food is actually quite good. You're not the only one who has forgotten to do their shopping." She petted Gertie one more time, then rose so he wouldn't hesitate. "Come on. We can talk and eat." She gathered up her notes and laptop. "We'll get much more accomplished if we aren't starving."

"With Gertie?" Henry sounded anxious at the possibility of being parted from her.

Noel looked down at the content dog. She had no idea whether or not Gertie would be welcome in the caff, but she would take responsibility for the mistake if not. For heaven's sake, she thought, the dog had already wandered throughout the museum to reach these offices; why not the cafeteria too?

"Of course she may come," she said with more confidence than she felt.

"All right then," he agreed. "Food would be good."

To avoid any friction with the cafeteria staff, Noel quietly asked the department administrative assistant to ring down and let them know a dog would be joining her and her artist guest. When they arrived, the food and beverage manager himself greeted them and led them to a table off in a back corner where there would be space for Gertie to stretch out without fear of being stepped on or tripping the other diners. If the manager was at all fazed by the four-legged guest, he didn't let on.

Gertie carried herself with a great amount of dignity and stayed at Henry's side. Once at the table, Noel and Henry took seats opposite each other and the dog snugged herself underneath, her body across Henry's feet.

Henry reached up and pushed a hank of brown, wavy hair back from his forehead. The gesture struck Noel as familiar, something she'd seen him do time and again, as if this young man was an old friend and not a new acquaintance.

"Shall I go up and bring us back some food?" she suggested. "If you give me an idea of what you'll eat?"

"Something hot would be great," he said. "Stodgy. Preferably vegetarian."

"I can do that," she said with a smile. Within minutes, she found a vegetarian shepherd's pie made with mushrooms and eggplant. That would get stodgy points for its mashed potato and cheese topping. For herself, she chose a salad with beets and goat cheese. "Beetroot," the server corrected, as if they were speaking two different languages.

"What are you smiling about?" Henry asked when she returned to the table. "Thank you," he added, reaching for the plate she offered from the tray of food.

"Beets, beetroot," she said, chuckling. "How rusty I am with British English after all these years."

Henry raised an eyebrow as he shoveled a forkful of pie in his mouth.

"I attended university here for two years, oh, almost thirty years ago." Noel twisted the top from a bottle of sparkling water.

"But enough about me. I'm here to learn more about you and your work so that I might do you justice in the catalog. I've seen all the images of your submissions. The articles, the reviews, your prizes. I've read your artist statement. Maybe you could start talking about how you work, your process and such, and I'll take notes, maybe jump in with a few questions."

Henry finished chewing and swallowed, followed that with a good swig from his own bottle of water. "I'm really very boring." He spoke with a broad Yorkshire accent. "And talking about myself is the worst. I'd like to know more about this secondment you're on. What's that like?" He shifted in his seat, startling Gertie for a moment. "This is good, by the way." He pointed at his half-finished lunch. "Exactly what I would have chosen." He smiled.

"Oh. Good. My secondment? I'm here for six months, brushing up on some skills so I can move out of collections management into curatorial work when I go back to the States. I was working toward that many years ago, but . . ." She paused. "Are you sure you want to hear all this?"

Henry nodded and kept eating, his eyes on her.

"But when my daughter was young, I wanted to spend more time with her. Collections work let me do that. Regular hours, limited travel."

"Is your daughter here with you now?" Henry asked.

"Stepdaughter, actually. And no." Noel's voice caught when she said the word and she cleared her throat. "She's home with her dad. School. Friends. All the things an eleven-year-old doesn't want to leave." She moved her notebook in front of her. "Shall we?" she asked, picking up her pen.

Henry set down his fork, pushed his now-empty plate to the side, and wiped his mouth. "I'm going to get a coffee first. May I bring you one too?"

Noel looked back at him. He was sidestepping her questions, and yet she found herself more curious than frustrated. "I should stick to my water. But thank you."

When Henry stood, Gertie stirred. He held up a hand for her to stay and she sighed but did as she was told.

Noel stared at Henry's back and then peeked under the table at the dog. "Maybe I could interview you, huh, girl? What do you say?"

"Are you talking to that dog under the table?"

Noel looked up to find Cal beside her. He wore a different protective mask today, one that looked like a portion of Mondrian's *Composition with Red, Blue and Yellow*.

"Guilty," Noel replied. "But only because her owner has disappeared." She nodded in Henry's direction.

"Is that . . ." Cal turned his eyes toward the young man leaning against the espresso counter. When Henry saw them looking, he lifted his hand.

"Henry Bell. Yes. He came in for his initial meeting with me, decided he was hungry, and here we are. He's very charming, but a little . . . reluctant to talk about himself and his process. All we've talked about is my secondment, in case you're wondering how it's going. Cal?" she said when her friend didn't respond. He was still watching Henry, waiting for his coffee. "Cal," she repeated. This second time got his attention. "Were you looking for me?"

"No, I came down for some lunch myself and saw you here." His eyes drifted back to the coffee bar.

She followed his gaze. Henry's back was now to them. "I know you like his work. Would you like to meet him? You could sit with us while we chat."

"Oh, I couldn't," he said, returning his attention to Noel. "I only came for a coffee to take back to my office. But how are you settling in? Any luck with bringing the family over for a visit?"

Without thinking, she gave a loud, wry laugh, then clamped her hand over her mouth.

A look of confusion on his face, he asked, "What have I said?"

She shook her head. "I can't go into it now. Henry's on his way back."

Cal looked over his shoulder, and they both watched Henry walk back to the table, balancing a large and wide coffee cup on a larger and wider saucer. His eyes weren't focused on his destination; instead, he seemed to be staring off into space or back into the recesses of his own mind. It was only when he reached the table—walked into it, nearly—that he snapped out of the reverie.

He set down the cup and saucer and slid back onto the bench seat. "Hello," he said to Cal as if he was surprised to see another person there.

"Hello. Look, I won't disturb you two any longer. Noel, I'll ring you. We have some catching up to do." He raised his hand in a brief wave and departed for the food line across the room.

"Bye, Cal," Noel said in his wake.

"Who was that?" Henry asked.

"Calum Paterson. A colleague. An old friend." She smiled.

"From your time here when you were in uni?"

"Yes, in fact."

"Boyfriend? Partner?"

"Cal? No. There was a time when he was my best friend, though." She changed the subject. "Did you have enough to eat?"

"I did. Let me finish this and I'll be ready to discuss anything you want. It feels a bit wrong to have a cappuccino in the afternoon, but it's delicious."

Noel raised an inquiring eyebrow.

"I was in Italy in September," he said. "Took my dad. He'd always wanted to see Rome but Mum wasn't keen, so he put it off. Then he didn't go anywhere for years because she was ill. After she died, there was a good amount of time when he could barely function. Then COVID. Finally, this fall the timing was good for both of us. I said, 'Right, Dad. Up on your feet. I sold a painting, I have some money. Off we go to Rome.'" He chuckled to himself. "Our first day there, after the train ride from the airport, all Dad wanted to do was sit at a café in the Piazza Navona and drink a cappuccino, but it was after eleven in the morning and the Italian waiters wouldn't hear of it. They pretended to not understand our order and brought Dad an espresso instead. No milk after eleven is not a suggestion." He shrugged. "We got him his cappuccino the next morning, and it was otherwise a lovely holiday. Brief, but lovely. Have you been?"

"To Rome?"

He nodded. "Rome, anywhere in Italy? Most art people make their pilgrimage to the Uffizi at some point."

Noel didn't answer straightaway. Florence was where Bryn had begun his Italy tour in 1992. The only correspondence she'd received from him, a postcard, had come from there. She remembered it clearly, word for word. "You'd love it here," he'd written. "The cypress stand tall in the distant landscapes, and their green can look darkly menacing in the right light."

After everything that had happened in that period of her life, she had avoided Italy. She'd gone to museums in Paris instead. Amsterdam. Vienna. Madrid. New York. Everywhere but Italy. When Andy had later suggested that they honeymoon in Tuscany, she'd responded with a quick and unequivocal no, suggesting instead that they take Alice and go to Quebec City. Not even the Uffizi could lure her to the country she'd lost Bryn to. So be it if she had a gap in her professional development.

"You know, I haven't," she answered, her tone light. "Maybe while I'm here, I can fit in a trip." She latched on to what he'd said about his mother to change the subject. "I'm sorry you've lost your mother. I lost mine when I was young and had to go live with my grandmother. I probably never got over losing her. I find myself missing all the time we didn't have together, if that even makes sense? Anyway, what am I saying?" She flapped a hand in front of her, as if to clear the air. "This conversation isn't supposed to be about me."

Henry tipped his head to one side, as if considering. "Why can't it be about you? And yes, to answer your other question. You make perfect sense. 'Missing all the time we didn't have together,'" he repeated. "That's very appropriate . . ."

His voice trailed off as he looked to his left out the window to the courtyard, pensive, and Noel could see he'd gone somewhere else in his mind, as he had earlier when walking across the cafeteria. All she'd intended to do was get him to open up about his work; instead, she'd invited melancholy. Hers. His. Time to brush that aside.

She cleared her throat. "Shall we take a walk to visit your paintings?"

At the word *walk*, Gertie perked up. She stood and wiggled, back end then front, her toenails tip-tapping on the floor tiles as she danced back and forth between them.

That was all it took to break the spell. Henry returned from wherever his mind had taken him and laughed. "Keeping me on the straight and narrow, Gertie." He looked up at Noel. "The paintings, then. If we must." He picked up the coffee, drained it. "Let's go."

Back in her office, Noel looked at the notes she'd taken during her meeting with Henry. Instead of the pages she had accrued with the other artists, the jottings regarding him and his work fit one side of lined paper. It wasn't because he was dull. He was witty, charming, and curious, and they'd ended up talking for longer than the allotted ninety minutes. Still, she'd come away with very little content beyond the few biographical details he'd shared. The names of his parents. His early art instruction. Not venturing far from home when it came time to go to university. How he felt art school at Leeds had shaped him. He'd fluctuated between reticent when she asked about his early awards ("Talking about all that is prat territory") and downright embarrassed when she'd praised *Yours for the taking* ("It's like seeing oneself on film or hearing one's voice on a recording").

When he hadn't wished to discuss something, he'd turned the questions on her. Henry Bell now knew that she had soft spots for both cheese and Kandinsky's early landscapes. That she'd never had a pet but was fond of cats as well as dogs. That she'd finished university near the top of her class and that the focus of her master's thesis had been in the realm of American primitive art, although in recent years she'd begun to wish she'd researched something different ("women artists, women's issues"). He'd even been curious about how often she'd been to London since she left. ("Only three times," she'd told him, counting off on her fingers. "2007. 2012. 2019. Traveling with artifacts on loan to museums. Very quick trips, though. This time is much different.")

"You saw nothing in previous trips?" he'd asked. "No plays? No exhibitions?"

"You know, in 2019, I was given a pass for the comprehensive Blake show at the Tate, and I did go. It was the week it opened, I think, and I walked through late morning. It was a zoo. But after, I went straight to the airport. I'm afraid I never made much time for exploring." She'd cocked her head then. "We really should be talking about your work. When it comes time to write the review of your work in the guide and the object labels for the walls, I'll be wishing for more of your input. What if you think I've gotten it all wrong?"

Henry had only smiled at that. "I'm curious to read what you have to say," he'd replied, and then asked another question.

She liked him, she'd decided after they parted and she returned to her office, even though he'd left her a bit frustrated.

She was thinking about all this when there was a knock on her door. "Come in!" she called out—and was surprised when Calum popped his head in.

Since their longer talk over breakfast last month, they'd only spoken when meeting by chance around the building, just as they had earlier today in the cafeteria. Noel feared her shortness with him had made him retreat from her. She wished she could take back that entire conversation. She turned her notes over on her desk and gave him her full attention.

"Shall I come back another time?" he asked, studying her face. "You seem . . ."

"No, come on in. One of my afternoon meetings was canceled and I'm only looking over my notes from the meeting with Henry. He didn't say much, so I'm basically looking at nothing. I'd love a diversion." After a moment, she added, "And it really is good to see you. I didn't like how we left things after breakfast on my first day."

"No. I didn't either. I should've checked in on you sooner, forgive me. This gave me an excuse to drop in." He reached over and placed a tabloid-size newspaper on her desk.

"What is this?" She drew the paper closer to her and turned it around. The paper was open to the headline, "New Eyes on the Prize: The Addison Gallery Enlists Visiting Help."

"Oh. My *Art/Source* interview? Do I want to read it?" Curious, she began skimming the paragraphs before he answered. "Well, she got the important parts right and I don't sound like a complete novice," she mused aloud.

"She did a nice job, but she had a good subject. Jean will be pleased, although the word around the building is, she already is thrilled with you and the work you've done thus far. Listen," he added, lowering his voice, "I have an ulterior motive for dropping in. My offhand remark about your family visiting? It really seemed to upset you. Is everything all right?"

She continued to stare at the words in the article until they blurred.

"Noel?"

At her name, she looked up. Cal's eyes were flashing with a concern she probably didn't deserve. Years ago, she had confided almost everything in him, and then she'd stopped, become secretive and protective of those secrets. She might keep him at arm's length now, except she really needed a friend—although it was a lot to expect that he might want that too.

"No, everything is not all right," she said. And then the tears flowed. She pressed her fists into her eyes to make them stop, but they seeped under instead and stung her face.

Cal handed her a beautiful handkerchief—white, starched, monogrammed, oversized—and she wiped her cheeks with it. "Thank you."

"Don't mention it. Do you want to talk about it?"

"How much time do you have?" She sighed. "I should have told you when you asked the first time that they're not coming at all. Andy and I are in the middle of a divorce. When I suggested that Alice could fly here by herself for a visit, Andy refused to allow it. She's his, not mine. I suppose he's punishing me for leaving."

"He's hurt and he's figured out how to hurt you back."

Hearing someone affirm this brought a fresh round of tears. Cal stood silently by. When they finally subsided, Noel held up the hankie.

"I'll wash this and get it back to you," she said. "I'm sorry."

He smiled. "It's only a handkerchief."

"I'm not only apologizing for that."

"Ah," he said. "Water under the bridge. If I've learned anything over these past two years, it's that connections are too important to suffer under grudges." He reached out and squeezed her shoulder. "Listen. Guess what you're doing tonight?"

"Going home and scrambling an egg," Noel told him. "Drinking a lot of wine. Then wallowing."

"No—coming to mine," he countered. "For a supper slightly more sustaining than an egg. And so I might make good on my intent to get reacquainted."

"I'm not great company lately." She gestured to her tear-stained face.

"Never mind that. You're coming. Come prepared to talk and drink and maybe not in that order. I'm emailing you the address as we speak." He took out his phone and a second later, there was the ping of the email in her inbox.

"Received." She smiled. "You're sure about this?"

"Put yourself in a taxi and come. Seven o'clock. Don't be late."

CHAPTER 21

CALUM'S FLAT, DECEMBER 2022

"Come in, come in," Calum said from his glossy black front door. He had opened it before Noel rang the bell and she wondered if he had been watching for her. As if reading her mind, he pointed above their heads. "Camera. I've been watching anxiously from my phone. Come in," he repeated, stepping aside to let her through.

"You have a lovely home," she said, walking into a long and sleek hallway. In front of her was the kitchen, its range centered in the doorway. To her left, stairs up. To her right, a living room. *Reception room,* she reminded herself, smiling. There would be a snug further on, she suspected, the British equivalent of a more relaxed family room space, complete with comfy chairs and television.

"Yes, well, it wasn't when we bought," Cal said. "Tim and I paid a relative song for the place in the aughts and then spent years doing it up. Tim was very talented with color. Here, let me." He relieved Noel of the paper shopping bag she carried and then her coat.

"There are some things in the bag for you," she said. "I wasn't sure about the wine so I added a couple of extras."

He peered into the bag, which held a nice bottle of red and several small, wrapped pieces of cheese. "You found a cheese shop without any trouble, and clearly couldn't control yourself." He smiled.

"You know me and cheese."

"I do know you and cheese." He leaned to kiss her cheek. "I'm happy you're here."

"Thank you for inviting me over," she said. "Now that I've got the sleep thing down, I feel it's time to tackle my eating habits. It will be lovely to share a proper meal with someone."

"Come into the kitchen, then. There's an English sparkling wine to toast with, and I'm putting a vegetable tian in the oven."

She raised an eyebrow.

"Tim's influence. Remember when I would argue chips were the only veg I needed?" He laughed. "Tim was horrified the first time I tried that on him. He was a gardener and took his vegetables seriously." He pointed to a pair of tall glass sliders at the very back of the house. "You may find this hard to believe too, but in the summer, there are things growing back there. I've kept up the vegetable patch and the raspberries in Tim's absence. Although I've drawn the line at putting up raspberry preserves. Jam was and shall remain his domain."

"I wish I'd known him," Noel said.

"There we are together." Cal pointed to a large, framed black-and-white photograph hanging on the wall just outside the kitchen doorway. In it, he had his arm around a radiantly smiling man. They stood together on a mountain in an arid-looking landscape. The sun was bright, creating starburst reflections on both pairs of reflective sunglasses. Both men sported a few-days-old beard growth, wide grins, and floppy sun hats with neck protectors. It was hard to tell for certain from the black-and-white photo, but Tim looked very fair—blond, or perhaps gingery like

Cal; his arms and the part of his face not covered by the beard were heavily freckled.

"That was taken in 2014, at a scenic stop on the way to Taos, New Mexico," Cal said wistfully. "We enjoyed traveling together too. That particular trip was when we decided to get married. It wasn't long after we got home that we did, and then I lost him. Those years flew by and I'm left wishing I had ten, twenty, thirty more."

"I'm so sorry, Cal. It's very sad and unfair."

His eyes welled up and he turned away briefly.

Still raw, Noel thought. She reached out and touched his back.

When he looked at her, he forced a smile. "That wine, then."

"Of course. That would be lovely." She followed him into the kitchen.

As he moved toward the fridge for the wine, he gestured to a row of seats at the huge kitchen island—it looked like it was made of a repurposed farmhouse table—and Noel sat. She ran her hand along the wood top. It felt satiny with wear and warm, a change from the cool granite of her own counter back home. She stopped caressing the tabletop and folded her hands in her lap. "This kitchen is very comfy."

On the other side of the expanse, Cal loosened the metal cage on the sparkling wine and worked out the cork. It slipped out with a gentle pop. He carefully filled two flutes and handed one to her. "Thank you. It was a true labor of love, emphasis on labor: ripping up lino, tearing out an ancient, unusable green range, knocking out a wall that was there." He pointed into the small snug that was on the other side, separated from the kitchen by a chimney with a wood burner. "It gave us the feel of more space in here. The whole project was madness, but also good fun. Listen to me," he said, shaking his head, "cataloguing our renovation project and not letting you get a word in edgewise."

She looked into her flute, watched the small bubbles, rising, rising, rising. She took another sip of the sparkling wine. Everything she had to talk about was so depressing. "I like hearing about you and Tim."

"Oh, well, here's a good one. For our honeymoon, we hired a vintage VW bus and drove through the Scottish Highlands. After, we ditched the car for the Fort William ferry to the Isle of Skye, where we took long rambles. The trip culminated with us singing with a local church choir in a cave on the island. The whole affair alternated between completely embarrassing and utterly brilliant. And now it's unforgettable."

She smiled. "As it should be."

Cal sipped the sparkling wine and looked at her over the rim of his glass. "Do you really not want to talk about what's happening to you?"

"I will, but right now? Anything but," she assured him. "In fact, I need something to do to keep me busy. You should put me to work."

"Easy. Would you like to set? We'll eat right here, I think, rather than move to the table." He set down his glass and slid the linens and plates topped with cutlery her way.

"Happy to." The cloth napkins were folded in quarters, and she folded them in half again before placing the silverware on top. "How did you meet Tim? He wasn't at college with us, was he?"

"No, no. We met, of all places, on one of those sightseeing boats on the Thames."

She laughed. "What? The ones we swore we wouldn't be caught dead on?"

"Hand to heart," he said, eyes crinkling. "A group of colleagues and I were entertaining someone visiting from Bilbao with just forty-eight hours of layover. This was a previous job. We were doing a quick-and-dirty, see-as-much-of-London-as-possible tour. Tim had just moved down from Durham and he had decided to play tourist, that very day on that very boat. He heard us talking art and struck up a conversation, and, well, the rest is history."

"So he did museum work as well?"

"No, no. Art was more a passion of his. He was a finishing carpenter by trade. Much sought-after by people like us who'd bought something that needed renovation." A timer bell pinged. "Ah. There's our starter." He turned away and walked to the oven.

"It smells delicious," she said.

"Thank you." He set the individual casserole dishes side by side on a cooling rack. "We'll eat this first and then I'll cook the fish, if you don't mind taking our time?" When Noel shook her head, he added, "Poached salmon and peas next. I harvested early in the summer and froze what I couldn't possibly eat by myself."

"I love salmon," she said. She picked up the wine bottle and topped off her glass.

"Don't take this as a criticism, but you may want to slow down with the sparkling wine. I have another bottle of white chilling that we'll have with supper."

"Oh, right." She brought her hands up to her cheeks. They felt hot and she hoped her face wasn't flushed. "I'm feeling anxious, I guess. Or maybe a better word is unmoored."

He looked at her. "Is it being here? Or everything back home?"

"Trust me, it's not being here in your home. Or being at the Addison. I needed the change of scenery, and the distance from Andy. I keep thinking maybe he'll have a change of heart while I'm away. Or Alice will. She was very upset the last time I saw her. First her birth mother left her, and then I did too." She winced at the thought. "But I am finding it a bit hard to be in London, to be honest. Reminders, everywhere, of so much I've worked hard to forget."

Cal's eyes widened slightly at that.

"Sorry," she offered quickly. "I said that without thinking."

"But you meant it, didn't you? You've stayed away for the past thirty years."

"Twenty-nine and change," she corrected, hoping he would smile. He did.

"It's not a terrible thing to talk about this now," he said. "The world won't end if we do."

It was tempting, she thought as she looked at his familiar, kind face—this idea of unburdening herself by telling him everything he'd never known. Bryn's betrayal. The baby. Her grandmother's solution. The regret she had lived with since. But was it fair to subject a person she'd purposely kept at arm's length to the torrent that might start pouring out once she dismantled the dam?

"Staying away was never about you. It was all me and my inability to cope."

"What was I to think, though, when you withdrew from the course without a word and then I never saw you again?"

She looked away.

He pressed on. "We wondered if having your letters returned twice made you angry enough to leave. We wondered if you left because you were ill. Did you go to hospital after I saw you in September? Did you go home in October to recover? We just didn't know what to think. Or how to find you, for that matter."

October. Of course he'd wonder if she'd left right after withdrawing from university. "No, I didn't leave in . . ." Wait. She frowned in confusion. "Who's 'we'?"

"Bryn and I," Cal explained. "He was frantic when he came back from Italy and found you'd gone. I mean, he'd have to be frantic to decide to ask me, knowing how I felt about him."

"Bryn?" Noel repeated. She heard a pounding in her ears. "Bryn came back?"

"Of course he did. Look." Cal reached across the table and took Noel's hands in his. "You know I resented that he took up so much of your time. But he loved you, and of course he came back. He was beside himself with worry about you and concerned about all the possible reasons why you wouldn't have waited for him. We both were, we had that in common."

"No, no, no, no, no." For a moment, her mouth couldn't form any other word—and then word after word began to spill out. "This is all wrong. He did not come back. I waited for months . . . I was still in the flat on Boxing Day. When you came knocking to check on me? I was there, waiting. He never came!" Noel said in a panic. "I left because he left me first."

Cal squeezed her hands tighter, tried to get Noel to meet his eyes. "You have to listen. Bryn was days late because he'd been stuck in an Italian hospital for three weeks. But he did come home, and the very first thing he did was look for you. Everywhere."

Stuck in a hospital. Frantic. He looked everywhere. Fragments of Cal's explanations pinged her like ice pellets falling from a harsh sky. The words stung. This can't be happening, she thought, but it was. Everything she'd thought when she was muddled, confused, alone, and frightened in a body that, swollen out of recognition, no longer seemed like her own had not been true. She had allowed herself to lose faith in Bryn, to lose all perspective, in his extended absence. She had allowed herself to give up their child . . . and for no good reason. Oh, god, the baby. Her baby, Sammy: given away, any time she might have had with him relinquished. She remembered the day she handed him over to the midwife; she remembered telling Gran she couldn't do it alone. The way his head smelled at that moment. His long, slender fingers gripping hers. Any future she imagined—the three of them together, here or in Wales—stopped before it had a chance to materialize. Stopped by her.

She took her hands from Cal's and covered her face.

"Noel," he said, "look at me. What is it?"

After a moment she did, but instead of Cal, all she saw was the magnitude of her mistake.

"He . . . came back. I left and Bryn came back. You can't imagine what I've done!"

"You didn't do anything wrong," he said. "You'd been waiting all that time with no word—anyone would have believed what you did, that he had left you. Even Bryn understood why you might have been angry enough to go home. He blamed himself for falling ill, for trusting the Italian post. He blamed himself for going away in the first place. I blame myself for not attempting to find you, somehow. There's plenty of blame to go around, but you—you are not to blame here. It was all a terrible, terrible series of events. Maybe if you talked to him, like you're talking to me now . . ."

She just stared at him for a few seconds, silent. When she finally spoke, her voice was flat. "You don't know what I did because I didn't tell you everything that was going on with me back then. I tried to tell Bryn, but my letters kept coming back to me unread. He didn't know what was going on either. I felt so . . . alone."

"What was going on with you, Noel? Tell me. I didn't help you then; let me try and help now."

His face was so kind; the open, friendly young man he used to be still was present in the more mature face, there beneath the weathering and the wrinkles and creases. Her old friend. But he might be horrified when he learned what she'd done in her despair, and there was nothing he could do to help even if he pretended he wasn't. What's done is done. As soon as that old adage popped into her head, she felt a bubble of hysteria take shape in her throat, as if she might laugh, and she took a deep breath to hold it down and make it stop.

But why? Why should she hold anything in anymore? For so long, she had lived with these mistakes and missteps and regrets held deep inside. Even if she never examined them, they were part of her—a buzzing, restless part. Try as she might, there was no escaping that. Maybe it was time to let it all out into the air and light. If she did and Cal wanted nothing more to do with her after, their friendship would be little different than it had been for the past thirty years. But what if, just what if, she spoke and he understood and she felt . . . relief? What if her truth might relieve him, too, of the burden he'd carried all this time?

"There was a reason why I didn't open the door after Christmas," she began, "and it wasn't that I was upset with you. I couldn't let you see that I was pregnant."

"Pregnant?" Cal's mouth dropped open.

"Almost eight months, at that point. I knew I was pregnant that last time we had tea."

"Your illness, then—"

"Was morning sickness," she interrupted. "I had months of it."

"But why couldn't you tell me?"

"I don't know! I don't know! I was afraid your doubt of Bryn would make me doubt him? No." She shook her head. "That's not right. Those doubts were already in me, and you were a mirror. When I found out I was pregnant, I got caught up in the fantasy of what it would look like to make a family with him, what our future would look like, how happy he would be when he came home and learned about the baby. When I couldn't reach him with the news, I started to worry what he'd feel when he came home to find a baby on the way. Would he resent me for not telling him, not giving him some say? For trapping him? I worried he wouldn't want the baby, and then what? If I kept alone in my bubble, I wouldn't see my worries reflected in your face, and then maybe I could stop believing all that and . . ." She shook her head again. "I can't adequately describe the state of my mind back then, except to say it wasn't right. I loved Bryn so much, and I was alone too much, and then he never came home. It . . . broke me."

"But what about the baby?" Cal looked pained. "Did you . . . lose the baby?"

"Sammy." She looked away and off into the distance and smiled. "I named him Samuel. Everyone says this about their own babies, but Sammy really was perfect. He looked so much like Bryn I couldn't stop looking at him. He had a lot of dark hair and these beautiful long fingers . . ." She turned back to look at Cal. "No," she said, her voice hollow, no longer wistful. "I didn't lose him. Two days after I gave birth to him, I gave him away."

CHAPTER 22

SHOREDITCH FLAT, JANUARY 1993

It was January, about a month before Sammy was due to arrive, and it was harder and harder for Noel to explain Bryn's absence to herself. The words she'd repeated to herself in late December—maybe he'd gotten sick, maybe he was lying sick somewhere and had been for weeks; maybe he'd been robbed of all his belongings, injured and unidentifiable, maybe that was why he was late in coming back—no longer sounded convincing.

He's left you. This voice had been with her for days now. *He's left you. If he was coming back, he'd be here by now.* She was alone, she had to face it; there was no one to help her. Cal hadn't come back either, and she couldn't blame him. She couldn't reach out to anyone in her department or Bryn's without revealing what a mess she'd gotten herself into.

And then a thought came to her: *Not true, not no one.* There was one person who could take charge and help her now.

On the day of this epiphany, she willed her large body out of bed and went to the corner phone box. She phoned her grandmother.

"Help. You have to come. I need you."

Three short, sharp raps on the door. Then a pause. Then someone calling her name. "Noel. You need to let me in."

Gran. Here for her! Just as she'd been all those years before. Noel had been so angry with her grandmother after they'd last spoken. Gran had been dismissive of her relationship, implying she was too young to know her own mind and too inexperienced to get so serious. But she, not Bryn, was the one who'd come in the end, and the pull of the practicality she offered, had always offered, was too great and Noel was too tired to resent it.

She took the few steps across the room to open the door. Framed in the doorway, her size was on full display.

"I'm thankful you called me, my girl. You shouldn't be doing this alone."

Within five minutes of entering her flat, Gran had Noel sitting at the kitchen table while she made tea.

"It's properly stewed," she said, carrying the pot over. "You have no cups and saucers that I can find, so these mugs will have to do," she added as she poured a cup for Noel.

"They're all I have, sorry." Noel drew the filled mug toward her. "I do have milk if you—"

"Black is fine." Gran took a seat opposite. She lifted the pot again and poured the steaming hot tea into the second mug. Before she took a sip, she reached her hand across the kitchen table and laid it over Noel's. "We've got a lot of talking and planning ahead of us."

"Do we?" Noel asked. "Aren't you tired after your flight?"

"I'll manage. Now," she continued, "we're not talking about bringing you home to have the baby there. Clearly that's not in the cards, not when you're this far along. But I do have another idea. Will you listen?"

Shaken by her doubts, Noel wavered. Gran was measured; she had a plan, where Noel only had dreams. She nodded. "All right, I'll listen."

"I have distant cousins up north," Gran said. "I rang the one closest in age to me for some advice. We met once or twice many years ago, when we were children, but she was just that much older that we didn't play together at the time. These days, the age difference no longer matters. She's very nice, very easy to talk to. I thought she might be a good resource for us as we look for . . . solutions. And you know what? She's already had an idea, something I think you should consider."

Noel waited, unsure what to expect.

"She has a nice family, three daughters, several grandsons—I forget how many she said—but only one granddaughter. Your generation in the family tree, Noel, although this girl is almost ten years older than you. She and her husband own a shop, and they run it together. A very comfortable life, a nice home, my cousin said. The only thing lacking is a child. And they want one, desperately, only they're unable to have their own. I didn't ask for details."

This was such a lot of noise, such a lot of talking about people Noel didn't know and would never know. So much nice—nice cousin, nice family, nice home—that Noel had almost, almost missed the message within. Now that Gran had stopped chattering, however, the implication dawned on her. She was suggesting that this couple would give her Sammy a nice life, these two parents with their settled living who wanted him more than anything. Whereas she, Noel, would give him . . . what? Something far more precarious?

Gran was being so gentle, so calm, but unspoken in the many, many words she had just said was how reckless Noel was in her eyes.

And yet, surprisingly, Noel wasn't angry at any of the interference. She was too weary to raise her voice. If Gran stopped talking, she could go to bed and sleep for days.

A thought occurred to her. Curious, she asked, "Did you suggest my mother give me up too?"

If Gran had made the same urging, how had Ellie resisted being worn down by the rational arguments and promises of nice things for a baby who had done nothing more egregious than show up at an inopportune time? "Did you want her to let me go?"

"Twenty years ago"—Gran shook her head slowly—"I wasn't so slow, so achy, and so close to the end of my life that I couldn't help her raise you. So, no, to answer your question, I didn't suggest this then. But given where I am in my life, all I have to offer to you this time around is a chance for a fresh start."

Noel just listened, too tired to engage.

"Your mother wasn't you," Gran continued, growing more riled up as Noel remained impassive to her answer. "She was never going to college and graduate school to make a career for herself. But you—you have all this ahead of you, so much promise! What is the alternative, love? Such poor attendance at school that you have to withdraw and never finish? You can't stay here and work here if you have a dependent and no degree. You'll be coming home with me either way, so why not by yourself, unencumbered? You walk away and get yourself back on track at home. Take time to heal and get back to your junior year in the States in the fall. Apply to a master's degree program after that. My understanding is that for a familial adoption, all it takes is a legal appeal made by both parties and the baby will be placed within our family. Wouldn't you like that? Knowing he's with blood? Say yes, and it's all but done and dusted."

"I'll know where he is, then?" Noel asked, a spark of hope entering her. "They'll let me know him? I could send him letters? Meet him someday?"

"I don't think that's a good idea, love. You'll want him to be happy, yes? And settled?"

Never see Sam? Never know Sam? The idea jolted her out of the stupor Gran had lulled her into, and her eyes filled with tears. Why was she even listening to this plan, all its steps, every one of them leading to giving up her child? She loved Sam. Being tired and worried that Bryn had been hurt or worse didn't excuse how quickly she was folding to Gran's will. If Bryn did eventually come home, he would be upset to find she'd had his baby but left him with strangers. At the least, she and Sam would be a family. They would be fine as long as they were together.

"My answer's no," she said loudly. "I'm sorry for this couple, but no. This is my boy, not theirs."

Gran rose from her chair and moved around the table to sit next to Noel. She laid a hand on her arm. "I know this is hard for you now, you feel torn, but you can have your own family a few years down the road, once your education is behind you and you're settled into a successful career. You can put this Bryn out of your mind and find someone you feel secure in, a real partner." She looked into Noel's eyes. "Let me get the process underway. Please."

"I don't feel torn," Noel said. "I feel certain. My answer is no. And if you try to bring this up again, I'm afraid you'll have to leave."

Easily said, harder to stick to. With each day that passed, Noel grew more and more anxious. Her nails were bitten and ragged. She stopped sleeping through the night and stopped washing her hair in the sink, claiming her unwieldy stomach was an impediment to both. Her spirit, though, was the true culprit, the true heavy and unwieldy thing—a spirit like a sack of stones and nothing else, no more soaring, no more elation. Bryn's absence began to feel like loss, like she was a widow who was, she realized, starting to forget what her partner looked like and felt like, who was feeling the distance from those memories as a rebuke to her faithlessness. What kind of bad person was she? What had he meant to her, really, if she could no longer call up the exact color of his hair or eyes or the feel of his hands on her?

She was standing in the kitchen, staring out into the room but focusing on nothing. Her emotions felt like they were behind a gray scrim, obscured and unknowable. The big nothing. Physical sensations were blocked too, as if her entire body had been dosed with novocaine. She didn't register when it happened, the gush of warm water running down her legs, barely felt the accompanying cramps that made her double over. It wasn't time, it wasn't happening. She could barely hear her grandmother calling her name, telling her they must get to the birthing center.

How could Sam be coming when she felt nothing?

CHAPTER 23

MATERNITY CENTER, JANUARY 1993

They brought Sam to Noel's breast while he was still slippery and red. He had a white, curd-like substance matting down his dark hair. All she could think was, *Is there something wrong with him?* She must have asked the question aloud because the midwife smiled and told her he was small but absolutely perfect. They'd clean him up in a few minutes and he'd be beautiful. For now, she was supposed to let him find her nipple, get used to her.

Instead, he started crying. She was such a failure that her son didn't want her.

"That's not true," the midwife said. Noel had spoken aloud again, although she couldn't remember opening her mouth, forming the words. "He's had a big day, he needs a good cry and a rest. And so do you. Here," she said, "let me take him to get cleaned up. We'll bring him back to you when he's all swaddled and settled."

Tucked up in her bed, Noel fell deeply asleep. She dreamed she was back in an art history lecture, reviewing art slides, but she was standing instead of sitting. No one noticed her, even when she held up her hand, even when the lecturer asked questions about Titian's use of underdrawing and underpainting and she shouted to be noticed.

When she woke, Sam was in his basket next to her bed. He was sleeping, wrapped tightly in a flannel blanket.

"You're awake."

Noel looked to her right to find her grandmother sitting in a chair next to her. She pulled herself upright to sitting. "Yes. But I'm tired, Gran. Really tired."

As she said that, her midwife walked in. "No doubt you are," the woman said in her jollying voice. "You just completed the most arduous work humans can do." Her eyes wandered to Sam and then back to Noel. "How about we give the feed another go, then you can rest your eyes again."

"But he's sleeping."

"That never stopped a hungry baby before. Listen," she added, taking in Noel's look of confusion, "we should get him used to latching on sooner rather than later. Some babies don't take to it right away, and it's best to jump right in and keep going until they do."

"I'll wait outside." Gran rose to leave the two women alone with the baby.

"Oh, don't leave on our account," the midwife said. "You'll be wonderful encouragement for Mum while she's learning."

Gran dropped back into her seat.

"Here we go." The midwife lifted the bundled baby, holding him along her forearm with his head resting in the cup of her hand. She used the knuckle of her free finger to gently stroke the corner of his mouth. He responded by rooting around in search of something to suckle. "You know what you need to do, little man. You're a clever big boy, aren't you?" she crooned. "A clever, big, hungry boy. How about your mum instead of my finger, eh?"

Mum. Noel froze, the baby in the other woman's arms looming over her. She was this baby's mum. She was responsible now for feeding him, making him happy, keeping him alive—but she had no idea how to be anyone's mum. She had no template for it. Her mother had been a free spirit, fun and flighty rather than reliable. Gran had overcompensated, setting goals for each of her days and keeping her to routines. Noel wasn't unloved, but she'd never been mothered either. Had her mother breastfed her when she was an infant? What had days been like? Nights? Had they played together, gone for walks, read books? Had she been overjoyed when Noel arrived, or as heavy and low and as incapable of moving as Noel was right now?

The baby kept coming to her, lower and lower, until he was at arm level. No—not "the baby," not "he." Sammy.

"Sammy," she said.

"That's right," the midwife said. "Here you go, now. Remember to support his neck in the crook of your arm."

He was coming to her whether she was ready or not. Somehow she got her arms to move and she made a cradle of them, and all of a sudden he was in them. His eyes opened with the movement, taking her by surprise. They were blue and piercing like Bryn's, although lighter in color. With his dark hair cleaned and lying slick against his skull, he reminded her so much of Bryn that her heart hurt.

It wasn't his fault that she couldn't look at him. Instead, she looked at the soft spot on his head, counted its pulses.

"Now let's get this gown lowered for you," the midwife said, untying the garment and tucking the shoulder flap of fabric below her breast, assuming the task Noel had failed to do.

From her right side came the sound of Gran clearing her throat. Oh yes, Gran was here. Noel had forgotten.

"Gran?" she said.

"Yes, love?" She moved forward to the edge of her seat and put her hand on Noel's arm. "What is it?"

"I— I can't. I can't do this."

On her left side, the midwife said, "You can. I know this is daunting at first, but let's give it a try. Just one try."

"Gran. Please. Help me." Noel took a deep breath, exhaled slowly. "I can't do this."

Her grandmother looked at her, comprehending. "Are you sure?"

Noel nodded.

Gran squeezed her arm and then stood. When she spoke again, she spoke to the midwife. "I think you should take the baby to the nursery. He can have a bottle. Noel needs some rest right now, she's got a lot ahead of her."

The midwife hesitated only a moment before taking the baby from Noel. When he was settled in his basket, she wheeled him out of the room.

"I'll go talk to them out there in a minute," Gran said. "But are you sure about this? Once it's done, you won't be able to change your mind. That wouldn't be kind to his new parents."

No, she wasn't sure, not at all. The thought of someone else holding Sammy, loving him, hit her like a body blow. But the thought of keeping him, harming him with her inadequacies, marking his life with her pain, was unbearable. He deserved to be loved and celebrated. He deserved so much better than someone so empty.

She'd held him twice. She wouldn't hold him again. But at least she had that. And he had that too, from her, the best she could give him right now. Maybe he would know he'd been loved. Maybe his new parents would tell him that much.

"Do you think they will get here soon? I don't want him to be alone too long."

CHAPTER 24

CALUM'S FLAT, DECEMBER 2022

More wine—Cal opened a bottle of red. Noel suspected it might turn out to be a mistake in the morning, but she held out her glass anyway.

She drank and she lost track of how many times she refilled her glass. Work would roll around in the morning and she would have to get through it, hungover or not. She had run out of tears, at least, and was thankful to feel numb now, as if the pieces of her, every single piece with nerve endings, had been scooped out and set aside. She was a dry husk.

"We should eat something," Cal said. "I'm happy to cook the salmon—or serve up the starter with a little bread and butter, and maybe some of your cheese?"

She looked at her friend. She had derailed his entire evening and here he still was, rallying around her. "All your lovely food," she said.

"Everything will keep. But here. You should have something." He cut a few slices off the baguette that had been resting on a cutting board off to one side and unwrapped one of the pieces of cheese. "I'll eat if you do." He slid the board closer to her, and followed that with a butter knife.

She cut two thin wedges of cheese and picked up one. He took the other.

"Do you remember," he began after taking a small nibble from the corner of the cheese, "when I was sick at the end of first year and you asked what you might bring me? I told you 'Scotch broth' but you had no idea it was soup you could get in a can, so instead you made me a hot toddy concoction from Scotch whisky and cinnamon sticks?"

"And fuzzy honey." She managed a laugh. "Don't forget that. Lots of honey for your throat."

"'Here's your Scotch broth!' You were so pleased with yourself." He smiled.

"Of course I was. I thought I'd gotten it right." She rolled her eyes. "Little did I know."

"If you remember, I drank the toddy and asked for seconds. It wasn't the soup I'd asked for, but I remember thinking how brilliant it was, how right. Sometimes we don't know what we really need until we're offered the truly right thing, even if it's by accident."

She broke the rind off her slice of cheese and set it down on the edge of the cutting board. She popped the rest of the slice in her mouth and let it melt between her tongue and palate. Its sharpness made her mouth water.

"I don't know what's right anymore, Cal. My gran and I decided we'd go back home, where I'd put the birth behind me. She kept calling it 'the birth, the birth,' until soon Sammy wasn't a real person. I could keep that period of my life in the past and move forward. It felt cold, but it felt necessary, too, and after a while I almost forgot the entire experience was something I'd gone through—it was like it had happened to someone else. I thought that was right. Now, I'm not sure I'm a good judge."

Cal reached for her hand. "I think you might be better than you think. Remember, this didn't happen to someone else. This horrible, horrible sequence of events happened to you. And Bryn. And your son. But you now know what happened. There's pain in knowing, and I imagine part of you wishes you never found out. But could you go on and continue to keep the experience locked up inside you now that you know about Bryn? Would you want to? Maybe the right thing is freeing the truth."

"Free it how? By finding Sam? Telling Bryn?" She shook her head. The sharp movement made her dizzy and she pushed her wineglass aside. "Maybe they don't want to know. Maybe they're perfectly fine and all the news would do is disrupt their nice lives. Besides," she added, "this is all so muddied up with the way I've left things with Andy and Alice. Everywhere I look, there's so much I have to fix, and I hardly know where to start."

"How about you start by changing that sentence to 'so much that needs fixing'? These aren't situations you are solely responsible for." He released her hand and poured himself more wine. He took a big sip. "I once worked very hard to fix a relationship with someone who wasn't ever going to approve of anything I did. I said to myself, *Fix this one more thing and we'll be fine.* Then it was one more, and one more after that. I'm a pleaser, Noel, in case you hadn't noticed." He smiled and drained his glass. "It took me years to realize I wasn't responsible for making everything right. Nor are you. You may have to pick one thing that matters to you—the one thing that heals you—and do that. Then, after, the way forward may become clear. It did for me. And now," he said, with a flourish of his hand, "we have officially reached the woo-woo stage of the evening, a clear sign I have had too much to drink. Food. You'll eat, then you'll spend the night. No arguing."

He stood up and headed for the fridge. He pulled out a bottle of water. Next, he brought the vegetable tians to the island and inspected them. "Lukewarm, but so what."

Noel smiled. "They'll be delicious."

As Cal worked to put a meal on the table between them, she thought of the quiet flat that awaited her across town, the work she'd brought home to fill the time, the solitariness that she had been encouraging with her secrets and omissions, the loneliness she'd created that ran counter to the family life she had always wanted for herself. The only person who could change the dynamic was her.

What if she could find him, her son? Her heart lifted at the thought. She'd never known the details of the adoption; Gran had arranged it all, telling her she was better off putting it behind her so she might heal. It wouldn't be easy, but what if she worked hard and figured out where he was? A picture flashed in her mind: smiling as she boarded a train bound for some quaint village in a place she would have to learn about, finally knocking on a door that would be opened by her Sam.

"Do you think there's a way I might find Sam?" she asked. "If he wants to be found, that is. I think I'd like to start there."

Cal looked up from the food he was prepping and smiled a wide grin. "We'll find out if there's a way. First, we eat. If we're not too shattered after dinner, we can get on the computer and look for some answers. It's a start."

It's a start, she repeated to herself. *Looking for Sam.*

Once she started, Bryn would need to hear about Sam from her. There was so much to do, but she didn't have to do it all now. For now, she only needed this one place to start.

There was a moment in my life, a moment before my brain made memories, when I hung between worlds, belonging to no one. Even though I can't remember it, this is fact. I imagine this as two people watching me leave them, two others watching me approach, while I wait in between, alone. That is the moment I think of when I hear the words "childhood" and "parents." Not the birthday cakes and candles, the clean clothes, or the tender way Mum laid plasters on my skinned knees. Not the worry or the looks of pride or anything that came after I was taken home. The first thought is: in the time between relinquishing and claiming, I was alone. It is fact; I cannot unknow it; it is who I am.

Time has since filled in faces. Ruth and Douglas, naturally. Yours in later years, once I knew who you were and the internet gave me a face to add to the name. But I'm ahead of myself. Imagine me first finding the records of my birth, filed so efficiently in the General Register Office. Your name, the name you'd given me, father unrecorded. Still, the person helping me navigate the process told me I was lucky! "Some mums remove their names. Others are firm about no contact. But you, lucky boy, you now know one parent. She can tell you the rest." My girlfriend at the time was so excited for me. I remember how eagerly she grabbed the copy of the original birth certificate out of my hands when I returned home with it, as if it was her news, not mine. I took it right back from her before she'd had a chance to scan for your name. "But it's wonderful news," she protested. "I want to share it with you." And later, when I secured the certificate away, "I don't understand why you looked at all if you had no plans to find your parents."

No answer I could give would ease her disappointment. It's difficult to explain to anyone who was born to one or two parents and came home with the same why a person might want to know but not seek. It's difficult to explain those moments of being no one's and how the feeling lingers despite not being able to remember the actual abandonment. Say all that and watch eyebrows draw together and the eyes underneath emit skepticism. If you're lucky, you won't see the twist of a mouth, a twist of scorn that can do nothing but confirm your suspicion that someone thinks you are ungrateful and churlish.

When I requested those birth records, I had just turned twenty-six years old. I wanted a name, but I did not know then if I wanted to find you. My life was fine. My mum was gone but I knew she had loved me; my dad continued to love me still. I was beginning to emerge in the art world, on an even keel. What more did I need? What if you rejected me again because I reminded you of your mistakes? What if you couldn't look at me because my father was unknown to you, someone who had done a horrible thing to you? What if I pressed to have you in my life, and for whatever reason of your own you denied me and my life went off the tracks? What then? Perhaps asking these questions is the definition of ungrateful and churlish; I simply don't know.

I did what I thought would satisfy my questions while still buffering me from rejection. I took the name I'd been given and found you through a web search. I learned you are a professional; your photo accompanies your name in several registries and small newspaper articles. I have looked at your photos a lot since then. You have a kind face. We do not look much alike—your hair is a similar shade of brown but very straight, your eyes smaller and deeper set—although in your chin and jaw I can see the outlines of my own face. It surprised me not at all to learn you too belong to the art world. If I could tell Dad what I'd been researching without hurting him, I could finally say, "My genes are why I am who I am. This woman holds answers to all the questions."

Whenever I could, I went back to my bookmarked searches and looked at you and looked at you until your face was etched in my memory. It felt incredible that you were across the ocean and yet my life went on as it always had. Winter, spring, summer. Breakfast, lunch, dinner; work, walk, sleep. Months out, my girlfriend and I made reservations for the opening week of the William Blake exhibition at Tate Britain, and then, shortly after, she left me. When October came, I attended the exhibition alone. What phenomenon was it when I saw you in the profile of the woman who stood next to me, gazing as I did on one of Blake's earliest engravings? Was it you? Or was I imagining things, hoping for you so much that I would see you anywhere?

Lately I have been reworking the sketches I did back then of the sea of faces at the exhibition, of people passing each other as strangers in a crowded space. My premise is, as folks mingle about, connections are discovered. Several people are not strangers at all.

One pair in my sketches might find out during a polite chat while in a line for coffee that they have a connection through a former lover, someone they both strolled art galleries with at different times in the past.

Another pair is made up of one person who makes an offhand remark at the coat check about a Klimt exhibition in Vienna years before, and another person standing close by pipes in that he, too, saw the exhibition. As the two begin to chat, they realize they were at the Belvedere on the same day while on separate trips to Vienna.

One more pair is made up of an art historian and a painter, there in a museum on the same day at the same time, stopping next to each other to admire the same engraving, something from Songs of Innocence. *The poem is "Spring," the engraving of a mother, child, and baby lambs—the pastoral Blake, fit for warm laps and small bodies being held close to larger, comforting ones. This pair looking at this art are mother and son, although only one of them knows it.*

The Law of Truly Large Numbers states that within a large enough sample of people, you'll find coincidences that seem at first glance extraordinary—someone in the crowd has won the lottery several times, or the people on either side of you share your birthday—but are not extraordinary at all, given the size of the sample. Coincidence is even more likely when the sample is concentrated with people who hold, say, a common interest in art. It's all statistics and probability.

This means anything can happen in our world, even in a city this size—or is it especially in a city this size? Anything at all.

I remain—
Your son

PART IV

TOWARD THE DOOR WE NEVER OPENED

CHAPTER 25

SWN Y MOR, DECEMBER 2022

Bryn listened as the kettle on the gas ring began to rattle and hiss, the water coming to a boil. He set down his paintbrush again and went after it. He didn't need more tea but his hands felt the cold, and he hoped holding a hot mug might loosen his fingers enough so he could keep working this morning. The room had a small wood burner, but it made little difference today against December's damp.

But can I even pour my tea? he wondered with a look down at his fingers, curled as if he still held his brush, each knuckle knobby and swollen. The damp was aggravating the arthritis. He shook his head. Everything aggravated the arthritis: dressing, bathing, cleaning up, cooking, sketching, painting—all of it.

He sighed, switched off the gas, and flipped open the spout's whistling lid with his elbow. His fingers were not completely useless, but he tried to spare them excess movement to stave off pain and conserve whatever flexibility he could for his painting.

"How long do you think you'll be able to continue painting?" Delaney, his agent and sometimes his lover, had asked months ago when they were in bed. She had picked up one of his hands then and made a point of kissing each deformed knuckle.

Only moments before, relaxed after sex and not thinking clearly, he had invited her to stay for lunch. That morning, he'd bought good bread in the village and come home to make some carrot soup—something that he liked that was also easy to cook, easy to blend with the stick contraption he'd bought—but lunch would require ferrying bowls and utensils and a bread board to the table while using his wrists to lift. Delaney would probably offer to lay the table for him, which would only make matters worse. Whyever had he offered a meal when he couldn't carry dishes properly, let alone hide the curl of his grip on the spoon, like a talon grasping a branch?

"I'll be fine," he had answered, rising from their embrace, the moment broken. "I'll get in to see the doctor."

He hadn't kept his promise yet, but he would. And this time, he would give whatever medication was prescribed time to take effect and his hands would get better—well, as better as it was possible for them to get. Better enough to continue painting. No, the newest canvas wouldn't be his last. Critics might note the changes in his technique—the increasingly looser outlines, the blurring and blending of color—but they would attribute it to aging eyes, perhaps, or the freedom from convention that comes with growing older. Neither Bryn nor Delaney would challenge the assumptions. The last thing he wanted made public was the gradual creep of the joint disease that had afflicted generations of his family and now him. He wanted no pity and certainly wanted no art world debates about diminishment of talent. He simply wanted to paint. Painting was his life, his entire purpose.

With the tea steeped, he poured himself some and took a seat at the small, cluttered table. He wrapped his hands around the mug. Its warmth soothed. The day was not so cold, but remnants of yesterday's rain, compounded by the salty, wet wind off the ocean, made for a persistent damp. It found the gaps in every one of the windows cut into the thick white stone walls and seeped in.

Once upon a time, damp and drafts had seemed a small price to pay for the abundance of light to work by and landscape to inspire, and nothing an extra cardigan or jumper wouldn't solve. But that was back when his hands worked better, and back when this home was only his summer escape. He had never intended to live here in his granddad's old place year-round, but then had come the pandemic that prompted his move out of his flat in densely populated Swansea. He was now quite content here—alone and secluded, save for the occasional visits from Delaney that satisfied the physical itches. His inclination for years had been to withdraw, and the few obligations he had to meet with dealers and the public were more and more carried out grudgingly, only out of his sense of responsibility. The pandemic, while destructive, had provided cover for his natural instinct to retreat.

A rumbling noise caught his attention and he looked over to the gas ring, wondering if he'd maybe forgotten to turn off the heat under the kettle. The cooker was ancient in appliance years and lately he had become rather nervous about the bottled gas sparking a fire, setting the studio and his paintings alight.

But no, he wasn't becoming forgetful on top of everything else. As he stopped to listen to the noise, growing louder by the second, he realized it was the motor of a car making its way up the lane to Swn Y Mor.

He wasn't expecting anyone, and it was too early for the post. He walked to the studio door and peered out, there in time to see the front end of a car coming round the bend in the lane. Delaney's car, as if by thinking of her just now he had conjured her.

"Bloody hell," he whispered under his breath. "Bloody interruption." He immediately drew his shabby cardigan close around him, though, and stepped outside to greet her.

Delaney stopped the car and hopped out, waving to him. A tall, handsome woman, she was casually dressed in corduroy trousers and a long sweater, clothes that shouted "ready for a stay in the country." Not here, he hoped—and then, feeling guilty, he raised his hand in return and tried to clear the scowl from his face. But it was too late. She noticed.

"Before you say anything," she called as she approached, "I'm on my way to Caernarfon to see my sister and her family for the holiday. Stopping here doesn't take me that much out of the way. And I have news. With you, it's sometimes easier to pass it along in person." She stopped as she reached him, and she kissed his cheek. "I must say, the beard is growing on me."

He ignored the remark. "Come in, I suppose. I'll heat up the tea, but I warn you, it's cold in the studio." He stepped aside and let her walk inside first. "Go ahead and check up on me." He nodded at the canvases resting against the far wall.

"Truly, Bryn, I'm here for another reason. But as I am here . . ."

"You might as well have a look, right?" He shook his head; she was across the room inspecting canvases before he even got the words out. "You look, I'll get the water back on."

He sparked the flame and reached for the only other mug he had close by, all the while keeping watch over Delaney out of the corner of his eye.

After twenty years of working together, she knew the way he stored his work; she started with the smaller, finished pieces at the farthest corner of the studio. He waited for reactions, but as was her way, she kept her body language in check. Occasionally her gaze lingered on a piece of work, the only tell that something had piqued her interest, but that could mean she loved it or felt it needed a little more attention.

He shook his head again. He would find out soon enough.

The water boiled and he added it to the stewed tea in the pot. Leaving it to steep some more, he joined Delaney at the next grouping.

"Still finishing these," he said, unnecessarily.

"Yes, I can see." She moved toward the painting on the easel.

"I'd rather you not look at that yet. Early days."

She ignored him and walked around to the front of the easel. He watched her bring her face up close to it and then take a few steps back. After a few moments, she asked, "What are you calling this one?"

"Don't know yet," he replied—a lie, but he didn't want to get into a discussion about this work just yet. In his mind it was Ceridwen of Llyn Tegid, Ceridwen the witch, but he could only hope Delaney wouldn't see the outline of the woman beginning to take shape in the middle distance. "Early days."

"Yes, you said." She laughed and turned to him. "It's quite good. Better than good. It's easy to see how the arthritis is making your brush strokes looser, but you've made it work as a sort of new direction for you. But is that a figure I see going in there? An old trope for you, surely?"

He held back his sigh and changed the subject. "What was it you wanted to talk about?" He poured tea into her mug and held it out to her.

"Thank you." She, like he, wrapped her hands around the mug. "I'll tell you, but please don't say no in a knee-jerk response. It has to do with more travel to London. Your retrospective show opens on April first, and that's probably enough of the city for you. However, the Rising Artists Award ceremony comes in May. It's the thirtieth anniversary of the award, as you'll know, with the distinction of being held live for the first time since 2019. I've been asked," she said, "to ask you, the first recipient of the award, if you'd join the judging and also present the prize to this year's winner."

"No." He knew it was not what she wanted to hear, but there it was. He didn't need or want to think it over. It was bad enough he would have to appear at the reception marking the opening of the retrospective of his work, but at least he'd arranged to head straight home after to return to his quiet life. He hated being in London, and wouldn't go there any more than necessary. "No," he repeated.

Delaney sipped her tea. Bryn expected her to protest his decision, maybe cajole him into a change of heart, but all she said after a few moments' pause was, "That's disappointing, but I did tell them not to get their hopes up. Anyway," she added, "there will be someone else willing to take your place—clamoring, even. One of the front runners for the prize this year is a big draw, someone—like you in your day—who has managed to capture the imaginations of people beyond the art world. Come to think of it, he reminds me of you a bit, around the eyes, although not as brooding."

Brooding. He frowned. "I'm not bloody Heathcliff."

Delaney set down her mug and pulled her phone from her handbag. After some unlocking and tapping and scrolling, she held up the screen for him to see. Bryn leaned close. She'd pulled up a photo of a young man. Henry Bell. The name meant nothing to Bryn. Time was, he'd known everyone from accomplished artists to the up-and-comers, but keeping a finger on the pulse of the art world was also a thing of his past.

There were limits to his hermitude, however. As tempting as it was to limit all outside contact, alienating an agent and ally like Delaney could mean losing all avenues to income. There was a difference between "reclusive" and "forgotten," and maintaining his life up here, as simple as it was, required ongoing infusions of money. Maybe he'd want to fix these damn studio windows before next winter.

"May I?" he asked, reaching for the phone. Delaney gave it up easily.

The boy filling the screen indeed had eyes similar to his: wide-set, the outer corners raised higher than the inner corners, reminding him of a cat's. The color was more of a clear gray than Bryn's blue, but very striking against his dark hair. He was smiling in the photo, but Bryn got the sense it wasn't from simple happiness. Maybe instead from a sense of absurdity, finding the art life ridiculous sometimes and having a laugh at the inside joke.

He looked up from the screen to Delaney. In the interim, she had fixed herself another tea and was drinking it, a studied, blank look on her face. She knew he needed her as much as she needed him; she was giving him time to reach this conclusion on his own. He had already decided to walk back his reflexive no. This award presentation was something he knew he had to do. Still, he would make her think he had yet to be persuaded.

He returned the phone to his agent. "Can you find any images of his art?"

"Of course. Here's the prize entry. It's called *Yours for the taking*." After a bit more scrolling, she turned the phone around again to show him. "He terms it a landscape. As you can see"—she shrugged—"it's so much more."

An understatement. Bryn's eyes widened as he took in the painting's use of color, texture, layering, light, and shadow. Featuring the ruins of a factory of some sort—pylons, oversized weeds flowering in the rubble—this wasn't a traditional landscape, nothing at all like the ones Bryn painted of the Welsh terrains and coastlines. But the two men shared an urge to portray a space both within and beyond the natural world.

"It reminds me . . ." But he hesitated to share his thoughts. It did remind him of what he had aimed for with his own prize winner, *Lady of Llyn Y Fan Fach*, both because of the shared exploration of shadowy figures and the attempt to express an intimate, otherworldly moment within a larger realm.

"It reminds me of some of your work," Delaney said mildly.

"Not in style, no. Nothing like," Bryn said dismissively. "But somehow . . ." He frowned. "It captures the tension between two worlds, like in *Lady*, but he's done something entirely new to me. You do think it will win?"

She tipped her head to one side, considering. "I've been saying this is the best of the show. He should win. But things are not so straightforward in these competitions. One never knows what the judges will decide. There are several other very good entries as well."

He narrowed his eyes. "Is he your client?"

"I'd like him to be." She smiled.

"I really don't want to be in London any more than I have to be," he said. "A weekend, maybe. That's all. A nice hotel, close to the trains. Let me think about it for a day or two. Two at most."

"Listen," she said, "I don't have to be up at my sister's at any certain time." She moved closer and laid a hand on his arm, and there was no mistaking what she was communicating.

Sometimes Bryn needed the physical closeness of sex. He had never let himself fall in love after his twenties, after Noel, but that didn't mean he was celibate. There was his female friend who worked behind the bar of the pub down the road, a teacher from a school in Swansea, the quiet but wickedly funny woman who ran the local library—women who, like himself, favored no strings. Good sex both exhausted and exhilarated him the way steering a boat through the rocky coastal waters would.

But today he didn't possess the desire or the energy or the coordination required to even remove his own clothes, never mind attend to another person's body. He wanted, he realized, to save what he did have for his work. Henry Bell's painting had inspired him to dig deeper into the emotions of his work-in-progress, to aim for the contradictions within Ceridwen: witch, avenger, shapeshifter, mother. That sense of inspiration and, yes, competitiveness was something he hadn't felt in a long time.

He put his hand over Delaney's, still on his arm. "Another time?" he asked, although as he said it, he knew he wouldn't be sharing a bed with her again. "I really should get back to the canvas."

She looked a bit surprised to be turned down, but she recovered quickly. "Yes, of course. The agent side of me applauds your dedication to the retrospective. Next time, maybe."

"Yes," he said. But in his mind she was already on her way out the door, already in her car, already gone.

Instead of continuing out to her car, however, she set down her mug and said, "One more thing. There's a journalist—"

He groaned.

"Hear me out," she said. "Federica Mackintosh of *Art/Source*. Reputable, right? They're doing an in-depth series on the awards for the thirtieth anniversary. She'd like to profile you. Something brief," she emphasized. "Answer a few questions about your role as awards presenter—now that you've agreed to do it—and the first winner. That's it, and you can do it all via email, all right? I want you to do it. We'll be able to work in the details of your retrospective; win-win."

He grimaced.

"Hold on," she added, and she dug around in her large handbag. "Ah, here it is." She pulled out a print tabloid and laid it down on the table next to the deserted mugs. "A copy of *Art/Source* with Federica's first profile in the series. It's of someone the Addison has hired specifically to work on the exhibition guide—unimportant, really, but it will give you a sense of her style and show you how painless this will be for you, okay?"

He could no longer afford to reject publicity. Besides, he was tired of being petulant, more tired of being away from his work. "Yes, fine, I'll read it. If it's to my liking, you may have her send along the questions and I'll do my best."

"Excellent. Thank you, Bryn, I appreciate it. Now, I'm off. I hope you have plans for the holiday this year. Dinner with a neighbor. I know you say you hate Christmas, but it's good for you to see people."

"I'm fine, Delaney." He did hate Christmas; to him, it was another day, something to get through. It was easier to forget the holiday without a television—and, wisely, he'd stocked his pantry with shelf supplies weeks ago. All the better to avoid the reminders in the displays of lights and decorations and boxes of mince pies. "Enjoy yours," he added before he shut the studio door behind her.

Try as he might, Bryn couldn't return to the state of concentration he'd reached before Delaney arrived. He sat in the studio, drinking more tea and brooding despite his protests otherwise. Time had certainly marched forward. Thirty years.

He had been the first Rising Artists winner; he hadn't thought about that in years. When he walked on stage this time as presenter, he'd be the legacy artist, not the exciting new one. Surely that was the angle this journalist, this—he picked up the journal that Delaney had left to look at the byline—Federica Mackintosh would play up for her profile of him, under a similarly clever title. "New Eyes on the Prize," he read. What would she write for him, "Old, Bent Hands"?

He sighed. If he read this now, he'd have done as Delaney asked and could return to work without feeling guilty. He picked up the sheet of paper and began reading.

New Eyes on the Prize: The Addison Gallery Enlists Visiting Help

(This profile is the first in an 8-part series introducing the people behind the scenes of the 2023 Rising Artists Awards exhibition and awards ceremony.)

By Federica Mackintosh
10 November 2022

For years, the Addison Gallery, under the leadership of its head curator, Jean Rayburn, has developed a special and cooperative relationship with the Field-Lyons Museum and Sculpture Park outside of Boston, Massachusetts. Until recently, this relationship centered on the sharing of artworks and the joint development of major exhibitions. Nearly two years ago, however, when Ms. Rayburn was performing her duties remotely during gallery closure, she began to wonder if the two institutions might benefit from an exchange of museum personnel as well.

After finding a kindred longing in Deborah Stone, Deputy Director of Field-Lyons, Ms. Rayburn brought the idea of setting up formal secondments to the museum's Board of Trustees. Enter Noel Enfield. She is the first secondee to the Addison, becoming part of the 2023 Rising Artists Awards team as the member responsible for interviewing the competing artists and reviewing their work in order to create the exhibition guide . . .

Bryn felt the air leave his lungs, as if he'd taken a fist to the diaphragm. Noel Enfield? Seconded to the Addison? This Noel Enfield had to be his Noel—how many could there be in the museum world?—and she was in London right now, working on the events surrounding the prize he'd won and then pushed out of his mind because the win would always be tied to her.

The award had come to him ten months after he brought Noel on holiday to this very house by the sea and told her that he was going to Italy. That even though he didn't need to, he had to—by himself. He'd be home by Christmas. No matter that only weeks before they had signed a lease for their first flat together, in gritty Shoreditch. She could move in on her own in August, couldn't she? Set it up? Have it waiting for him?

Instead, he'd returned home late and found that she'd gone, left him without so much as a note of explanation. When he'd won the prize in April, for the landscape composed around a portrait of Noel, she hadn't been by his side to see his moment and hers.

So long ago, and so many awards and accolades since, each one overshadowing the last, propelling his career forward from the Bryn he'd been at twenty-three. He shook his head, thinking back. He had been so full of himself, walking onto the stage to accept the award. The swagger and conceit he'd walked arm-in-arm with that evening had surprised some in the audience—peers he had studied with, tutors he had learned from. He'd caught the tail end of whispers as he walked through the cocktail reception after the ceremony. *What's happened to him? What an ass. Believe me, it was always there under the surface.*

He agreed he'd been an ass, but that last one had hurt, for he knew it wasn't true. He would have told them the conceit was a shield—there for strength, for getting through the evening—if only they'd asked. Instead, they'd put on their false faces and congratulated him as if he had imagined their venom only moments earlier.

If the person whispering, *What's happened to him?* had had the balls to ask him to his face, he might have been vulnerable enough to their compassion to say, *I needed something to get through this evening alone.*

Noel was supposed to be by my side, he would have explained—she was why the canvas had succeeded. Instead, he had no idea where she was except gone.

CHAPTER 26

LA MORRA, DECEMBER 1992

The climb to the belvedere in the village of La Morra was challenging. Bryn had known it would be; the group of student painters had been informed so by their local guide when he'd stopped the van to drop them several meters outside the entrance to town.

Usually fit and nimble on foot, Bryn was struggling to keep up with his peers. *My goat,* his granddad used to call him as he leapt from boat to mooring, from rock to barnacled rock. On this path into town, though, his legs felt filled with cement and, in his chest, his lungs were no longer light but as ponderous as two sandbags.

He had picked up a cold about five days after landing in Turin—their final stop in the five-month sojourn across Italy that had begun in Florence, hopscotched east to Bari, and from there headed north. Despite the beauty of the city and the wealth promised by the region's grapes, he and the others had been lodged in a cheap hostel, six to a room, some boarding with travelers not in their group. The weather, misty and wintery, had permeated everywhere; the hostel, with its terra cotta-tiled floors, had been damp, and the thin bedding inadequate. Someone in the room for only one day at the beginning of the stay had coughed all night long. Even though the bloke left early the next morning, the damage had already been done.

In the last few days, Bryn had begun to have difficulty breathing deeply enough to fill his lungs. It hurt his ribs and his chest to take in air. Now, out in the misty countryside, he could no longer deny the germs had invaded him. He was miserable—shivering, coughing, full of a seemingly never-ending supply of mucus. Yesterday's trudge through the rain falling on Grinzane Cavour and the hills outside Diano d'Alba hadn't done him any good. But still he'd lingered, intent on sketching the ruins of a building that was either an old farmhouse or villa, indeterminate now with its crumbling chimney, staved-in roof, golden blocks of stone scattered here and there in the overgrown grass. He had even taken time to stop an older man coming out of a café with his curly-haired dog and mimed taking a photo. The man had assented and Bryn had shot the Polaroid; he'd worked from it for hours last night, sketching the pair while kept awake by his stuffed head, his mucus, and his cough.

One of the advantages of being dropped so far outside of La Morra's gates was that he might set up his painting anywhere along the way and capture vistas the others would not. Maybe stopping to paint somewhere on the trail was a good idea, he considered, until he paused briefly to look ahead and upward. The town above was catching the sunlight and the tops of its stone buildings glowed golden, transporting him back to Rome and the Doria Pamphilj and the awe and inadequacy he had felt while standing in front of *The Annunciation.* More golden light traveled through the gaps between structures and down the sides of the hills, illuminating rows of vines and their wooden braces in the surrounding vineyards, while other rows were darkened by the shadows cast by taller towers. If he was to have a chance to capture such light, he had to be where that light play originated, and he could only get there by finishing the walk.

He took as deep a breath as he could, heard a cellophane crackle deep in his chest, chose to ignore it, and began walking again. He could rest at the top.

The village, when he finally reached it, was charming, its belvedere wide open and flat enough. Everyone else had removed their equipment pack from their back and was already at work or getting to it.

As he walked to the railing of the overlook, he felt the ground beneath his feet roll and judder, the view ahead tipping back and forth before his eyes. He gripped the metal bar, certain this was an earthquake and the entire town was about to slide off its perch. He was sure in that moment they would all die and he would never paint again and he would never make it home to Noel.

For some reason the shaggy truffle hound he'd met and sketched yesterday bounded into his thoughts. If only he might make it home to Noel, he'd never leave again. Or at least not for a long while. He'd bring her to Wales again, and there they would stay and make a home. They'd find a dog of their own they could take to the pub with them. If only he survived this convulsion.

When the swaying passed, he opened his eyes and looked around, expecting to see his terror mirrored in his fellow students, but all he saw were the townspeople heading home from the market, the drivers of the small trucks making wine and food deliveries to the *trattorie*. Odd, he thought, and when he surveyed the belvedere, he blinked. No one was fazed but him. His coursemates were painting, the others were going about their day.

"Everything all right, mate?" The painter he'd become friendliest with, Sean, had paused mid-brushstroke. His forehead was creased with concern.

"You didn't feel that? That rolling?" Bryn turned from the railing, took a step forward, and the ground churned again. He planted his feet wide and tried to steady himself, but couldn't. When he reached back for the solid safety of the guardrail, his hand missed. The last things he remembered were Sean coming toward him with some urgency and how incredibly close his face was coming to the gray stone all around him.

CHAPTER 27

TURIN, DECEMBER 1992

"*Polmonite. Batterico streptococco.* P-noo-monia, in *Inglese*," the doctor added. "*E un'abrasione, e un livido—un grosso livido.*" He traced a big air circle with his finger in front of his own forehead, then pointed at Bryn, making sure he understood that this something big was all happening on his face. "*Ma, concussione? No.*"

Bryn was too depleted to care and too weary to demand translation. He got the gist: bacterial pneumonia and a cut-up face from his fall, but no concussion. Once he'd landed in bed in this very warm hospital room all he had wanted to do was sleep, and sleep and sleep he had done. But no, he couldn't continue to be in and out of consciousness. He needed to be somewhere by Christmas—home by Christmas, yes. Noel was expecting him. He had to stay awake.

He tried to push himself up into a sitting position.

"Uh-uh-uh!" scolded the doctor. Pointless, as it turned out. Bryn had so little energy, he couldn't complete the move. Blood rushing in his ears, he sank back against the pillow and closed his eyes.

"Christmas?" he asked, when he could speak—and then, after slowly searching his brain for the little Italian vocabulary he had, he added, "*Natale?*"

"*Si, Natale. Dopodomani.*" The doctor then turned to the nurse at his side to explain the instructions he had written for Bryn's care in the medical chart he held in his hands.

"*Dopo . . . ?*" Bryn asked.

This time, the nurse answered. "The day after tomorrow," she translated.

"No," he whispered. He was supposed to be home by now. He was two days late. He'd been in hospital for five days, if he was calculating correctly. Noel wouldn't know what kept him, she wouldn't understand he was lying here in a Turin hospital, sick and unable to get home. She would worry that he hadn't turned up on time. "I have to get home," he said. "To London. *Londra.*"

"I speak English," the nurse told him. "You will not go home for maybe two more weeks. We must clear your lungs and clear the bacteria from you, yes? You are very, very ill."

"Very ill," the doctor agreed, clapping his hands together for emphasis. He handed the chart to the nurse, and with a "*ciao,*" he departed the room.

"My girlfriend," Bryn said. "I need to tell her." But how? he wondered. They had no telephone in the apartment. He had to assume everyone else he'd been traveling with had gone home on time, so there was no way to send a message with one of them. Tears started to fall down his cheeks. "A letter," he said. "A telegram?"

"*Ai, ai, ai.*" Bryn's crying clearly distressed the nurse. She went to his side and held up her hands for him to stop. "*Dio mio*. Yes, yes, I will bring you some paper for a letter. You write, but later, after you rest. Okay?"

He was being punished, he thought, for leaving Noel to move in alone. For leaving for months when this course had been unnecessary, nothing more than a lark, really, something he wanted to do in a place he'd long wanted to see. For not being more attentive each and every time he'd taken off to paint and left her behind. He would write the bloody letter as soon as it was possible and cross his fingers it would arrive before she decided he was unforgivable. No, he couldn't even think it.

"Yes, all right. But please, paper, as soon as possible. Please."

CHAPTER 28

UNIVERSITY COLLEGE, JANUARY 1993

Cal was hard to miss around the college, given his wardrobe combinations. In a world of largely black-on-black clothing, Cal provided the splash of color, wearing things like bright vinyl moto jackets in a variety of colors or long, faux fur–trimmed coats. This made it easy for Bryn to spot him in the art history building, standing out this time in bib dungarees over a T-shirt advertising what looked like Heinz beans, the baggy dungaree legs cuffed about four inches above his ankle to show off shiny red Dr. Martens.

Cal with his flash and Noel with her limited and conservatively dark wardrobe made unlikely but inseparable friends. So close that of course Cal would know where she had gone, and why. She had left Bryn no note of explanation on their small dining table, only the ring he'd fashioned for her out of picture wire, a heart twisted into its center.

Cal gave off a cool, relaxed vibe as he strolled down the corridor, smiling to his right and to his left as he passed familiar faces. The smile froze for a brief second when he turned his head once more and made eye contact with Bryn. Bryn noticed the almost imperceptible pause and wondered if Cal was considering turning to escape him. They'd always been rather reserved with one another, but that had to be over now, Bryn thought. He walked swiftly up to Cal and planted himself in his path, giving him no chance to avoid an encounter.

"Where is she?" Bryn had planned to open with a more pleasant greeting, but that plan had gone out the window as soon as he'd seen the desire to flee on Cal's face.

Cal composed himself. "I have no idea who you're talking about."

"I don't have time for you being a prat, Cal. Noel moved out. If she's staying with you . . ."

Cal narrowed his eyes, clearly curious, although he quickly tried to pretend that he wasn't. "No use wondering that," he said. "She's not. I really can't help you." He tried to move around Bryn, but Bryn stepped in his way again.

"You must know where she is. You're her best friend."

Cal laughed. "*Was* her best friend. Noel and I last spoke about three or so months ago. Yes, that's right," he said when Bryn's face registered surprise. "Not that long after you left for Italy. Quite honestly, I'm surprised you're surprised, given that she effectively shut everyone out after she took up with you. Even me, her supposed best friend." He raised an eyebrow. "Did you two have a falling-out over the letters? Or was it about her leaving the course? My money is on the letters."

"Letters? What in the bloody hell are you talking about? I only wrote her one letter, from the hospital where I've been for the past three weeks trying to recover from pneumonia, and I found that sitting on the floor in the pile of post accumulated outside the front door to the flat. She hasn't even seen it, so how would we argue about it? And I haven't the slightest idea what you mean by her leaving the course."

Only after he stopped talking did Bryn realize he'd been shouting by the end of his speech and the stragglers in the hallway had gone quiet, their curiosity piqued. There was little to be gained by shouting at Cal, and judging by the look on his face, Cal was equally confused by the conversation.

"I'm sorry, I'm sorry," Bryn apologized, his voice lowered. "I'm only so bloody frustrated, and it feels as if we're talking at cross purposes. Might we start over, somewhere less . . . public? Do you have time now?"

Cal gave the suggestion a few moments' thought and finally nodded. "Ten minutes. That's all I can spare, and honestly, that's likely all the time it will take. Come." He took Bryn by the arm and led him outside to a quiet corner of the building's courtyard. Once there, he took a breath and said, "I'm not sure that what I can tell you will help, because—despite what you might believe—I really have no idea where Noel is. And I'm still not sure why you don't either. Are you telling me that you only now got back to London and found Noel gone?"

"That is indeed what I'm telling you. And you're telling me you had no idea that she'd left our home?"

Cal shook his head but he looked as if he had more to say.

"What is it?" Bryn asked.

"As I said," Cal said, "Noel and I spoke less and less once she started spending all her time with you, and at the start of the new term, I had very little idea what was going on in her life beyond the broad strokes. For the first couple of weeks, we'd see each other in class and pass the time, but it was always awkward. Then I saw her between classes one day, coming out of the toilets, and she looked awful. She'd been ill, she told me, and if I'm honest, she looked as if she was still ill. Peaky, gaunt. She said she wasn't eating much, but she'd been to the clinic and was on the mend. I took her out for tea. It was the first real conversation we'd had in ages. I was upset that you weren't coming back to take care of her. That's when she told me she'd mailed two letters to you in Italy, telling you she wasn't well, but the letters were returned to her, marked undeliverable. Some system you had for staying in touch, I must say. Even arranging a weekly call at the telephone box would have been more advanced than relying on the Italian post."

Bryn's blood began to boil, and Cal seemed to see it.

"All right, all right," he said. "I'll stop being sarcastic. I thought maybe Noel and I would get close again, but it didn't happen. I think she didn't like that I'd criticized you taking off and leaving her like you did. In her eyes, you could do no wrong."

That explained what he meant by the letters, Bryn thought. "So what's this about her leaving the course?"

"By October, I no longer saw her in class or even in the building. I heard later from one of the tutors that she withdrew shortly after the semester started."

Cal winced when Bryn's eyes narrowed at this news, perhaps expecting more anger. But the only person Bryn was angry with was himself.

"Could she have left the flat as early as that?" he wondered aloud. "Long before she knew I was delayed?"

Cal answered as if the questions were meant for him. "I went to your flat on Boxing Day, hoping she'd see me. I brought cake." He shook his head. "No one answered so I assumed you two were somewhere; Wales maybe, I don't know. But . . ."

"Go on," Bryn prompted, impatient.

"I thought I heard someone moving, but then I thought I was making it up. Could be she was inside the flat but not answering the door, I suppose. I don't like thinking she would have done that to me. And remember, she withdrew from uni in October; why would she hang around? I wish I'd . . . never mind."

He didn't bother to finish, and Bryn didn't push him. He knew what Cal wanted. It was the same as what he wanted. *Now that you know she's nowhere to be found you might have done things differently, Cal? Well, you can queue up right behind me,* he thought. There are a million things he would have done differently too, starting with turning back the clock and changing his decision to go to Italy altogether.

"What a mess," he murmured, and he ran his hand over his face. She wrote to him, he wrote to her, neither one of them got those letters, she left. Two mix-ups and . . . over. Could the course of a life teeter on something so capricious as mail withheld, mail delayed? If so, life was crueler than he'd ever believed.

"Could she have been so angry about the returned letters that she'd leave? Or was she seriously ill? How would we even find out if she went to hospital?" Bryn shook his head. "None of this makes sense. Do you think there's something we're missing?"

"If she continued to feel poorly, I suppose she might have gone to hospital. If she were ill enough, though, she might have gone home."

Home. Bryn had assumed that he was Noel's home, but of course. Her grandmother. "The States, you mean? Whether it's that or hospital, how do you imagine we'll find out? No one at uni will give us that information, if they even have it; we have no standing. Unless you have an address or telephone number for her grandmother?"

Cal smiled wistfully. "Why would I ever have asked for that? Somehow, I thought she was here for good. I thought she loved it here. She was so much a part of . . ." He didn't finish the sentence and his smile faded. Bryn saw his eyes were glassy, wet. "No. Not anymore, she wasn't, largely because I resented you coming between our friendship. I've been thinking the worst of you for ages, Bryn Jones, but it turns out we've both been useless."

It was not enough but would have to be enough, Bryn told himself as he watched Cal walk away until, finally, the bright red shoes were gone.

CHAPTER 29

SHOREDITCH FLAT, FEBRUARY 1993

Lady of Llyn Y Fan Fach was out of Bryn's hands. The painting had been accepted by the jury for the first Rising Artists Award before he left for Italy; it had made it through the early rounds of competition to the shortlist. It was now February, the canvas had been gathered up by the Addison weeks ago, and there it would reside until the night of the awards reception in the spring.

When people, mainly journalists, asked him if he dreamed of winning the inaugural prize, he laughed in their faces like a madman. Maybe he *was* mad. He certainly couldn't tell the questioners what he really did dream. At night, as he lay alone in his too-big bed in his too-big flat, he wished so hard that he had the painting back that his hands itched for it. He fantasized about destroying *Lady* so he would never have to see Noel's face in the lake or remember the inspired weeks when she sat for him and he painted her into his beloved Welsh landscape, when they—two outsiders, two uprooted children—fell in love. Acid, fire, his hands made into fists. All those would get the job done.

Only a few short years ago, an ex-soldier had shot at a Da Vinci cartoon hung in the National Gallery, shattering the glass and tearing into the art. So obviously a gun would do some damage too, but guns were too hard to come by. One night last week, he'd thought about visiting the Addison with a Stanley knife in his pocket and getting down to the work of destruction in front of stunned gallery workers. The painting was his property, after all, and if he wanted to cut it to ribbons, he should be able to cut it to ribbons.

The simplest course of action would be to withdraw from the competition. Once the painting was back in his studio, he could crack it over his knee and be done with it. But the pull of winning was too strong, or his ego was, or the idea that Noel—wherever in the world she was—would read about the competition and come back to him. That pull, in particular, was much, much too strong. He fantasized about it, when he wasn't imagining all the ways he could mutilate *Lady*—that the competition publicity might be a call to her, one she would hear and answer. All he wanted was a chance to explain to her what had happened.

All he wanted. He shook his head. That made his need sound so simple when in fact it was fiery, vehement, as violent as his fantasies for his painting. The truth was, he worried that if Noel returned to hear him out he might grab her by the shoulders and shake her. Shake her, or pull her close and crush her in his arms. The impulse was so wrong, like some wiring inside himself had shorted then rerouted as a fix, creating a person he'd never been before. He'd never hurt anyone in his life, but now he had a list of people he would take his frustration out on, given the chance. Cal, for hating him and losing track of Noel because of it. The pompous Italian doctor who'd taken ages to get his treatment right. The nurse who'd made him believe she would treat his letter to Noel with urgency. Noel, for giving up on him so quickly. Himself, his self-centered behavior.

Had the urge to do damage been dormant in him since his parents left him with his grandfather? Granddad had distracted him with busy tasks as a boy, and had loved him well once he'd brought him into the safety of the little cottage by the sea. But Bryn's father had been a petty criminal who'd ultimately met his end in a street fight, his mother an alcoholic who'd dissociated after his father's death. Maybe the gentle Bryn, the one who'd ached to throw the caught fish back, the one who'd met orphaned Noel with tenderness, was the fake.

This new awareness would inform Bryn's way forward. He would hurt no one at all, ever, if he made himself into a person who no longer needed or wanted anyone close. A person cannot hate that which he does not desire. Work would have to be enough. The land would have to be enough. A life contained in the cottage by the sea would have to be all he needed.

CHAPTER 30

SWN Y MOR, DECEMBER 2022

Noel was back. Bryn could hardly take it in. For a long time she hadn't been real to him, he hadn't even allowed her to be a memory.

He had looked for her several years back, long after the internet had arrived and made it easier to find people, and he'd found her professional listing. She was, he noted, back on her home grounds outside Boston, working in the museum world, as she'd always planned. He'd looked again more recently, advanced searches, and turned up a wedding announcement. Working and married, too, as she'd always wanted, with a child. It had taken her a while to get there, but she'd done it. Husband Andrew. Stepdaughter Alice. He'd read the wedding announcement carefully. The internet service he'd had at the time was unreliable but he'd stuck with the search until he'd exhausted every trace of her.

After, he'd felt it was underhanded, what he'd done, intruding on her privacy like he was a stalker, and he'd known he wouldn't look ever again. She had started over; it didn't matter why. He would have to continue living his life as well. There were all the pressures on him to produce, and once he began working, all concerns of the world outside his studio melted away. No more remembering, no more London visits that prompted memories.

The discipline of his life—wake up, paint, walk, lunch, wash up, then paint again until it was time to sleep—filled every minute for days, weeks, years.

When younger, he hadn't been reclusive, hadn't been dour as he was today, but the years and the disappointments that came with them had shaped him. Being hurt could stunt a person. Most days he accepted this, that living came with hurt and that hurt led to unexpected changes. Like a tree that loses a limb only to form a scar in its place instead of something new that reaches for the sky. There were days like today, though, days when the gray outside the window cultivated a bleakness in his soul, when the suggestion of a warm body for company fell short, when the past would invade his mind and torment him, replacing his bewildered anger at Noel for leaving with rebukes for himself for getting sick and then stuck in an Italian hospital, unable to get word to her. When he wondered what might be different now if he had agreed to write to Noel from each painting outpost along the trail of his *al fresco* trip instead of telling her he wasn't sure he could afford to lose the time it would take to find the post office or to wait for her replies. *"We'll see each other soon enough."*

How difficult would it have been, really, to add a sheaf of the serviceable blue air mail tri-folds that came so cheaply at the post office to his pack, pen a few words, find a post box? That way, when he had been unable to communicate for those last three weeks, she might have worried enough about the silence to track him down—or at least confident enough to continue to wait. Maybe she wouldn't have assumed he'd left her; maybe she wouldn't have left.

He felt a tear escape his eye. He used the back of his wrist to wipe his face. Even if all that were true, what was the point of wallowing in it? She might be back, but she wasn't back for him. He would call Delaney tomorrow, he thought, and bow out of the additional commitment in London. Stick to the schedule of one overnight in April to celebrate the launch of his career retrospective. Bell—or whoever ended up winning—would neither need him there nor miss his absence, and he didn't need to torment himself with ghosts from his past.

He set down the mug he was holding and pushed it aside. He held his two hands out in front of him, looked at the knobby, gnarled, liver-spotted whole of them, front and back. He looked up from his hands to the easel holding his newest work. He should get back to the canvas while he could. Everything else was an unnecessary entanglement. It helped to remember that.

He pushed back the rickety chair and rose. Yes, back to it.

CHAPTER 31

MARYLEBONE, DECEMBER 2022

The gap between cobblestones was wide enough to fit a shoe heel but not wide enough to release it easily, something Noel realized after she'd yanked her shoe free and found an exposed nail where the plastic heel guard should have been. She was on her lunch break, taking what she'd intended to be a long walk to blow off steam after an unsatisfying call with her attorney. Andy wasn't budging about visitation and he wanted her to stop contacting Alice; her "pretending to care," he said, was confusing her. Besides, if she really cared about her daughter, she wouldn't be in London.

The "pretending to care" business infuriated her; as if she'd write to her daughter out of anything but love. Despite Andy's guilt-tripping, she had stood her ground, instructed the lawyer to find a mediator who might take the temperature down a bit, and then hung up the phone. As she did, she'd realized she didn't even know if Alice had received her Christmas gift.

At least she had a plan forward, she'd thought, but by then her body had been so flooded with adrenaline from arguing that she could no longer concentrate on her work. It was lunchtime and a swim was out of the question, so she had settled for a long walk—but now that plan was scotched. The best she could hope for was a walk to a nearby same-day cobbler, if there was such a thing, and a good long fuming while she waited for the repair.

She pulled her phone from her handbag and searched the vicinity for a cobbler on the map app. Nothing. There was, however, a TK Maxx north of her, near Regent's Park, where she might pick up a pair of inexpensive shoes. She couldn't walk on the nail for the rest of the day. Not only was it loud, it was also slippery, and the only thing that could make the day worse would be taking a header on the tile floor in her office.

With the way her luck was going, she wasn't hopeful about finding a cheap pump or loafer in her size. A pair of sneakers, then—clunky but sufficient. Who did she need to impress, anyway? She started walking in the direction of the park.

Step-tap, step-tap. The nail rang out on the paving stones but she didn't slow down. Moving so determinedly felt good; perhaps she could restore the mood she'd been in before making that ill-advised call.

In the days since the dinner at Cal's, she'd been on a cloud, buoyed by hope. They had sobered up enough that evening to find the pages pertaining to adoption records on the government's website, and Noel had been able to apply online right then to add her contact details to the Adoption Contact Register. She'd also made an extra application to an intermediary agency that would help her in the search, if it came to that. So far, Sam hadn't done the same, and she wouldn't be able to find out his details until he indicated he was agreeable to being found. But it was a start, and she'd felt optimistic. *Channel that,* she told herself as she marched along, *not the frustration.*

Somewhere behind her a dog barked, but Noel didn't think anything of it. Dogs were always headed to the park with their owners. But the dog barked again, short and insistent, and this time the barking was followed by someone calling her name. Noel turned quickly and her right leg almost slipped out from beneath her. She caught herself just as the dog reached her side and licked her hand. The dog's owner jogged behind, smiling, his hand raised as he tried to catch up.

"Gertie," Noel said. "And Henry. What are you two doing here?"

"Noel, hello!" Henry held up the large shopping bag swinging at his side. "On the way to the park, with an impromptu bit of Christmas shopping for Dad. Where are you off to?"

She rolled her eyes. "Nothing nearly as fun. My shoe heel was eaten by the cobblestones. I'm off to the discount store for a new pair."

"We'll walk with you, then."

"I'm sure you have better things to do than walk me to the shop."

"We'd planned to have our long walk before heading back to the studio, so really, we're free for the next hour or so." He whistled to Gertie and she fell in step.

Noel smiled at the eccentric sight the two made, even for London—this dark-haired, slightly round-shouldered young man with such a large dog following freely at his side. Her shoe heel was still an annoyance, but she felt her mood improve in spite of it. Running into this pair was the best kind of coincidence. Something about them put Noel at ease. His earnestness, maybe, or his even temper, and Gertie's sunny disposition.

In their presence, the problem Andy presented seemed further away with every step she took.

"This is me," Noel said when they arrived in front of the store. "Thank you for walking with me." She scratched the dog's ears. "You turned my day around, Gertie, good girl."

"Join us for our walk," Henry suggested. When Noel hesitated, he said, "A loop around the canals, fresh air, no rain. You can tell me how your work is going."

"I don't know how long I'll be . . ." she began to protest.

Henry shook his head as if it didn't matter.

She supposed the work back at her desk could be put off another hour. "If you're sure you don't mind waiting."

"We don't. Off with you. We'll wait."

Henry and Gertie, now on her leash, were waiting across the street in front of the food hall when Noel left the discount store wearing her new shoes. She looked at her feet—trainers had turned out to be the best option available, just as she'd thought, but they were also perfect for walking through Regent's Park, a space she had once been very familiar with. Why not enjoy herself, the company? Her old shoes were in the shopping bag and she could take her time with the repair.

She waved and crossed the street when the walking man popped up on the lights. When she made it to the other side, she held up her foot and turned it this way and that. "Not too ugly, Gertie, are they?"

The dog licked her hand again in response.

The day had played out in unexpected ways, but now that they were meandering toward the park and Noel was no longer intent on her errand, her mind wandered back to the phone call with her lawyer. She resented that Andy held all the power and tried to manipulate her decisions with it. She groaned aloud.

Gertie cocked her head and looked at Noel. Henry did too.

"It's fine, lovely," Noel said, her cheeks coloring. "I'm fine."

"Gertie's not convinced." They had arrived at the Gloucester Gate entrance; Henry paused before continuing on. "Problems at work? New shoes uncomfortable?" He smiled, but Noel could tell he expected an answer.

"Shoes, A-plus. Work is great—busy, which is how I like it. Things back home are . . . not great. I'm in the middle of a divorce that I'd rather not talk about." She tipped her head in the direction of the canal towpath and the zoo. “It’ll feel good to move.”

Once they were well into the park, she asked, “Do you have plans for Christmas?”

“I’ll go up to Leeds, muddle about the kitchen with Dad, probably make something halfway edible.” Henry lifted a shoulder. “It’s quiet these days. Well, it always was, if I’m honest. Me, Mum, Dad—that’s it. We weren’t big on large family gatherings. I won’t stay long because I have work to get back to.”

“New paintings?” she asked.

He nodded. “I started a new series of sketches recently and I’m trying to figure out how best to get the ideas I’ve sketched onto the canvas. I haven’t found the best way forward yet, but I will. Maybe you’d like to come to the studio someday and see the work in progress? I’d value your input.”

“Oh—w-well,” she stammered, taken by surprise by the invitation.

He looked at her curiously. “Too big a favor?” he asked. “I know how busy you are and I wouldn’t want to impose on your time.”

She didn’t answer right away and they walked on. She looked off to her left at the canals and the row of moored narrow boats, all painted in glossy jewel colors, some strung with garlands of lights. She remembered how pretty the canals looked at night, all lit up, the worn parts of the houseboats hidden in the dark. Thirty years ago she had imagined this would be her life—living in this city, taking walks just like this, associating with people in the art world here, being asked for her analysis or opinion, perhaps writing articles in between curating shows. That life hadn’t panned out that way, and yet it was doing so now, left her feeling strange, as if maybe an alternate Noel had been doing this all along while she had split off for the States, and only recently had they met in some sort of time meld where each could see the path the other had taken.

She shook her head. "It's not an imposition at all, Henry. I'd be happy to have a look, once Christmas is behind us. This all feels a bit surreal to me, that's all." She gestured around her with her hand. "That I'm here, doing what I always intended to do but didn't. I'm probably making no sense at all."

"No, you make perfect sense," he replied. "We tend to think of life as a straight line until we're reminded it's lines that sometimes fold back on themselves or go in circles and figure eights." He looked at her. "Tell me. How did you find your way to London in the first place? You were young to leave home—eighteen?"

She nodded.

"That was brave," he said.

She laughed. "I didn't think of it as brave. Gran was nudging me out of the nest. She was tired by then, ready to retire, and she knew I had goals. London was, in a way, the logical choice." When Henry looked at her quizzically, she counted off the reasons on her fingers: "I didn't need a visa. We had family here, if I ever needed assistance. And then there was the art."

"Did your grandmother encourage you to study the history of art?"

She shook her head. "Gran encouraged swimming lessons and getting an education, didn't matter in what as long as I could support myself. Save myself, support myself—those two things were important to her. I found my way to art history on my own. She would have been worried if I had told her I wanted to paint; she thought artists were ne'er-do-wells. Sorry. But becoming an art historian was an acceptable career goal."

"Did you want to paint, though?" he asked. "Are you a frustrated painter?"

"Not at all, to both of those questions." She paused, deciding whether or not she would say more. Henry was looking at her, though, waiting for an answer. "I simply fell in love with looking at paintings and sculpture, starting with the day we took a school trip to the Museum of Fine Arts in Boston. I was fourteen. Our class had its own docent from the museum who took us around to see all the major works and helped explain them to us—the artistic elements, sure, but also the historical context of the paintings and how the artist brought everything together on the canvas. I couldn't believe that a person could make a living studying art, surrounded by art. I remember the massive Turner she took us to—*The Slave Ship*." She shook her head. "The other kids in the class were fidgeting by then, but I couldn't take my eyes off of that painting as the docent pointed out the details, the color, the light, the movement. That was the moment when I knew what I wanted to do with the rest of my life. Where that came from? Who knows. Maybe my mother was the frustrated artist. Or my father. I never knew who he was, so it's possible."

She laughed self-consciously. "Anyway, probably more information than you wanted or needed."

Henry shook his head. "Don't say that. I asked, and I'm glad you told me." He gazed out across the park. "It's an interesting question—where the desire, or in my case the need, to pursue art comes from. My parents weren't artists and they didn't always understand why I was driven to make art, although they were marvelously supportive. Maybe it's inherited, maybe it isn't. Maybe it's one big mystery never to be solved. Like you, I don't know my real father either. One more thing we have in common."

He kept walking as if what he'd dropped was some minor detail. But Noel stopped in her tracks.

"So your father in Leeds . . ." she called after him.

He looked over his shoulder. "Douglas," he said, "isn't my biological father. He adopted me."

He kept walking until he reached a nearby bench. As he stopped and turned to face her, Noel roused herself from the initial surprise of his revelation and caught up. Ahead of them, in the middle distance, several dogs greeted each other and began playing. Gertie began to whimper.

"Do you mind if I let her off the lead to see her friends? We can sit if you'd like."

Noel nodded and Henry unclipped Gertie to let her free. She took off, gathering speed to meet up with a beautiful black and tan hound, and after a few sniffs they set off on a game of chase, running circles around one of the large, old plane trees.

Oh, to be as carefree as these playful dogs, Noel thought to herself as she took a seat next to Henry to watch the cavorting. Instead, she turned over and over what she'd just been told. Neither of them knew their fathers; neither of them had any real idea what—or who—had made them into the people they were today, sitting here on this bench. Without thinking, she asked, "Your mother never told you about him? Your biological father?"

Henry turned to her, a sad smile on his face. "Did yours? Did your grandmother? No?" he concluded before she even shook her head. "There's no name where a father's should be on my original birth certificate. I suppose they thought it wasn't necessary to give me answers. Two people loved me. I knew what I needed to know, as far as they were concerned. And Douglas is a great dad. He could help me with my maths, which, at times, was more useful to me than having someone who might help me with my drawing or give me a leg up."

Noel looked away so he wouldn't see her face and the blush she could feel creeping up her neck. "Sorry. That was intrusive."

"It's really not. It's fine that you asked. I put it all out on my canvases anyway, so none of this is exactly a secret. And may I tell you one more thing? Because I think maybe you'll understand?"

"Of course."

"Most of the time, I think I've made peace with not knowing where I come from and how I came to be who I am, although of course that not-knowing is rife with all sorts of horrible possibilities. You know: What if the man who fathered me was a murderer? What if he did something awful to my mother? What does that make me?" Eyes on Gertie, he continued, "But what if, just what if, he was decent and my mother simply didn't want me to know him or want him to know me—whatever her reasons? Wouldn't that decent man now, wherever he is, whoever he is, want to know who I am? Wouldn't he want to know I exist?"

Each of Henry's questions stung Noel. He was talking about his situation, but every word he spoke could have been about hers, and Sam's, and Bryn's. Because she'd thought she was entitled to move forward from her past, Sam was somewhere in this world holding the same questions about his identity. And Bryn, a decent man, was oblivious to the fact he had a son. She'd done that, her choices had done all that, and it had all been for naught anyway. No matter where she went, no matter how hard she tried to escape it, her past came bubbling up. It was as forceful as a stream of water running underground, persistently looking for its outlet.

Noel turned to look at Henry but he didn't see her. He had lifted his fingers to his mouth and now whistled for Gertie's return.

Gertie paused, as if making up her mind whether she would obey or ignore. Noel raised her hand and waved, and in a split second she decided and came running. But instead of going to Henry she stopped at Noel's feet, eager for a good ear ruffling. Noel obliged.

"She really likes you," Henry said, sounding almost surprised. Pleased, but surprised.

Noel leaned over and buried her face in the dog's neck. She hoped it would hide that her eyes had welled up with tears.

After a moment, she pulled herself together. "Well, I like her too. And you." She rose from her seat. "I really should head back to work. But thank you, both of you, for the walk and the talk. And Henry? He would want to know you exist, trust me. He would want to know you. And I hope someday you'll find him."

CHAPTER 32

THE CITY, DECEMBER 2022

But Noel didn't return to the museum. Instead, she rang Jean's office and left a message that she would be out for the afternoon—something personal had come up, she said, leaving Jean to imagine a doctor or dentist appointment or banking glitch or family crisis. Instead, she started walking, in her comfortable new shoes, south and east from the park to Bloomsbury and straight into her past.

The trip was long overdue. She should have known this well before Henry told her his background and asked all his existential questions, but all she'd been thinking about up to that point was how best to protect herself. She now had to think about how best to strip those protections away.

She walked south until she reached the first street name she remembered—Clipstone—and turned left onto it. Looming ahead of her was the telecom tower, framed between several-story buildings—office or apartment—she had never seen before. The tower was blue against a sky that was even bluer, save for an airplane's jet stream streak of white. She recognized very little else around her. She couldn't even recall ever having been so close to the tower, or where it was planted on the ground.

She took another left. The gardens at Fitzroy Square remained, but the heavy traffic was jarring. Tottenham Court Road was also busier, and the shops had all changed. Once upon a time, during her first few weeks in the neighborhood, that street had been the touchstone, the landmark that, coming down Goodge Street, had helped her find Foyles farther on in Charing Cross. She had met Cal for the first time in Foyles, right before classes began, when they both had reached for the same books. She smiled at the memory, but she would leave Foyles book shop for another day; today, her plans didn't include detouring in that direction.

Instead, she continued eastbound, only stopping when she got to Gower Street and the long row of university buildings ahead of her. The Slade School. The Octagon. The art museum. Noel stood across the street, buffered by the wrought iron fencing surrounding the ramp up to the library, and looked. So much of her young-adult life had been formed here, set into motion here.

As she took in all the activity surrounding her, time fell away and she was thirty years younger. The students milling about just inside the gatehouses might have been her classmates. Bryn might have been in a studio arts class or waiting for her to come out of her class, tapping his foot or sitting on a step and sketching. If she closed her eyes, she could imagine Cal was on his way to pick her up for a coffee. Or perhaps he was meeting her here so they could cut through the Octagon to go to class or head back to the halls of residence or, later, one or the other's bedsit in the grotty area just north of here in between the rail stations.

After a few minutes, she pushed off the railing she'd been resting against and walked around the row of buildings to reach Tavistock Square. The familiar seated Gandhi sculpture remained at the center of the gardens, while a new (at least since she'd last sat here) bust of Virginia Woolf had been erected in a corner not far from the home Woolf had shared with her husband, Leonard.

She sat at a bench where she could look at this version of Virginia, her doleful Modigliani face. It wasn't hard to imagine the demons that must have been with the writer every single day of her life.

Not far beyond the sculpture was the Tavistock Hotel, where she and Bryn had once cadged breakfast, pretending to be hotel guests partaking of the steam table buffets of overpoached eggs and cold toast. When the dining room manager—an older gentleman they'd nicknamed Lord Tavistock—had taken notice of them and approached, suspicion clouding his up-until-then hospitable eyes, they'd taken off with a few bacon baps stuffed in their pockets.

Noel smiled and shook her head. It was nothing she'd done before or since. What had made them grab hands and brazen their way into breakfast service after almost two years of passing the hotel without giving it a second thought? Hunger? Lack of funds? The audacity of it? The motivation was lost to time, but not the act itself. As hard as she'd worked at repressing all this, the memory returned to her as vividly as if it had happened yesterday.

And yet, it hadn't. It had been years since that escapade—years in which her life had taken many unexpected turns. And what about Bryn? Had his life changed as significantly? As for Lord Tavistock—he would be lost to time, wouldn't he? He'd seemed to them ancient thirty years ago, but maybe he'd been sixty or seventy. If he hadn't passed on by now, he was surely closing in on one hundred and most certainly long retired.

Noel closed her eyes and tipped her head back to feel what warmth she could from the sun on her face because the reality was cold, sobering. An old man, dead. A former lover as old as she was now—older, she reminded herself, by two years—and no longer the twenty-two-year-old she'd waved goodbye to as he got on the coach heading for the ferry to mainland Europe. Likewise her baby, once small enough to hold, even as briefly as she did, had since been transformed by time. That son was a man, not the infant she'd frozen him as, perhaps a man with a family of his own. Maybe she was a mother-in-law and a grandmother and Bryn a grandfather. And instead of imagining everyone at all these stages, enriched and complicated by life, she had stunted them all, every last one. Her refusal to wonder about them had fixed them like fossils in amber.

She had trapped her essential self, too, in that one period of time. The life she'd gone on to live, full of its striving and unrequited longings, held nothing of the girl she once was, the one who'd felt easy and happy. To find remnants of that girl, there was one place she could go—and it was only about a half-hour away on foot.

She rose from this latest bench and loosened her limbs. One more stop, then, before heading home.

In 1840, J.M.W. Turner had first exhibited *The Slave Ship* within these walls, albeit under a different title: *Slavers Throwing Overboard the Dead and Dying – Typhoon Coming On*. As a title, the lengthy original was more descriptive of the moment in history, sixty-odd years earlier, that Turner had aimed to capture. A ship carrying human cargo mistakenly sailing off course with limited supplies of food and water for survival. The despicably calculated decision to offload the cargo—living, breathing people—into the turbulent seas to save these supplies for captain and crew and also to collect insurance money.

When Noel saw Turner's work for the first time at the MFA, she'd been so moved by how the composition of light, color, and loose but intentional brushwork came together to depict the horror transpiring in the churning sea that she'd stood for ages after the group she was with had left the gallery with the docent. Eventually, someone had been dispatched to find her after a head count, and she'd never lived it down; on every field trip after, a few of her classmates would rib her about trying not to get lost again.

But she simply hadn't cared what they said or how they perceived her. She'd found her purpose.

The first time she visited this museum, she had been with Bryn. He had applied to study here, he'd told her on that visit, but had not been accepted—a source of frustration for him two years on, even though The Slade was every bit its equal and perhaps a better fit. It was the first time Noel had understood how alike she and he were, navigating the complicated world of higher education and aspiration and belonging without the guidance of someone connected and knowledgeable, without an advocate. *So what,* she'd thought. *We have each other*. "Someday you'll exhibit here," she'd said to him in the foyer during that first visit. "Someday they'll fall over themselves to buy your work."

And they had. The museum had acquired *Lady of Llyn Y Fan Fach* not long after it was released to accolades and won its prize. And although she'd never seen it in its new home, Noel knew where the piece hung.

Self-preservation had long made her keep tabs on Bryn's work, specifically any upcoming shows and any time a piece—or he—might be traveling somewhere she would be. For several years, poring over art magazines to gather information was cumbersome work. The advent of the internet, however, had made it easy enough to browse online professional journals and her own museum's intranet for worldwide exhibition information, and even easier to launch a Google alert for mentions of his name and *Lady*. There was never any need for in-depth image or website searches, and she'd never attempted either. She wasn't interested in following Bryn; she was instead vigilant about avoiding him.

Nine times out of ten, these alerts for the painting title had only yielded some article about or new translation of the Welsh folktale. But the tenth time had given her information about the tenth anniversary of the Academy's purchase of *Lady,* and a more recent search had informed her that the piece wasn't currently on loan, it was here.

She headed for the stairs and the first floor.

Lady of Llyn Y Fan Fach by Bryn Jones drew Noel to it as surely as if it were a magnet and she a mere pin.

There was a bench in front of it, and someone had parked herself there. An art student, by the looks of it. She had a sketchbook on her lap and a pencil in her left hand. The young woman had narrowed in on the boat stranded on the pebbled shore of the lake, copying Bryn's shape and perspective but adding details of wood grain to the bent planks making the boat's hull.

Noel stood behind and watched her look and sketch, look and sketch, then erase, only to start over. Sensing she was being observed, the artist paused and shot a dirty look over her shoulder.

"I wanted to sit but didn't want to disturb your drawing," Noel explained.

"Less disruptive if you'd do that rather than hang over my shoulder." She slid down to one end, making room.

"Sorry." Noel came around to the front of the bench and sat. "You have talent. Are you a student?"

"What, here? No." The young woman drew out the last word as if Noel's question was the most absurd one she'd fielded in her life. "I like this painting. I come when I can and draw a different section. Landscapes are all right. I'm crap at humans, though, human form. So I haven't tried her." She gestured to the wall with her chin—intending to point out Nelferch, Noel assumed.

"Nelferch," she said for the young woman's benefit, getting as close to the Welsh pronunciation as she could.

"If you say so." She turned her attention back to her sketchbook.

"Why sketch from this one, if you don't mind me asking?" Noel asked. "What is it you like about it? My name's Noel, by the way."

"Noel. I'm Lizzie." She blew air through her lips. "I don't know, really. I like looking at it, for starters. I don't get tired of it. It's both the real world and unreal at the same time, and I'm not sure how the artist did that. I like the way it makes me think—I mean, I think it's so beautiful and yet it leaves me feeling sad, as if something has just happened that they can't take back and they both realize that at the same time." She shrugged. "I'm not very good at this."

"You're doing fine," Noel said.

Lizzie looked at her. "You didn't paint it, did you?"

"No. Not me. I don't paint."

"What are you then, some kind of instructor here?"

Noel smiled. "No, not any kind of instructor. I work at the—"

"Noel? Noel Enfield!" A familiar-looking woman walked purposefully over to the bench Noel shared with Lizzie.

"Yes, I—"

"Sophie. Adler. We were at uni together years ago, but I'm also on the board at the Addison. We approved Jean Rayburn's secondment plans. I'm sorry I couldn't make it to your welcome breakfast, but let me tell you, I was thrilled that it was you coming over to take charge of the exhibition guide."

"Sophie, of course." Noel stood and offered her hand. "It's so nice to run into you. Do you work here now?"

"No, no. I worked in an art gallery for a time, but I haven't done much more than volunteer work since I had my children—boards and such. Keeping my hand in. I'm here because I'm taking a class. Watercolor. Not very good at it, I'm afraid, but I have always wanted to try and there's no time like the present. I can guess why you're here." Sophie nodded toward the canvas.

Noel noticed that Lizzie had rested her pencil on top of her sketchbook, more interested in listening in on the conversation. She kept her answer vague. "I had some free time, so . . ."

Sophie turned her attention to the painting. "It's still such a beautiful work. You know, there were quite a few of us who were a tiny bit jealous of you at the time, going out with Bryn Jones. More so after we learned he had painted you. But then—"

"We all went our separate ways," Noel finished for her, hoping to head the conversation in a different direction.

"I suppose we did. But we can all catch up this spring, at the awards ceremony. You, me, Calum Paterson, Bryn. We'll probably see scads of people show up. The prize committee has managed to talk Bryn into presenting this year's winner with the award. Quite a coup, really—he doesn't leave Wales often."

Noel froze at this news, stunned at the casual way information so important had landed in her lap, and she stared at Sophie.

Sophie, seemingly misinterpreting her surprise for discomfort at being put on the spot, asked, "You are staying through the big event, aren't you?"

Noel had planned on it, and she mumbled, "Of course." Inside, however, she understood that Bryn's appearance at the event would change everything. No—had already changed everything. She wished Sophie would go, would leave her to her thoughts and working out what steps she would take next. "Are you leaving class?" she asked. "Or on your way to it?"

Sophie took her phone from her handbag and looked at the time. "Oh! On my way. And if I don't hurry, I'll be late." She started walking but turned to Noel and added, waggling her phone, "Look, I'll ring you at the Addison and we'll talk more over lunch. Lovely to see you!" She waved, and then she was gone around the corner.

Noel dropped back onto the bench seat. She'd forgotten she wasn't alone until a voice next to her said, "So that's you in the painting, is it?"

Lizzie. Noel looked at her.

"I'm sorry, but it's not like I could turn off my ears while that lady was going on and on. It's really you?"

They both looked at the painting then. Noel nodded. "Yes, it's me. I was eighteen when I began sitting."

"Was the artist some old lech? Is that why her talking about him upset you so?"

Some old lech. Noel laughed in spite of her mood. "Bryn was a student when he started this. Twenty. A friend. Not old, and definitely not a lech."

"Then why—"

Noel held up her hand, cutting the young woman short. "You have too many questions, and I need a little quiet to think. Please," she added, softening her tone.

Lizzie nodded, picked up her pencil, turned to a fresh page, and got back to her sketching.

Noel put a hand over her face. The signs were all there, had been there all day and ever since she'd arrived and probably even before that, pointing out what she must now do. What would Bryn think—of the news and of her—when he found out he had a son? *When,* not if. She had to tell him. Henry and his wondering about his father had started her thinking of it. And now this news from Sophie had made it essential. She couldn't keep running.

She would leave work a day early for the holiday weekend and take the train up to Wales, to Swn Y Mor cottage. Everything had to come out in the open; all those kept from the truth had to be allowed to know the truth. Especially now that she'd set in motion the possibility of a reunion with her son. Their son.

She sighed.

Next to her, Lizzie gave up the pretense of being disinterested and closed her sketchbook. "It'll be okay," she said.

"Will it?" Noel asked, curious more than skeptical. Lizzie sounded so certain.

Lizzie shrugged. "Honestly, I don't know. That's what my nan used to tell me when I worried about something. 'Do your best and everything will come out all right in the end.' I remember it felt good hearing her say it, although come to think of it, things didn't always turn out the way I wanted. Still, can't be wrong to do your best anyway, can it?"

Noel smiled and laid her hand on Lizzie's arm. "It's good advice, no matter what happens in the end." She rose from her seat. "I have to go home and make a few arrangements. I'm glad I ran into you, Lizzie, and thanks for the advice. Here's some of mine for you: Keep drawing. You're talented."

With that, Noel departed the gallery and headed for home.

Gertie the dog came to me with her name. I didn't particularly like the name, but I didn't have the heart to change what she answered to. It was the way she answered when I first called to her—slowly, turning her shaggy, blocky head at the low cadence of those two syllables, staring lovingly at me with her golden-brown eyes. All I knew of her first home was that they'd made her spend much of her life alone and out of doors. By all rights, this dog should be wary of humans, but she is trusting and gentle with most. She claimed me as her person the instant we met. Still, I know she remembers life before she came home with me. Every once in a while, she meets a human she will back away from, instinctively placing herself behind my much larger body for protection. When she does this, I know to keep my distance from that person as well.

Gertie seems to trust that you are kind, and I will too.

Because of this, I have given you many pieces of information about my life—the names of my parents, where I am from, my age, and most recently the fact that Douglas is not my biological father—but you have not yet connected these facts to you, to you giving up your child. Do you have even less information about the adoption than I do? Did someone else make the arrangements—or the decision—for you? Why, when I get near to having answers, do I end up with more questions instead?

I came close today to telling you I was adopted by Ruth as well as Douglas in Yorkshire thirty years ago this January, thinking a full disclosure of the adoption and the timeline might stitch everything together for you. But I stopped short of that. You've shared a lot with me but never that you gave up your child. Pressuring you into that admission on the spot seemed unkind, and I couldn't risk losing you before I even had the chance to know more.

Instead, I told you that Douglas and I don't share blood, that I don't know who my biological father is. As you do not know yours. Will knowing we have a bond in fatherlessness shake something loose in you? Will my questions about my father's character, and what he might or might not know about me, and my need to know where I'm from and why cause you to think about the man who is a mystery to me? Will that prompt you to contact him, if that's even possible? Will any of this set in motion actions that might lead us three to each other? I feel it might. I feel we're very close.

I am fundamentally an honest person, but getting to know you before you know who I am to you is not honest. You will forgive me someday, I hope, for using Gertie as reconnaissance for our first meeting, but I had to know if you were someone I would be safe with. We're both wary, you and I (separated from our mothers, not knowing our fathers, what else would we be?) and our caution is simply another one of those commonalities. This is why I can believe you will understand why I came into your life this way, even if it takes time. I hope you do. I hope I'm not getting this wrong.

I am—
Your son

PART V

DISTURBING THE DUST ON A BOWL OF ROSE LEAVES

CHAPTER 33

SWANSEA, DECEMBER 2022

The train out of Tenby picked up speed as it left the town environs and headed toward Swansea. Bryn's car rocked gently back and forth as its wheels clacked along the length of track. He'd slept poorly the night before and had hoped to catch a nap on the ninety-or-so-minute trip, but the rhythms and white noise weren't lulling him. Instead, he remained agitated.

Delaney had called last evening with a last-minute request that he carry two early sketches he'd made before painting *Lady of Llyn Y Fan Fach* to the Swansea gallery that would be hanging a month-long preview of his retrospective before its final destination in London. The original painting was staying put at the Academy and would be hung in the April show, but she felt it was important for St. David's to have something representative of the work that had launched his career. "Bring the studies over, tomorrow if you can," she'd said. "Tell me what train you'll be on and Bethan will be ready for you."

Bryn had bitten his tongue and agreed. If he made it quick he could be back home early afternoon, so he'd looked at the timetables and picked a mid-morning train. But once he'd hung up with Delaney, he'd regretted agreeing to it. The prospect of a search through his grandfather's damp, cobwebby shed for the old crates had plunged him into anxiety.

As such, it had taken him a while to get to the job, but he'd finally laid his hands on the works, and now they rested between his knees and the back of the seat in front of him. Bethan and her staff could pry open the crates and worry about the state of the charcoal and pencil sketches. He hadn't looked at these pieces—one, an early rendering of the lake and Gwyn's boat; the other, a closeup study of Noel as Nelferch—in the twenty-five years since he'd angrily banged them into wooden frames and shoved them away, that time when anger had sunk its claws into him and taken forever to let go. All behind him now, or so he'd thought.

Being resigned to this task didn't mean he was sanguine about it. He gazed out the window, and instead of the landscape passing by, he saw himself walking into the empty East End flat; instead of wheels on tracks, he heard the echo of his voice as he called Noel's name to no avail. He watched on as the hands of his younger self balled into fists at the first sighting of Calum trying to avoid him in the halls of the university. Parading through, too, were his murderous feelings toward the finished *Lady* itself. And there he was on stage on the night of the award, making that terse, sullen speech. Then all the days that followed—days of alternately loathing himself, then Noel, then himself again. Drinking. Then not drinking and not eating. Not working. Then finally working again, but badly.

Eventually, his mood had evened out, but every choice, every new phase had added up to wasting time. He looked at his hands, resting on his thighs. He'd wasted a good bit of prime working time not working well at all, time he couldn't get back.

Ninety minutes of this ruminating and then the train pulled into Swansea Station. Bryn sighed, exhausted, and maneuvered the crates into the aisle. He stood and got a grip on the rope handle he'd fashioned—badly, he acknowledged with a shake of his head. Time was he could tie nautical knots almost as well as his granddad, but no longer. If he was lucky, the rope tie would survive the short walk from the station to the gallery.

Hoping for the best, he exited the train.

As promised, Bethan was awaiting him, smiling and holding the gallery door open as he approached. Bryn grumbled his greeting as he got the crates over the threshold, and then instantly regretted his bad manners. Gallery staff treated him so well, were always glad at his presence. He heard Delaney's voice in his head—"Would it kill you to be pleasant?"—and took a deep breath.

Once inside, he apologized. "The walk with these put me in a mood, I'm afraid."

"I can imagine," Bethan said. "But you're here now, the work is here safe and sound, and we're so pleased. I've made tea." Bethan waved over a staffer and gestured for him to take the crates.

"I shouldn't . . ." But then he thought better of begging off. The weather outside was raw, and the young woman had gone through all the trouble of preparing a hot drink for him. He nodded and thanked her. "I want to get the next train back, but a quick cup of tea would be most welcome." Somewhere up in Caernarfon, Delaney was smiling.

"We'll make sure you make your train," she promised. "Come."

He followed, and soon he was ushered into the administrative offices and a comfortable chair. For a few minutes they sipped tea as Bethan chatted to him about press releases and the show and the bubbling and building of interest in it. Bryn nodded, distracted from his earlier worries by the musical lilt of enthusiasm in Bethan's voice.

As he was listening, the staff member who had taken the crates from him earlier entered the room. He knocked on the doorframe and Bethan broke off mid-sentence to acknowledge him—"Yes?"

"We've uncrated. There was some mold on the wood braces but the sketches are surprisingly undamaged." His brown eyes glowed with excitement, and a smile broke across his dark face. "Would you like to look?"

"That's my cue to leave," Bryn said, hoping to make a smooth exit before being confronted with his work. He set his unfinished mug of tea on the desk between them.

"Stay, please," Bethan said. "Finish your tea. Yes, please, Huw, bring the sketches in." She stood and collected an easel resting in a corner of the office. She set it up at her desk and turned back to Bryn. "You might want to check them over too, make sure all is as you wish before we hang them."

Bryn felt his heart begin to race but Huw was back with the first before he had a chance to protest.

"*Llyn Y Fan Fach*," Bethan said as she settled it on the stand.

Bryn blew out a breath. The lake, the boat. He still had time to excuse himself before Huw brought in the sketch of Noel.

He looked up at the wall clock and stood. "My train," he said. "I trust you'll give them a good look."

"Oh, yes. Sorry. I will." When Bethan realized Bryn wasn't going to wait to make his goodbyes, she followed him to the office door. "Delaney said you might not want to come to the members' opening reception, but if you change your mind . . ."

"You'll be the first to know. Thank you for the—"

"Here's the next." Huw appeared at the door, slightly out of breath, as if he'd run in to catch Bryn before he could leave. He held up the work, blocking Bryn's exit.

After all this time, the charcoal work looked fresh, still vibrant with the excitement he'd felt as he drew, knowing he'd figured out how to make the composition work. The paper was almost as fresh, too—a bit dated, but as yet unyellowed.

He drew in a breath. Everything in the room around him receded as he stared at the multiple poses he'd captured on this one sheet, a slightly different angle in each one, but in all of them the curve of Noel's spine, the fullness of her hips, her profile, her downward gaze. "Pretend you're looking into the water and seeing the home you left behind, the place where you know how and who to be, all while knowing you're leaving your sons to go back there." There was such sadness on her face, caught as she was in the moment of recognizing the vast divide between her world and Gwyn's, between her desire and her need.

Nelferch had been vulnerable; Noel had too. He couldn't move for looking, remembering as he did the moment he had finished the painting itself and Noel had still been stuck in it, mired in all the emotion of the story and the sitting. Day in and day out, playing the role of someone who made the mistake of loving a man she should not because he could never understand what she was giving up to be with him. He had kissed her forehead and sent her out for a walk. When she returned, the sadness had disappeared, replaced with a sexual urgency he had never seen in her before. They had made love and it had been slower but urgent, closer but urgent, reverent but urgent. He knew that he wanted to—no, *had to*—spend the rest of his days with her, touching her and attempting to recreate that urgency every single time he did. He wouldn't take her for granted; he'd prove that to her. And then he'd failed.

"Is everything all right?" Bethan asked. "You're upset. The sketch—do you see a problem?"

Bryn brought a hand to his face. It was wet. He had been reduced to tears in the gallery office. He wiped his cheeks, pulled himself together. "No, no problem. I—I haven't seen this piece in a while and I didn't sleep well last night and I'm more nervous than I thought about this retrospective. I think this is relief, maybe, that nothing worse has happened to it than some mold on the wood crate. If you'd seen where I had it stored."

He tried to make light of the moment, tried a laugh at himself, but he could see that although Bethan and Huw smiled at his remark, they remained a bit uneasy. They might be worried enough to mention it to Delaney, but she would be easy to put off once she heard him say he was overwhelmed. She knew how he got when he started anticipating public appearances. That's all he had to say and she'd believe it and move on to cajoling him into a better humor.

"Everything looks fine, though," he said. "And I'll make sure Delaney lets you know what I decide about the opening reception. But I really must run."

A few minutes later, Bryn stood in line at the station's busy Costa Coffee. He'd missed the 12:01 home. The next train was due around half one. He had a little time to kill.

When it was his turn, he ordered middling coffee instead of their poor tea and received the travel cup in no time. Rather than sit in the oppressively overlit shop, he took his coffee out to the bustling waiting area. Like everyone else, he huddled near the departures board so he could see his train's platform number when it was announced fifteen minutes prior to boarding.

Just as he brought the coffee cup to his lips, an announcement for the next London train came across the loudspeaker. Platform 3. The people around him began peeling off and heading to the ticket gates to wait for the train to pull in, the doors to open.

Bryn paused. London Paddington. From there it was a short tube ride to the Addison. And Noel. The departures board told him passengers on this train would arrive in London after four; from Paddington, he might make it to the museum before the end of the workday. He looked across the expanse and considered his options. He could go home to the empty house or he could—finally—get all the answers he'd been avoiding for decades.

He tossed the cup and started walking, no longer thinking about the wisdom of the trip or worrying about it or weighing his options. He just walked, through the ticket stile with a touch of his train pass, and on to the platform. He kept going, past the crowds, hoping to reach a spot where eventually he'd connect with a door that would lead to a sparsely populated second-class car. He had no reserved seat, and that could present a problem.

Far down the track, he stopped. As he did, he heard the noise of the slowly approaching train, followed by a squeal as it stalled and stopped several meters up the track. He groaned in frustration. Now that he'd made up his mind to get on the London train, he wanted it here as quickly as possible.

"Hurry up and wait," he muttered under his breath.

To pass the time, he did what came naturally. He looked. At the steel arches overhead, the litter and pigeons on the ground, the crowds, all the shades of black and grey from the steel to the concrete to the clothes on his fellow passengers. The only break in the monotony came from the raised yellow warning strips running the length of the platform, trackside. And also from a woman in a bright winter coat, the golden yellow of the gorse growing wild on the coast, as she walked briskly to a different set of ticket stiles. The arresting color held his eye and he watched the woman stop, as he had, under the departures board. She had light brown hair that brushed her shoulders, then fell below them when she lifted her face up to look up at the train information.

Just as he was about to look away, the woman turned and scanned the platforms, maybe looking for numbers. Bryn could see her profile as she started walking to what he believed was the Tenby platform he should have been at.

No, he thought. He closed his eyes, shook his head, and blinked. When he looked again, he saw the same woman, but his eyes had to be playing tricks. After a jarring afternoon of looking at old sketches and seeing old ghosts, he was surely seeing resemblances where none existed. *No,* he assured himself this time. *It's not possible.*

His train was moving now, underway again, and he focused on its approach.

But not for long. Unable to shake the feeling of familiarity, he looked in the other direction and saw the woman in golden yellow pass through the stile in front of the Tenby platform, saw her tuck a stray lock of hair behind her right ear. She was a few tracks over but he was certain he did know that profile and that gesture, and would know both anywhere after any amount of time.

Overhead, the London train's approach was announced, along with a warning to stand behind the yellow lines, but Bryn barely heard it. He only heard his breathing and the sound of his feet as he ran to catch a different train.

CHAPTER 34

SWANSEA, DECEMBER 2022

The ticket wasn't cheap and the trip would take almost five hours with a layover, time enough for Noel to start doubting her impulse to travel west to speak to Bryn. By the time she reached Swansea to change trains, she had talked herself in and out of continuing at least half a dozen times. Why had she decided seeing Bryn was a good idea? What if he wasn't receptive? What if he wasn't home?

Once past the ticket gates, she looked at her phone. She then glanced up at the departures board above her. Her connection would leave for Tenby at noon, a half hour from now, and it was running on time. So was the next train back to London. What if she got that one instead, just admitted her nerves and the foolhardiness of this trip and went back to her flat?

As she debated, her stomach growled; maybe she would make her best decision on a full stomach. There would always be another train, whether she decided on London or Tenby after lunch. When the voice in her head accused her of delaying the inevitable, she quashed it. Lunch, a practical lunch, she repeated to herself—not a stall, not an avoidance. She remembered Swansea as a lovely, lively, artsy seaside community, and lunch in town would give her a respite from the train and a chance to regroup from the anxiety that had built up during the ride. She looped the strap of her large handbag over her head, crossbody, and made it to the information desk in no time. Someone with local knowledge could give her a recommendation for a nearby restaurant.

A few moments later, Noel had a tourist map with a restaurant name circled—a casual breakfast and lunch spot named for its building's former life as a police station. She thanked the information-desk clerk and followed signs for the exit.

The winding walkway out to the street was pasted with ad after ad for area attractions. The Dylan Thomas Center, Swansea Market, The Waterfront Museum. The city was even richer in culture and activities than she remembered, but today she had no time to explore. She kept walking with the crowds to the way out, until she reached the next sign and its advertisement stopped her in her tracks. *Wales: Land of Mountains and Myth, Lakes and Legend. The landscape art of Bryn Jones. St. David's Gallery, Swansea. February 1–28, 2023.*

As she stared at the reproduction of one of Bryn's landscapes, people walked around her. She hardly noticed when someone jostled her arm and glared at her for blocking their progress. She only cared about the poster. The name of the arts gallery was familiar because she'd visited all those years ago. Bryn had taken her there one day during their summer holiday in Tenby to show her the museum's collection of Kyffin Williams landscape paintings. And now, soon, they would be displaying his.

Without hesitation, Noel turned and headed back to the information desk. Approaching the same clerk who'd helped her before, she said, "You recommended a lunch spot, but I've changed my mind. I just saw a big advertisement for a show at the art gallery; do you have directions to that building instead? Is it far?"

"From here? No. It's the same walk as the café, one street over. Five minutes and you're there." She took back the map she'd handed over earlier and marked the gallery with an X. "There you are." She slid the map around so it faced Noel. "But the show doesn't open until February. If you'll be in the southwest area later this winter, you might like to come back. The artist is a local. Famous. The show will go from here to London in April, but we get it first."

To London in April. That Bryn would soon be exhibiting in London, as well as participating in the awards ceremony, could be interpreted as another sign. Sign upon sign. She nodded. "Thank you, although I'm not sure I'll be back. I'll have to see the regular collection today."

"Ah. Shame about February. But the regular collection is worth the stop. It's a lovely spot for seeing Welsh artists in particular. They'll have the Christmas tree up!" she called after Noel, who was already walking back in the direction of the exit.

Once inside, in a matter of minutes, Noel found the Kyffin Williams painting Bryn had once lingered over. *Snowdon from near Harlech.* Williams, she recalled, was from the far north, off the coast in Anglesey, and the rugged northern landscapes were the ones he'd captured once he turned his attention to his home country. Bryn had told her the man painted largely with a palette knife, and the thickly applied paint confirmed it. Much of his work was almost Cubist in texture, each swatch of paint in the work's details applied in a rough square. "Slade," Bryn had stated with pride, no longer hampered by thoughts of his art school as second best.

Noel had been drawn to this particular painting immediately. The subject was simple—snow-covered Snowdon and its range, the surrounding fields—but the technique was not. The sky was turbulent with clouds and weather. What sun there was in between breaks of gathering storm clouds lit only a few peaks and a field; the rest of the landscape was blanketed by moody shadow. With a palette of grey, black, white, rusty brown, and muddy olive, the result was a terrain that felt lonely and perhaps a bit ominous, dangerous. She remembered how, gazing at it for the first time, the mood of isolation had settled over her and brought tears to her eyes, how she had taken Bryn's hand to feel a connection because she'd felt like a speck herself, always at the whim of an unforgiving landscape. Ever since her mother had died, Noel had felt that. Thinking back, she wondered if she'd responded so emotionally to the painting because she'd been in the early stages of her pregnancy then, though she hadn't known it—her body already in flux, her hormones surging.

Her whole adult life could be distilled down to that pregnancy. Her decision to leave Sammy behind was the struck bell that continued to ring through every part of her life. Even when she'd pretended all of it was behind her, even when she'd tamped down the sneaky memories, the bell echoed on and on. The experience had shaped who she was today, the woman on the train and walking alone through Swansea and standing in front of this painting. She'd come up for a reason. This woman was done with her grandmother's worn adages, she was done with outrunning her mistakes. This trip today, she reminded herself as she headed for the museum's front door, was the first step in the long process of changing course, whether or not those changes might change anything, or anyone else.

The Tenby train was running on time and the platform had been posted. As she got closer, Noel could see that the train was there and waiting. Good. She'd get to her seat and settle in for the last leg.

With her mind finally calmer, maybe this time she could relax enough to read the book she'd bought at Paddington before she left; with any luck, she'd find herself in an uncrowded car where she could read in peace.

She registered some kerfuffle behind her, a voice above the din of white noise calling, "Wait, wait!" Someone running for the train, no doubt—nothing to do with her. She kept on to find her assigned car.

When she did, there was someone in her seat—no, not her seat. Her face flushed with embarrassment when the other passenger pointed out: correct seat number, wrong car, a right at the door she'd entered instead of the left she'd taken. "How did I do that?" she wondered aloud.

The passenger was very polite about it, calling it an honest mistake that she'd made herself a time or two. Noel apologized once more and turned back. She pulled the ticket from her pocket and double-checked her reservation. Yes, the correct car was the one behind, and it was easy enough to pass through the automatic door where the two cars joined.

A bearded man was standing in that vestibule, though, standing still between the two cars' doors, looking at her, his eyes wide with surprise, with something she thought was recognition, until they softened and crinkled as his face broke into a wide smile and she knew it was in fact recognition.

Oh my god, she thought, *I know you too*—but she couldn't speak the words or his name aloud. Was she imagining, was her mind playing tricks? Had all her thoughts drawn him here or was it an inevitability, in this place so close to his home?

Her voice managed, "How . . ." And that was it, nothing more.

The man made up for her inability to form words, saying over and over, "It is you. I knew it. It's you. It's you." And then he opened his arms, he stepped forward, she stepped forward, and then they were clasping each other—as if no time had passed, as if no mistakes had split them apart.

"Bryn, I . . ." But again, she couldn't finish her thought. She'd prepared herself for knocking on his door and taking a deep breath before uttering rehearsed opening lines, not for this. At a loss, she shook her head.

"Would you like to sit?" Bryn whispered into her ear. "Would you come home with me to talk? For now, I'm happy to sit quietly with you on this train. *Cariad.*"

Noel nodded, her face against his. The train hiccuped and shuddered, a whistle blew, and then it was moving. They were still wrapped together, moving with it, heading home.

CHAPTER 35

SWN Y MOR, DECEMBER 2022

"I almost missed you, you know. I'd made up my mind to get on the London train to see you at the Addison, and I would have been well on my way, if not for your coat catching my eye."

Bryn opened the front door of the cottage and stood aside, letting Noel enter first.

She stepped in. Although still familiar, it was snugger inside than she remembered it to be. When she'd stayed here the place had been drafty even in the summer, but no longer.

"I weatherproofed this main part of the house," he said as if reading her mind, "once I moved out here full time. Central heating, new windows, new log burner. Not in the studio, though. Not yet." He reached out his hand. "Here, let me have your coat. Your beautiful, bright coat that I spotted halfway across the train station." He smiled.

She slipped out of her coat and handed it to him as if she'd only been away from here for a weekend and not a lifetime. No different than the way she'd moved right into his arms in the train car's vestibule, just as if no time had elapsed. There had always been this ease between them, and that hadn't changed.

Other things had. They'd aged, of course. Lines in their faces, gray strands in their hair. She'd noticed the disfiguration in his hands when he asked if he could hold hers as they sat next to each other on the train, but at the time she'd said nothing but yes to his question. He'd slipped one hand under hers, the other on top to cover, and she'd seen his knuckles were overly large, a few of his fingers crooked. Arthritis, she assumed. In his talented hands.

"Go on through to the sitting room. I'll bring us a drink, shall I? I have tea. Or whisky. I think I might need a whisky."

"I might too," she admitted. She didn't move. "If you tell me where you keep things, I'll get the drinks."

"Ah," he said. "You've noticed. I mean, how could you not?" He looked at his hands. "It's not as bad as it could be. I'm still painting and I take something for the pain. Well, sometimes."

"I'd like to get the drinks anyway. I insist." She wanted a minute alone to acclimate now that she was here—now that she was *home*, as she'd thought on the train when falling into Bryn's arms. While it was true that being here felt like the most natural thing in the world, it was also most unsettling to be back in this house, with everything that had happened here. The marriage proposal, her unequivocal yes. The ring he'd made her, twisting sturdy wire with his younger hands. The first bouts with the upset stomach she'd written off as a bug; Bryn's confession that he'd be leaving for Italy instead of being home for the move into the new flat; the way he'd hemmed and hawed because he knew he'd done it again, made a decision that would leave her alone. The beginning of the end.

After Bryn directed her to the glasses and the whisky bottle, he took the step down into the snug and disappeared behind the wall that separated the spaces.

Noel took a deep breath and put her hands on the cabinet to steady herself. Now that she was alone, she could look around her and take it all in. There were changes everywhere in the small house. Bryn—someone—had decluttered. Gone was the bowl that once held fishing hooks and all the other traces of the home's past as a working fisherman's retreat. Had there been a partner who'd helped him fix up the place, she wondered? Was there still?

The walls had been painted—somewhat recently, she thought, judging by the freshness of the white—and maybe had been replastered as well. Of course, Bryn had already pointed out the new windows and the addition of heating. But the place was still familiar enough to her that her hands shook as she poured some whisky between two glasses. Her heart was racing too. Now that the surprise of meeting had worn off, everything that needed saying loomed large, left her uncertain and overwhelmed. She thought Bryn might be very upset when he heard what she had to say.

It was late afternoon, already darkening outside. It dawned on her that she had no plans for lodging that night, and she wasn't sure she even had enough battery life left in her phone to call for a taxi. Unless Bryn had a compatible charger to replace the one she'd forgotten to bring . . . which meant what? She would be staying here? Or would she say her piece and then Bryn would ask her to leave? Would he make her walk miles in the dark?

Pour the whisky, she told herself. *Walk it into the other room.* She was here, and for now she wanted to be here and her company was wanted as well. One step at a time.

This was enough to get her moving, although she did double back and tuck the bottle under her arm, thinking they'd probably need more than one drink.

Bryn was sitting already, his elbows on his knees, his hands on his forehead, shading his eyes. Maybe he, too, was having second thoughts, she thought.

The floor creaked as she entered the room and he looked up. Instead of doubt, his face radiated happiness at seeing her.

"No ice or water," she announced, handing him a glass, looking away from his intense eyes. Her hand free, she took the bottle out from under her other arm and set it on the coffee table. "But I can get you one or the other if—"

"No need. Sit. Please."

Noel took the worn leather chair opposite the sofa where he sat. For a few moments, they sipped their drinks in silence. Then, both of them at once: "I—"

They broke off at the same time with a laugh.

"You go first," Bryn said.

Earlier, she had thought it might be easier to tell him about Sam and her horrible decision straightaway—simply blurt it out and face the fallout—but now that she was with him and could see how happy he was, she couldn't do it.

"I can't believe you were getting on a train for London," she said.

"I found out that you're working at the Addison when my agent brought me a copy of *Art/Source* to get me ready for an interview with one of their journalists. The article she wanted me to read was the profile about you. Of course, she had no idea I knew you. Complete serendipity." He paused, meeting and holding her gaze. "Once I knew, though, I planned to let it be—to let you be, I mean—but I was looking over some old sketches this morning, getting ready for a show in Swansea, and I—"

"St. David's," she interrupted.

His eyebrows shot up in surprise. "Yes. That's why I was in Swansea today, to bring the sketches to St. David's."

"I was there today, too. Only briefly, in between trains. To look at the Kyffin Williams paintings. To see them again."

He looked at her in wonder. "We must have been in the building at the same time. The sketches I brought to the gallery were studies from *Lady*. They'd been crated for years, but when I saw them again, they made me think of you. So I made the split-second decision to go to London to see you. Instead, I found you heading for the Tenby train. Coincidence after coincidence."

"Yes. No. Sorry. I'm making a mess of this." Her cheeks reddened. "Yes," she said, "there's a bit of coincidence. The train. But the rest . . . well, I didn't come all this way for Kyffin Williams and a seaside day trip."

"So, I get my reckoning after all this time. I thought after the train trip back here that—well, never mind what I thought." He drained the whisky from his glass. "You deserve to have your say and to have me listen to it. I need to hear it."

"No. That's not why I'm here. I mean, I planned to let you be too, but it turns out I couldn't."

Bryn leaned forward. He looked curious.

She took another deep breath, exhaled quietly. "It's a long story, starting with . . . When I arrived, I reconnected with Cal. Calum Paterson. Believe it or not, we're colleagues at the Addison while I'm on secondment. In one of our conversations, he told me you looked for me once you returned from your painting trip. He—he also told me the reason why you were late returning. That you got sick in Italy and were in the hospital for weeks. All those years ago."

"Ah." He leaned forward and reached for the whisky bottle. "This is where we need another drink." He poured a measure in both glasses, just missing her rim at first, spilling a little. After he set the bottle down, he took another sip before speaking. "All those years ago. I'm afraid I grilled Calum when I returned and found you'd gone. I thought he knew where you were. That's when he told me he hadn't seen you for months and that you'd been sick too, sick and alone and had withdrawn from your course, and then he told me off for not being around to take care of you." He stared down at his drink. "And I'm so ashamed that I wasn't, Noel. This, you and me"—he pointed his glass at her, then at himself—"we ended because of my selfishness. After I saw the sketches of you today, I thought maybe you being in London was a sign that I should find you and tell you how sorry I am. I'm sorry I wasn't with you when you needed me. I don't expect you to forgive me, I truly don't expect anything from you. I know you have a life, and a family. It's enough to see you, to have the chance to tell you that I have regretted what happened every single day since."

"Please," she said, holding up her hands and waving them, trying to make him stop talking, stop apologizing. Between his self-centered decisions and her insecurities and the Italian postal system, there was certainly enough blame to go around. In different circumstances, picking their way through the missteps and the bad luck now that they were face-to-face again might have been cathartic. Instead, at the end of all the missteps and bad luck was Sammy—her giving him up, keeping his existence a secret from Bryn, and trying to keep his existence from her own thoughts as well. They had moved well past the catharsis of apologies. It was time instead for truth.

"Let me finish, please. It's important. Cal thought I was sick, because that's what I told him. But I wasn't sick." She picked up her glass and finished what was left of the whisky in one swallow. "I was pregnant."

Confusion clouded Bryn's face. "Pregnant? But why . . . where is . . ." He shook his head. "I don't even know what I want to ask you first."

"Then let me keep telling you the best way I know how," she said, her voice low. "Why didn't I tell you? I only found out myself after you left. And once I knew, I did try to tell you. I wrote letters to you. Two. They both came back, undeliverable."

"The letters," he said, barely above a whisper. "Cal mentioned letters coming back to you. Now I know what was in them." He ran a hand over his face. "I wish I'd known you were trying to reach me."

"I wish I'd done more to track you down—got someone at the university involved, maybe, to see if they could find out where you were staying. I screwed up, I know I did. But the longer I waited, the harder it was to justify asking you to come home. You'd be home soon enough, I told myself, and I didn't want to be responsible for cutting your trip short. I thought I could handle it on my own, like I had always handled things. But then . . ."

He put his face in his hands. "But then I didn't come home."

"No. You didn't come home."

"And you had our baby alone."

"Not alone. My grandmother came to help me. I had him right after the new year. Samuel. I called him Sammy." Noel took a breath and then continued. "A few days later, Gran took me home with her. For a fresh start, she said. I . . ." She looked down at her hands, clutching her glass. She only realized she was crying when tears plopped into the whisky. "This is hard. This is the hardest thing I've ever had to tell someone."

Bryn left his seat on the sofa and knelt on the floor before her. He took the glass from her hands and set it on the table. He wiped away the tears that were streaming down her cheeks, but more kept coming.

"Noel. *Cariad*. Tell me now. I have always loved you. I promise, there is nothing you can say that will change that."

She looked at him then. Once he knew the rest of the story, his feelings might change, but no matter what happened next, she would stay here and face it all—no more burying memories and moving on.

She might lose him again. But he deserved to know about their son. She owed him that.

Slowly, her tears subsided and she caught her breath. When she nodded, he seemed to understand she was ready to talk and he pulled away just a bit.

"Okay," she said. "But you might want to sit for the rest of this." She pointed to the sofa and he went back to it, giving her room. "And we might need another drink," she added.

The hangover would be brutal, she thought, but at least she'd be feeling something.

And then, once they settled in with their drinks, she told Bryn all she could about their son.

Bryn was back down in the sitting room after tucking Noel into his bed. They'd had a lot to drink and she wasn't used to brown liquor. It had taken an hour or so for her to settle, for her head was spinning. Or the room was spinning. She'd said she couldn't be sure which.

"I'm sorry it took me so long to tell you about Sammy," she'd said as she finally drifted off.

"Hush," he'd replied. "You told me and I'm glad you did. But now you need to rest. Our heads will be clearer in the morning." He'd repeated those words over and over, and stroked her hair away from her forehead over and over, until finally the rhythms of both had made her eyes heavy and then close. *Let the whisky do its work,* he'd wished as he kissed her forehead. *Let her have this break.*

Truth be told, he too needed the break to make sense of how he felt about what he'd learned and what must happen because of it. He sat down in his armchair, his back to the log burner. Its fire had long since burned out and the house was cooler, but he decided against adding more logs. He didn't have the will, and thanks to the central heating, he wasn't chilled to the bone anyway. Or maybe he simply didn't feel the cold because his nervous system was overloaded after the wild, eight-hour ride of emotions he'd been on since recognizing Noel on the train—emotions he had expected, plus many he had not, all surging through him.

He'd imagined the reunion going much differently. When he'd found her on the train, when she'd agreed to hold his hand on the journey, he'd been happy, simply happy. Back in this house, watching her move around it, feeling her body heat across from him—still happy. Looking at her sitting across from him, he had been transported to simpler times, just the two of them, her body under his hands. Until she'd spoken and brought him back to the present.

They had a son, Noel told him. She'd given him up because she thought she couldn't raise him alone. "You hadn't come back," she'd said. "When Sammy came, I realized how alone I was. My grandmother said a couple in her cousin's family would give him a better home, and because I was so low, I believed her. I left and I didn't look back. Until I came back to London and couldn't avoid the past any longer."

They had a son and Noel had named him Samuel and he'd been somewhere in England all this time. The news had gutted Bryn. He felt so responsible for everything that had happened once he'd decided to go to Italy. She'd had to move to a new neighborhood without him, manage morning sickness without him, and give birth alone. If he hadn't been sitting when she'd told him about Sam, out in the world somewhere and lost to them, he might have fallen to the floor and curled himself into a self-pitying ball. As it was, he kept going over and over all his failings. "If only," he'd said, the pain in his gut growing. "If only."

Noel had understood. She'd put a hand on his knee and made him look at her and said, "In the first few weeks after I went back to Gran's house, I couldn't stop thinking about everything I might have done differently, and how if I had, I might still have our son. Until finally, I stopped thinking about him and what I'd done altogether. I had to. Anything else was a torment. I wouldn't have been able to get out of bed."

Bryn knew something about avoiding the past and adopting that strategy as the best way forward. In his life, he had been at times stoic and self-reliant, both qualities thought to be personal strengths, but really these were the strengths of walls and fortresses, the kind of strengths that aim for nothing more than to keep harm away.

"But once I found out you'd come back and you'd looked for me," she'd continued, "I knew I had to tell you what I'd done."

"I'm glad you told me," he'd said. "I'm glad you're no longer alone with this."

But now he was alone, he and the empty bottle of whisky and the two empty glasses, alone with this news and more.

"I'm trying to make contact with Sam," Noel had told him as he helped her upstairs. "You should know that too." She was pretty drunk by then and he hadn't followed up with questions. But he had several now: What did this mean, "trying to make contact"? Did looking for him involve something like detective work to find her grandmother's family? And if Noel wanted to find the boy—no, not the boy; the man—did she want Bryn to be with her on the search? Did he even want this—finding his son, a stranger to him? Did his son want it? Could he even be anything like a father after all this time? He'd missed all the time that should have been spent bonding, hoisting a small body onto his shoulders for rides, teaching him to fish, watching as boy grew into man and found his calling. Was Sam an artist? Was it in his blood? Would they even understand each other? Did he live down the street, in London, across an ocean? Had he had a good life, good parents, a loving home? Did he hate the parents who'd let him go? Would he forgive Bryn and Noel? Would Bryn ever forgive himself?

As he sat in the quiet, he grieved all the unknowns and the losses and the cruel way some choices kept a person in their grip of give and take away, give and take away, over and over and over.

With that desperate thought, the ache in his stomach moved up under his ribs and he crossed his arms around himself to keep himself safe from it. But nothing could protect him. The pressure built, and the grief demanded release. He wailed with the pain of a wounded animal, and once he started sobbing he couldn't stop, his shoulders shaking uncontrollably as he hunched forward and doubled over himself.

Somewhere inside the noise of his howling, he heard heavy footsteps on the stairs. He looked up and saw Noel standing at the bottom, and still he couldn't stop sobbing.

"Oh my god. Bryn." She walked over and knelt next to the chair.

He held up a hand. "I'm sorry, I'm sorry I woke you. Please give me a minute." He stood. She wasn't supposed to see him like this. If only he could get to the bathroom to clean his face and wipe away the tears and strings of spittle. He was in a godawful state.

Before he could move, though, she stood up too, her arms out, reaching for him. When she was close enough that he felt her warmth, he pulled her into him. They held each other, swaying slightly. The closeness was familiar. Her skin smelled of whisky and—after sleeping in his sheets—him, but also her own scent, the one that had always made him think of wild herbs and pine resin. A balm.

She tipped her head back, as she always had when he'd held her, and his lips found her throat, her fluttering pulse, as they had time and time before. Noel exhaled and Bryn felt her body relax. He moved his hands to her shoulders and drew back a bit to make space between them. Their eyes met.

"You've had a shock. You shouldn't be alone down here. Come up to bed," she said, and without waiting for an answer, she wriggled free of his hold and began to walk to the stairs.

Bryn reached out before she got too far from him and grabbed her hand. "We've had a lot to drink. Are you certain this is all right?"

She nodded. "I am. Really. Really," she said again, emphatic, and squeezed his hand.

He smiled. He had missed her so very much.

CHAPTER 36

SWN Y MOR, DECEMBER 2022

When Noel came downstairs the next morning in yesterday's jeans and shirt and one of Bryn's heavy jumpers, it was well after ten. There was a log in the burner, and the bedding from Bryn's attempt at sleeping on the couch had been folded neatly and placed near the armrest, a pillow crowning the pile.

She called his name but got no answer. She wandered into the kitchen and found he wasn't there either. But he had left a note on the kitchen table—open flat, not folded, her name in his still-familiar scrawl across the top, a heart instead of his name at the bottom. "Off for supplies before the shops close for Christmas," he had written. "Back soon with breakfast. If you can't wait, there's instant coffee. Sorry about that."

She sighed with relief. *He'll be back,* she assured herself, even as she felt a flutter of worry that she'd always be on edge about any absence, any note.

"Stop," she told herself out loud. "What you need is coffee." She winced at the idea of Nescafé, but she wasn't sure she could wait for Bryn to get back with the real stuff. Her headache was calling for caffeine.

The gas flame needed to be lit with a spark lighter, handily sitting in a jar with the rest of the kitchen utensils. Once she'd put the kettle on, she found the Nescafé—she picked the correct cupboard on her first guess—sitting next to a tea caddy and a French press. The jar looked as if it had been hanging around a while, its red label worn, a corner of it peeling, and it probably had. Bryn was a tea drinker. He would have the press for guests and this jar for the odd craving, although that seemed rare, given the state of the coffee. Peering inside the jar, she could see the granules had formed a block so hard that it would have to be chipped at with the spoon handle before she could put some in her mug.

Once the water was added and the coffee dissolved, she stood with her back resting against the edge of the wood countertop. She blew on the surface of the coffee and waited for the drink to cool. Around her, the old house was still, the only noise the clicking of the radiators as they heated, but outside she could hear wind picking up, blowing off the water. The last time she'd been here it was early summer and birds had flitted around outside, singing their songs or occasionally squabbling. On one or two nights that June, they'd had some heavy rains and they'd listened to the water run off the roof in sheets.

Tired of standing, she took her mug to the table. When she pulled out a chair to sit, she found a small sketch pad on its seat, probably the source of paper for Bryn's note. Because of its size, small enough to fit in a jacket pocket, she assumed this was the pad he'd take with him on walks or excursions. Curious, she began leafing through the pages.

There were studies of vegetation and sand following the curve of the coastline, done in pencil, and outlines of a few of the iconic colorful Tenby homes drawn, for a change, using colored pencils. Ships at rest dotting the harbor. These were followed by charcoal sketches, small pieces that appeared to be details of a larger landscape. Maybe, she wondered, a landscape painting in progress?

He had always been obsessive about working out details, working at these small-scale pieces until what his hands made matched what he saw in his mind. A few of the sketches had notes, but these were either illegible or in some kind of shorthand. She wondered if he would let her see his studio if she asked.

Noel flipped through a few more pages and landed on a portrait. It was labeled "Noel at Night." Her, curled up in the big chair, the wood stove at her back, glasses and a whisky bottle on the table in front of her, everything composed using minimal lines and yet evocative of a night of drinking and difficult conversations. Had he conceived this sketch last night while they talked? Before or after she'd told him about Sam, about Andy, about Alice, about her shame at failing, her guilt? Had he then drawn it early this morning before going out for bread and coffee?

She rested the pad on the table and moved her coffee well off to her left to avoid spilling. In the sketch, her hair hung in loose layers to the nape of her neck. Her eyes were watchful and a bit sad. She traced a finger along the jaw of the woman in the drawing. *Her* jaw, she reminded herself, and its very own softness that had come with age.

Everything about her body was softer and slacker since they'd last shared a bed. Arms, stomach, thighs. Her neck. Noel had thought time and age might have dulled desire; she had no illusions regarding how she looked and felt at fifty. And yet, before they'd fallen asleep, he had run his hands and mouth over all of her as he had always liked to do, whispering as he did a constant stream of endearments into her ear until she felt bold, as if it were all true, as if she was the most beautiful and delicious woman in the world. Her cheeks warmed as she remembered, and she brought her hands up to them. She hadn't intended to bring him back to bed; she hadn't even come prepared to stay over. Her only plan had been to tell him the truth, finally, and give him a chance to decide if he would forgive her—to ask if he, too, wanted Sam in his life. But staying in this house and sleeping with him had felt natural and familiar, as if no time had passed and no secrets had been kept and no resentments stoked. And it had been easy to talk when loosened by the alcohol. But now, with the truth out, would they be wary, even resentful, of each other? Were they staving off the inevitable? Would the feelings of last night turn to dust when they came together in the light of day and fully clothed?

As she was sitting and looking at the sketch and thinking, she heard the crunch of a car approaching over the gravel. Bryn, home. With breakfast, she thought next, and her stomach growled in anticipation. She shook her head at her body's hierarchy of needs. It wanted what it wanted.

She stood and brought her mug to the sink, where she rinsed out the bitter instant brew before filling the kettle with fresh water and putting it back on the heat. That done, she left the house and went down the walk to meet Bryn. "Let me help with the bags," she said.

"Hello!" he called, a wide grin on his face. He opened the boot of the car. "Take that one," he said, pointing to one of the reusable shopping bags. "It's got bread and eggs in it. That bag's heavy with some bottles and a cabbage," he warned when she grabbed a second one as well. "Will a vegetarian meal suit for Christmas dinner? Do you like cabbage? Better yet, do you have any fancy cabbage recipes up your sleeve? I'm afraid I should have shopped sooner. This was about all that was left in the shop." He pulled his head from the boot and looked at her, hopeful. "Of course, I haven't asked if you'll stay the weekend. You will, won't you?"

Noel smiled. "I love cabbage. If you have cream and cheese and an onion of some kind, I can make the most delicious cabbage gratin you've ever tasted."

"Can you now? Come here," he said, and he kissed her when she stepped closer. "Hello."

"Hello to you. Now, let's go in. It's freezing out here."

By the time Bryn had gotten his coat and boots off, Noel was already unpacking, setting the small carton of eggs off to the side. She smiled when she pulled out the bag of ground coffee, and hugged it close. Bryn saw her and smiled back. "You make your coffee. I'll get the rest put away."

"Do you want coffee? Or tea?"

"Tea, please."

A couple of minutes later, she brought his mug of tea, along with a pitcher of milk, to the table. "Why don't you sit and I'll make breakfast?"

He acquiesced without argument. As he sat, his eyes landed on the open sketchbook and he pulled it close. "You were looking through."

"I did," she said, moving toward the stove. "I hope that was all right. 'Noel at Night,'" she said. "Specifically, last night."

"What did you think?"

"I think you captured a moment. You don't do many portraits, and I think it's a nice change." She broke some eggs into a bowl.

"Ah, good. If you're willing, I'd like to do a more formal sketch than the one I tossed off this morning. Would you sit today?"

Noel paused in her task of beating eggs, fork over the bowl. The first time he'd asked, she had been self-conscious because they'd barely known each other. The same could be said for today, given this long absence between them, and yet she felt none of that earlier awkwardness. "If you'd like," she answered. She poured the beaten eggs into a skillet of melted butter, lowered the flame, and gave them a stir. She already had bacon going in a second pan. "Everything will be ready in a minute," she announced when she went back to stir the eggs.

Bryn took that as a cue and got up to fetch plates and utensils. He paused, his arms full, as he passed the window that looked out onto the back garden. "We'll eat, then get into the studio, if that's all right. The light is promising."

The studio was even colder than Bryn had expected, and he saw Noel shiver despite the heavy jumper she'd found to wear. He sat her on the stool and went back into the house for the wool blanket he'd meant to sleep under last night. Once back with it, he draped it across her shoulders. She pulled it closed, her hands tucked up under her chin.

Bundled up, she looked so young, like the guileless girl he'd once photographed sitting on the edge of his bed, the girl who had given him the ideas for the painting that had gotten him started.

As if she'd listened in on his thoughts, she asked, "Do you still have that old Polaroid camera?"

"I do!" he answered. "Tucked away somewhere, though, for I haven't used it in ages. The film is expensive and mobile phone cameras are equally instant and much more convenient. It was big and awkward, remember?" He finished positioning his easel and sketch pad, and then stepped over to Noel. "Could I?" he asked, motioning with his hands to the blanket she had clutched under her chin. "If we might loosen this—just a bit."

She didn't object and he parted the ends of the blanket, exposing her neck, some shoulder, some collarbone, and the hollow of her throat. "If you're too cold like this, tell me, and we'll move back inside in front of the fire. But if we could take advantage of the light in here for the next hour or two . . ." His eyes went to the windows, where a silvery, early-afternoon light flooded in, bathing the room in a rare mercury shimmer. Noel glowed in it. He couldn't capture the glow with only charcoal pencils, but he could sketch the play of light and shadow on her neck and across the bone structure of her face. He could do more with it later, when he began the portrait in earnest.

"I'm going to take a few photos now, before I start, to preserve the light for later. Bear with me?"

A few minutes later, satisfied, he set down his phone and they got to work. He had her look at different points in the room, but with each, she projected either wistfulness or distance, and neither quality worked for him.

"Noel," he said.

She turned, inquisitive eyes meeting his, and once they did, her face relaxed, the look on it settling into recognition and comfort and finally confidence—*I know you, I trust you.*

"Yes," he said, "that's perfect."

They worked until his hands began to seize up around a fine-point graphite pencil. He set it down and sighed. "I guess the light has gone anyway."

"And my backside is asleep. May I see?" she asked, easing herself off the tall stool.

He nodded. "Between this and the photos, I've got enough to start working from once you've . . ."

"Once I've gone. You can say it." She joined him, standing at his side, the blanket hanging from her shoulders now like a cape. "It's me this time, not me playing Nelferch. It's a funny feeling."

"I think I'd like to add this portrait to the show. It would bring the thirty years full circle, with you first as Nelferch, and now this most recent portrait. Like bookends."

They stood quietly, looking at the afternoon's work together.

"I won't use your name in the title if that's too much for you," he said, "and of course, if you say no to exhibiting the finished painting at all, I won't. But I do want to finish it regardless."

"Finish it—show it," she said after a moment more.

He held his hand out and she took it.

"You're cold," she said, holding his hand to her cheek. "Let's go back in the house and I'll make us some tea."

Bryn lingered in the studio when Noel went inside to make the tea; he had an idea. After some searching, he found what he was looking for.

He found her in the snug with a full tea tray, the log burner crackling nearby.

He held up the envelope in his hand, a triumphant smile on his face. "A Christmas present," he said, placing the envelope on her lap.

She looked from her lap to him. "A present? But I don't have anything for you."

He waved that off. "Don't forget you're making the most delicious cabbage in the world this weekend. And really, this pales in comparison."

She gave him one last sideways glance before opening the envelope. Inside was an opaque sleeve, something for holding a fragile document. Or, in this case, a photo.

"You found it," she said, removing the old Polaroid photo of herself in Bryn's bedsit from its protective covering.

Bryn hadn't looked at it in years but every detail was as he remembered, down to Noel's fuchsia mandala shirt from Oxfam, its richness only slightly faded.

She brought a hand to her face. "Oh, I was so young. And limber." She laughed. "I'd try to make that pretzel pose again, except I'm afraid I'd get stuck." She studied it for a moment longer. "Thank you. I'm so glad to have this."

He sat down next to her and looked at the picture with her. "I thought our son, when we meet him, might like to see what you were like in uni, as I saw you."

She slid the photo back into its sleeve and held the envelope to her chest. "You want to look for him, then? With me? I thought since we weren't talking about it—the search, making contact—you might need some time. It's okay if you do. If the fact of Sam hasn't sunk in yet."

He thought about what she'd said. What does one make of meeting one's child for the first time as a grown man? What does one make of an abstract—this son, this hazy, small form, this bundle he never had the chance to hold? Noel was real to him, their bond interrupted but long-standing.

He raked his fingers through his hair and pushed it back from his face. He remembered a game he'd played once as a boy, at a rare birthday party for one of the rare friends he'd had, a boy who'd been part of the kind of family that was foreign to Bryn: a father who had dragged furniture and toys out onto a large lawn with good humor, and a mother who had thrown herself into baking a cake and laying the table and creating party games.

The game he was thinking of had involved a web of strings the mother had painstakingly woven throughout the trees and shrubs in the garden, each string a different color. She'd handed out small cards in matching colors to every child at the party, then instructed them to follow the string that matched the color of their card all the way to its end. At the end, she'd said excitedly, clapping her hands together, a prize. It had looked easy until the boys began following strings and ran into tangles and snarls, realizing they'd need patience to slow down and tease their string out of the jumble.

For years now, Bryn had believed that too much time had passed, that their lives had moved on independently of each other. But Noel's presence back in his life now said otherwise; they'd stayed connected somehow, by some string like the one in the game. They'd only needed to sort through the twists and turns to see that at the end they were still tied together.

His joy at this had indeed overshadowed the idea that they had created a human together; Noel was right that it hadn't sunk in. But she was very real, a part of him, and she wanted this.

"You hold on to the photo and keep it safe," Bryn said. "We'll find him."

CHAPTER 37

SWN Y MOR, DECEMBER 2022

On Christmas morning, they went swimming.

"We call this a 'polar plunge' or sometimes a 'polar bear plunge,'" Noel said as Bryn helped her into a newer version of the wetsuit she'd once worn when swimming in the local cove.

"Ah. Here it's a 'stampede to the sea.'" Bryn laughed. "Hundreds do a rush in–rush out on Boxing Day. We're missing the crowds going a day early."

The suit kept the cold water at a remove, something Noel appreciated. The guarantee of a wetsuit was the only thing that had allowed her to be coaxed into the Welsh waters thirty years ago, and that was true again now. But it was lovely to be in the sea again rather than a pool lane, and the swim brought back memories of the best parts of her childhood—the long and languid days of summer vacation, receiving her grandmother's full attention for the three weeks they spent in the small rental house on the Cape. Paradise, for Noel, had been that three-week escape from being pigeonholed as the poor orphaned girl living with her hardworking grandmother. It had likely been a welcome respite for her grandmother, too—no alarm clocks going off at five in the morning, no rushing to get out to her bookkeeping job at the small manufacturing firm where she worked, and no pressure to find care for or entertain her solitary grandchild. The seaside had given them both what they needed.

Back at the cottage, she let Bryn strip the suit off her and wrap her in a towel. He smiled as he gave her damp hair a fluff. She smiled back at him, thankful for his care. It still bothered her a bit that she had no present to give to him, and as she got dressed into what she now thought of as her cottage outfit—her jeans and an old shirt of Bryn's, with his heavy fisherman's sweater over it—she had an idea. In addition to the simple pot of braised lentils and the cabbage casserole she was making for Christmas dinner, she would make dessert.

"Do you have fruit in the house?" she asked him. "Apples, maybe? Or anything dried? Oh, and flour and sugar?"

"Yes, an apple or two, I suspect," he said. "And yes, there are sultanas. And flour. Sugar, now, I'm not so sure. I definitely have honey."

"Honey will be fine."

In the end, Bryn found three apples and the sultanas, and even a little bit of caster sugar in a small bag—clumped by the damp like the instant coffee had been, but easily pulverized with a few whacks of a rolling pin. The apples had no brown or bruised spots and were only a little wrinkly.

She shooed Bryn out of the kitchen once he'd brought her all the ingredients, and he decamped to his studio. Before she addressed the lentils and a cabbage that needed coring, she whipped up something she was calling apple cobbler but which was more like an apple and raisin pie with only a top crust. Once that was in the oven, she crossed her fingers and started in on the rest.

Soon, both bean pot and casserole dish were ready for the oven, and she set these aside while the pie finished baking. In the lull, she brewed herself some tea. Now that the meal preparation was done and the mug of tea was warming her hands, her mind started wandering in the quiet. It was Christmas, her first as a woman on the way to divorce. Had Alice received the coat she'd shipped? Had she sent Noel a card? Had she tried to phone? Was she missing a call from Noel?

Her phone had died the morning of her first full day here without its charger. Bryn's wasn't compatible. And although she hadn't minded being unplugged while lazing about in bed with Bryn or sitting for hours in the studio, her regrets found easy breeding ground now, in a mind without distraction. Would Andy use this holiday weekend's absence against her in visitation mediation? Her argument for the minimal time she'd requested was already tenuous. Maybe she should borrow Bryn's phone to call . . . but what if Alice didn't answer? And if she then called Andy, would he grill her about the strange number?

She shook her head at that last question. Instead of simply doing what she wanted and calling her daughter on Christmas, she was second-guessing everything. This might be exactly what Andy wanted—for her to question herself into inaction and slip as quietly from Alice's life as Marisa had. But her daughter needed the constancy of a mother in her life, no matter what Andy had decreed. Alice needed Noel to try harder, and she would. She would borrow Bryn's phone, no matter the consequences; she would make the call.

By the time the kitchen timer rang, she had made her plan. She would ring Alice before dinner, late morning back in the States.

The pie coming out of the oven cheered her up some. It was brown and bubbling and smelled good. If the rest of the food went in now, they could be sitting down within a couple of hours.

As she closed the oven door on the lentils and the cabbage, she heard what she thought was a car coming up the lane. She stilled herself and listened. Yes, it was a car. Who would be driving here on Christmas?

She went to the door and opened it to see an unfamiliar car parked and a long-legged, unfamiliar woman working her way out of it.

"Oh, hello," the woman said, closing the car door behind her. "Are you the new cleaner?"

"Am I . . ." Noel stepped outside and shut the door behind her. "No. I'm not the cleaner. If you're looking for Bryn, he's in his studio. I'll go—"

"I'll find him, shall I? No doubt he's seen me drive up already, although pretending he hasn't." She started to walk around Noel and toward the cottage.

Noel stepped to one side and blocked her. "I can't let you in. I don't know who you are."

"And I don't know who you are either, so I suppose we're even." When Noel didn't budge, the woman reached into her large handbag and waved about a business card. "Delaney Jenkins. I'm Bryn's agent. Do you think you might let me in now? It's a bit raw out here."

Just then, the front door opened and both women turned to it. Noel breathed a sigh of relief to see Bryn. He went down the walk and joined her.

"Delaney," he said. "I wasn't expecting you. I thought you were up in Caernarfon with your sister for the holiday."

"They had a houseful, which I wasn't expecting. Her children and their cousins were driving me mad with their noise. I thought you wouldn't mind if I stopped in to have a quiet Christmas dinner with you, but of course I didn't know you'd have company." She darted a look at Noel. "You never have company."

"Noel's not 'company,' she's a friend. This is Delaney, my agent," he said to Noel, and then he sighed. "You've been driving a while, so you may as well come in. I'll fix you a drink."

Taking Noel's hand, he led the way into the house. Delaney followed.

"Coffee or tea?" Bryn asked as they entered the kitchen. "Wine? Something stronger?"

"Tea, if I'm getting right back in the car. Although I did leave my sister's before breakfast."

Noel turned from pulling a bottle of wine from the cupboard. "Why don't you join us for dinner, then?"

Bryn looked at her, his eyes wide. Noel smiled and shrugged at him. He sighed again in return and said to Delaney, "Yes, of course, stay. But I'm warning you, I shopped late, so dinner is lentils and Noel's famous cabbage."

"Red okay?" Noel asked, holding up a bottle of Spanish wine in front of a flustered Delaney.

"Yes, please," Delaney said, sitting down at the table. She met Noel's smile with scrutiny, her eyes narrowed. "You look familiar. Have we met?"

Bryn, reaching for the glasses, jumped in to answer. "I shouldn't think so. This is Noel Enfield, an old friend up to visit for the weekend."

"Noel Enfield," Delaney repeated. "Why does your name sound familiar too?"

"She's the art historian from America seconded to the Addison. The *Art/Source* profile you wanted me to have a look at?" he added when she continued to look puzzled.

"Oh. And you read the article, as I asked, and realized the subject just happened to be your old friend? That's quite a . . . coincidence."

Bryn didn't answer. Noel brought Delaney's glass to the table. "Bryn, why don't you sit with Delaney and I'll clean up a bit."

He gave in without argument, and Noel didn't miss Delaney's look of surprise as he did. Then the agent's eyes landed on the open sketchbook and she pulled it close. "Did you do this just recently? 'Noel at Night,'" she read aloud.

Bryn took the book away from her and tucked it between his back and the chair back. "I wish you wouldn't look through my unfinished work."

"It was open," Delaney protested. "Will it be a portrait? A portrait is something different for you. A departure. It's quite nice." She called to Noel, raising her voice to be heard over the running water, "Have you posed before?" When Noel looked over her shoulder to answer, Delaney's eyes widened and she said, "Oh my goodness, you have. I'm so thick." Her face brightened. "Are you here to model for his Ceridwen, then? As kind of a follow-up to *Lady*? We could make a lot of that in the lead-up promotions for your retrospective, Bryn."

"No," Bryn said firmly.

"No to which?" Delaney laughed. "You always say no immediately when I make suggestions, so I'm going to ignore you and remind you to have a think on it. The publicity we'd get from tying your old work to the new, especially if Ceridwen is finished in time to show in April, would draw in crowds. Noel, you could be the special guest. I can see the headlines: 'The Lady of Llyn Y Fan Fach comes out of the shadows after thirty years.' You will still be here in April, won't you? Mid-May at least, if you're staying right up through the Rising Artists Awards?"

Noel paused in her task of scrubbing a saucepan. "I will, but it's really not my place to agree to anything Bryn hasn't endorsed. This is between the two of you."

"No, she's not posing for Ceridwen," Bryn said, returning to Delaney's suggestions. "I've put that painting aside for now. And also, no, I don't think that kind of publicity is what we want."

Noel turned to watch their face-off. Delaney raised an eyebrow but Bryn met her curiosity with a long stare. After several moments of this staring contest, Delaney picked up her wineglass and looked away, deterred at least for the moment.

"Agreed," she declared. "No more talk of your show or the publicity."

Bryn approved with a nod of his head.

"Noel," Delaney pivoted, "do you mind talking about your work at the Addison? I'd love to hear more about what they have you doing."

"All right." Noel dried her hands, poured herself a glass of wine, and joined Bryn and Delaney at the table.

When the conversation turned to Noel's work on the upcoming exhibition's guide, Delaney zeroed in on a few of the artists, asking for thumbnail bios and information about each. Then she reached into her large handbag again for a few of her business cards. These she pressed on Noel with instructions to give them only to those artists in the group. "Discreetly," she cautioned. "I don't want the others to think they can contact me. I am specific about my preferences."

"You are relentless." Bryn laughed as Noel pushed the cards back across the table. "Noel's not your employee, mind."

"It's okay," Noel said to Bryn, covering his hand with hers. She looked back at the agent, unsure what she might be wading into. Delaney was a stranger to her, but something about the give-and-take made her uncomfortable; it was a reminder that she was both missing something and acutely aware of all she had missed. She took her hand back from Bryn and reached for her wine. "I can't recruit people for you, Delaney," she said after taking a sip. "I've worked too hard to be objective. But if you make it to the party after the ceremony, I can introduce you to all the artists. This is a talented and interesting group of people, and I think you will like them." She stood. "Now, do you think I might get you both to move to the other room while I finish getting dinner ready?"

Delaney took the hint and stood also. "We'll leave you to it. Bryn, we can go over some details for your Swansea show.

Coming?" she prompted when he didn't immediately rise out of his chair.

"Yes, of course." He got up slowly and kissed Noel on the cheek as he passed her. "Thank you for doing this. Give a shout if you need a hand."

"Of course," she answered.

Delaney followed him but paused at the doorway. "Yes, thank you, Noel, especially for asking me to join. It's very kind."

Noel watched from the window as Bryn walked Delaney to her car after dinner. There they stood chatting, Delaney standing close, the white clouds of her breath as she talked wafting into Bryn's personal space. Noel exhaled loudly, relieved to see her go. The surprise visit had thwarted the plans to call Alice before dinner, and she reached for Bryn's nearby phone while she had the next few moments to herself.

The call went unanswered for several rings and then, just as Noel was about to disconnect, there was Alice's voice, thin across the miles and tentative at the unfamiliar number. "Hello?"

"Alice." She smiled, relieved to hear her daughter's voice. "Alice, it's Mom."

"Mom," she repeated without any enthusiasm. "This isn't your number."

"You're right, it's not. I had to borrow a phone because my own—that doesn't matter," Noel said, reminding herself to stay upbeat. "I'm glad you picked up. Merry Christmas! Are you having a wonderful day so far? Did your dad make your favorite chocolate chip pancakes? And did you get the package I sent?"

A few moments passed with no answers from her daughter. She wondered if the call dropped.

"Alice? Are you there?"

"I'm here. But I have to go."

Alice's tone remained flat and Noel's heart sank. Still, she pressed on. "I understand. It's an exciting holiday and you must want to call your friends to talk about your Christmas presents. But I couldn't let the day go by without calling. I miss you. I wish—"

"If you missed me, you'd be here," Alice interrupted. "I have a wish too, you know. I wish you wouldn't call me again. Ever."

This time, Noel knew the silence that followed Alice's last words meant her daughter had ended the call.

"Alice," she whispered aloud, and she held the phone to her chest.

She turned her attention to the window again, to the people beyond it. Outside, the conversation had come to an end. Delaney kissed Bryn on both cheeks before bundling herself inside her car. Then, with a three point turn on the drive, she was off.

Bryn lingered outside, watching the car disappear around the corner at the end of the gravel drive, making sure Delaney got off safely. He was closer to his agent than he had let on. They had been, and maybe still were, physically intimate, Noel realized. Even after all this time, his body had the same tells—his muscles looser, personal boundaries erased. Oh, this man was so familiar and, at the same time, such a mystery to her. This life he had built in thirty years—there was so much about it that she didn't know and wouldn't know . . . or would only have a finite time to learn. Would this be what would happen between her and Alice going forward, days stretching into years stretching into decades—time they would work to bridge someday, or not? And what about Sam? Was she a fool to think they might ever know each other, even if they met?

She was brooding about this when Bryn came in a minute later and found her at the window. He put his arm over her shoulders and pulled her close. "Sorry about that. I thought we'd have the day to ourselves. I hope you weren't worried by Delaney's idea of bringing you into the promotion for my show. I made it clear where I stand."

"I'm not worried. She's a force, though."

"Yes, she is that. She's happy about me painting your portrait. She thinks it's her idea, and I find letting her have her beliefs is sometimes the path of least resistance." He nodded at the phone still clutched to her chest. "Were you calling someone?"

Noel smiled briefly and then looked away.

"Something is bothering you. Are you certain it's not Delaney?"

She shook her head. "It's not her and it's not her ideas for promoting your show." She swallowed down the knot in her throat. "I called Alice . . . and she didn't want to talk to me."

Bryn pulled her close. Noel shrugged.

"It's all right. She's angry. Still, it makes me think about time. How much has gone by, how much more will. All this time I missed or will miss. With Alice, with Sam. Even with you," she added, smiling sadly. "At least you and I have a past together that we'll either build on or remember each other by. But I'm afraid of always being a stranger to my children." Another lump grew in her throat. "May I tell you something?"

"Of course."

"My head wasn't in a good place for a while after Sam was born, and I got through by thinking all I had to do was be patient and I would have my own family at the right time. Gran gave me that idea to hold on to, as a sort of permission to think about the future, not the past." She looked away from Bryn and back out the window. "But the things we've done aren't erased simply because they are behind us. The past lingers, it shapes our present and our future, even if we think we won't allow it to. I'm afraid of that, the way the future is going to play out because of the past."

"*Cariad*. Hey." He put his fingers under her chin and turned her face to his. He smiled at her. "You're very hard on yourself, aren't you? You're here now. You could have stayed away but you're here, you found me and told me about Sam. You want to be in your daughter's life. You've taken steps to find our son."

"Maybe it's more about being here in this cottage for the weekend," she said, scanning the room before looking back at Bryn. "Celebrating the Christmas we didn't have in 1992. Sleeping together, cooking breakfasts together. You sketching me the way you always did. I worry I'm puttering about here as if the past thirty years never happened and all is right with the world."

"Maybe all is right with the world, for now. Look, I don't know what comes next, my love." Bryn took Noel's face in his hands. "Maybe more mistakes. Maybe we'll be together until one of us dies. Or end up cordial and kind to each other and that's it, nothing more. Maybe Alice will come around and I can get to know her too. Maybe we won't find Sam, or we'll find him and he'll reject us. Maybe he'll want to know us and we'll finally be his parents. The only thing I am certain of is, the moment I saw you on the train platform, I knew you'd been a part of my life all this time, even though you'd been gone, and that you will continue to be, however the future looks. So."

Noel looked at him. Yes, she thought. He'd been part of her too, and would be as long into the future as she could see. As would Sam. As would Alice. Even Andy—part of her. They populated her mind, her memory, her heart, and there they would all stay, whether beside her or not. How had she ever thought that moving on meant she could leave anything behind?

She reached up and held on to Bryn's wrists. She lifted his palms from her face and brought them, one at a time, to her lips. "So," she said.

CHAPTER 38

NOEL'S FLAT, BOXING DAY 2022

A dramatic sky greeted Noel as she walked out of Paddington Station. Above, gray clouds hung in heavy clusters, while farther ahead rays of sunlight and blue sky broke through. She chose to walk to her flat for the exercise after the long train ride, risking the intermittent rain bursts without an umbrella. The temperature was moderate, but the air felt damp and raw. She pulled her coat around her, buttoned it, and picked up her pace for home. The sidewalks were full but no one lingered, the only reason to be grateful for the storm clouds.

Inside the warm flat, the air was still and slightly stale. Someone somewhere in the building had been frying food, and the old oil smell had made its way into her space. Before she took off her coat, she was at the windows, opening them a crack. The smell reminded her she'd need to find an open grocer later today and stock up for the week. She sighed. Back to reality, back to her routines—and that meant checking for emails from her colleagues, even though most were away for the long weekend, as she had been.

Her phone charger was where she'd left it, next to her closed laptop on the dining table, and it was quick work to plug in the dead phone and boot up the computer. Devices taken care of, she hung her coat on a peg in the bathroom to let it dry. Tea, she thought then, to stave off the chill that had settled over her. At least there were tea bags in the kitchen.

As the kettle heated up, so did her cell phone. Now that it had some juice in it, notifications started pinging, one after the next. She had hoped for some activity—a call from Alice, Cal checking in from Glasgow—but this much? Had there been a work crisis? Her pieces of the project were up to date, she was certain of it. If plans had hit a snag somewhere else, the problem must have been big and all-encompassing if someone had tried reaching out to her this many times over the holiday weekend. But unplugging from work for the long weekend was expected—encouraged, even. She couldn't imagine . . .

Dread came over her in a wave. What if something had happened to Alice?

No longer in the mood for a relaxing cup of tea, she switched off the kettle, went for her phone, and began scrolling through her messages. The most recent one was from Bryn—*Let me know when you're home safe and sound. x*—but she left it unanswered and dropped into one of the kitchen chairs. The rest of the texts began on Friday. She could hardly believe what she was reading.

Tried calling you today.
Twice.

But you didn't answer or call back.
Did you go away for xmas?

Nice to know I can count on you.

I had to call your office. Admins
underwhelming, no help.

Come to find out you took vacay days
thru Boxing Day? WTH is Boxing
Day?

You need to hear this. Stop going
around me and my atty
to hire a mediator. Alice doesn't
want to see you. She's upset
and we're done.

Coat you sent is totally
inappropriate for school.
What were you thinking?

No way for us to return or exchange
either. Thanks for that.

Why can't you be bothered to reply?

This is a real eye opener Noel.

Are you even alive?

You know what? Never mind.
Don't bother calling.

Since that flurry of texts on Friday, Andy had sent nothing more, though she hardly wanted to see more proof he was furious. She scrolled through the rest of her unread messages. There was one from her lawyer. *Call me. Problem.* The last four were from Cal—the first two sent within minutes of Andy's rant, the last two yesterday.

Are you sitting down? Andy called your office. Gave your admin an earful.

Call me if you can.

Did you stay in Wales longer than you planned? I bet you did. Happy Christmas.

A tad worried about you but assuming you've had no phone service. Call when back. xo

Cal answered on the second ring. "There you are." He sounded relieved.

"I'm back. Sorry if I worried you. My phone's been dead since early Friday," she explained. "I missed every text. Andy's. Yours about Andy. He's angry that I tried to hire a mediator for visitation talks."

After a moment, Cal said, "I did hear he was very upset when he rang the museum. You won't ring him back, will you?"

"I don't know. Maybe he'll listen to me if I do. Otherwise, I feel like I'm bound to lose Alice. As it is, she's very angry with me too."

"Noel, forgive me, but when some people feel their worlds spin apart, they do all they can to maintain the upper hand. I know you love your daughter and you want to see her. But perhaps it's time to stop expecting something different from Andy and start thinking about what is within your power to do for Alice."

But that's it, Noel thought. *What exactly* is *within my power anymore?* She had no power, right? She had "no claim." Andy had said as much after they'd first separated and she'd pleaded for one day a week to take Alice to and from the ice rink and then on to dinner. No claim, when she'd asked if Alice could come to London to visit over her vacation week. No claim on the girl Noel had sat up nights with when she was ill, or had comforted when she'd argued with friends or done poorly on a quiz or had a nightmare. Noel was expected to walk away, she had been told she must walk away, but all the while her heart was being shredded and her head certainly did not understand what or who this ultimatum served. Certainly not Alice.

"You've gone quiet," Cal said, interrupting her thoughts. "I'm sorry. I shouldn't have spoken so bluntly when I know you are hurting."

"I'm glad you did. You're right, someone needs to think about Alice and not winning arguments. I'll—I'll think of something."

"You raised her, Noel Enfield," he said. "Maybe all that's in your power right now is to be certain that when she needs you, she'll be able to find a way back to you. Don't let this cast a pall over your own plans, or over the weekend I imagine you just had in Wales? You were gone longer than I expected."

"Longer than I expected, too, or I would have packed my charger and a change of clothes," she said, her voice softening.

"Ah. Good trip?"

"Yes," she agreed. "Weird at first, but good. I told him about Sam and he was remarkable, really. I'm glad I went."

"As I said, you did the right thing. You're doing all the right things."

"Although it meant missing your very Scottish Christmas. I hope you had a good time with your family."

"It was a smaller group than usual, but a good time was had by all. Although I admit, I'm worn out from being entertaining for the past three days. Someone has to, but why is it always me? I'm glad you rang, I was concerned—but now, if you don't mind, I'm going to go watch some mindless telly. Get yourself settled, get comfortable. If you need anything from me, you may wake me up.

Otherwise, I'll check in with you tomorrow and we'll make plans for another supper."

After Noel disconnected, she sat and stared off into nothing for a few minutes, thinking about what Cal had said—thinking about Alice's needs and how best to be her mother.

In the middle of all this, it dawned on her that she hadn't replied to Bryn and she typed a quick text to him: *Got home about an hour ago, safe and sound, settling in now. xx*

It wasn't nearly all she wanted to say but it would have to do for now, and he'd be happy enough to know she'd made it back to her flat. She hoped he was working, keeping his hands warm, eating well. The weekend felt almost unreal now that she was miles away. It was hard to believe she'd last embraced Bryn in his little car earlier that very morning and not days ago. The immediacy of Andy's angry texts had overshadowed the peace of her weekend.

She sighed. As much as she wanted to avoid thinking of the divorce, she knew it would be wise to send her lawyer a quick message too.

I am home, she wrote. *I'll call you to say more, but please know I'm done fighting with Andy*. Then, for good measure, she texted Alice: *I am so sorry I hurt you. I know that's not enough, but it is true. If you ever need me, I am here for you. I love you.*

After she hit send, she made a quick wish that Andy wasn't monitoring Alice's phone, but she knew she couldn't control his actions. Embracing that thought, she powered down her cell. Enough.

Cal was right. Andy could persist in alienating Noel from Alice, but sooner or later, Alice would be old enough to make up her own mind about who she saw and who she didn't. Noel considered Cal's advice. There was strength in being a steady presence, in being the person who continued to show up however she could and without an agenda. Being Alice's mother in those ways was still within her power.

CHAPTER 39

SWN Y MOR, MARCH 2023

Bryn set down his phone. Bethan had just assured him that the plans for packing and moving his paintings to London were in place—the gallery rooms at St. David's had been closed off and the canvases taken down to be packed over the coming week—and with that news, he had one fewer responsibility to worry about in the days leading up to the London show.

March would be a busy month, April even busier, and for someone who appreciated his quiet and his routines, the anticipation of so much activity stirred his anxiety. One thing at a time, he told himself, and he knew which one must come first. While Bethan and her staff were taking care of twenty-eight of his paintings, he still had the twenty-ninth in his studio, almost but not quite finished.

Noel had visited twice in January and he'd had her sit both times. Each time she'd gotten on the train bound for London, he'd missed her a little more. He'd been toying with the idea of making the next trip—meeting her in London to finish it, and then perhaps staying on through the awards presentation in May. The painting needed finishing, but also he liked the idea of them being together if—*when*—news of their son came in. Her work was getting more intense and she couldn't travel as frequently, while for his part there was nothing keeping him in Wales now that the show was coming down and the packing underway. He worried some about the effect of the city on his ability to focus after being holed up in solitude for so long, but he knew it would be better to work from life and not a photo—seeing the light in her eyes, the way they flickered with her different thoughts, the kindness in them when she smiled, even the worry.

Calling the portrait a landscape wasn't a gimmick, a way to shoehorn a personal painting into the show's theme. He thought of Noel's face as the topography of a life lived in ways she couldn't have anticipated. Everything that had happened to her, everything she had seen and done and thought, was all there, in every line and every hollow. He could look at her for hours and never see the same landscape twice: the clouds descended, the clouds broke, the sun struggled and even came out through the storms; on occasion there were calm skies and tranquility.

While he was pondering this, his phone rang again. Delaney.

"Ringing to let you know St. David's is ready to pack for shipping," she said, foregoing pleasantries. "I've had a call from Bethan."

"She rang me as well."

"Ah, good. What of the portrait? She said they're packing twenty-eight crates, but will you have them ship that as well? If so, you need to get it to them today or tomorrow."

"It's not finished, Delaney. My hands aren't as fast as they once were. Plus, I need another sitting. At least one."

"I see." She said nothing further, and the silence grew between them.

Discussion of this work was awkward because any discussion of his relationship with Noel was awkward—had been since Delaney's surprise visit at Christmas. She covered her feelings well, but Bryn could see she'd been embarrassed by showing up and stumbling into a part of his history she'd never known about. She didn't like being caught off guard, and she had been. Yes, he had stopped sleeping with her months before that, but he had never formally announced an end to that aspect of their relationship. Yes, their arrangement had been, by mutual agreement, without strings, but there was attachment, and Bryn knew he owed her something anyway—an apology, an explanation, clarity, *something*.

"Delaney, I never told you—"

"Because there's no need to," she interrupted. "Relax. I never had any illusions. You were never the only one, nor was I to you. But let's stick to business, shall we?" she said, pivoting. "If you need another sitting, will you be seeing her soon? You're cutting things awfully close."

"Neither of us has had a minute to travel this month, but now that this show is coming to an end, I'm thinking . . . You'll think I've gone mad, but I'm thinking of following my paintings down to the city when they go and staying with Noel. I can finish the portrait there, and maybe stay on through the awards presentation in May."

"All those weeks in the city? You?" Delaney laughed.

"If she'll have me."

After a moment, she said, "You in London for the next several weeks isn't such a bad idea. Especially if we can use that for some publicity. You said no before, but please listen. I think you need to reconsider talking to a journalist about the history of Nelferch and Noel, of Noel and yourself, to create some excitement before the retrospective opening. Noel will be with you at the opening party, won't she?"

"We've not talked about it."

That was true. They spent their precious time together learning how to be together again and planning for the day when they might reunite with their son—something he could hardly discuss with Delaney.

"We're not thinking that far ahead," he explained.

"Maybe it's time to start, then. You know, there has always been speculation about the identity of the woman who posed for *Lady*."

He did know. And at the beginning of February, a South Wales arts journalist had revived this speculation when he reviewed the show at St. David's. Bryn and Noel had read the article together and shrugged it off, but perhaps people were more interested than either of them thought. Certainly Delaney read such situations better than he did. Left to his own devices, he shied away from publicity altogether—but he wondered if he should take Delaney's advice this time. Maybe a little story was warranted to keep the gossip in hand, if Noel was agreeable.

Without waiting for an answer, Delaney continued, "Once you're in the city, your relationship will be out in the open anyway, at least within the museum world. So let me set up an interview for you. We'll make sure the message is clear and straightforward, something that highlights the show and the release of the new painting, not gossip. A story like this adds depth to your show, and the coverage of it in the press."

"Maybe. Listen, I'll speak to Noel about her feelings. If she's not keen to speak publicly, then I won't."

Delaney sighed. "I'll have to be satisfied with what you both decide. But please do your best to convince her it will only be good for the show. And please get down to London and get that painting finished." With that last directive, she ended the call.

As if it was that easy, Bryn thought as he stared at the phone in his hand. Crate the canvas well, carry it on the train with paints and brushes and knives in a rucksack, get down to work, and hey, presto. Done and dusted. He hadn't exaggerated the way his hands hampered his progress. But it was more complicated than mere speediness. He worried that asking Noel if he might stay with her through May would remind them both that her six-month secondment would come to an end right at the same time he prepared to go back to Swn Y Mor. What would happen after the secondment finished was something else they hadn't discussed. Nor had they discussed the possibility that Sam wouldn't contact them during the next several weeks—or at all.

What then? Would she leave? Could she?

"*Duuuuuw*," he growled aloud. He was getting ahead of himself, making trouble where none existed. They would have several weeks, time enough to sort through all the open questions. He had to call her. More than anything, he wanted to see her. Once he was with Noel, all would be well.

CHAPTER 40

NOEL'S FLAT, MARCH 2023

It was approaching six o'clock and Noel still sat at her desk. Jean had been home for the past week, recovering from COVID, trying as best she could to direct her team via the teleconferencing platform. But her fatigue was evident, and Noel had stepped in to pick up the reins.

She liked being busy, as it kept her from brooding. An unoccupied mind had too much to worry over. There had been no updates from the General Register Office or the intermediary after Bryn had added his contact information, meaning her son hadn't made any moves toward reaching out. Nor had he placed an absolute or qualified veto on any contact, so Noel supposed that no news at this point had to be good enough, despite her impatience. She and Bryn had taken steps to amend Sam's birth certificate with Bryn's name, and that felt like progress.

To keep the anxiety at bay, she threw herself into Jean's work of scheduling and leading the team meetings, requesting updates from her colleagues, monitoring the galleys of the exhibition guide, and updating the master calendar as each new deadline was met. She also began editing both the exhibit labels and the longer copy that would accompany the artwork in the show. She hadn't spoken to any of the artists since Christmas, and she decided to check in on them now that the results of the judges' panel were almost in. Many had celebrated the holidays with family; Henry, she remembered, had been with his father in Leeds. Others had planned to stay in their studios and work instead. There would be much to catch up on.

With her list for the days ahead completed, Noel packed up to walk home. Most evenings she loved coming home from the museum to find Bryn cooking in the flat. Her day, no matter how stressful, was improved the instant she walked through the door to the aromas of something simple but delicious bubbling away in the kitchen. He said doing the marketing and preparing the food made for a nice transition from painting, and Noel had no objections. She was eating better than she had in months. On the two Fridays they'd had together since he'd moved in, he had even resumed his thoughtful trips to buy her favorite cheeses, a gesture harkening back to their cheese-and-plonk nights of old, although these days they drank a better class of wine.

Tonight, though, Bryn was joining the reporter from *Art/Source,* Federica Mackintosh, online in—she looked up at the wall clock—only three minutes to discuss the link between his new painting and *Lady of Llyn Y Fan Fach.* In other words, her; they would be talking about Noel. She had offered to pick up food from a favorite spot on the way home—to save Bryn from having to cook tonight, but also to give herself a detour on her walk. She didn't want to get home until she knew the interview was ending.

She didn't mind, she had told him when he'd announced he was considering taking Delaney's advice to discuss how and why he had painted Noel thirty years ago and again just recently. And she didn't. Although he'd offered her the chance to veto the interview, and she appreciated that he had included her in the decision making, she believed it should be up to him to market the retrospective as he thought best. But her approval didn't extend to being in the other room listening in on his conversation with the journalist.

This article could only usher in the larger world of the press and its promise of wide readership and a wider interest, a big, public world colliding into the little, private one that currently included just the two of them and the hope of Sam. Come April—not so far away now, it struck her—their lives would become hectic beyond their four walls. And with April came the guarantee of May and the contemplation of difficult realities: a parting, nothing resolved here with Sam, and nothing to return home to. Memories of glorious winter days faded. Present hectic ones inched toward dire. Why wouldn't Noel want to hold on to this unadulterated little world for as long as possible?

The world inside the little flat was a fit boat bobbing on a calm sea, safe enough for the time being. Bryn and his delicious meals and his bits of cheese and his steadiness kept Noel buoyed. She hoped that her optimism amid the long odds and the smiles she had for him when she walked through the door at the end of the day lifted him likewise. For now.

The only hint that they were both anxiously watching how quickly the days passed was in the fevered edge their lovemaking now had. Every night they pulled each other close, and hands and mouths began roaming soon after, committing features and form and taste to memory. Those languorous nights in bed, running a lazy finger down a spine or along the inside of a thigh without minding the clock, belonged in another world and another home—a place by the sea where it seemed they could stop time.

The bag of takeaway food hit the counter with a thud and Bryn laughed.

"Yes, I ordered too much," Noel said. "Onion bhaji, chana masala, aloo gobi, a biryani, garlic naan, and coconut naan as well. Online ordering is a hazard. I don't know when to stop."

She began to unload the containers. Bryn caught her hand.

"Come here," he said.

Noel set down the wrapped naan and walked into his arms.

"I have missed you," he said, and they swayed together for a moment. "The interview went well," he went on. "It should be out in two or three days, two weeks before the opening reception. Would you like to hear about it?"

"I'd like to eat first," she answered, and she pulled away to finish setting out their supper. "Would you grab some plates?"

He did this while Noel gathered utensils from the drawer. Soon they had filled their plates and they took these to the small dining table.

"Water?" Noel asked before she sat down.

"Lager, but I'll get it," he said. "Water for you?"

"Sure. Or, is there an open bottle of white in the fridge? If so, a glass of wine, please."

While he poured drinks, she tore a piece from her naan and popped it in her mouth. "I've changed my mind," she said. "Tell me about the interview."

He set their glasses on the table and took his seat. "Federica asked after you. She was a bit taken aback, I think, to learn from Delaney that you were my model for both *Lady* and the new painting, but she was prepared and asked good questions. She expects she'll be able to condense this story into about one or two paragraphs within the larger story about the retrospective, and the focus will be mainly on the art—why I saw you as Nelferch, how this idea I had about you influenced the entire landscape, and, more recently, making the departure from landscape to paint your portrait. A little bit about losing touch, meeting again by chance in Swansea. I also may have told her we first met over a dance in the disco." Bryn smiled before piling some chickpeas onto a torn piece of naan.

Noel managed a smile in return, but hearing the condensed story—hearing that all they had gone through across the decades could be reduced to a couple of paragraphs, knowing that she'd given up their child and they were trying to find him and they would all have to reckon with the fallout of that, knowing that people would wake up one morning and read the barest outlines of this story and judge it all very romantic or at the very least sappy instead of complicated and poignant and maybe even tragic—made her feel hollow. "That's almost everything, then," she said, but her voice caught on the words.

He wiped his hands and reached across the table to grip hers. "*Fy duw,* no. It's the surface. The outlines. No one needs everything but us. The story is ours."

Ow Wers. When Bryn got passionate about something, his speech became slower and more deliberate, his accent more pronounced.

He looked into her eyes. "I shouldn't have agreed to the interview, should I?"

"It's only an interview. Don't mind me, I'm . . . I'm tired and out of sorts after a long day. Jean's still ill, and there's suddenly a lot of pressure to meet deadlines." *There was more to say, though, wasn't there,* she thought to herself. They had to talk about it, they had to. "And Deb Stone, my boss at Field-Lyons, is beginning to email me about returning to work in May, after the exhibition launches. Eight more weeks here seems like a lot of time, until it doesn't."

He pushed his plate aside and set his elbows on the table. "True. But it's a good amount of time for thinking about what you want."

Noel took a sip of her wine. She knew what she wanted. She wanted this life with Bryn to go on and on. She wanted for it never to have ended in the first place. She wanted Sam in her life. She wanted Alice. She was aching and aching for one child she had no claim to and another whom she could have claimed as her own but had given up. She wanted to turn the clock back, but to what point? Where could she set the hands that would make this all right?

"You don't have to decide everything tonight, on an empty stomach and after a very long day."

She looked at Bryn, so earnest. Maybe the answer was as simple as that.

"Are you still hungry?" she asked.

"Still?" he asked, a smile on his face. "I've hardly eaten anything. But no, not hungry right now. We can reheat everything later, I suppose."

They looked at each other. After a moment, he waggled his eyebrows suggestively. She laughed, and the weightiness of earlier lifted. Across the small table, they clasped hands. Together, they rose.

Supper could wait.

It's Mothering Sunday. I'm at a café drinking my second flat white with Gertie at my feet. My laptop is open; thirty minutes ago, I accessed the Wi-Fi at this outdoor terrace on a tree-lined street in order to read the latest issue of an arts journal I like to keep up with.

Around me, magnolias are already dropping petals, while the pollarded plane trees have yet to leaf. Each different planting comes to life after winter on its own particular schedule. Isn't that remarkable? We may put plants in the ground at any time in the year, but in spring, they awaken when they will. Buds and flowers and leaves come when they must.

For years, I have wanted answers to my questions about my birth parents, but now I must admit to you that I have wanted these on my schedule and on my terms. Before I made myself known to you, I wanted the chance to decide if inviting you into my life would hurt me. I wanted to be prepared for what you might tell me about my father and your relationship, if any, with him. I thought I was in control, first learning about you, then taking my time to get to know you. Funnily enough, I found I have missed you over these several weeks that our work together has gone quiet, and I have looked forward to working with you again as the exhibition and awards deadlines approach. I like you, you see, and Gertie likes you; you are genuine and clever and thoughtful and kind. Late last fall, when I learned you were looking for me and were open to meeting, I felt close to revealing to you who I am. I felt ready to hear why you left me. I felt the story you had to tell would be one I could understand, even as I continued to feel conflicted about learning why we were parted in the first place. I went so far as to determine I would wait until the awards were behind us—there should be no hint of favoritism in your work on the exhibition or the guide; I was firm with myself about that—but I was ready to say yes.

But like those buds and flowers and leaves, answers come not when I am ready or the time is right but when they must. "Truth will out," as Mum used to say when some intrigue in our little world was revealed for all to see. This time, the truth is out on the screen in front of me, in black and white. Bryn Jones is my father, I am certain of it, although this interview with him that I've just now finished reading mentions only that you knew each other as students, you posed for him, you lost touch thirty years ago.

"Until last fall, when she came back to London to work. We ran into each other at a train station and we've been together since. I'm painting her again too. Her name is Noel. Noel Enfield."

Nothing about you and he having a child together. But the timing adds up. Thirty years ago, and I am thirty years old.

I think I've always known the answer would be something like this. Someone like this. Of course, talent arises from all sorts of situations. Non-musicians end up with a piano prodigy. The tone-deaf might birth an opera singer. It's not such a lift to believe that you with your love of art and someone like your uni friend, Calum, might have made me. For a time, I believed he might be my father, even after you told me he was nothing more than a friend. That early on, I wasn't sure I could believe you. There was the way he looked at me in your cafeteria, you see, as if he'd seen someone familiar, and that ease you had with each other—believe me, I read all sorts of things into those facts. But the more I came to know you and trust you, the more certain I was that you had told me the truth about your friendship. Also, I can see myself in you a bit, in the shape of your face and the coffee brown of your hair, but there's no likeness in gingery Calum. Nothing.

But with Bryn Jones, there's more than a passing likeness. We share the shape of our eyes, the touch of olive in our skin, and the wave in our hair. And the compulsion to create art.

I should be happy. This answer is what I wanted. Judging by the way he speaks of reconnecting with you, I think he loves you, and that there is a story behind the two of you that I need to hear. However,

Bryn Jones complicates everything in my life right now. He is both my father and a judge for the art competition. If I tell you who I am now, how can I possibly compete for this award? If I reach out to you after, how will anyone believe that you didn't know who I was during the judging? If I remain in the competition, is the price of staying forever saying nothing to you?

Which do I choose? Is it even a choice? Has my life always been in hands other than my own?

Yours,
Henry Bell

PART VI

OTHER ECHOES INHABIT THE GARDEN

CHAPTER 41

THE LONDON ACADEMY OF FINE ARTS, APRIL 2023

The crowds arriving for the opening night of Bryn's show never let up, and it wasn't long before each gallery was full of people taking in the paintings while holding their glasses of wine or waiting on the sidelines to get a word with the artist. Art critics and collectors and curators from museums all over milled about. Noel had been happy to meet the head curator from St. David's Gallery in Swansea, Bethan, and they'd had one of her favorite conversations of the evening—not about her and the paintings she featured in, but rather about the collection the woman oversaw. Bethan had asked her to lunch the next time she was in Wales, and Noel was genuinely excited by the prospect of having a quieter conversation with the woman.

The people Noel worked closely with at the Addison cycled in and out, most still expressing their surprise at her role in Bryn's art and life, although Sophie Adler expressed surprise at the surprise. "I thought surely everyone knew," she had exclaimed. "We all did at uni."

When Noel felt overwhelmed by the conversation and the crowd she would escape to a corner with Cal for a few minutes, and there they'd stay, chatting, until someone came over to draw her into conversation or pull her over to a painting to get some insight into the work. She'd hardly spoken to Bryn since they'd arrived and Delaney had taken him over.

Whenever there was a lull, Delaney brought a new pair or trio of art patrons over to introduce them to Bryn. Noel wondered if he felt the walls closing in as she did amid the din and stifling heat. She caught his eye across the room and he looked as pained as she felt, in need of rescue or at least a respite. Neither of them was an extrovert, and she thought a break for fresh air might give the both of them a few moments of restorative quiet. She also needed to feel his hand in hers, even if only for a moment, so she abruptly excused herself from the clutch of people who had been hanging around her for what felt like hours and crossed the room.

When she was almost at Bryn's side, Delaney stepped in front of her.

"Give him a minute more with those two, will you?" she asked. "They're collectors."

She looked past Delaney. The couple had only half of Bryn's attention; the other half was on her. He smiled ruefully, gave a slight shake of his head. She looked back at the agent. "All right. But he should have a break after, just a minute or two. Thanks, Delaney," she said, quickly, before Delaney could make any objections. "I'm going outside the front doors for some air."

Noel stopped at the cloakroom and picked up the colorful woolen wrap she'd worn in place of a coat. As she walked through the front doors and down the steps into the plaza that allowed the museum to be set back from the busy main street, she drew it close around her.

There were benches on either side of the stairs, and she sat down on one. Settled, she took a deep breath. The cooler night air was reviving, and she was grateful the evening's earlier sprinkles had let up so she might sit a while and enjoy the few moments of solitude.

She smiled. In her newfound quiet, she could appreciate what a rush all this was—bringing art to people, watching them connect with a collection. Working behind the scenes for so many years, she'd forgotten that electric feeling of launching a show, of knowing intuitively it would be a success. Naturally, opening receptions tended to buzz with people hoping to see and be seen, but at tonight's, even the most social of art butterflies seemed captivated and moved by the work itself. And as overwhelming as the night had been, Noel knew the presence of enthusiastic crowds was a good indicator that the show would do well over the next few months. With thirty years of hard, solitary work behind him, Bryn deserved the attention. And this was only one night, as they had repeated to each other all day. Life could get back to normal as soon as they got home to her flat and closed the door behind them.

As normal as could be, that is, given that the awards exhibition Noel was responsible for was close on tonight's heels.

She shivered and pulled her wrap tighter around her. She looked up, hoping to see stars overhead, but of course the city was full of too many lights. As she was looking in vain, she heard, to her right, coming from the direction of the street, footsteps—shoe soles hitting stone. Not Bryn, then; wrong direction. She sighed. She had hoped he would follow her out here after a minute or two, but he seemed to be stuck in Delaney's loop of never-ending introductions.

She looked in the direction of the noise and saw a figure approaching. One more person showing up for the reception, albeit late. She should get back inside, she thought, and she rose from her seat to make her way in. The footsteps picked up speed once she started moving—not running, but walking at a clip. Anywhere else and Noel might have felt nervous. Instead, here, out in the front of this venerated spot, she was merely curious. She stopped and turned.

"Noel." She couldn't yet see the man walking through the plaza, but he knew her. "I thought it was you," he said. "I could see you pretty clearly with the floodlights around your seat." A few more strides and he stepped into that light.

"Henry!" She took a few steps toward him. "This is a surprise. I didn't know you planned to come to the reception. And where's Gertie? I don't think I've ever seen you without her."

"I didn't want Gertie to see you. She's too fond of you, and I wouldn't be able to say what I need to and get away after."

Noel's smile faded. What could he mean by that?

"I haven't come for the reception," he said. "I thought I'd have to catch you inside, but it's better that I found you out here. Please, stay there." He stopped a few feet from her and held out his hands so she wouldn't come any closer. "I need to talk to you. I won't take much of your time."

She heeded him but she frowned. He was worked up, so unlike him. "Henry, I don't understand. Would you rather come into the museum tomorrow and we can speak in my office? Or at least come inside the front doors and warm up. We can talk there. You have no coat on, and it's chilly tonight. You'll be cold," she added, fussing over him like a mother.

He looked down at his clothes as if only then realizing he'd left his flat and traveled all this distance without a jacket. "I'm not cold. Listen," he said, looking back at Noel, "I've come to a decision. I'm withdrawing from the competition, and—"

"You're what?" She couldn't have heard him right. He had decided to drop out of the running for the Rising Artists Award? She knew her colleagues would worry over all the completed print work that would need redoing, but to her, none of that mattered. Only Henry did, and whatever distress he was feeling that might have led him to make this rash decision.

"Is everything all right at home? With your dad?"

"My dad?" he asked, and then he gave a short, sharp laugh. "Ha! My dad. I guess you could say something's wrong."

Noel's forehead wrinkled with concern.

"Sorry," he apologized immediately. "I can tell you don't think it's funny, and it's not. I'm not going to compete. I wanted to tell you as soon as I decided, that's all."

"Here? Why tonight?"

"So you'd have as much time as possible to, I don't know, fix whatever you have to fix, because I'm leaving. I knew I would find you here tonight. I don't mean to cause you problems, Noel, but I can't stay in. I can't."

"Henry." She took a step toward him. He held up his hands again and she stopped. "I'm not worried about what needs fixing. I'm worried about you. Please sleep on this and come see me tom—"

"Noel? Is everything all right?"

Noel and Henry both looked in the direction of the voice. Bryn was exiting the museum, on his way finally to get some air. How much of this frantic exchange had he seen?

"Jesus," Henry said under his breath. "I've said all I wanted to say. I have to go."

"Stay," she urged. "Look, my . . ." She searched for the best word to use and decided on his name instead. "Bryn Jones is coming to meet us. Tell him what you told me." When Henry began to protest, she said, "Oh, I know you know he's one of the judges, and I'm sure it's not appropriate for you to talk to a judge, but I don't care about that right now. Maybe he can help you, if you're having a, a crisis of confidence. I guarantee he knows everything you're going through."

Henry smiled. She thought it looked as if he pitied her.

"No," he said. "He doesn't know a thing. Good night, Noel. Thank you for listening." With that, he turned on his heel and walked back toward the street.

By the time Bryn reached Noel's side, Henry was passing through the archway. He hadn't looked back.

"What happened? Who was that?" Bryn slid his arm around her waist. "Are you all right?"

"Yes. No. I'm not all right." She leaned into Bryn. "That was Henry Bell."

"The artist?"

She nodded. "He came here to find me and tell me he's leaving the competition."

"Leaving the—is he mad? Sorry, sorry, that was inconsiderate. The person who wanted to slash his awards entry to ribbons is the last person who should call anyone mad." He gave her a reassuring side hug, pulling her close. "Can you ring him in the morning? Perhaps he's overwhelmed by the pressure and needs some time to think."

"I suggested exactly that to him." She thought about Henry's pitying parting smile and his odd laugh when she mentioned his father and she shivered again. She felt certain this wasn't a crisis-inspired decision he would think better of when he woke up in the morning. But she told Bryn, "Yes, I'll call him."

"That's it. Now, you're catching cold. Let me take you inside for a few more minutes. I promise we'll leave soon."

Noel nodded and let herself be led back inside. It hardly mattered anymore if they left soon or stayed. Her mind was going to be on Henry either way.

CHAPTER 42

THE ADDISON GALLERY, APRIL 2023

Noel was back at her desk at the Addison on Monday. True to his word, Bryn had excused them from the reception on Saturday evening not long after Henry had walked off. Sunday had been a blur—rising too early after not enough sleep, ringing Henry and listening to his phone go to voicemail each time. She'd stopped leaving him messages after the first three. It was obvious he had turned off his phone to avoid her calls.

After that, Bryn had walked her over to Hyde Park, claiming the exercise would do them both good, but she'd spent all her time scanning the greens for dogs and their owners—hoping to spot Gertie, hoping the dog would appear from out of nowhere and run right to her side.

"It was all so very strange," she had said about the encounter to Bryn as they walked back along the Serpentine. "Am I somehow responsible for his change of mind, do you think? I can't think of anything I've done or said that led to this, but why track me down to tell me—and on your special Saturday evening, no less? Why not wait until Monday? Or simply email the awards committee itself? The Addison is only responsible for the exhibition, not the prize. And the thing he said about his father? It felt so cryptic, as if he was trying to tell me something without actually telling me. Should I call his father, do you think? I could probably find him. How many Douglas Bells could there be in Leeds?"

Bryn had let her talk and speculate for a long while as he listened, and then, before they departed the park gates for home, he had offered some perspective: "Give the lad some time to sort through his decision. This is a very high-pressure time for the competing artists. All sorts of things go through their heads, not the least of which is self-doubt. I remember feeling like a fraud; maybe that's what's plaguing Henry in the moment. I'm sure it's nothing to do with you. If anything, he seems very comfortable talking to you, and I think that means you are the safe person for him to express his fears to. Perhaps give him another day or two. Ring from the Addison."

Noel had nodded at the measured advice, but the worry lines on her forehead hadn't gone away.

Bryn had tried to smooth them away with his thumb. "You really care about him. He'll know that."

Would he? Noel wondered, now that it was Monday and she was back at work and Henry remained unreachable. She sighed. Bryn was right; she cared about the young man. Every so often in the course of a life, friendship bonds develop quickly, easily, deeply. She'd been lucky this way more than once—with Cal, with Bryn. There was all that with Henry, and more than that, too. She felt protective of him, like his champion, maybe because—like her, like Bryn—he was a motherless child who needed someone in his corner at this momentous time in his life.

Maybe what Bryn had suggested was true, that he had confided in her because he knew that she cared, but something about the way he'd told her continued to nag at her. His words, his manner, physically keeping her at a distance—it all felt very personal, a personal rebuke. Had she put him off somehow? Had she been presumptuous in assuming they were friends or that he would welcome her support? Had he felt some favoritism despite her efforts to stay evenhanded? Had he learned about her relationship with Bryn, one of his judges, and decided he wouldn't win on his own merits?

She groaned and buried her face in her hands. She didn't think she could stop turning these questions over and over in her mind, but maybe it was time to turn the why of his declaration over to someone else. She did have to do her job, and until Henry decided to answer her calls, that job was preparing to amend the exhibition plans as if he really meant to drop out. She knew she needed to pass the news on to Jean and let Jean go to both the museum and the awards committees, maybe even to Henry himself. Before she did that, though . . .

She reached for the telephone and dialed the number for the publishing press in charge of printing the exhibition's softcover book. When she was put through to her contact from the sales and marketing department, she skipped the pleasantries and went straight to the burning question.

"Freya, has our book gone to press yet?"

When she was assured it hadn't but it was on the print schedule for the next day, she said, "Would you hold it another twenty-four hours, please? Just the one day, and I need your promise this won't cause a delay. Yes, even if it means we ultimately expedite and pay more for the job. I may have some changed pages for you, and I need the twenty-four hours to make those changes."

Agreements reached, Noel cut the call. As soon as she released the button, she dialed the head curator's office.

"Aditi, I need to see Jean as soon as possible. No, eleven won't do. Yes, I understand she's got a full calendar, but if you'll tell her this is about a potential crisis with the awards exhibition, she may want to reschedule her morning. I'd like to be there within the next fifteen minutes. You can get me in now? Excellent. I'm on my way."

CHAPTER 43

NOEL'S FLAT, APRIL 2023

With the wrap of the departmental meeting at four on Friday, Jean declared that the hectic week had finally reached its end and she sent everyone home. "There have been several late nights this week. Please go home, enjoy the weekend. And fingers crossed the crises are behind us!" she added as staff rose from their places at the conference table.

Noel smiled sympathetically as she collected her materials and prepared to leave.

The news she'd passed along on Monday had come as a shock to Jean. For several minutes after, Jean had sat silently with both her hands clamped over her forehead while she absorbed the ramifications of Henry's announcement. When she looked up again, Noel could tell her thoughts had already pivoted.

Jean's only concern from that moment on was managing their way through the crisis, and that she had, mapping out each step of the way forward. She had been pleased to hear that Noel had anticipated changes to the guide manuscript and had negotiated a pause in the printing schedule until they confirmed Henry was serious in intent. To carry out that confirmation, she had said, she would turn to the awards committee.

"For obvious reasons," she had explained to Noel at the end of their impromptu meeting, "further contact with the artist has to be out of our hands." She had been as bewildered as Noel by Henry's actions but had been far less eager to try and make sense of them, given all the other details that required her attention. "I'll make sure the awards committee updates us with the artist's final decision within the next twenty-four hours so you might restart the printing process. Until then, we focus on what's within our control. For you, Noel, that means making necessary revisions to the manuscript and identifying all mentions of the artist in our print material in the event we must excise those."

Now, five days later, the exhibition plans were back on track and the excision was complete. All traces of Henry were gone, as if he'd never taken part. *The artist,* Noel reminded herself as she entered her office and gathered her coat. *The artist, the artist, the artist.* Wasn't it better to follow Jean's lead and remain impersonal, now that both their professional relationship and their friendship had ended? Henry hadn't been in touch since the Saturday evening of Bryn's opening, and likely wouldn't be again. He hadn't even indicated when he might come to collect his painting, nor had Noel authorized it to be packed up for shipping to him at home. She suspected Henry's motive was avoiding seeing her at the museum, but her own? Packing the work was more final than she was ready to accept.

The artist, the artist, the artist, she repeated to herself all through her walk home. If she forced herself to think of an abstract instead of a person, maybe she might hasten some of that acceptance.

"You're home early, *cariad.*" Bryn looked up from his sketchbook when she walked in the door. He put his things down and rose. "I have some cheese and wine for you. It will only take a minute to get it ready."

"Jean sent us home early to make up for the late nights this week." She tucked her bag and coat in the hall cupboard. When she arrived in the kitchen, Bryn handed her a glass of wine and she smiled gratefully.

He led her to the table, where he'd laid out the cheese with a few dried apricots and salted almonds. She lifted her glass. "Here's to the end of a brutal week."

She watched him fiddle with an unopened packet of cream crackers—her favorite, despite all the fancier options available. She reached out and laid her hand on his, and he stopped tugging at the package seam and looked up.

"Will you be terribly angry if I check my email before I shut down my phone for the evening?"

He smiled, but she thought she saw a flicker of worry pass across his face.

"I promise to give you and this cheese my full attention once I've had a quick look," she said.

"Of course," he said as he laid some crackers on the board. "It'll give me time to light some candles." He left her to return to the kitchen, where he started rooting around in the drawer where they kept their candlesticks.

Smiling, Noel took her phone to the sofa and perched on the edge of a cushion.

A quick look at her work inbox revealed no new communications about the week's crisis. It really was put to bed. With nothing more to follow up on, her thumb hesitated over the shutdown icon. Before tapping it, she looked over at Bryn; he was setting the candles in their holders on the table. She had a minute to check her personal email too, something she hadn't done since the start of the week. There might be an update from her lawyer. Best to look in case something was time-sensitive, since she'd already been out of touch for days.

Most of the emails in her inbox were advertisements—a relief. Nothing from the Boston lawyer. She was about to log out when an address she'd missed in the first skim of her inbox caught her eye. She clicked on the email and read. For a moment she thought she was suffocating, and it was a struggle to draw in some air.

From across the room, Bryn called, "Should we sit down?" When she didn't respond, he prompted, "Noel? Is everything all right?"

She shook her head. "There's an email from the adoption intermediary. Dated Wednesday. I haven't checked in days. I've been . . ." She couldn't say it out loud. Too busy. Too busy to even remember their ongoing search for Sam, never mind check in on it.

She looked back at Bryn, still standing at the table and about to strike a match. He looked strangely calm. Her eyebrows drew together as she read to him, "'Adoptee has registered a qualified veto and does not wish to meet birth parents at this time, but perhaps would be prepared to make contact in one year.' One year?"

"All right," he said. "That's not the worst news, is it? He hasn't registered an absolute veto." He set down the box of matches in his hand and came over to where she sat. "He hasn't told us to piss off. He just needs time. That's how I read it, anyway."

"How you read it?" Her head snapped up. "This email was sent two days ago. When did you read it?"

He sat down. "Shortly after it came in, I suppose."

At least he looks sheepish, she thought. *Don't get angry with Bryn, don't do it,* she coached herself. Checking was her responsibility, and she'd dropped the ball. Still, two whole days had passed with him knowing and yet saying nothing. "Why didn't you tell me on Wednesday?"

"I made a decision to wait until your workweek was ended," he said. "What good would it have done to give you one more thing to worry about while you were already trying to solve the problem of Henry Bell?"

He was right, of course he was. And yet. "So you decided for me that I couldn't handle more than one piece of bad news in a week."

"No, I—"

"Because that's what it feels like," she said. Her nerves felt like they were on fire; she got to her feet.

"I decided," Bryn said carefully, "that I didn't know if you had seen the message already and were setting it aside to deal with once the work crisis was out of the way. I decided that if you didn't bring it up when things had quieted down, I would. Now you've seen it and we're discussing it." He reached out a hand to Noel, but she didn't move.

"Why are we arguing?" he asked after a moment. "This is a blow to both of us. Maybe we should be talking about writing a joint reply to the intermediary. 'We understand our son might be feeling overwhelmed right now. Please let him know we'll be here if or when he changes his mind.' Doesn't that sound about right?"

Of course it did, Noel thought, but she was close to furious that Bryn was so rational, so measured, that he couldn't see how futile any response, and especially that one, would be. "He's never hinted he wasn't interested, then he backs off the minute he's heard we are?" she said. "Why do you think he'll come back around? There's something about us, something he doesn't care to get to know." She flapped her hands. "No, forget that," she said, now talking faster, "it's *me* he doesn't care to get to know, and I can't blame him. He was a tiny, helpless thing and I. Gave. Him. Away. I kept him from you, I kept you from him. I don't know, maybe if I bow out of the whole thing, it will make it easier for Sam to reach out to you."

"Bow out?" Bryn shook his head. "What are you talking about?"

"Bow out. I withdraw my request. You keep yours in. Why wouldn't he want to know you? It wasn't you who screwed everything up."

"Noel. *Cariad*. Please sit down. Sit."

She hesitated, but after a moment, she took a seat on the opposite end of the sofa from him.

"Instead of talk of bowing out and withdrawing your request, why don't we talk about getting out of the city for a break? A few days, a week. Work remotely for the week, yes? You can breathe at Swn Y Mor, you know you can. We can walk and swim and put all this in perspective." He inched closer to her. "And you can also stop in to see Bethan at St. David's. She told me she'd like to talk to you when you're up there next. She said she mentioned it to you on Saturday?"

Noel frowned, perplexed. They had enjoyed each other's company, but when Bethan had suggested a visit, Noel had assumed she meant for lunch or coffee—a friendly get-together. Bryn was making the request sound more formal than she had assumed. "Bethan wants to talk to me about . . . what?"

"I should let her speak for herself," Bryn said, "but I believe she wants to ask you about working at St. David's."

"You mean, another project like the one at the Addison? Some collaboration type of work? Because you know that's totally out of my control."

Bryn shifted so that he was facing her. "I think she means to offer you work—maybe as a curator, I don't know—thinking you'll be staying on after your secondment ends."

Staying on. Thirty minutes ago she could have imagined at least considering an offer of work so close to Bryn's home, but with the news about Sam, she wondered if she might as well go back to Massachusetts and deal with her pain and disappointment alone, as she always had. For a moment, she let her mind consider what a future here might be like—constantly wondering if she might be passing her son on a sidewalk, wondering if he might ever be ready to forgive her, wondering if Bryn's extraordinary grace might just turn to resentment.

"I feel like you're trying to manage me right now," she said coldly.

"Manage you? Whatever do you mean?"

"Manage me. Tell me what's best for me and what I should do." The minute the words left her mouth, she regretted them. It was a terrible thing to say, terrible to want to wound Bryn that way, for no reason but to punish herself. She covered her face with her hands.

"You honestly think that's what I'm doing here?"

"No, I don't think that," she said through her hands.

"It's like you're poking a hornet's nest, hoping to be stung. What are you pushing me to say? That this setback with Sam is all your fault? That I'm angry with you? That I'm glad you're this angry with yourself, because you deserve it? Or is it that you think *I* deserve it?" Bryn slid down the couch, took Noel's hands from her face, and made her look at him. "I can't say any of those things. I can't be angry at you. And I won't continue to wallow in my own self-pity, either, for the things I did and didn't do thirty years ago. I want reasons to keep looking forward. I want us to keep going forward, preferably together. You need to decide if that's what you want too, because I'm sure it's not good for us to keep reaching this point."

"I think I need a walk," she said before she said another thing without thinking first. What she really needed was a swim and the sensory oblivion the pool offered, but she hadn't reserved a lane and didn't care to argue her way into securing one last-minute on a Friday evening.

She rose, went to the coat closet, and shrugged back into the coat she'd taken off not so long ago.

"I think a walk is a good idea," Bryn said from his spot on the couch. "We'll be here when you get back."

Noel paused at the front door. "We?"

"Me and the cheese." With that, he shot her a sad smile and lifted his hand in a wave.

CHAPTER 44

CALUM'S FLAT, APRIL 2023

Noel walked into Little Venice and stopped when she reached Rembrandt Gardens. Instead of taking a bench overlooking the canal—her original plan—she pulled out her phone. Calum was up the road. It was early enough to have a sit in his garden. She couldn't turn around and walk back to the flat, not yet. She hoped Cal was home.

He answered on the second ring and, eschewing any greeting, asked, "Don't you have better things to do on a Friday night than ring this old fart?"

"I'm down the road. Would you like some company for an hour or so?"

"Is it only you? While Mr. Jones and I seem to have made inroads, I'm not sure I'm up for happy couples tonight."

"I'm alone, and I'm miserable, if that helps."

"Ah, miserable. Excellent. Me too. Come up. I'll watch for you."

Sure enough, Cal was already at his front door when she arrived. He ushered her inside, through the flat, and out into his back garden. His patio pots were lush with hyacinths, blooming in all colors and full of fragrance, several variegated hosta, and an assortment of lovely tall and wispy wildflowery things Noel couldn't identify. He'd already set a bottle of wine and two glasses on the outdoor dining table, along with a bag of cheese and onion crisps.

"Thanks for letting me crash your quiet evening," she said.

"You've saved me from a night of anticipating a telephone call that will likely never come, hence my misery. What's your excuse?"

"You first. Tell me about this telephone call."

He smiled, slid an empty glass over to her, and said, "I've met someone."

"You have? When? Where? Who?"

He held up a hand. "One question at a time. First of all, at the opening last Saturday. We were both in line at the cloakroom at the same time, the attendant was mixed up and handed us each other's coats. We got talking and ended up walking most of the way home together, although he had to double back because he lives along the way in St. John's Wood." He gestured with his hand in a direction that could have been east.

"Posh."

"Quite. We spoke a few times this week and I was expecting him to ring this evening, perhaps come over. But so far, nothing. Maybe it's for the best. I feel it may be too soon to feel this excited about a new relationship."

She reached across the table and squeezed his hand. "Give it a chance," she said, "give yourself a chance. So who is he? Is he with one of the museums?"

"Oh, lord, no. He's a landscape architect for the parks with a 'dabbling interest in landscape art.' Someone he knows gave him their ticket when they couldn't go, which is why he was there on Saturday. I'm almost glad he hasn't come over to see my pitiful turn at making things grow. Don't you think a professional gardener will be full of scorn for my pedestrian plantings? Hosta isn't very daring. Listen to me. I'm nervous." Cal reached for the wine and corkscrew and opened the bottle. "Now it's your turn," he said as he poured. "What is your misery?"

She picked up her wineglass and took a few big sips. "Bryn and I argued this evening. Well, I did the arguing. I said some horrible things to him." She slumped in her chair. "You know about Henry Bell withdrawing from the competition, of course."

Cal nodded.

"I was consumed all week with the fallout from that, and today, when it finally seemed it was all in hand, Jean sent us home early to relax and refresh. That lasted about ten minutes." She was trying to make light of her evening, but tears began stinging her eyes. She should be home with Bryn—drinking his wine, eating the cheese he'd so kindly bought—but she'd had her tantrum instead, choosing to be angry with him rather than sit with her sadness and frustration with Sam's decision. It had been easier to gin up indignation—over his reluctance to tell her about the decision earlier this week, over what she'd implied was his plot to get Bethan to hire her at St. David's—than admit to him she might never be able to trust he had forgiven her for giving up their son. She looked away from Cal.

"What happened? Noel?"

"On Wednesday, the intermediary agency we've been working with to reach out to Sam sent us a message that he's changed his mind. He's vetoed contact for now. What they call a qualified veto; not an absolute decision, but one with parameters. The parameter he's established is time. Maybe in a year, they told us he'd said. I only found out about it tonight, though, because I've been too busy to check my messages. I claim news of Sam is so important to me, and then I don't make time to check for emails? I feel like such a terrible person. So of course," she continued, "when Bryn admitted he'd read the email on Wednesday and didn't tell me, I picked a fight with him instead of talking about how hurt and sad I am that Sam said no, and that I'm worried Bryn may never forgive me for all this. What is wrong with me?"

"Maybe you're hurt and sad and worried?" Cal smiled, pulled open the bag of crisps, and offered them to her.

She took the entire bag from him and reached in for a handful.

"You've had a stressful week, topped off by a setback," he said. "I think your reaction was, uh, a little fraught, but surely normal enough in the circumstances."

"I'd let myself feel so hopeful. We both had. The 'Sam will be as excited as we are' kind of hopeful. Pie in the sky, because of course he's not. Why did we think he would be?"

"What did Bryn say about the setback?"

"He was maddeningly calm. He says he understands how Sam could be overwhelmed with learning about us and our eagerness to meet him, and that he probably needs time to process it all."

"To be fair, that interpretation does track with what the intermediary wrote, doesn't it?"

"Maybe."

Cal raised an eyebrow.

"Probably," she relented. "Yes. But what if the intermediary made a polite translation of Sam saying, 'Fuck off, lady. I never want to know you'? Excuse my language. We have no idea what Sam will decide in the end. He may close the door for good. Isn't it safer for us to be cautious going forward?"

"Easier, I think you mean. Easier to choose protecting yourself rather than risk getting hurt."

"I'm taking risks, Cal. Coming back to London. Opening up about Sam. Taking a chance with Bryn. All risks." She sighed. "And things are so good right now that I'm sure something is bound to go wrong. I'm even inventing conflicts so I have my confirmation that I never deserved anything good in the first place, not after giving up my child."

After a moment of silence, Cal let out a loud whoop of laughter. "I have never heard such ridiculously self-pitying nonsense in all my life. Give me back those crisps." He made to snatch the bag from Noel, which made her laugh in return.

With the mood lightened, she said, "I'm not saying I'm right to think these things about myself, just that this is where my mind goes. I hate that it does, but it does."

"Then turn the tables on that mind of yours." He laughed at her look of puzzlement. "Only a minute ago," he reminded her, "you said things are good right now. So, ask yourself, how did I get to this place where things are so good? I'm sure you'll see there's only one answer: you got right here, right now by living your life, your most unexpected life, with its every up and every down. Tell that to the punitive part of your mind whenever it tries to dictate to you what you deserve. Everything you did and didn't do brought you exactly here. To something good, to old friends, hopefully to the son you're eager to know. And I'll drink to that." He lifted his glass.

Noel touched her glass to Cal's and thought about what he'd said. She had arrived where she was meant to be. The long and serpentine path wasn't an obstruction on her way to this life; it was the path she was meant to follow. Earlier, in her despair, she had told Bryn she might as well go back home. But the truth was, reaching home didn't require a trip back. Her home was now, her home was here—with work, with friends like Cal, with Bryn, and with the hope of Sam, even if it did take him an age to feel ready.

She set down her glass. "I think I can go back to the flat now."

Just as she said this, a bell sounded in the distance.

"That's my door," Cal said. "Did you tell Bryn you were coming here?"

She shook her head. "Maybe it's your mystery man, come to sit with you in your garden after all?"

"Never." Cal took his phone out of his back pocket and checked something. He breathed in sharply. "The doorbell camera. Look." He showed Noel his screen. A handsome, slightly younger man stood there, his hands clasped in front of him, although a second later they unclasped so he might brush some invisible thing from the front of his jacket. He did this two more times. Clasp, unclasp, brush. Clasp, unclasp, brush.

"Mystery Man?"

"He's called Gavin."

"Gavin. He's lovely. He looks slightly nervous but excited to see you. Come on, see me to the door. I've got to get home to tell Bryn how stupid I've been. Or how lucky I am." Noel stood and pulled Cal to his feet. "Up you get. He's waiting."

Gavin looked surprised to see two people answer the door but he recovered quickly. "Am I interrupting? I can come back another time."

"Not at all," Noel said quickly, "I'm on my way out. Noel Enfield." She shook his hand. "Somehow I missed meeting you last Saturday night, Gavin, but it's lovely to meet you now. Sorry to make it so brief, but I must get home.

"Cal." She turned to her friend and hugged him. "Thank you for everything you said. I needed to hear it. Now go enjoy the rest of your evening."

CHAPTER 45

NOEL'S FLAT, APRIL 2023

The door to the flat had been left unlocked; Noel opened it slowly, calling out, "Hello?" as she did.

No answer.

She moved into the large, open main living space and saw the flat was much as she'd left it well over an hour ago: wine bottle on the counter, partially filled glasses next to it, the cheese on its board, the lights dimmed. The only difference was the silence. Bryn wasn't here, smiling, walking over to her, his bare feet padding across the hardwood.

A sob caught in her throat. She'd done it this time.

"Noel?"

She turned. At the other end of the hall, coming through the door she'd just opened, was Bryn. He was carrying a tote bag, as if he was coming back from the shops.

"I thought you'd gone," she said.

Bryn smiled and lifted the bag in his hand. "Only as far as Flying Tiger to buy some candles."

"Candles?"

"Votives. I thought we'd start the evening over. The extra light will be nice, don't you think?" He walked down the hall and stopped when he was in front of her. He took another step closer and kissed her. "You taste like crisps. Cheese and onion."

Her cheeks warmed. "I walked to Cal's and I ate all his crisps while he told me what a self-pitying fool I'd been."

"A worthwhile walk, then?" he asked, an amused smile on his face.

"He's a good friend."

"I know now that he is."

"I'm sorry I took my frustration with myself out on you. I shouldn't have. You did nothing wrong."

"No. It was the wrong call, not telling you about the message sooner. I'm sorry I upset you after a difficult week. Come and sit."

Bryn held out his hand. Noel took it and followed him to the table, where he'd laid out the cheese and a couple of sharp knives. Seeing the cheese, her stomach spoke up despite the snack she'd polished off.

"You'd better have something in you."

Bryn handed her one of the knives and left her to the cheese while he began placing candles all over the flat. Tall sticks into the holders on the small dining table, and everywhere else—kitchen island, coffee table, hearth—votives. He improvised with the flat's ample collection of juice glasses, turning them into holders. Once he'd gotten all of them lit, he stood behind the island, admiring his handiwork. Noel smiled at the candlelight flickering all over.

He walked over to her and handed her a glass of wine. "Let's try this again. Here's to a fresh start."

"To a do-over. Thank you." She looked at him for a moment longer and then picked up the cheese knife to cut another generous slice of the farmhouse cheddar she'd cut into a moment ago. This she set on a cracker, which she handed to Bryn. "You should have something in you too."

They both sat at the table, wineglasses in hand.

"Cal met a new man on Saturday, at your show," Noel shared. "Gavin. He came by Cal's flat just as I was preparing to leave. Gavin looked nervous but happy. We watched him fidget on the doorstep via the doorbell camera." She smiled. "Cal told me he was nervous too—understandable—and he said he was worried he was jumping into something too soon after Tim. But I could tell he was also excited for what lay ahead, and really, really happy." She cut another piece of cheese. "On my walk home, I thought about how I could relate to all that. I'm sad, of course; insecure; worried; anxious about taking risks and being hurt. But, like Cal, I'm really, really happy too. I thought the happy feelings had to take a backseat to everything else, but now I think it doesn't have to be that way. Maybe all these feelings can coexist within me, with the happy part keeping all the rest of it in check a bit. You know, let happy be front and center every once in a while." She popped the cheese in her mouth.

Bryn nodded as he finished his bite. After, he asked, "Only once in a while?"

"Maybe more than that." She smiled. "What you said about going up to Swn Y Mor? I'd like that. I'll email Jean that I'll be working remotely for the week. We can leave tomorrow morning." She offered Bryn a sheepish smile. "And I would like to talk to Bethan while we're there. You know, in case there really is a job in Swansea in the not-too-distant future."

Bryn reached for her hand. "You know I still have the flat in the city."

"I do know that. I'll need a place to stay during the week. If there is a job—I don't want to be too confident and jinx it."

"There will be a job. The gallery and the collection are a bit smaller than you're used to, mind. And Swansea isn't London. And Swn Y Mor might as well be on the moon, especially in the winter. And I can be very absent when I'm working, even if I'm physically present. I think you already know this." He let go of her hand and held out his two in front of her, as if in offering. "And I worry what will happen, who I will be, if—when—I can no longer work."

She smiled at him. Who would they be, she wondered, in a week, a month, a year? Who would they become when they grew too old to work, or too forgetful? Who might they have been if circumstances had never parted them? Parents to more children? An art world power couple? Divorced? With the arbitrary way coincidence and happenstance had woven its way in and out of the tapestry of their timelines—those lines that would always remain separate and distinct, and those ones that overlapped and blurred—could they ever hope to answer those questions?

She thought of some of the last words Cal said to her that evening, right before he'd walked to his front door and opened it to see what could be a new future standing on his doorstep: *Everything you did and didn't do brought you exactly here.* Here was pretty good. And what did answers matter, anyway?

"Who knows what will happen?" she asked, looking into Bryn's eyes. "Maybe all we'll do is swim a lot. Swim, and complain that we're getting old. That wouldn't be so bad, would it?"

He laughed. "No, not bad at all. In fact, I'll drink to that." He lifted his wineglass, his fingers grasping the stem, his knuckles boldly gnarled but somehow beautiful, a marker of both time gone and who he'd become with every passing day she'd missed—a chronology just for her—and he tipped his head at Noel's glass so she, too, would take part in the toast. "*Iechyd da, cariad. Caru ti.*"

She clinked her glass against his and listened for a moment to the music they made. "I love you too," she said. "*Caru ti.*"

CHAPTER 46

SWN Y MOR, APRIL 2023

"You've tried, Noel. We've tried from Jean's office. Henry Bell isn't responding to our messages, and we do need him to collect his paintings. Have you any thoughts about what else we might try?"

Noel pinched the bridge of her nose. Aditi wasn't hiding her frustration, and while Noel understood the woman was under pressure to tie up these loose ends, she didn't know what more they could do. "We could take responsibility for having them transported directly to his studio, but I'd want to be certain he was present to sign for them. And we can't guarantee that if he won't answer a phone call. Can this wait a few days? It's Thursday; I'm back in London on Monday. If I have to, I can walk to his studio myself and confirm he is present for a delivery."

"Jean won't be pleased to let this linger until Monday."

Well, she won't be pleased to wait forever for a reply, either, Noel thought but didn't say. "I'll smooth it over with her. It's the best we can do, I think. In the meantime, keep ringing him. Of course, if he answers a call or miraculously shows up on your doorstep before then, it might be resolved by Monday."

"Let's hope so." With that, Aditi rang off.

Noel sighed.

"Frustrating phone call?" While she had been on the phone in the sitting room, Bryn had wandered in. He'd been working all morning and now here he was, coming in for lunch.

Noel looked at her watch and grimaced. "Is that really the time?" It was well after noon, and she'd barely noticed the hours passing because she'd been on the phone or on meetings since eight o'clock. "Slightly frustrating, yes," she answered Bryn. "Jean is peeved that Henry Bell is unreachable. He simply won't answer anyone's calls, and she doesn't want the responsibility of storing his work indefinitely. But"—she closed her laptop—"we have a plan, and I'll try and take care of it when I'm back in the city on Monday. I'm not going to let this problem interfere with enjoying your company at lunch. I'm going to miss you when you're away."

Bryn smiled and held out his hand. When Noel took it, he drew her close.

He was driving to Porth Ysgo after lunch, something like a four-hour drive, with plans to spend the next two days sketching and photographing. His car was loaded up, save for a few art supplies and his daypack. "I know it's not ideal timing, but I want to take advantage of the forecasted fair weather up on the coast," he said. "But if you mind . . ."

"I don't. You need to work. I have plenty of my own to keep me busy tomorrow, and as long as nothing blows up I plan to read all day on Saturday, maybe take a walk."

"I'll get an early start on Sunday, get back late morning, yeah? We'll have the day together." He kissed her on the forehead. "Are you still leaving for London early on Monday?"

"I was, until that phone call." She stopped herself and then waved away her concerns. "Never mind, I'll sort it out. Either very late Sunday or very early Monday. Either way, we'll enjoy what time we have on Sunday."

"Soon enough, you'll bring your bags for one last time and unpack them."

As well as shipping some things currently being stored back in the Massachusetts suburbs, she thought. She was doing it—moving to Wales when her secondment came to an end, moving into Swn Y Mor, at least on weekends. On weekdays, beginning in June, she'd be in Swansea, where she would manage and grow St. David's North American art collection. There was money in the form of a large gift, Bethan had told her when they'd finally met, that would pay for her role and a decent few new pieces, if she managed the budget carefully and made wise purchases.

Deb was letting her go reluctantly. At first sour about Noel's jump, she eventually softened her stance, admitting she'd always known that this secondment might mean Noel would find advancement elsewhere. "Even Jean wants you, although I'm glad to avoid that outcome," she said. "Her poaching you might have ruined our friendship."

Jean hadn't told Noel about her desire to have her join the Addison permanently; she was too circumspect to do so. But she had pointedly asked if she was sure St. David's was the place for her. What more could she want, Noel had thought, smiling at Jean's question, than to move forward, than a challenge like this, than a new chance at life with Bryn? Together they might do anything—withstand anything or welcome anything. Whatever happened, they would be together. Yes, she had told Jean, I am sure.

She would have to make a brief trip back to Massachusetts for her things, though there wasn't much she wanted to bring from her old life into this new phase. A few of her seasonal clothes, her now imperfect Meissen bowl. Neither of Bryn's houses were wanting in the way of furnishings. Maybe she would sell or donate the rest. While there, she would of course also try to see Alice—though if Andy's current attitude toward Noel held, her managing to do so would be very unlikely. She might even have divorce papers to sign by then.

"*Cusana fi,*" Noel said. Bryn's eyes opened in surprise, and she shrugged. "Bethan's asked if I'd consider taking a few conversational Welsh language lessons, so I thought I'd get a head start on YouTube."

"Ah, YouTube, where one learns all the important phrases first, I see." He chuckled. "Your pronunciation could be better, but you got your point across. Yes, of course I'll kiss you." He leaned in and did just that. "Now, we'd best go have some lunch or I will be leaving here hungry."

With Bryn gone, the normally quiet house was even more still. The rest of the afternoon's work was easier to manage than the first half of the day had been.

At five minutes before five, her mobile phone rang. Aditi again. Inwardly, Noel groaned. *Please not a crisis,* she said in a silent wish, *not five minutes before this workday comes to an end.* She let the call go to voicemail and played the message once the recording icon appeared on her screen.

"Noel!" Aditi sounded excited rather than frazzled or annoyed. "Good news! Henry Bell came for his paintings late this afternoon. He took us by surprise, but thank goodness we had them wrapped and ready to crate. He left fifteen minutes ago, satisfied everything is now in his possession and in good condition. You can abandon those plans to catch him at his studio on Monday. It's all taken care of, and I hope you have a lovely weekend."

She hit the pause button, then for good measure replayed the message. No doubt Jean was just as relieved as her assistant, but their good mood wasn't infectious. Melancholy settled over Noel in the cottage. Although it would have been additional work to travel to his studio, she had wanted to see Henry to confirm he was well and perhaps persuade him to open up about his reasons for withdrawing. And now there was no longer any legitimate excuse for her to drop in on him. Henry Bell would be just another person lost to her.

"Shall I tell you what your painting makes me wonder about?" We stand in front of Yours for the taking, *the show is any day now. The exhibition guide is done. You want to give me a first look, but for some reason, you are nervous about showing me. For the last few minutes, I have watched you as you survey the canvas, your eyes darting back and forth, occasionally pausing—but on which details, I want to know. What is grabbing your attention in this moment, in this painting? What do you recognize? How does it make you feel?*

Before I can open my mouth to ask all these questions, you ask yours.

No one has asked my permission before offering me their interpretation. You are the first and the question catches me off guard, as does the deference it implies. Too many art historians, art critics, competition juries are willing to offer their assessments with full confidence that they know my intent. But you, your question reminds me instead of the best drawing instructors at uni, the ones who saw us painters as individuals with ideas and impulses to be nurtured even as our techniques needed nudging toward improvement. Gentle, lest they stifle any creativity. I like that.

"Yes, of course," I say. "Please."

"After all this time with it, analyzing it, I'm nervous I haven't gotten things right. I worry I see things in here that maybe aren't."

You point to the tall shadows, you point to the shadows in the windows, you point to the basket and then make a circle in the air in front of it with your finger. "I see four figures altogether between the shadowy bodies and faces. Two people looking on the scene, perhaps, and two looking out from the building at it? A possible fifth in the small, highlighted bundle here, in its softness against the hard stone.

Caretakers, and something—someone?—found. Or lost? It's hard to say."

Your hand returns to your side. Gertie stands close to your hip and you begin to stroke her head, perhaps not even aware you are doing so. She is aware; she's loving your attention.

You look at me. "And that's where I am with your work, wondering if I've written the right things about it, if I have done it justice. When I looked at the painting for the first time, I felt an overwhelming sense of loss. I began to question this initial reaction because, objectively, the title hints that something has been found—in this case, the basket and whatever's in it, ready to be collected by some lucky person. But then I started thinking that, if the basket is there, it must have been left behind or abandoned by another person. Behind one person's gain is a terrible loss. And what of the object in the middle, with its fate tied to everyone's whim?" You shake your head. "Maybe I've seen things that aren't there. I worry that, because I've lived with so much loss since I was young, I'm bringing baggage to my interpretation. Too much information?" you ask, smiling, before you turn back to face the canvas.

The smile fades, and you stop stroking Gertie. Displeased, she nudges your hand with her nose . . .

None of this has happened. You know I never showed the painting. We never had this conversation. It only exists in my mind, a daydream.

Throughout my life, I used to think about this moment, the moment when I would be right next to you. When I was very young, I believed you would know me, instinctively, the moment you saw me. You would gather me up and hold me tight because you had always wanted me and your leaving me was a terrible accident. Older, I knew you wouldn't know me if you saw me; I would be a stranger to you like any other stranger you walked past. Older, I was angry with everyone, but especially you—for not wanting me enough, for not finding me worthy enough to make a family with you, for keeping me from knowing where I came from. Every painting I have created in the last ten years was an attempt to reach you and communicate this to you: "I am here, here I am, please come for me."

Yours for the taking, *this painting I imagine you standing in front of, has my childhood letters to you affixed to the canvas with diluted glue, the paper manipulated in places where you see the raised lines. They are the painting's bones, my words to you there underneath all the paint. Excitement, hope, longing, connection, mistrust, confusion, anger . . . It's all in there. Years of words to a woman who gave me away, sealed my fate. Or, as I've imagined you saying about the object in the painting, as one who tied me to others' whims. If you did see all this when you looked at my work, when you wrote about it, I can assure you, you're not seeing things that aren't there. You've gotten nothing wrong.*

I know from my birth certificate you called me Samuel. I know you did not name my father at first. But there is so much I do not know. Even so, something I sense now is that everything that happened to you and happened to me is much more complicated than I have imagined. And despite it all, I like you. Gertie likes you. She doesn't like everybody, but she has taken to you. And I think—I am sure—you like me too. It's a place to start.

So I imagine one more moment. I reach for your hand and take it in mine.

Surprised, you look at me. "Henry," you say, but instead of taking your hand back, you squeeze mine.

"For what it's worth," I say, "I think we all bring our baggage to interpreting any kind of art. I certainly do when I paint. How can it be any different? We are our experiences, and we bring our entire selves to our work." I turn to face you. "Look, I need to tell you something."

Because it feels like the time to do just that; it feels as if I am facing a starting line. I wiggle my toes, testing my will to go ahead and take that first step over. I know the minute I do I'll be on a course, racing into the truth—there'll be no going back.

PART VII

WORDS ECHO THUS IN YOUR MIND

CHAPTER 47

SWN Y MOR, APRIL 2024

Today, Saturday, was the day for getting kitchen herbs into pots. The sun was shining, the temperature was mild, and Noel was anxious to plant, although the helpful people at the garden center had warned her of the potential for a cold snap. On a day like today, with its blue skies and cottony clouds, the threat of snow or frost was hard to take seriously.

She stuck her hands in the bag of soil and got to it.

She was alone, having arrived the previous night to an empty house. Bryn was away painting, due back later in the day. He usually tried to be home for her Friday arrivals, but the timing of his trip couldn't be helped. He'd put off leaving early in the week because of heavy rains at his destination, and then, days lost but forecast clear, he'd gone with some urgency. He was accommodating the changes in his hands with changes in his technique, but he did feel time speeding up, coupled with a fear of what would come next. He liked to keep busy.

Noel was busiest during the week as well. Bryn had warned her that year-round life here at the cottage would be quiet; it was, and she'd felt it especially so in her first full winter here, but she liked it. A year after first deciding to move to Wales, she still looked forward to her weekends at the cottage. These weekends with Bryn, with an occasional full week, seemed to be the right amount of time for them to spend together for now. Those days together, they cooked and shopped and walked and swam, their work and thoughts of work left for the days when they would be alone again. She missed Bryn when they were apart, and they talked almost daily, but blending their lives had posed challenges. Bryn wanted to marry; Noel wasn't sure she did. She *could,* however. Her divorce had finalized rather swiftly and smoothly once she'd stopped pressing Andy to change his mind about visits with Alice.

Noel mourned her loss of Alice, and sometimes, when she was alone in the city flat, listening to the heat clicking on and off, she allowed herself to think, *What if? What if I had stayed in my old life to give her stability? What if I had left Andy but at least stayed closer? What if I had come back to London sooner, before meeting Andy in that restaurant? What if I had left Andy alone that day and sorted myself out instead?* There had been much to sort out, after all.

With that her mind turned to Sam—how she'd come here with no intention of looking for him and yet searching for him had ultimately become her purpose. Now that it had, she couldn't imagine doing anything differently; how could she have gone any longer without looking for him? She mourned Sam too, her child. A year had passed and no word yet; still, she and Bryn held out hope.

She sighed heavily, her hands stuck in the good dirt. Everything she'd done in her life may have brought her here, where she was her happiest, but those things she'd done had left others hurt, bewildered, even alone. Bryn. Cal. Andy. Alice. Sam. That bitter irony was, some days, difficult to reconcile, and was at the root of her hesitancy about marrying again. Marrying Bryn was a choice she couldn't see around the corner of—would she hurt him or someone else somehow, somewhere down the road, simply by saying yes, by standing up with him and taking vows? Could she be certain nothing bad would happen? Being here, loving him, was not so much making a choice as it was fulfilling a necessity, like taking breaths, and she was fine with that for now.

Bryn seemed to be too. Although he had asked, and kept asking.

Finished with the planting, Noel stood up from her stool and surveyed her work. The stones outside the front door would need to be swept, and the pots rearranged—brought closer to the door in case they needed to come in from the cold—but she was happy with the results. Lemon thyme, mint, some flat parsley, sea fennel, nasturtiums for their salad—not herbs, but edible and colorful. Sage and anything that needed more warmth would wait. She'd made a start. Bryn would smile when he came up to the door later.

Without thinking she wiped her hands on her trousers, leaving dirt trails. "Ugh." She rolled her eyes at her carelessness and went inside to wash up and change.

The water ran and ran, taking the soap and dirt with it. When she shut the taps, she heard something—a car down the lane—and she smiled. Bryn was home earlier than she'd expected.

She dried off quickly and went back outside to meet him. But the car, when it rounded the curve, was unfamiliar. She hoped it wasn't going to be someone looking for Bryn, or for a story—someone who would mistake her for the cleaner, as Delaney had that one Christmas. The last thing Noel wanted to do right now, on her lazy weekend, was stand guard at her own door.

The car pulled to a stop in the full sun, the light reflecting off its hood. For a moment, she couldn't tell who was stepping out, but when he came around the other side of the car to open the passenger door, the silhouette became a clear person.

"Henry," Noel said to herself, and her hand went to her chest. "And Gertie," she said louder this time, a smile in her voice as the familiar dog bounded over to her.

"Hello," Henry called, raising a hand—but the wave was tentative, and unlike his dog, he approached carefully.

Now that the initial surprise had passed, Noel realized how happy she was to see him, and how natural it felt that he was here. "Henry, please come here. It's so good to see you. I'm a mess because I've been gardening, but I'll change. Then I'll make tea. I'll get Gertie some water. How did you find us?" She shook her head. "You know what? Never mind that now. Come in, come in. Welcome to Swn Y Mor."

Noel fussed at the kitchen counter, gathering milk and sugar and cups and saucers and a small plate for biscuits, until the water was boiling. She poured this over leaves in a pot. Gertie, ignoring her bowl of cool water, went off to explore the house.

"Do you mind?" Henry asked.

"I don't think she can get in much trouble. I'd be worried about her getting into paint or varnish, but the studio door is closed. I'll take you around after tea. Here we go." She brought the pot to the table, then everything else together on a tray.

"I should have rung. Or emailed."

"Don't be silly. But how did you know where to come?"

"Delaney Jenkins. We've been talking because she fixed me up with a gallery for a solo show."

Noel smiled, remembering the agent handing her a small stack of her business cards, hoping Noel would pass them to the competition's artists. Who else had she swooped in on since the Rising Artists show? "Is she representing you now?"

"I haven't committed," he said. "I suppose you could say she's trying to win me over. I should say yes and be grateful, given that I threw such a bomb into my career last spring, but I really don't know yet if it's a good fit."

"She's good at what she does, but, yes, she takes some handling or before you know it, she's got you doing all sorts of things outside your comfort zone. Bryn seems to take her in stride."

Henry took a sip of tea. Noel noticed his hand trembled a bit as he set the cup back down. "Is he here?"

"Bryn? No. Out painting, but back later today. If you can stay a while, I know he'd like to meet you. He is impressed with your work."

"Mmm," Henry answered, noncommittal. "I can stay for a bit. It's really you I wanted to see. That's why Delaney gave me directions here. I told her I had a long-overdue apology for you. I think she took pity on me."

"Henry, you don't need to apologize. If it didn't feel right to you to compete, then you shouldn't have. Simple as that. But I was worried about you."

"I know you were. I heard it in every one of your voice messages." He smiled.

"Maybe I overdid it with the calls. Have a biscuit." She slid the plate his way.

Henry took one. Before he bit into it, he said, "I brought you something. A housewarming gift of sorts. It's in the car. Not that this house needs another painting."

"Well, we don't have a Henry Bell, but you really didn't need to bring me anything but yourself. And Gertie," she added as the dog came padding back into the kitchen.

"Do you mind if I—?" Henry asked, pointing to the door, as Gertie settled herself at Noel's side. "I'll just be a moment." He set the uneaten biscuit on his saucer and went outside.

Noel looked at Gertie and the dog returned the look with a cock of her head. "Is he okay, Gertie? I'm sure you're taking the best care of him." She scratched the dog behind her ears until Henry returned with a wrapped painting under his arm.

Something about the size of it made her curious. "It's not . . ." she began to ask, but immediately Henry was shaking his head.

"No. I sold it. A private collector. I did all right. This is something newer. The one I talked to you about when we ran into each other on the way to Regent's Park. I want you to have it." He began pulling at the taped brown paper, but Noel put her hand up.

"How about we open it in the studio and get it up on an easel? The light is perfect in there." She stood and beckoned the young man and the dog to follow.

A crowd of people—an art exhibition, and a large one by the looks of it. An air of Romanticism in the fluid lines of the human forms, in the colors. An explosion of color, activity, details, joy. There was an otherworldly quality to the composition. Despite the very human activity of people gathering in a museum, it evoked a feeling that some in the crowd were fairies, ethereally flitting among bulkier humans in the galleries. So very different from the heavy atmosphere in *Yours for the taking*, although even here she could see Henry's signature in the raised lines. Subtler, but still crisscrossing the canvas, adding dimension.

She pointed, her finger tracing the topography. "I think of these as the bones of your work. Before I'd seen the work in person, I thought this might be impasto. I know it's not now . . . but is it some kind of plaster under the paint?"

Henry smiled. "Not plaster, exactly. A kind of papier-mâché, made from old notes I'd held on to. I think of them as the bones too, the structure behind everything."

She stepped closer to the canvas. She saw two central figures standing next to each other, both looking at a painting, indistinct but suggestive of a mother in a pink dress, a baby reaching outward, a field of lambs. "This is the Blake exhibit. I recognize the layout. And this engraving—'Sound the flute now it's mute,'" she recited.

"'Nightingale in the dale,'" he said. "I'm sure there's another line in between but I can't think of it. Yes, it's the Blake show, at the Tate. I saw it in October that year."

She turned to look at him. "You never said when I told you I'd seen it. Remember? I was on a rare trip transporting two pieces of art to the Addison. I bought a copy of *Songs of Innocence* at the gift shop and brought it home for Alice."

"Your stepdaughter?"

"Yes. She was about eight then; it may have been a little young for her." She remembered back for a moment. "That show was special, a sensory overload of Blakes." She pointed at the canvas. "I'd like to know what those two are thinking as they stand there. They're the only two not going in one direction or another. Are they together? They don't seem to be from the angles of their bodies, and yet something's drawn them there at the same time. What are you calling it?"

"*The Law of Truly Large Numbers.* I had this idea that everyone passing through had some connection with another person in the room." He shrugged. "It was a bit of an experiment."

"I like that idea." She gave it some thought. It reminded her of the moments before she knew Bryn was in the same train station as her, and yet he was there. Of Cal at her welcome breakfast, unknown to her before he removed his mask. *What else do we not know?* she wondered. *What connections are out there, waiting to be discovered?* "I love it, Henry. Thank you."

He smiled. Then he looked around him and, changing the subject, said, "You were right about the light in here. It's a wonderful studio."

"Have a look around. Then you can see the rest of the cottage. We can walk to the beach after, if you'd like."

At the word *walk,* Gertie stood, looking at both humans.

"Yes, a walk," Henry said. "In a few minutes." He began moving around the studio, stopped when he came to the charcoal and pencil studies Bryn had made of Noel as he worked out the composition of *Lady of Llyn Y Fan Fach.* Next to these were similar practice sketches for what had become the more recent portrait he'd done of her. "You've known each other for over thirty years," he said.

Noel smiled. "It's more accurate to say we knew each other in the early 1990s and met each other again when I returned here for work. In between, we never spoke. It's complicated."

"I'm sorry, I didn't mean to bring up a sore subject."

"No, it's fine. I—we worked things out in the end. Some things, anyway. Others . . ." She looked away. Of the four people who'd ever known the full story of those intervening years, one was dead, one was Cal, and the other two lived right here in this house. She'd never considered telling anyone else, and so years of her life continued to be held secret. What she held inside, though, felt like an impediment to every part of moving forward. She wondered if finally telling the story to someone—to Henry, who felt so safe and so like in her many ways—and releasing the pressure that comes with holding things in for no reason other than shame, might let life flow forward as if it was a river freed from a dam.

"Would you like to go for that walk now?" she suggested. "I'll tell you a story."

In minutes, they reached the shoreline. Gertie ran ahead to sniff at the water's edge. Once they were within sight of the water, Noel began talking. Henry listened.

Over the next hour, she told him everything, perhaps more than she could expect him to handle or want to know. When she finished, Henry looked at her for several seconds, and then he looked down the beach, finding Gertie in the distance.

"Will you excuse me?" he asked. "I'm going to put Gertie on the lead." And then he left.

Noel hugged her arms around herself. She had to admit, she felt lighter with the telling, but at what cost? She wondered if Henry would simply walk back to the cottage with the dog, get in his car, and drive away as fast as he could.

She turned her back to him, giving him the freedom to sneak back to the footpath without her watching. A few moments later, though, she felt a nudge on the back of her calf. Gertie, looking for a few ear scratches.

Noel squatted, coming face-to-face with Gertie, and rubbed her ears. As she did, her eyes filled with tears and they spilled onto the dog's snout.

"Please don't cry," Henry said. "Please."

"I'm all right," she said, wiping her eyes with her sleeve. "I thought you were going to take Gertie and run away. These are tears of relief." She laughed a little and then stood up.

He reached for her arm and steadied her. "I won't run away. It's a lot to take in, but it hasn't changed what I think about you. But it is a lot."

"Even if you'd run away, I'd be glad I told you," she said. "My ex-husband didn't know anything about this part of my life and I know the secrets kept us from being close. I don't want to be the person no one can get close to anymore." She glanced in the direction of the house. "Shall we walk back?"

He nodded. Noel linked her arm through his and they set off for the cottage.

When they came out on the other side of the footpath, Noel stopped. Bryn's car was in the drive alongside Henry's.

"Bryn's home," she said, grinning, and she sped up a bit. She felt twenty again, her whole life ahead of her. "Come meet him. We'll look at your painting together. Or not," she added as she looked at his face and saw him hesitate. "You're anxious about showing him, so we'll leave that. But come in and meet him. He's heard so much about you."

"It's not that. I—I have to tell you something first, something I should have told you last April, when I dropped out of the competition. I . . ." he began, but he got no further. Just then, Bryn walked out the front door and spotted them coming up the lane.

"Company! How lovely," he called out, waving.

At the sound of his deep, singsong voice, Gertie pulled on her lead. Henry dropped it, a look of surprise on his face, and the dog ran up to Bryn and danced around his feet.

"And who's this?" He looked from the dog to Noel. "Did you bring home a dog in my absence, *cariad*?"

She laughed, pulling Henry forward. "That's Gertie, Henry's dog. And this is Henry Bell, here for a visit."

Henry stopped and Noel stopped with him. She looked at him.

"Samuel," he said looking back at her, looking from her to Bryn. "I believe you called me Samuel."

AUTHOR'S NOTE

Londoners, savvy London travelers, and my British friends and readers: You'll see I have kept true to the map of London and train trips between cities. But I have played a little fast and loose by creating museums and changing the names of venerable institutions to suit the story. Likewise, art prizes had to be created, jobs tweaked or invented to fit the people taking them, meetings and conversations arranged where perhaps none would have taken place in quite the same way. And perhaps it's only wishful thinking that a good dog like Gertie would be able to move so freely indoors and out. I hope the liberties I've taken cause no hard feelings. All were in aid of telling the story.

CREDITS

Epigraph and chapter headers: lines from "Burnt Norton", from Four Quartets by T. S. Eliot. Copyright © 1936 by Houghton Mifflin Harcourt Publishing Company, renewed 1964 by T.S. Eliot. Copyright © 1940, 1941, 1942 by T.S. Eliot, renewed 1968, 1969, 1970 by Esme Valerie Eliot. Used by permission of HarperCollins Publishers.

Epigraph: lines from "Stolen Moments" by Kim Addonizio. Copyright © 1999. Used with permission of the author.

Naked In The Rain
Words and Music by Martin Glover and Pamela Carol McBroom
Copyright © 1990 by Universal Music MGB Ltd. and Truelove Music International
All Rights for Universal Music MGB Ltd. in the United States and Canada Administered by Universal Music – MGB Songs
International Copyright Secured All Rights Reserved
Reprinted by Permission of Hal Leonard LLC

Includes lyrics from
"Naked In The Rain"
Written and Composed by Pamela McBroom
Published by Truelove Music

ACKNOWLEDGMENTS

Do writers ever thank their fictional characters? I am going to, right here. Noel, Bryn, Henry, and Calum were vivid and noisy and easy to summon every time I sat down to write. They did what they would and let me watch while I captured it all on paper. Thank you, wonderful people, for visiting me and staying a while.

The next unorthodox thank-you goes to the city of London, my favorite place in the world. However, setting part of the book there was about more than writing a love letter to a place I hold dear. Despite being enormous and cosmopolitan, at times London feels very much like a small town. One can wander its streets and run into friends, or see the same faces over and over, or find close-knit worlds within which everyone knows everyone else. So, for a story in which I wanted to write about all the remarkable things that can happen within truly large populations and subsets of those populations, London made the ideal setting.

Thank you to everyone at She Writes Press for empowering authors and launching good books into the world. Brooke Warner is every writer's dream publisher, and her team is a dream team. My thanks to the entire team—Brooke; Associate Publisher Lauren Wise; Project Managers Shannon Green, Addison Gallegos, and Megan Milton; and Art Director Julie Metz—for your dedication to showcasing women's writing. Publicist Crystal Patriarche and her entire team at BookSparks got the word out in so many innovative ways. They truly understand the changing times in book publicity, and I am in awe at the work they put into advocating for this book. My deepest thanks go to Rebecca Kinzie Bastian who carefully read through the manuscript and suggested ways to tell a clearer, better story. This is my second time working with the wonderful copy editor Krissa Lagos and I hope there will be many more collaborations in the future. Both women were as invested as I was in putting out the best story possible. I am so grateful. I am also grateful to proofreader Julia Denardo Roney for her sharp eyes.

Thank you to the lovely Grace Yanucci for spending a summer vacation from Fordham doing exhaustive research into British adoption and family law and briefing me on her findings. Any misinterpretations or missteps are my own.

When it came to writing about the process of creating art, I had generous help from two extraordinary artists. Thank you to Seattle painter Sarah Guthrie for the joy she spreads and for the art newsletters that offer glimpses into what she does and how she does it. Thanks also to western Massachusetts painter Sue Fontaine, whose practice of including dress patterns as the "skin" of her paintings helped me explain my idea of Henry using his letters as the bones of his art. I appreciate the time Sue gave me in her studio to discuss this.

A very special thank-you to childhood friend Elena McCarthy for reconnecting with me in London after decades had passed since our time together in Brownie Scouts and elementary school. I pictured the layout of her Maida Vale terrace when I wrote about Calum's back garden. Thanks also go to her for introducing me to a Royal Parks landscape architect during a good old-fashioned London pub crawl, thus confirming this is an actual profession. Thank you, too, to Karen and Adam for the hospitality that same evening.

I must thank the writers I have close by who provide support and friendship even when we don't get together as often as we'd like: Holly Robinson, Carla Panciera, Lori Haskins Houran, Elisabeth Elo. My mother always told me to surround myself with supportive, smart women, and I have.

I could not have finished this book without the guidance of Gail Randall Aspinwall, Ellen Graham Weeren, and Charlie Watts. Thank you for reading portions of this book in progress and making suggestions that pointed me in better directions.

My sincere thanks to all the booksellers, librarians, and readers out there who will pick up this book, or any book, and keep the love of reading alive.

To the usual suspects, John and Bennett: Let's keep making delicious meals together, wherever life takes us.

ABOUT THE AUTHOR

photo credit: Jason Grow

Jane Ward is the author of *Hunger* (Forge 2001), *The Mosaic Artist* (2011), and *In the Aftermath* (She Writes Press 2021). After graduating from Simmons College, she worked in the food and hospitality industry; later, she became a contributing writer to an online food magazine and a blogger and occasional host of cooking videos for an internet recipe resource affiliated with several regional newspapers. Most recently she has contributed book reviews to *Story Circle* and *Mom Egg Review*. She loves to travel, and to document her trips through travel photography. Jane lives in Ipswich, Massachusetts.

Looking for your next great read?

We can help!

Visit www.shewritespress.com/next-read or scan the QR code below for a list of our recommended titles.

She Writes Press is an award-winning independent publishing company founded to serve women writers everywhere.